YOJIMBO™

— THE SHROUDED MOON —

Created, Written, and Illustrated by
STAN SAKAI

Introduction by
SCOTT SHAW!

DARK HORSE COMICS®

Usagi Yojimbo

Introduction

I was extremely surprised and pleased when Stan Sakai asked me to write the introduction to *The Shrouded Moon*, this latest collected volume of *Usagi Yojimbo*. Stan's Federal Express pick-up-and-delivery person probably has more to do with the production of *Usagi Yojimbo* than I do, but his schedule was probably too busy for him to write an intro.

However, it occurs to me that I've actually had a *lot* to do with *Usagi Yojimbo* over the years. In fact, I may be the single person most responsible for convincing Stan to pursue what would become a stellar career in comic books — at least, instead of him becoming yet another overlooked talent working on animated cartoons.

I first met Stan in 1979, when he was one of an entourage of Hawaiian cartoonists visiting the San Diego Comic-Con (now known as Comic-Con International) led by Oahu's much-loved cartoon *sensei*, Dave Thorne. The following year, Dave's group (including young Stan) returned to the convention, as well as taking a side trip to Los Angeles. There, they dropped by Hanna-Barbera Productions, where I was working in the layout department on new *Flintstones* TV cartoons. I was delighted to give my new friends an insider's tour of the studio, where my co-workers greeted the newcomers with the same sort of poo-flinging (thankfully, not literally) that's usually unleashed upon unsuspecting visitors to a zoo's monkey house! Years later, Stan confided in me that the sight of dozens of animators laboring in identical cubicles is what convinced him that the one career he definitely *didn't* want to pursue was making animated cartoons!

And — other than co-creating a backup story ("Digger Duckbill" in Fantagraphics' *Usagi Yojimbo* #13, with Mark Evanier) back when Stan often spotlighted work by his cartoonist friends — I'm proud to claim I've had yet another effect on everyone's favorite rabbit *ronin*.

For decades, in addition to my own cartooning career in comic books, animation, and advertising, I've collected and studied what I refer to as "Oddball Comics." These include mainstream comic books of all genres that, due to various nutty aspects, make one wonder how they ever got published in the first place! (If you're curious about these, please visit my week-daily Internet column, "Oddball Comics," featuring the world's craziest comic books at <*www.comicbookresources/columns/oddball/*>.) One of the most popular — and certainly most ridiculous — categories of Oddball Comics that I've identified are funnybooks bearing what I call "fish-in-the-face" covers. These four-color oddities feature cover scenes of people (usually bad guys) getting hit smack-dab in the face with a fish! Apparently, Stan's a big fin, er, fan of these fish-in-the-face covers, too, as his cover of *Usagi Yojimbo* #49 — reprinted within this volume — attests. And if you think that's a fluke (ow!), check out my guest appearance on pages 13 through 16 of "Three Seasons." (Stan's portrayed me as that thug with the crewcut and the aloha-print kimono!)

Finally, here're some observations about Stan himself. When I first met him, his work certainly showed great promise. But I can think of no one in comics who has worked harder than Stan to bring his level of writing, drawing, and sheer storytelling to the heights of excellence he delivers with each new issue of *Usagi Yojimbo*. I'm equally impressed with Stan's ability to produce consistently outstanding work with the flawless self-discipline of a *samurai*. At our traditional Friday afternoon cartoonist lunches, many of our gang relate sob stories about creative blocks, clueless bosses, layoffs, or missed deadlines. Meanwhile, with a little smile on his face, Stan calmly hands out copies of the latest *Usagi*! Amazingly, Stan is also able to maintain a full life away from the drawing board as a wonderful husband and father. Everyone who knows Stan seems to respect and admire him; he's certainly the most "balanced" person I've ever met. (As for his rotten side, well, you'll just have to wait for the Fed Ex man's introduction to the next *Usagi Yojimbo* collection to spill the beans about that!)

We're all lucky to have Stan's *Usagi Yojimbo* to enjoy on a regular basis, but I'm especially lucky to have Stan as one of my best friends. And that's better than getting a fish-in-the-face any day!

Scott Shaw!
September 27, 2002

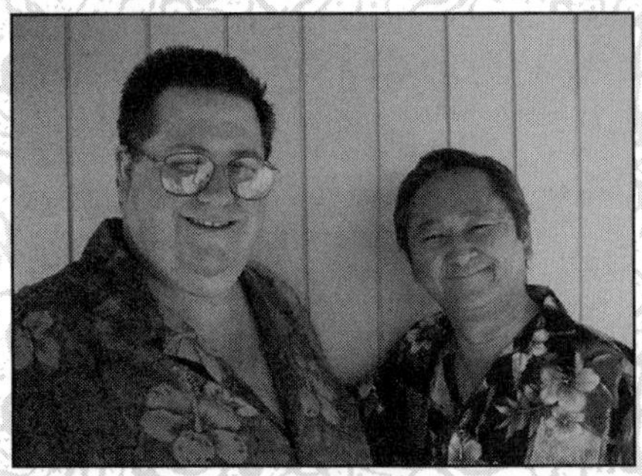

Friend and colleague Scott Shaw! with Stan Sakai

CONTENTS

THIS ONE IS DEDICATED TO
KEISO AND MIRIAM SAKAI.

SHOWDOWN

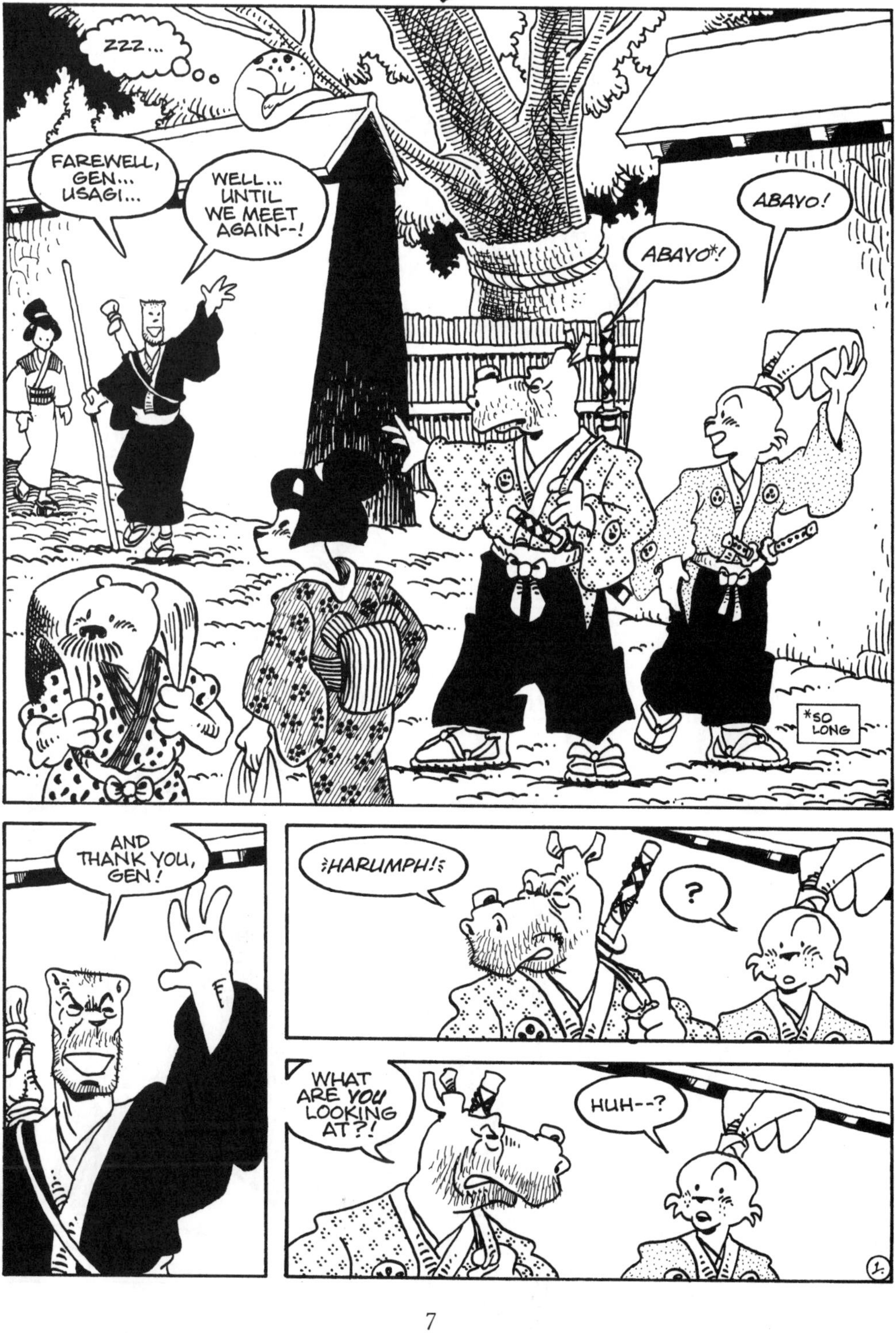
ZZZ...
FAREWELL, GEN... USAGI...
WELL... UNTIL WE MEET AGAIN--!
ABAYO*!
ABAYO!
*SO LONG
AND THANK YOU, GEN!
HARUMPH!
?
WHAT ARE YOU LOOKING AT?!
HUH--?
1.

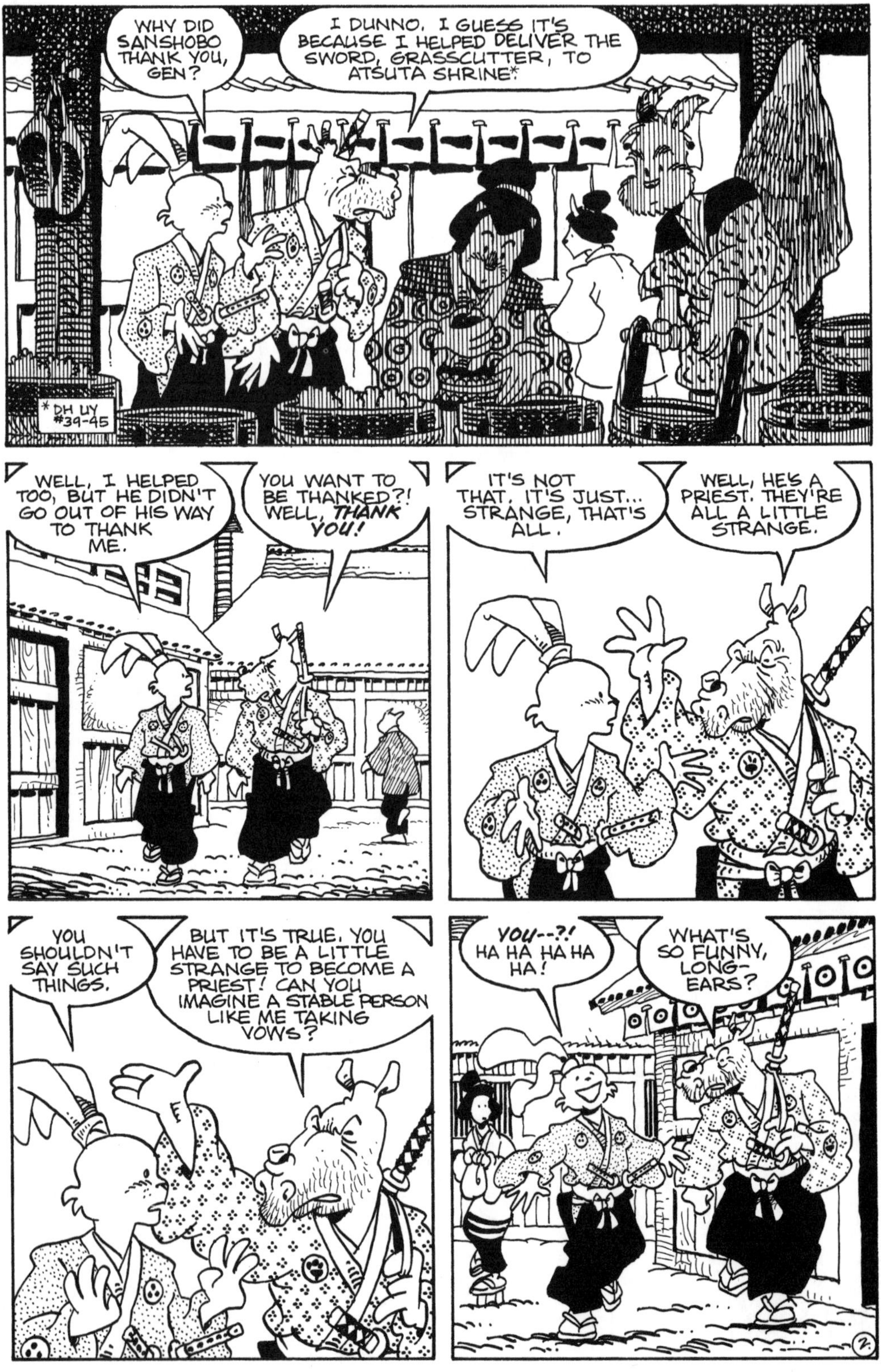

WHY DID SANSHOBO THANK YOU, GEN?
I DUNNO. I GUESS IT'S BECAUSE I HELPED DELIVER THE SWORD, GRASSCUTTER, TO ATSUTA SHRINE*.
* DH UY #39-45
WELL, I HELPED TOO, BUT HE DIDN'T GO OUT OF HIS WAY TO THANK ME.
YOU WANT TO BE THANKED?! WELL, THANK YOU!
IT'S NOT THAT. IT'S JUST... STRANGE, THAT'S ALL.
WELL, HE'S A PRIEST. THEY'RE ALL A LITTLE STRANGE.
YOU SHOULDN'T SAY SUCH THINGS.
BUT IT'S TRUE. YOU HAVE TO BE A LITTLE STRANGE TO BECOME A PRIEST! CAN YOU IMAGINE A STABLE PERSON LIKE ME TAKING VOWS?
YOU--?! HA HA HA HA HA HA!
WHAT'S SO FUNNY, LONG-EARS?
2.

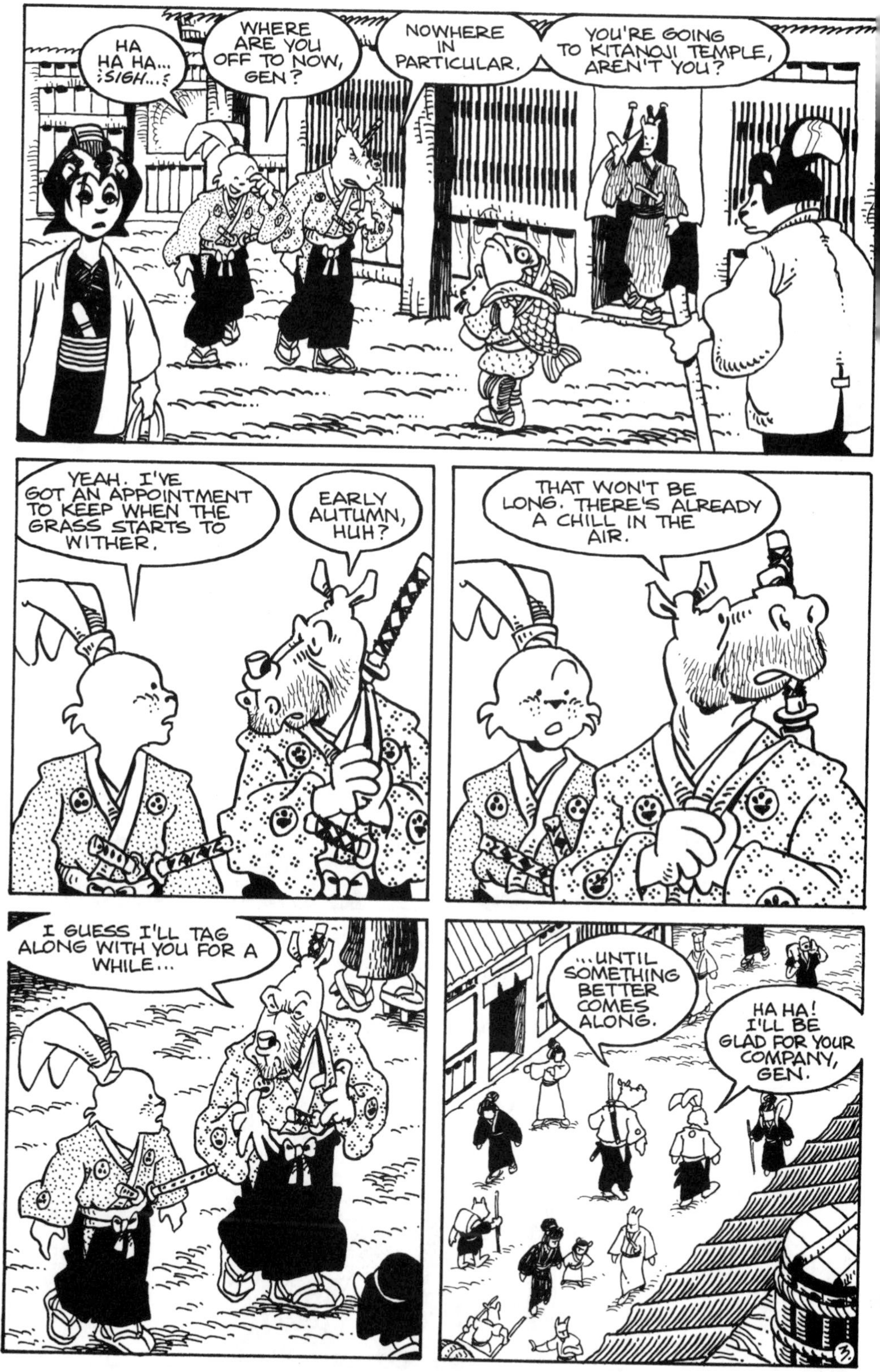

HA HA HA... SIGH...
WHERE ARE YOU OFF TO NOW, GEN?
NOWHERE IN PARTICULAR.
YOU'RE GOING TO KITANOJI TEMPLE, AREN'T YOU?
YEAH. I'VE GOT AN APPOINTMENT TO KEEP WHEN THE GRASS STARTS TO WITHER.
EARLY AUTUMN, HUH?
THAT WON'T BE LONG. THERE'S ALREADY A CHILL IN THE AIR.
I GUESS I'LL TAG ALONG WITH YOU FOR A WHILE...
...UNTIL SOMETHING BETTER COMES ALONG.
HA HA! I'LL BE GLAD FOR YOUR COMPANY, GEN.
3

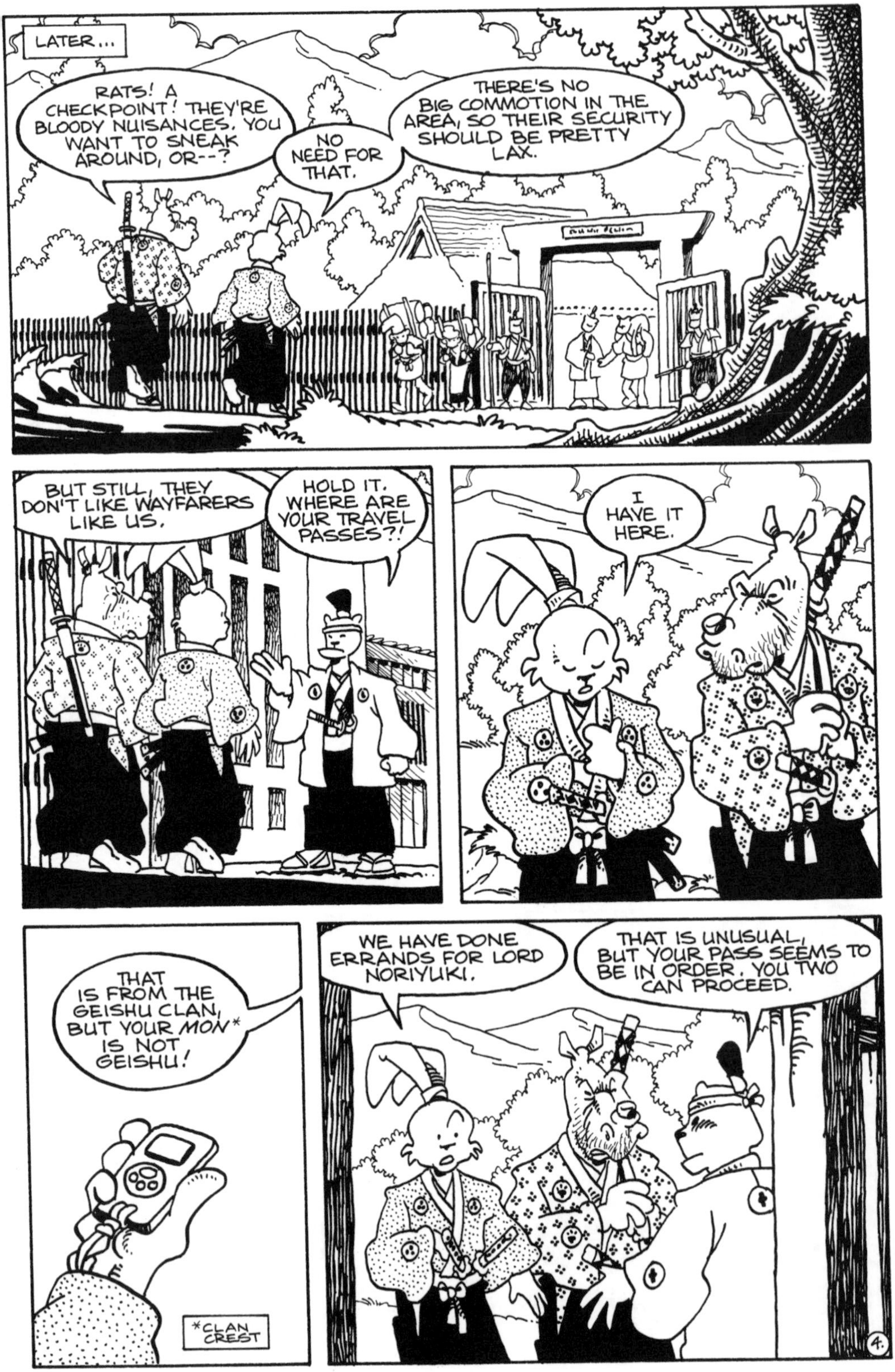
LATER...
RATS! A CHECKPOINT! THEY'RE BLOODY NUISANCES. YOU WANT TO SNEAK AROUND, OR--?
NO NEED FOR THAT.
THERE'S NO BIG COMMOTION IN THE AREA, SO THEIR SECURITY SHOULD BE PRETTY LAX.
BUT STILL, THEY DON'T LIKE WAYFARERS LIKE US.
HOLD IT. WHERE ARE YOUR TRAVEL PASSES?!
I HAVE IT HERE.
THAT IS FROM THE GEISHU CLAN, BUT YOUR *MON** IS NOT GEISHU!
*CLAN CREST
WE HAVE DONE ERRANDS FOR LORD NORIYUKI.
THAT IS UNUSUAL, BUT YOUR PASS SEEMS TO BE IN ORDER. YOU TWO CAN PROCEED.
4.

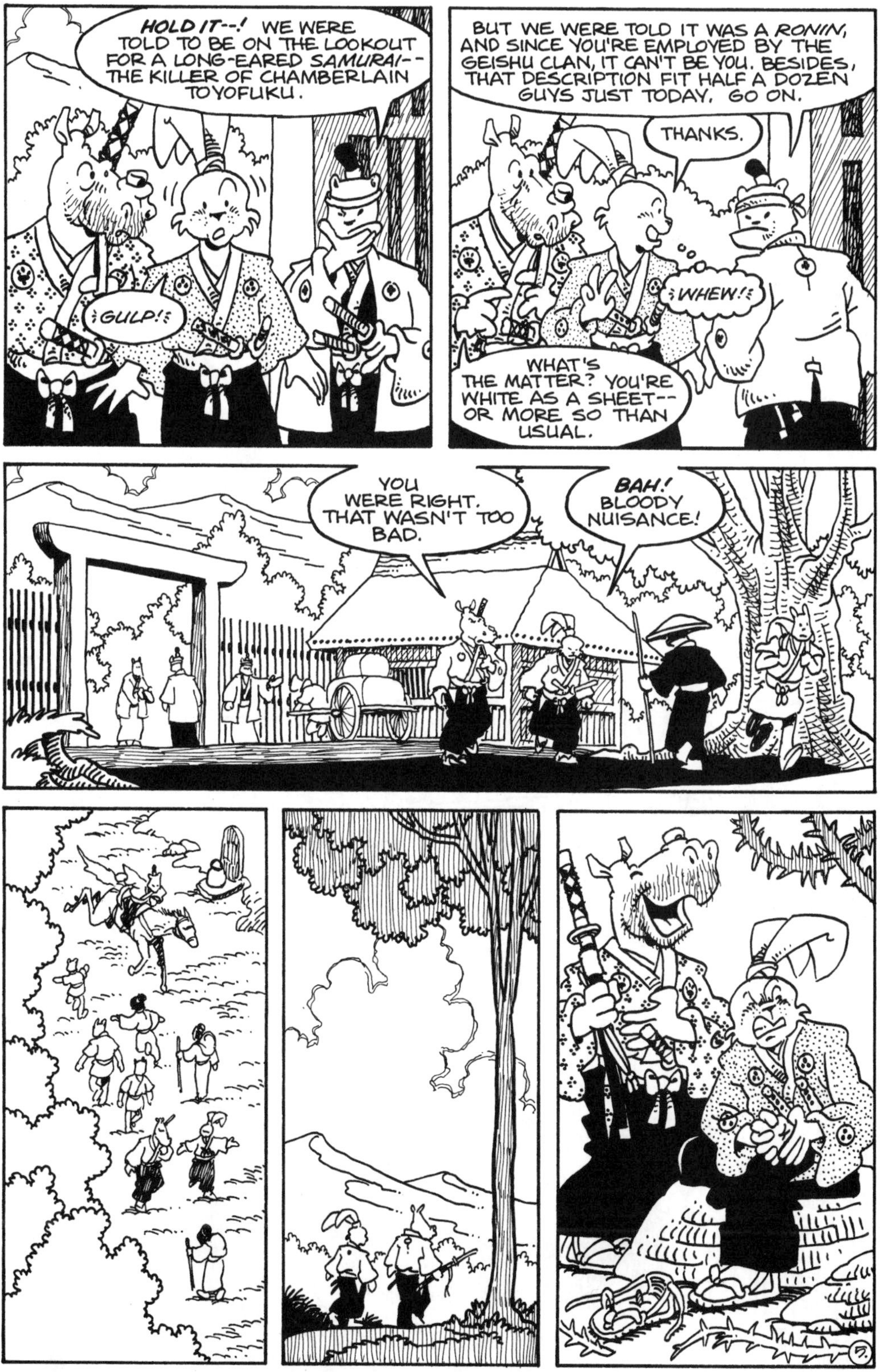
HOLD IT--! WE WERE TOLD TO BE ON THE LOOKOUT FOR A LONG-EARED SAMURAI--THE KILLER OF CHAMBERLAIN TOYOFUKU.
GULP!
BUT WE WERE TOLD IT WAS A RONIN, AND SINCE YOU'RE EMPLOYED BY THE GEISHU CLAN, IT CAN'T BE YOU. BESIDES, THAT DESCRIPTION FIT HALF A DOZEN GUYS JUST TODAY. GO ON.
THANKS.
WHEW!
WHAT'S THE MATTER? YOU'RE WHITE AS A SHEET--OR MORE SO THAN USUAL.
YOU WERE RIGHT. THAT WASN'T TOO BAD.
BAH! BLOODY NUISANCE!

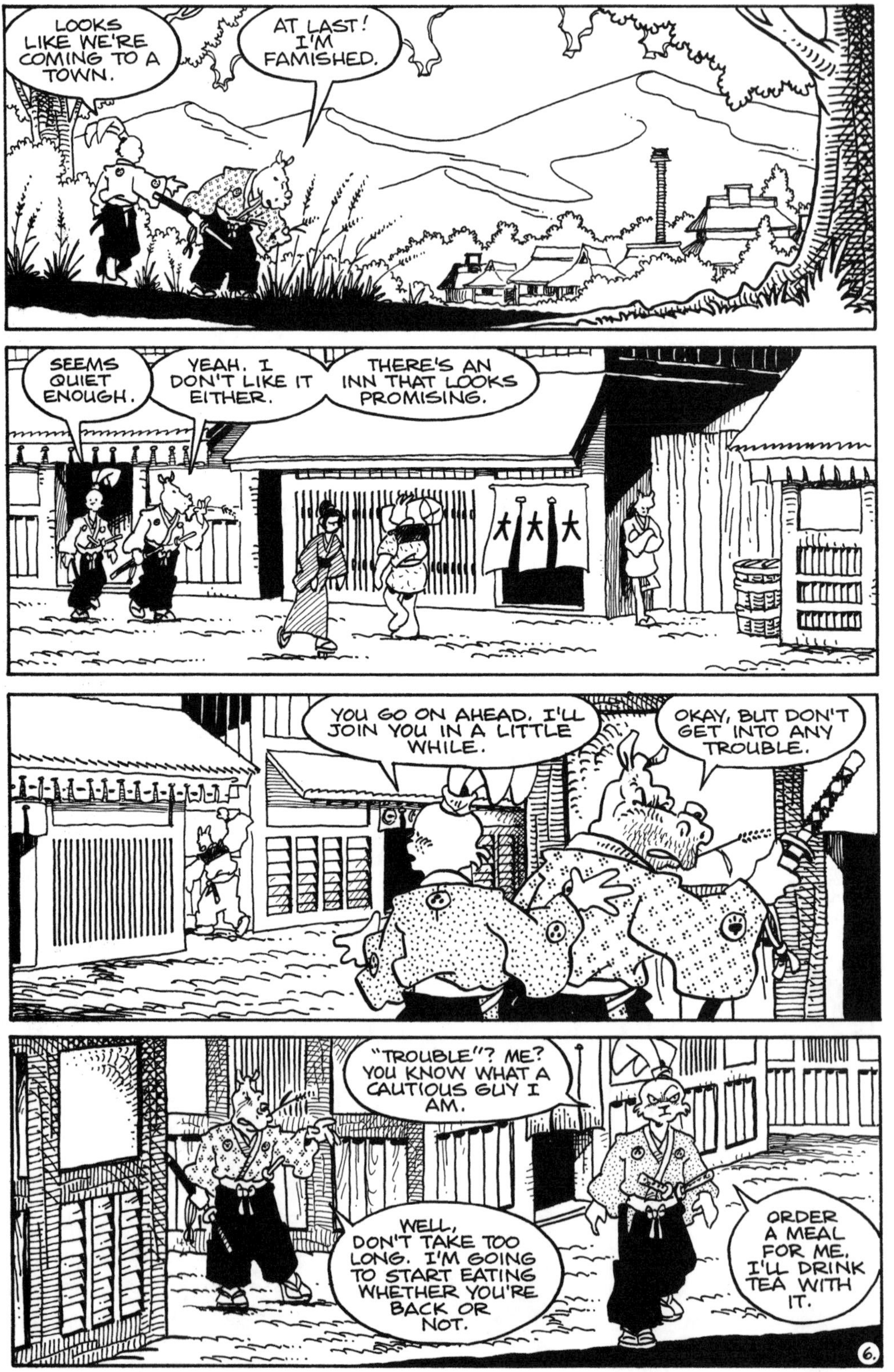
LOOKS LIKE WE'RE COMING TO A TOWN.
AT LAST! I'M FAMISHED.
SEEMS QUIET ENOUGH.
YEAH. I DON'T LIKE IT EITHER.
THERE'S AN INN THAT LOOKS PROMISING.
YOU GO ON AHEAD. I'LL JOIN YOU IN A LITTLE WHILE.
OKAY, BUT DON'T GET INTO ANY TROUBLE.
"TROUBLE"? ME? YOU KNOW WHAT A CAUTIOUS GUY I AM.
WELL, DON'T TAKE TOO LONG. I'M GOING TO START EATING WHETHER YOU'RE BACK OR NOT.
ORDER A MEAL FOR ME. I'LL DRINK TEA WITH IT.
6.

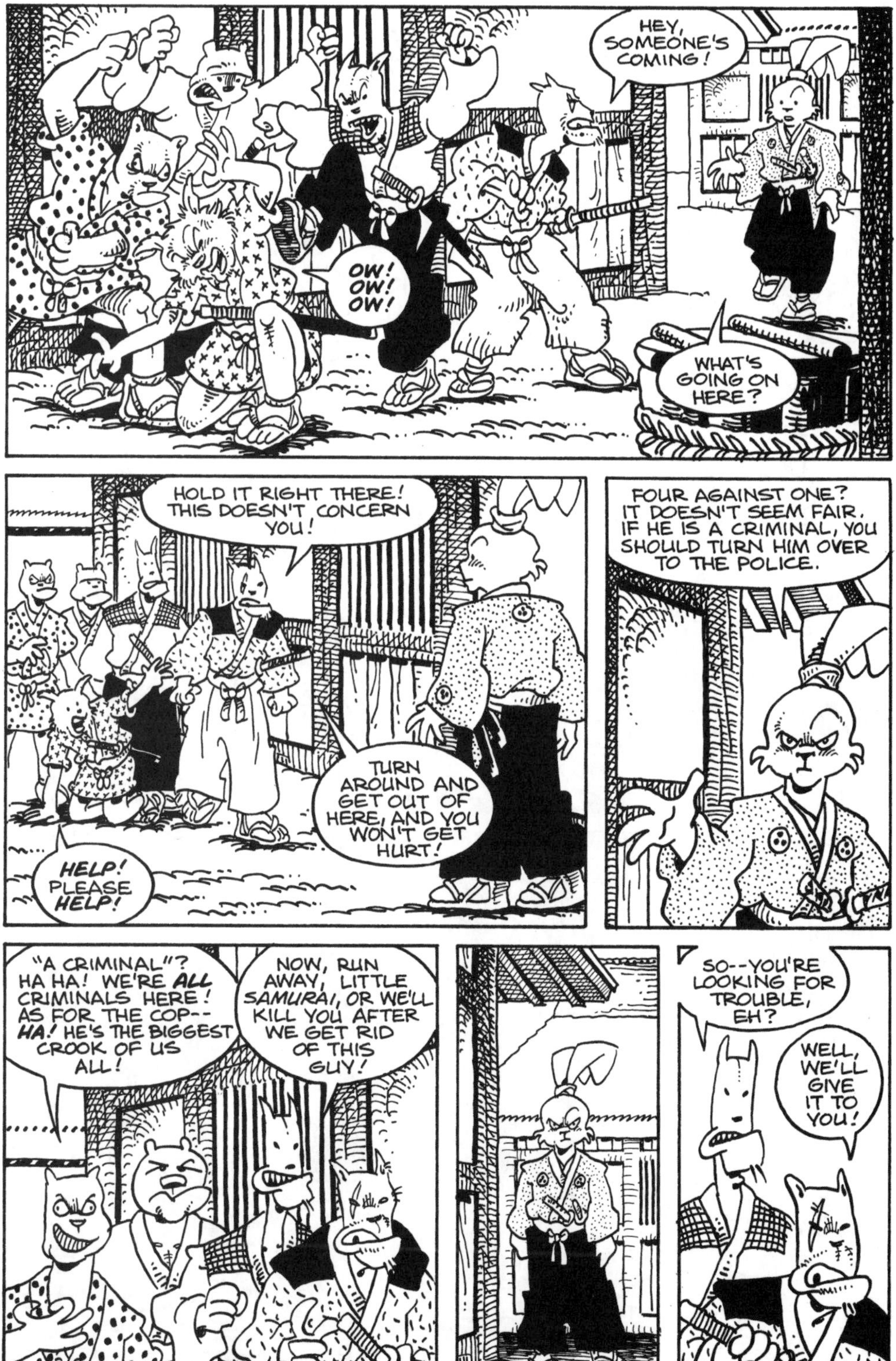
HEY, SOMEONE'S COMING!
OW! OW! OW!
WHAT'S GOING ON HERE?
HOLD IT RIGHT THERE! THIS DOESN'T CONCERN YOU!
TURN AROUND AND GET OUT OF HERE, AND YOU WON'T GET HURT!
HELP! PLEASE HELP!
FOUR AGAINST ONE? IT DOESN'T SEEM FAIR. IF HE IS A CRIMINAL, YOU SHOULD TURN HIM OVER TO THE POLICE.
"A CRIMINAL"? HA HA! WE'RE ALL CRIMINALS HERE! AS FOR THE COP-- HA! HE'S THE BIGGEST CROOK OF US ALL!
NOW, RUN AWAY, LITTLE SAMURAI, OR WE'LL KILL YOU AFTER WE GET RID OF THIS GUY!
SO--YOU'RE LOOKING FOR TROUBLE, EH?
WELL, WE'LL GIVE IT TO YOU!
7.

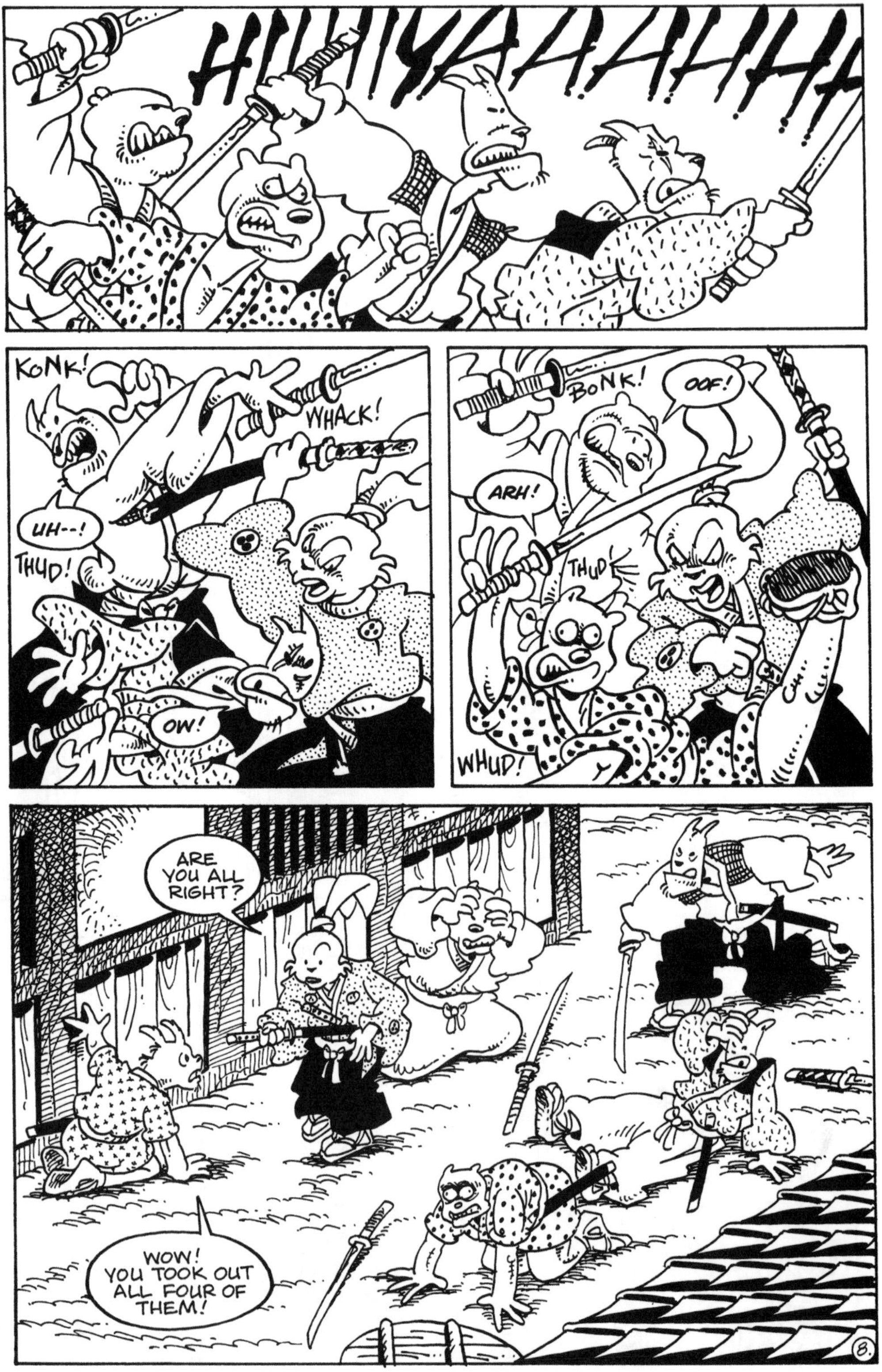
HIIIYAAAHHHH
KONK!
WHACK!
UH--!
THUD!
OW!
BONK!
OOF!
ARH!
THUD
WHUD!
ARE YOU ALL RIGHT?
WOW! YOU TOOK OUT ALL FOUR OF THEM!
8.

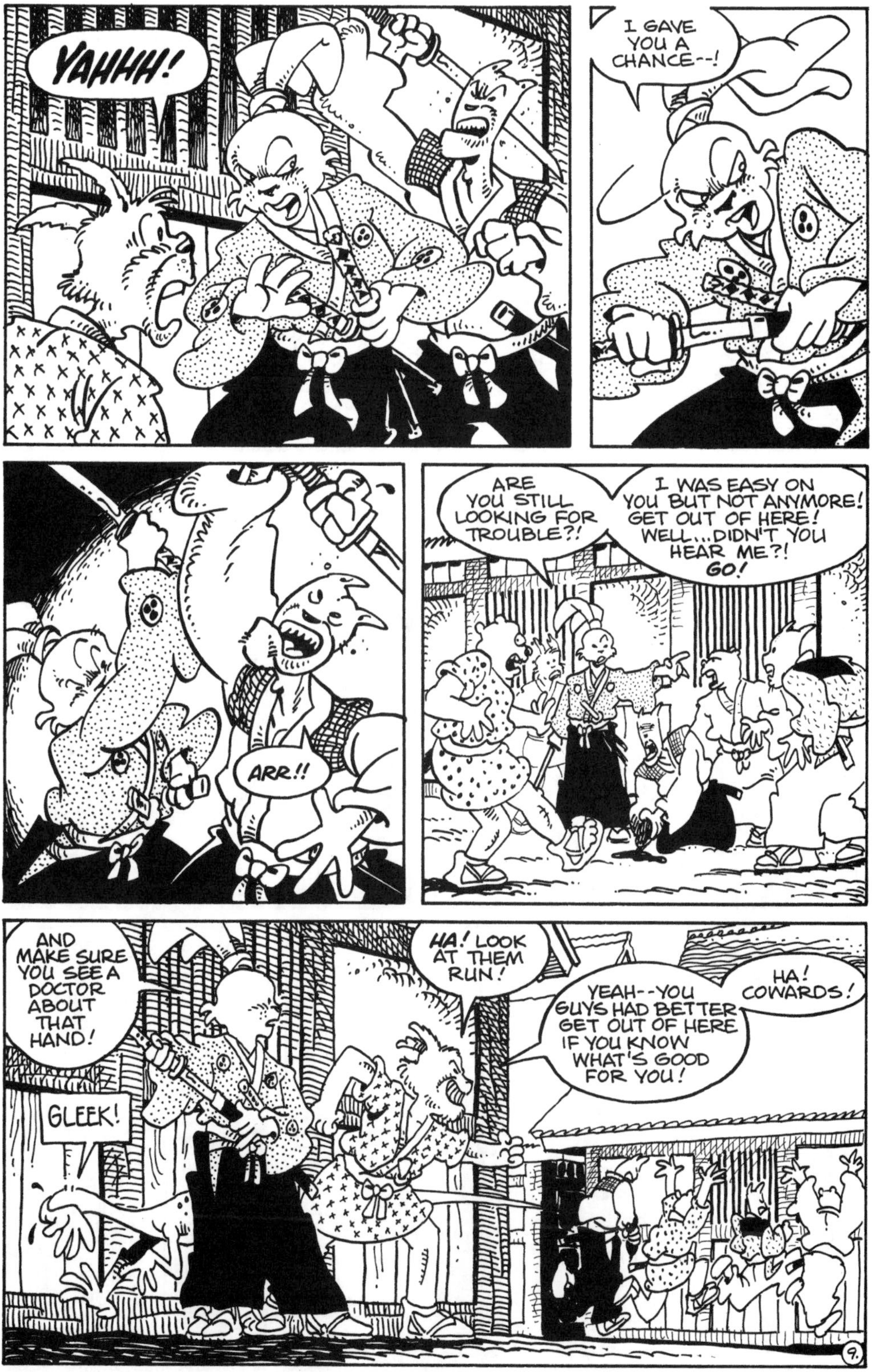
YAHHH!
I GAVE YOU A CHANCE--!
ARR!!
ARE YOU STILL LOOKING FOR TROUBLE?!
I WAS EASY ON YOU BUT NOT ANYMORE! GET OUT OF HERE! WELL...DIDN'T YOU HEAR ME?! GO!
AND MAKE SURE YOU SEE A DOCTOR ABOUT THAT HAND!
GLEEK!
HA! LOOK AT THEM RUN!
YEAH--YOU GUYS HAD BETTER GET OUT OF HERE IF YOU KNOW WHAT'S GOOD FOR YOU!
HA! COWARDS!
9.

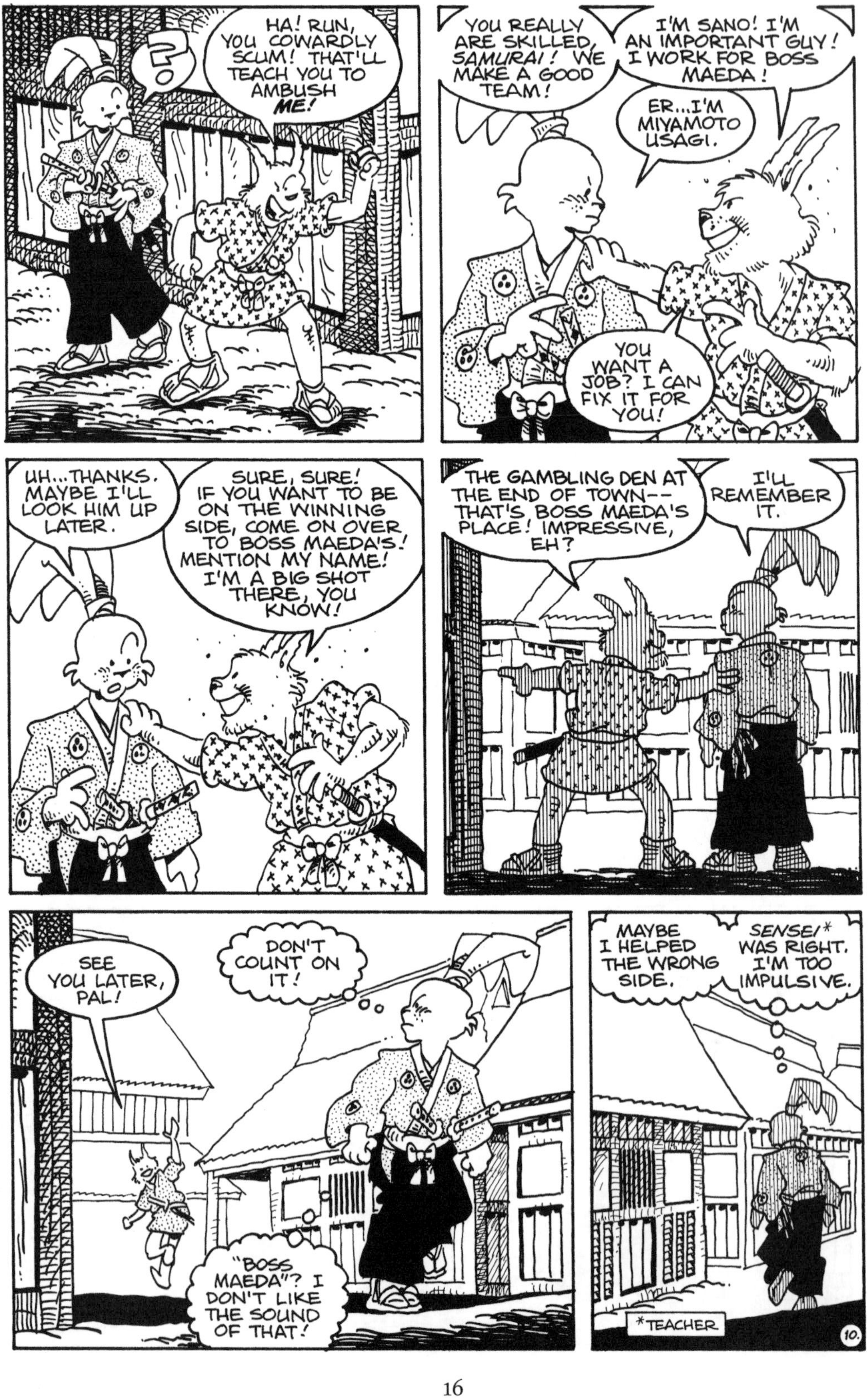
?
HA! RUN, YOU COWARDLY SCUM! THAT'LL TEACH YOU TO AMBUSH *ME!*
YOU REALLY ARE SKILLED, *SAMURAI!* WE MAKE A GOOD TEAM!
I'M SANO! I'M AN IMPORTANT GUY! I WORK FOR BOSS MAEDA!
ER...I'M MIYAMOTO USAGI.
YOU WANT A JOB? I CAN FIX IT FOR YOU!
UH...THANKS. MAYBE I'LL LOOK HIM UP LATER.
SURE, SURE! IF YOU WANT TO BE ON THE WINNING SIDE, COME ON OVER TO BOSS MAEDA'S! MENTION MY NAME! I'M A BIG SHOT THERE, YOU KNOW!
THE GAMBLING DEN AT THE END OF TOWN-- THAT'S BOSS MAEDA'S PLACE! IMPRESSIVE, EH?
I'LL REMEMBER IT.
SEE YOU LATER, PAL!
DON'T COUNT ON IT!
"BOSS MAEDA"? I DON'T LIKE THE SOUND OF THAT!
MAYBE I HELPED THE WRONG SIDE.
*SENSEI** WAS RIGHT. I'M TOO IMPULSIVE.
*TEACHER
10.

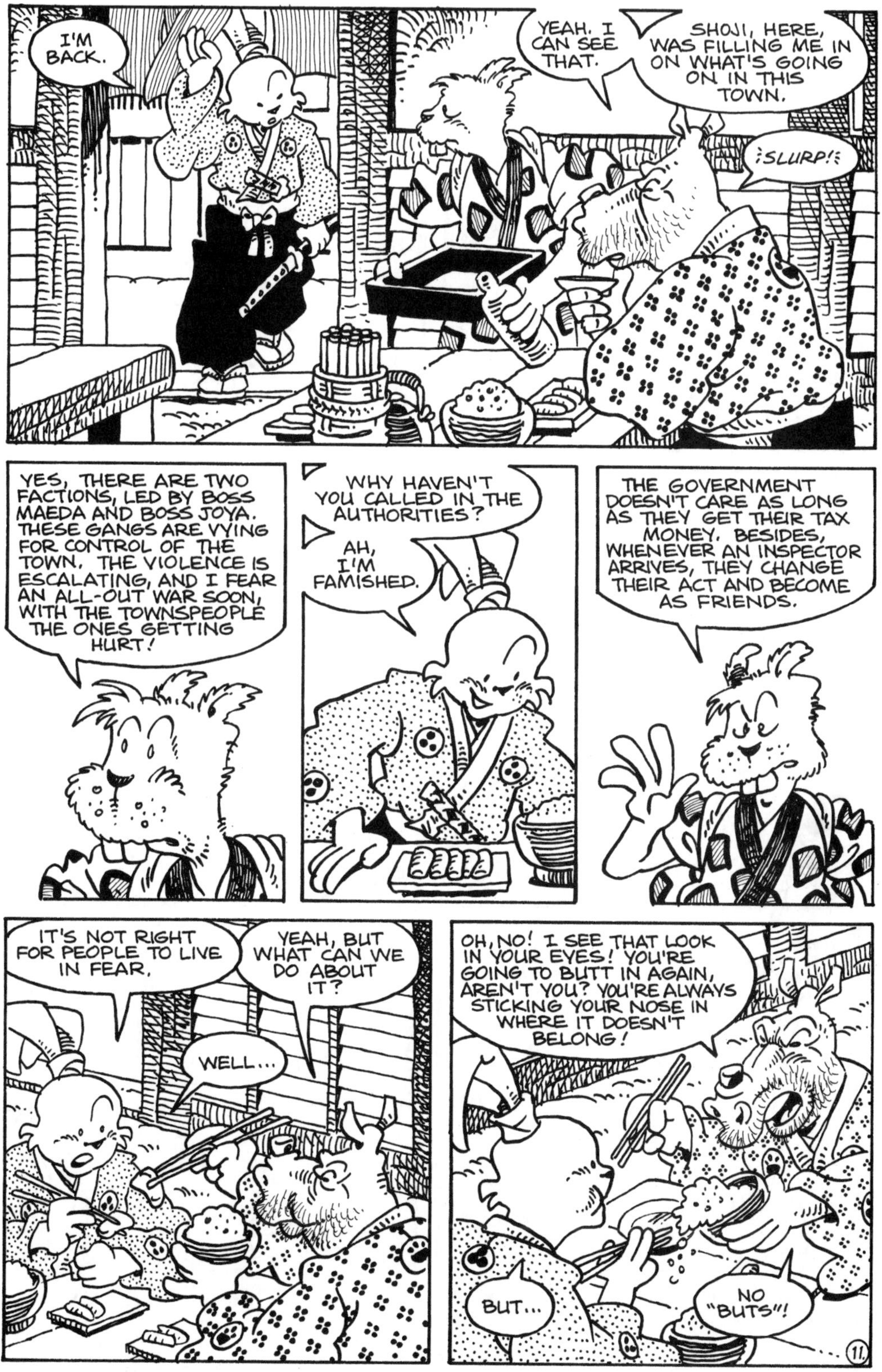
I'M BACK.
YEAH. I CAN SEE THAT.
SHOJI, HERE, WAS FILLING ME IN ON WHAT'S GOING ON IN THIS TOWN.
¡SLURP!
YES, THERE ARE TWO FACTIONS, LED BY BOSS MAEDA AND BOSS JOYA. THESE GANGS ARE VYING FOR CONTROL OF THE TOWN. THE VIOLENCE IS ESCALATING, AND I FEAR AN ALL-OUT WAR SOON, WITH THE TOWNSPEOPLE THE ONES GETTING HURT!
WHY HAVEN'T YOU CALLED IN THE AUTHORITIES?
AH, I'M FAMISHED.
THE GOVERNMENT DOESN'T CARE AS LONG AS THEY GET THEIR TAX MONEY. BESIDES, WHENEVER AN INSPECTOR ARRIVES, THEY CHANGE THEIR ACT AND BECOME AS FRIENDS.
IT'S NOT RIGHT FOR PEOPLE TO LIVE IN FEAR.
YEAH, BUT WHAT CAN WE DO ABOUT IT?
WELL...
OH, NO! I SEE THAT LOOK IN YOUR EYES! YOU'RE GOING TO BUTT IN AGAIN, AREN'T YOU? YOU'RE ALWAYS STICKING YOUR NOSE IN WHERE IT DOESN'T BELONG!
BUT...
NO "BUTS"!
11.

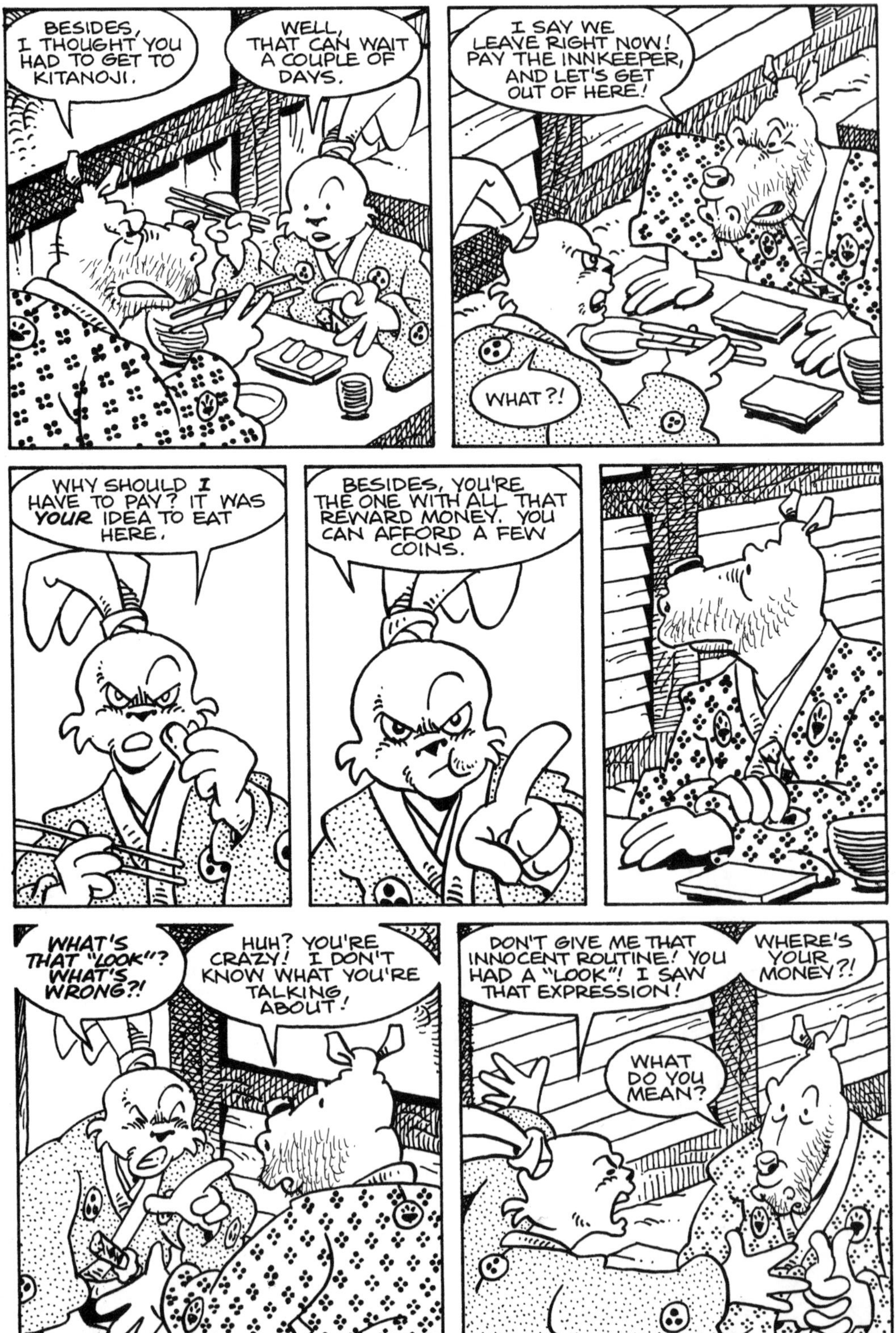
BESIDES, I THOUGHT YOU HAD TO GET TO KITANOJI.
WELL, THAT CAN WAIT A COUPLE OF DAYS.
I SAY WE LEAVE RIGHT NOW! PAY THE INNKEEPER, AND LET'S GET OUT OF HERE!
WHAT?!
WHY SHOULD I HAVE TO PAY? IT WAS YOUR IDEA TO EAT HERE.
BESIDES, YOU'RE THE ONE WITH ALL THAT REWARD MONEY. YOU CAN AFFORD A FEW COINS.
WHAT'S THAT "LOOK"? WHAT'S WRONG?!
HUH? YOU'RE CRAZY! I DON'T KNOW WHAT YOU'RE TALKING ABOUT!
DON'T GIVE ME THAT INNOCENT ROUTINE! YOU HAD A "LOOK"! I SAW THAT EXPRESSION!
WHERE'S YOUR MONEY?!
WHAT DO YOU MEAN?
12

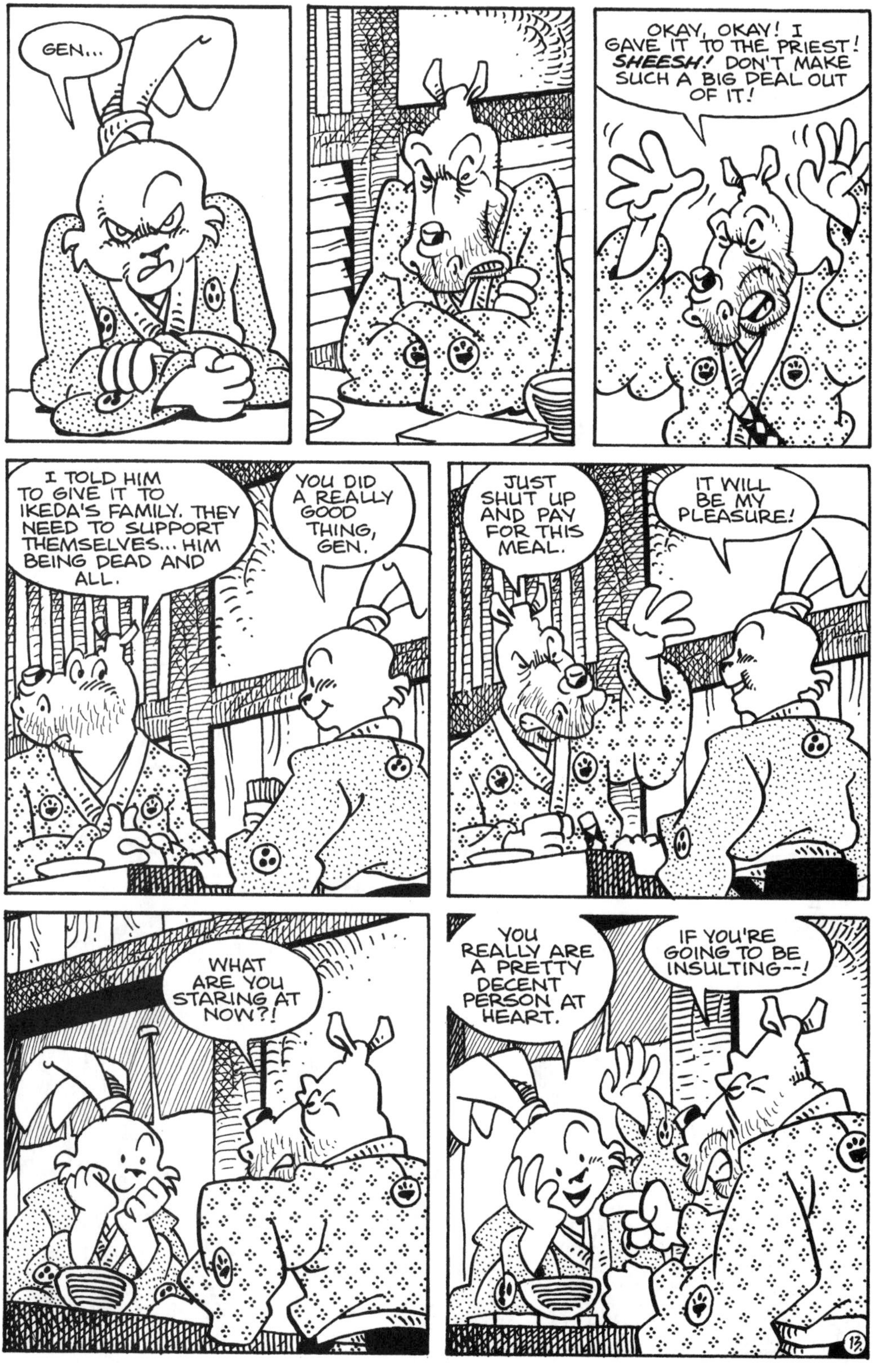
GEN...
OKAY, OKAY! I GAVE IT TO THE PRIEST! SHEESH! DON'T MAKE SUCH A BIG DEAL OUT OF IT!
I TOLD HIM TO GIVE IT TO IKEDA'S FAMILY. THEY NEED TO SUPPORT THEMSELVES... HIM BEING DEAD AND ALL.
YOU DID A REALLY GOOD THING, GEN.
JUST SHUT UP AND PAY FOR THIS MEAL.
IT WILL BE MY PLEASURE!
WHAT ARE YOU STARING AT NOW?!
YOU REALLY ARE A PRETTY DECENT PERSON AT HEART.
IF YOU'RE GOING TO BE INSULTING--!
13

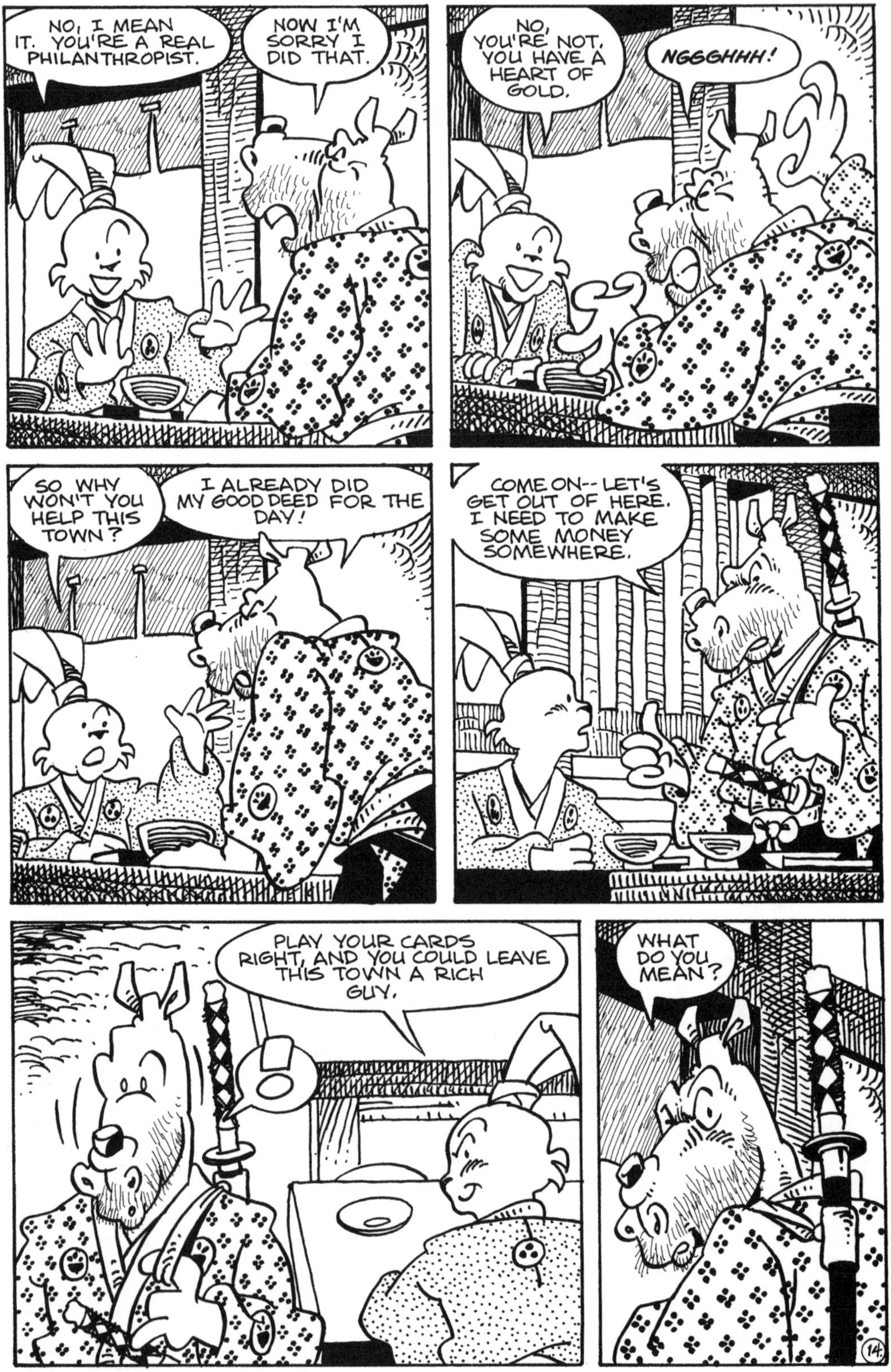
NO, I MEAN IT. YOU'RE A REAL PHILANTHROPIST.
NOW I'M SORRY I DID THAT.
NO, YOU'RE NOT. YOU HAVE A HEART OF GOLD.
NGGGHHH!
SO WHY WON'T YOU HELP THIS TOWN?
I ALREADY DID MY GOOD DEED FOR THE DAY!
COME ON-- LET'S GET OUT OF HERE. I NEED TO MAKE SOME MONEY SOMEWHERE.
PLAY YOUR CARDS RIGHT, AND YOU COULD LEAVE THIS TOWN A RICH GUY.
WHAT DO YOU MEAN?
14

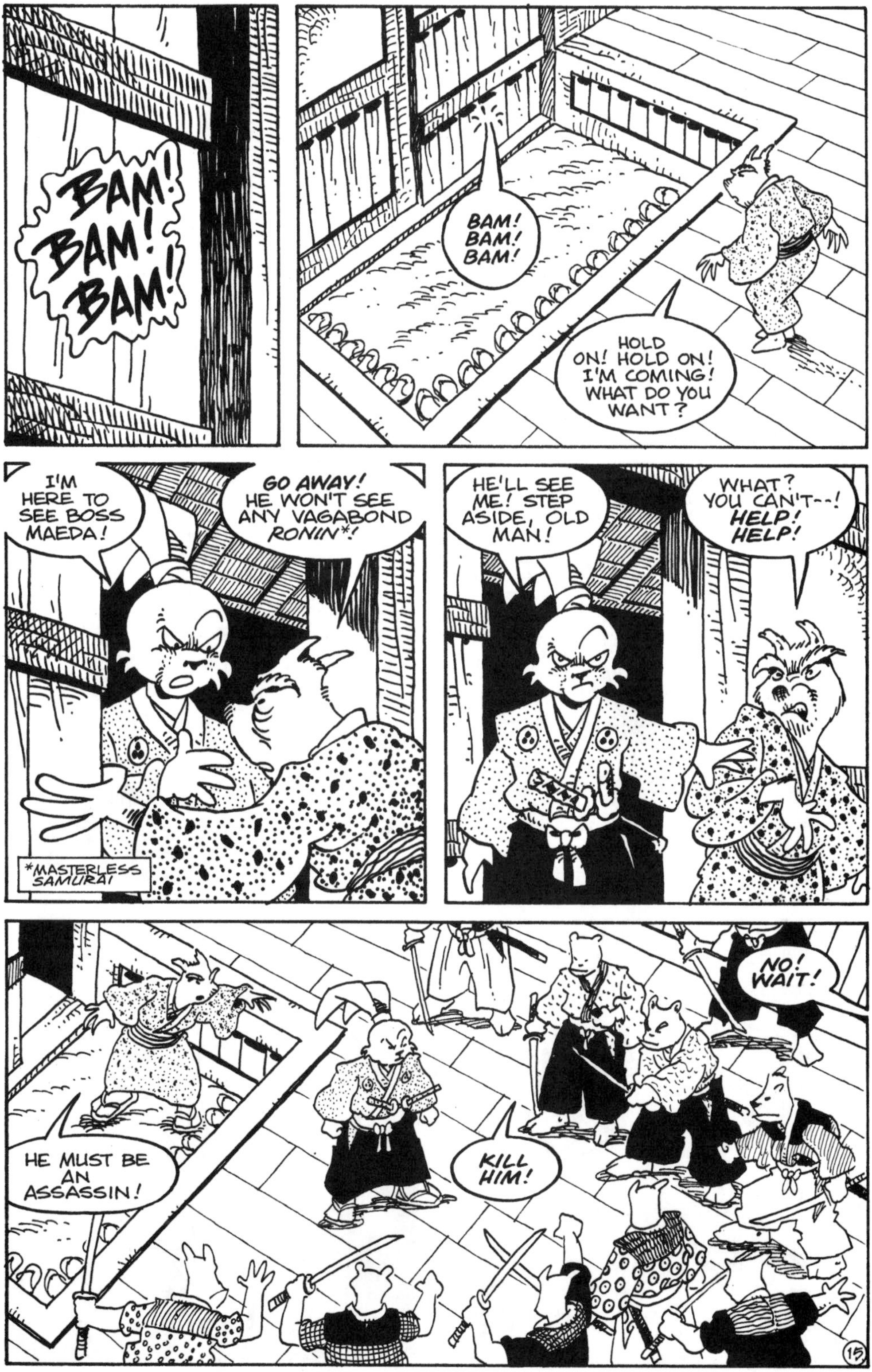
BAM! BAM! BAM!
BAM! BAM! BAM!
HOLD ON! HOLD ON! I'M COMING! WHAT DO YOU WANT?
I'M HERE TO SEE BOSS MAEDA!
GO AWAY! HE WON'T SEE ANY VAGABOND RONIN*!
*MASTERLESS SAMURAI
HE'LL SEE ME! STEP ASIDE, OLD MAN!
WHAT? YOU CAN'T--! HELP! HELP!
NO! WAIT!
HE MUST BE AN ASSASSIN!
KILL HIM!
15

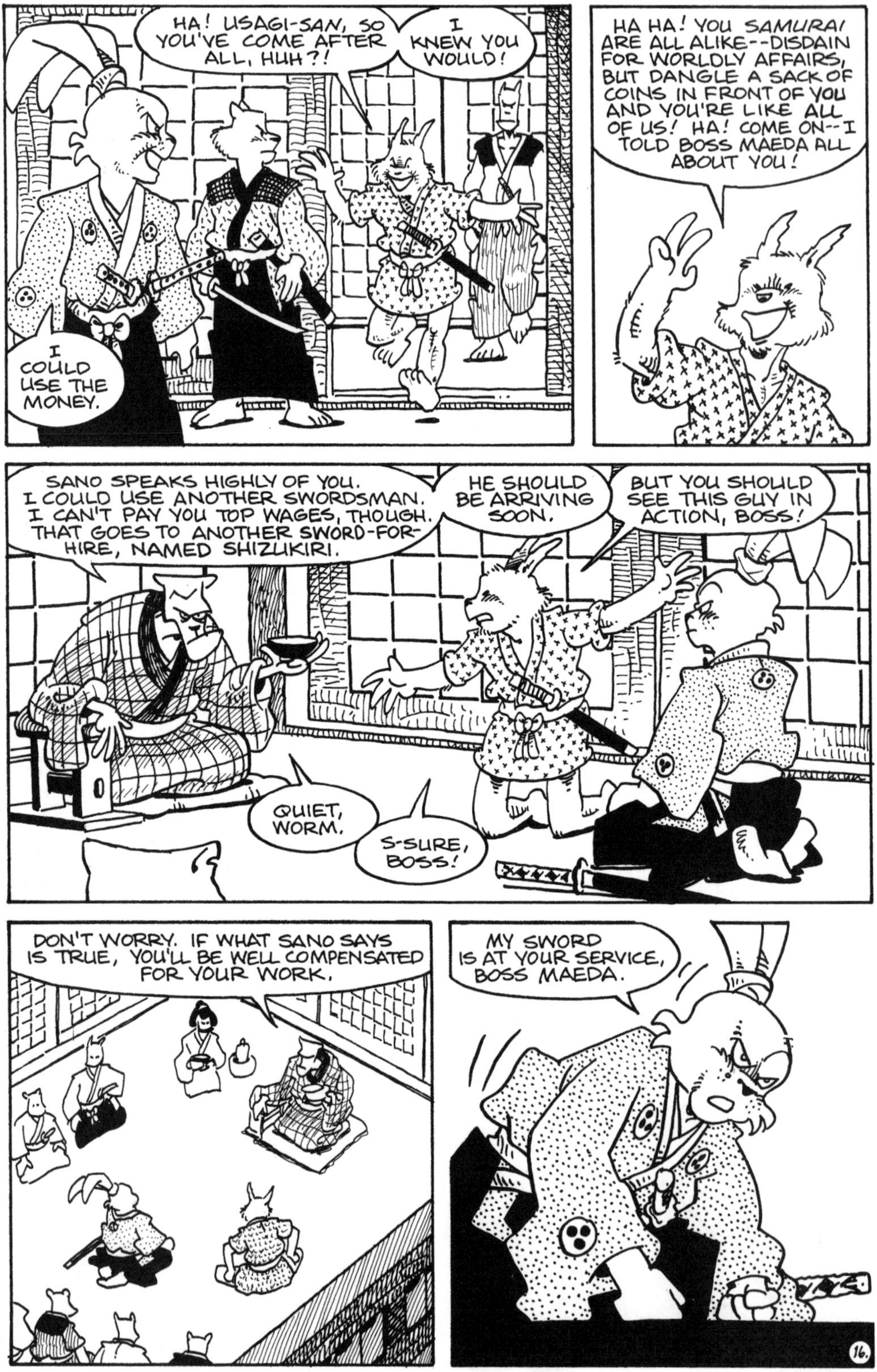
HA! USAGI-SAN, SO YOU'VE COME AFTER ALL, HUH?!
I KNEW YOU WOULD!
I COULD USE THE MONEY.
HA HA! YOU SAMURAI ARE ALL ALIKE--DISDAIN FOR WORLDLY AFFAIRS, BUT DANGLE A SACK OF COINS IN FRONT OF YOU AND YOU'RE LIKE ALL OF US! HA! COME ON--I TOLD BOSS MAEDA ALL ABOUT YOU!
SANO SPEAKS HIGHLY OF YOU. I COULD USE ANOTHER SWORDSMAN. I CAN'T PAY YOU TOP WAGES, THOUGH. THAT GOES TO ANOTHER SWORD-FOR-HIRE, NAMED SHIZUKIRI.
HE SHOULD BE ARRIVING SOON.
BUT YOU SHOULD SEE THIS GUY IN ACTION, BOSS!
QUIET, WORM.
S-SURE, BOSS!
DON'T WORRY. IF WHAT SANO SAYS IS TRUE, YOU'LL BE WELL COMPENSATED FOR YOUR WORK.
MY SWORD IS AT YOUR SERVICE, BOSS MAEDA.
16.

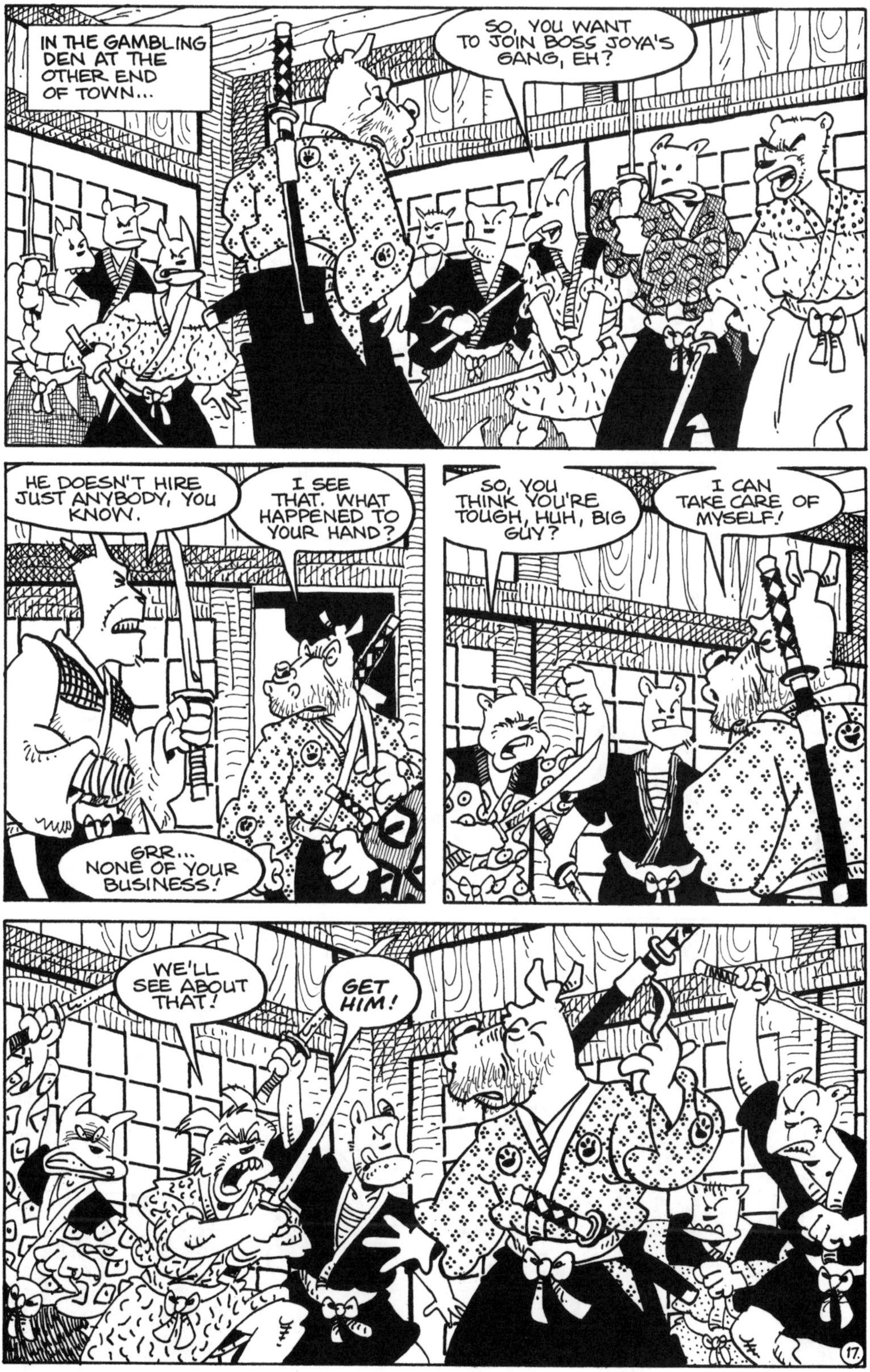
IN THE GAMBLING DEN AT THE OTHER END OF TOWN...
SO, YOU WANT TO JOIN BOSS JOYA'S GANG, EH?
HE DOESN'T HIRE JUST ANYBODY, YOU KNOW.
I SEE THAT. WHAT HAPPENED TO YOUR HAND?
GRR... NONE OF YOUR BUSINESS!
SO, YOU THINK YOU'RE TOUGH, HUH, BIG GUY?
I CAN TAKE CARE OF MYSELF!
WE'LL SEE ABOUT THAT!
GET HIM!
17

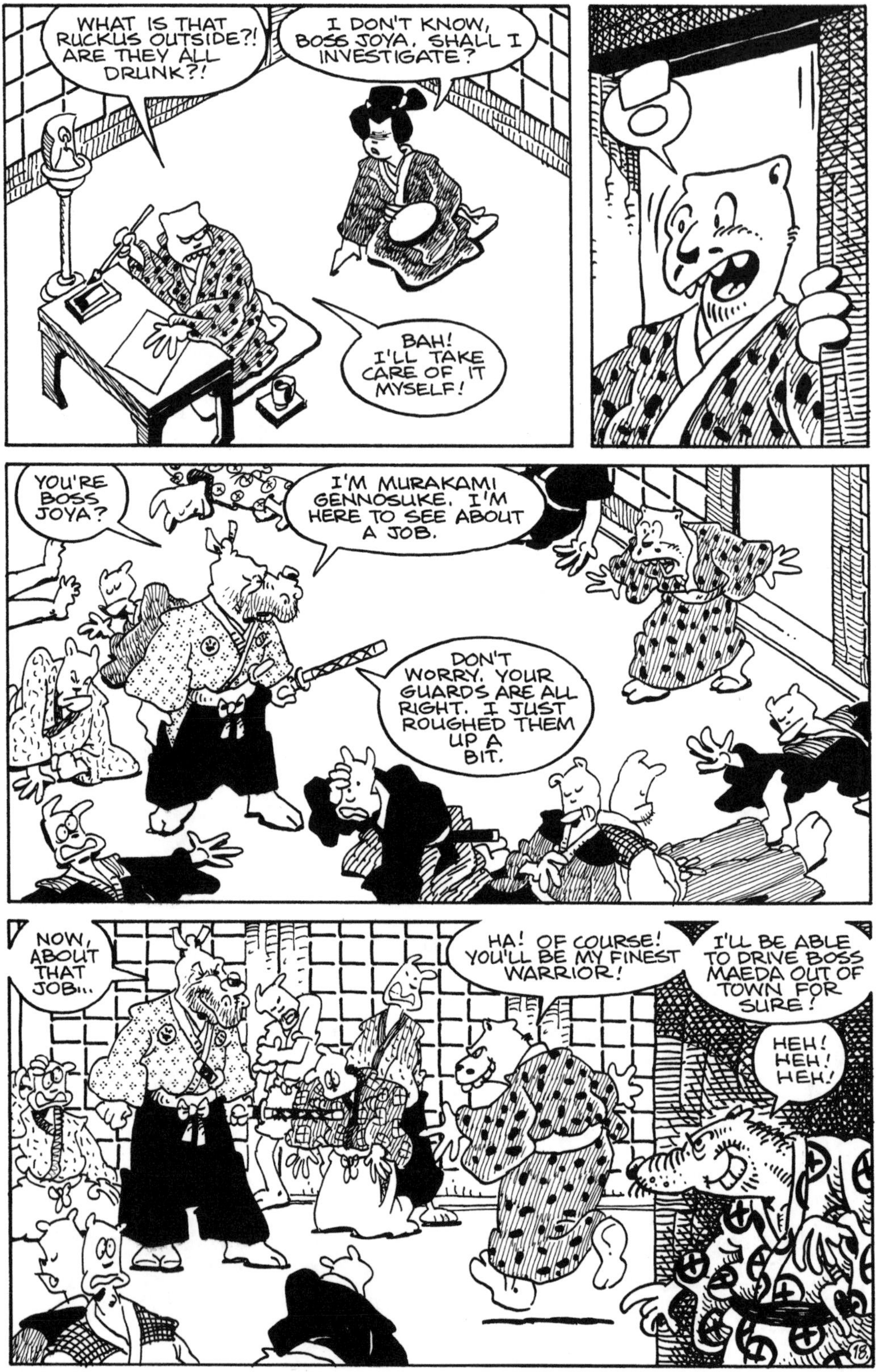
WHAT IS THAT RUCKUS OUTSIDE?! ARE THEY ALL DRUNK?!
I DON'T KNOW, BOSS JOYA, SHALL I INVESTIGATE?
BAH! I'LL TAKE CARE OF IT MYSELF!
YOU'RE BOSS JOYA?
I'M MURAKAMI GENNOSUKE. I'M HERE TO SEE ABOUT A JOB.
DON'T WORRY. YOUR GUARDS ARE ALL RIGHT. I JUST ROUGHED THEM UP A BIT.
NOW, ABOUT THAT JOB...
HA! OF COURSE! YOU'LL BE MY FINEST WARRIOR!
I'LL BE ABLE TO DRIVE BOSS MAEDA OUT OF TOWN FOR SURE!
HEH! HEH! HEH!
18.

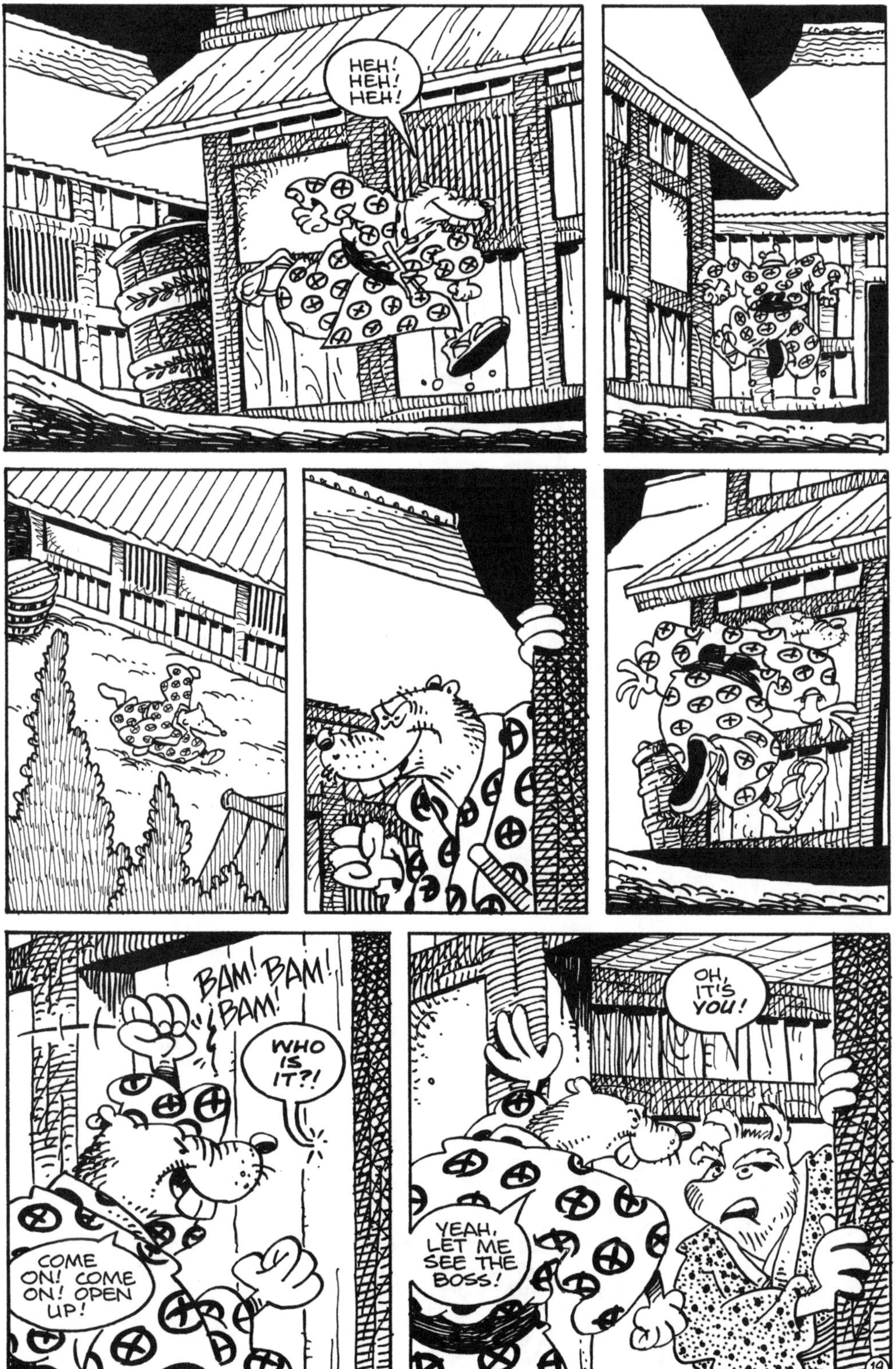
HEH! HEH! HEH!
BAM! BAM! BAM!
WHO IS IT?!
COME ON! COME ON! OPEN UP!
OH, IT'S YOU!
YEAH, LET ME SEE THE BOSS!
19

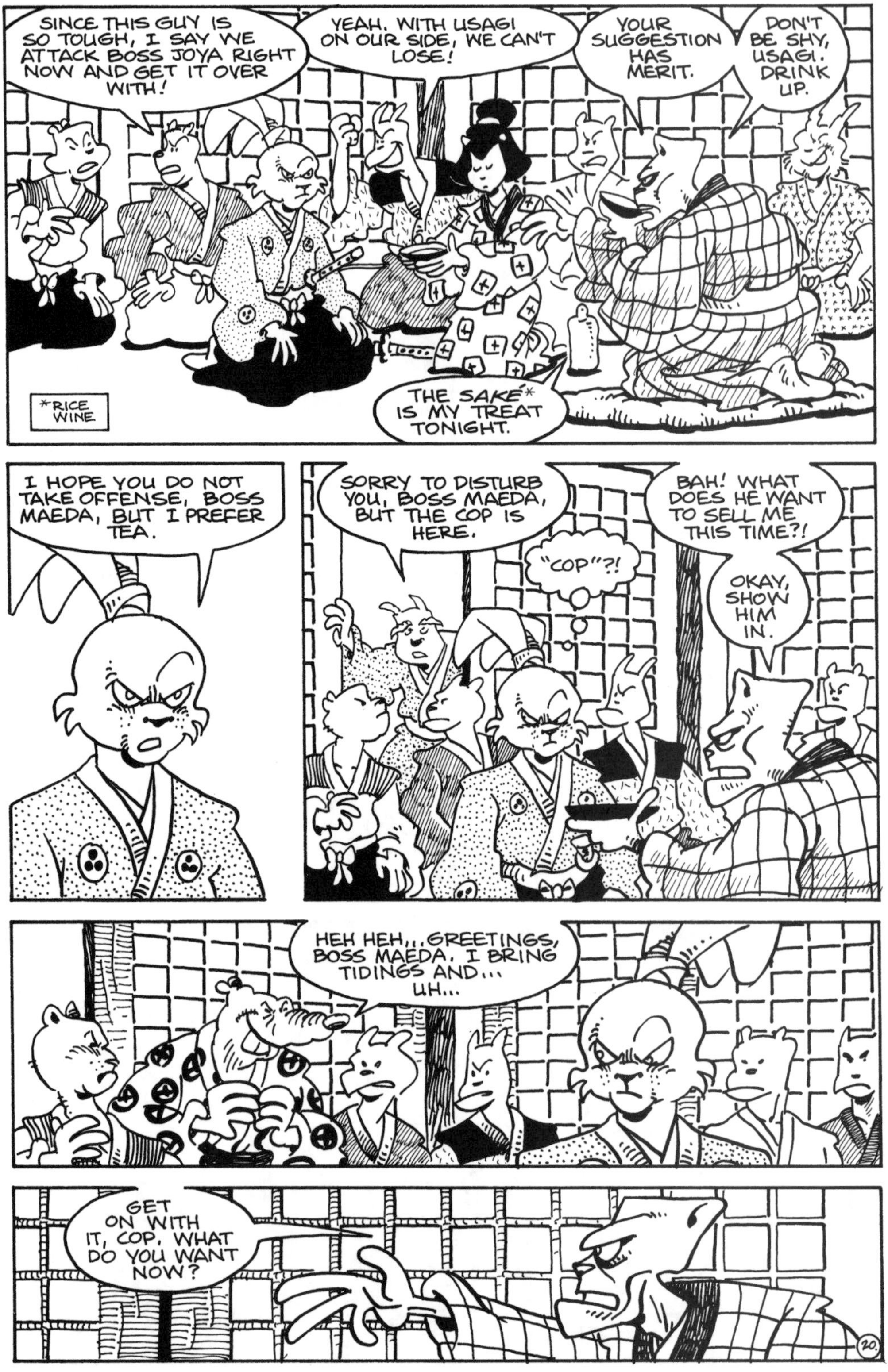
SINCE THIS GUY IS SO TOUGH, I SAY WE ATTACK BOSS JOYA RIGHT NOW AND GET IT OVER WITH!
YEAH. WITH USAGI ON OUR SIDE, WE CAN'T LOSE!
YOUR SUGGESTION HAS MERIT.
DON'T BE SHY, USAGI. DRINK UP.
THE SAKÉ* IS MY TREAT TONIGHT.
*RICE WINE
I HOPE YOU DO NOT TAKE OFFENSE, BOSS MAEDA, BUT I PREFER TEA.
SORRY TO DISTURB YOU, BOSS MAEDA, BUT THE COP IS HERE.
"COP"?!
BAH! WHAT DOES HE WANT TO SELL ME THIS TIME?!
OKAY, SHOW HIM IN.
HEH HEH... GREETINGS, BOSS MAEDA. I BRING TIDINGS AND... UH...
GET ON WITH IT, COP. WHAT DO YOU WANT NOW?
20.

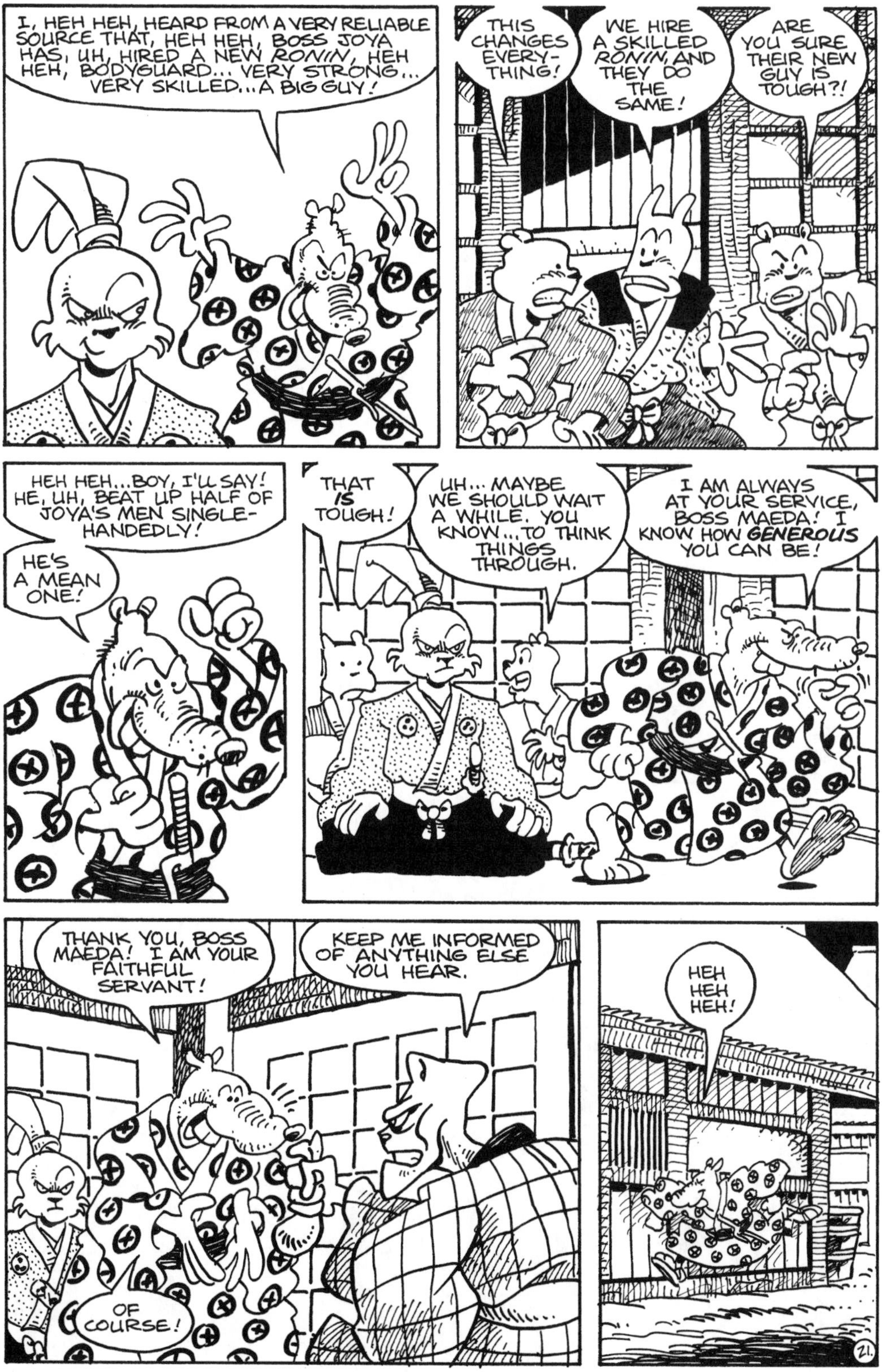
I, HEH HEH, HEARD FROM A VERY RELIABLE SOURCE THAT, HEH HEH, BOSS JOYA HAS, UH, HIRED A NEW *RONIN*, HEH HEH, BODYGUARD... VERY STRONG... VERY SKILLED...A BIG GUY!
THIS CHANGES EVERYTHING!
WE HIRE A SKILLED *RONIN*, AND THEY DO THE SAME!
ARE YOU SURE THEIR NEW GUY IS TOUGH?!
HEH HEH...BOY, I'LL SAY! HE, UH, BEAT UP HALF OF JOYA'S MEN SINGLE-HANDEDLY!
HE'S A MEAN ONE!
THAT *IS* TOUGH!
UH... MAYBE WE SHOULD WAIT A WHILE. YOU KNOW...TO THINK THINGS THROUGH.
I AM ALWAYS AT YOUR SERVICE, BOSS MAEDA! I KNOW HOW **GENEROUS** YOU CAN BE!
THANK YOU, BOSS MAEDA! I AM YOUR FAITHFUL SERVANT!
KEEP ME INFORMED OF ANYTHING ELSE YOU HEAR.
OF COURSE!
HEH HEH HEH!
21.

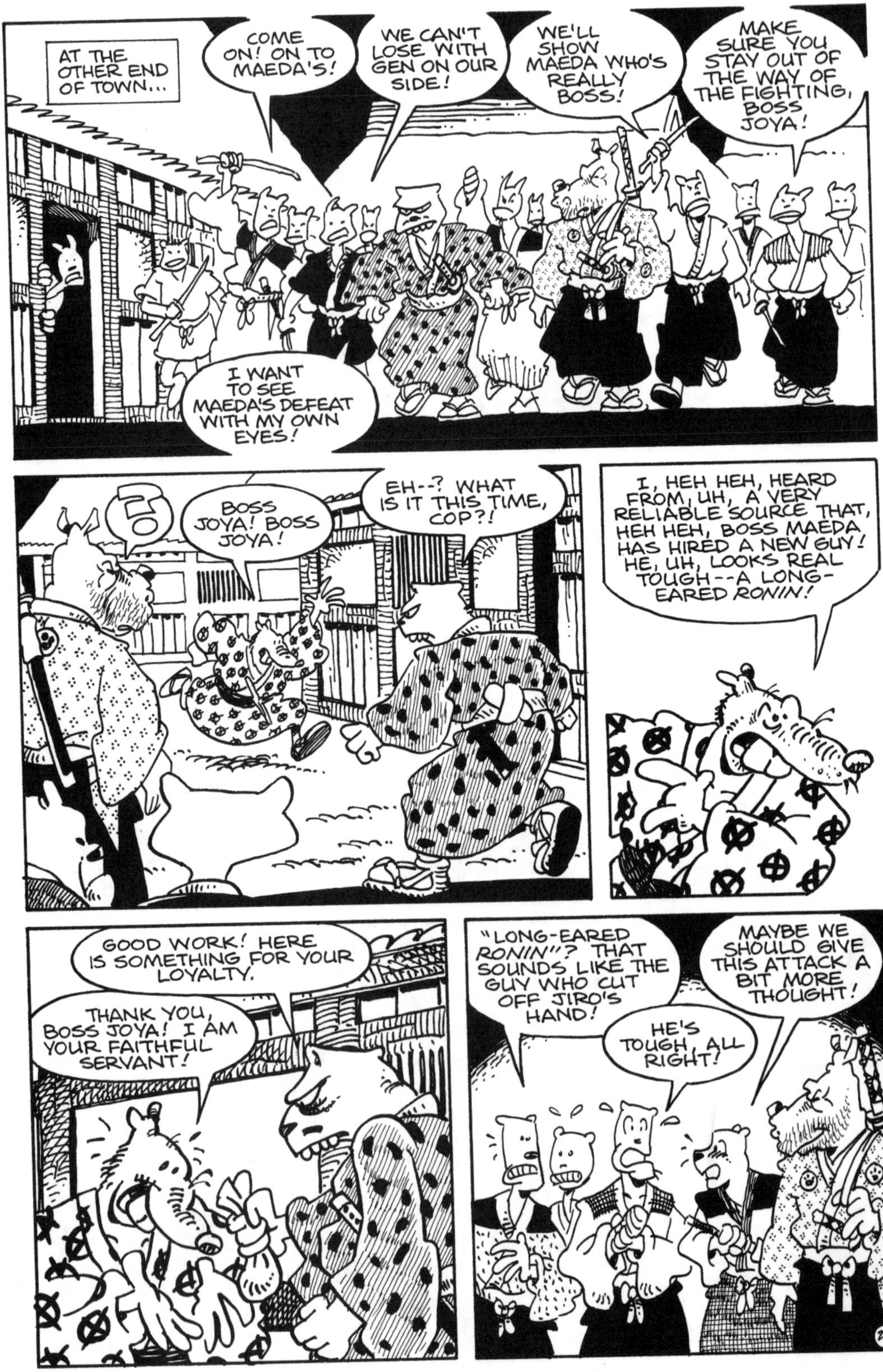
AT THE OTHER END OF TOWN...
COME ON! ON TO MAEDA'S!
WE CAN'T LOSE WITH GEN ON OUR SIDE!
WE'LL SHOW MAEDA WHO'S REALLY BOSS!
MAKE SURE YOU STAY OUT OF THE WAY OF THE FIGHTING, BOSS JOYA!
I WANT TO SEE MAEDA'S DEFEAT WITH MY OWN EYES!
?
BOSS JOYA! BOSS JOYA!
EH--? WHAT IS IT THIS TIME, COP?!
I, HEH HEH, HEARD FROM, UH, A VERY RELIABLE SOURCE THAT, HEH HEH, BOSS MAEDA HAS HIRED A NEW GUY! HE, UH, LOOKS REAL TOUGH--A LONG-EARED RONIN!
GOOD WORK! HERE IS SOMETHING FOR YOUR LOYALTY.
THANK YOU, BOSS JOYA! I AM YOUR FAITHFUL SERVANT!
"LONG-EARED RONIN"? THAT SOUNDS LIKE THE GUY WHO CUT OFF JIRO'S HAND!
HE'S TOUGH, ALL RIGHT!
MAYBE WE SHOULD GIVE THIS ATTACK A BIT MORE THOUGHT!
22.

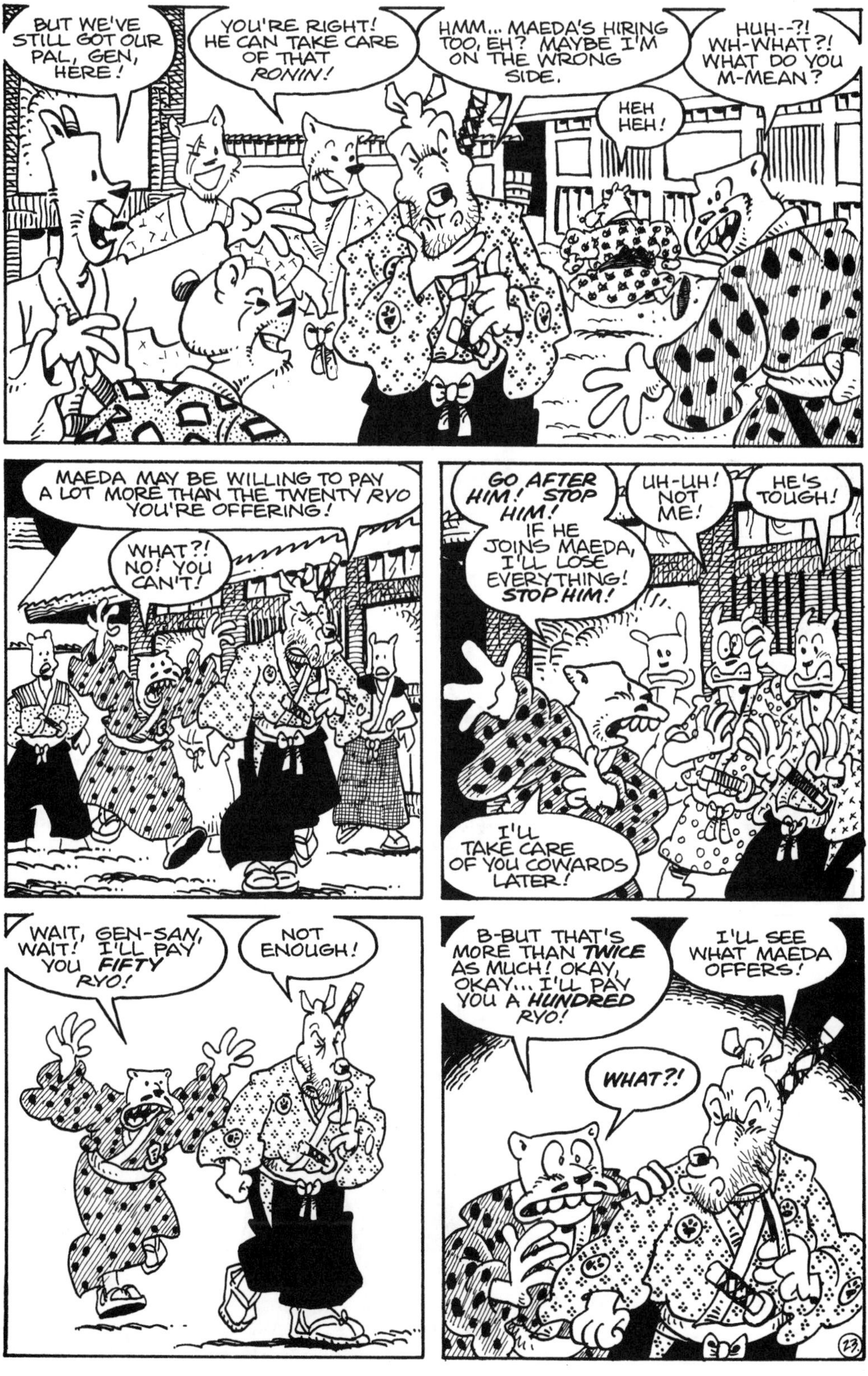

BUT WE'VE STILL GOT OUR PAL, GEN, HERE!
YOU'RE RIGHT! HE CAN TAKE CARE OF THAT *RONIN!*
HMM... MAEDA'S HIRING TOO, EH? MAYBE I'M ON THE WRONG SIDE.
HEH HEH!
HUH--?! WH-WHAT?! WHAT DO YOU M-MEAN?
MAEDA MAY BE WILLING TO PAY A LOT MORE THAN THE TWENTY *RYO* YOU'RE OFFERING!
WHAT?! NO! YOU CAN'T!
GO AFTER HIM! STOP HIM! IF HE JOINS MAEDA, I'LL LOSE EVERYTHING! ***STOP HIM!***
UH-UH! NOT ME!
HE'S TOUGH!
I'LL TAKE CARE OF YOU COWARDS LATER!
WAIT, GEN-SAN, WAIT! I'LL PAY YOU ***FIFTY*** *RYO!*
NOT ENOUGH!
B-BUT THAT'S MORE THAN ***TWICE*** AS MUCH! OKAY, OKAY... I'LL PAY YOU A ***HUNDRED*** *RYO!*
I'LL SEE WHAT MAEDA OFFERS!
WHAT?!
23.

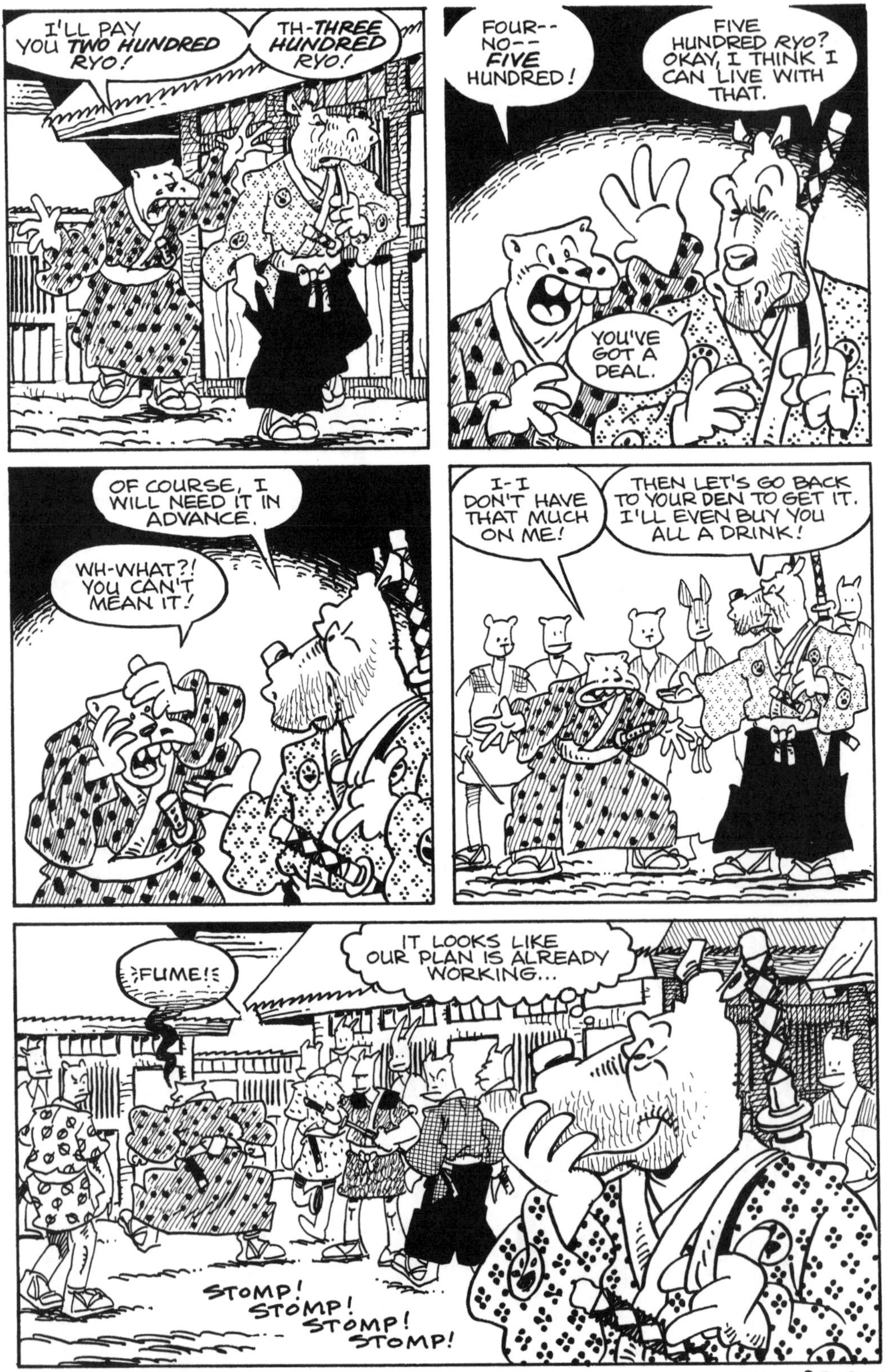
I'LL PAY YOU TWO HUNDRED RYO!
TH-THREE HUNDRED RYO!
FOUR-- NO-- FIVE HUNDRED!
FIVE HUNDRED RYO? OKAY, I THINK I CAN LIVE WITH THAT.
YOU'VE GOT A DEAL.
OF COURSE, I WILL NEED IT IN ADVANCE.
WH-WHAT?! YOU CAN'T MEAN IT!
I-I DON'T HAVE THAT MUCH ON ME!
THEN LET'S GO BACK TO YOUR DEN TO GET IT. I'LL EVEN BUY YOU ALL A DRINK!
FUME!
IT LOOKS LIKE OUR PLAN IS ALREADY WORKING...
STOMP! STOMP! STOMP! STOMP!

END of PART 1

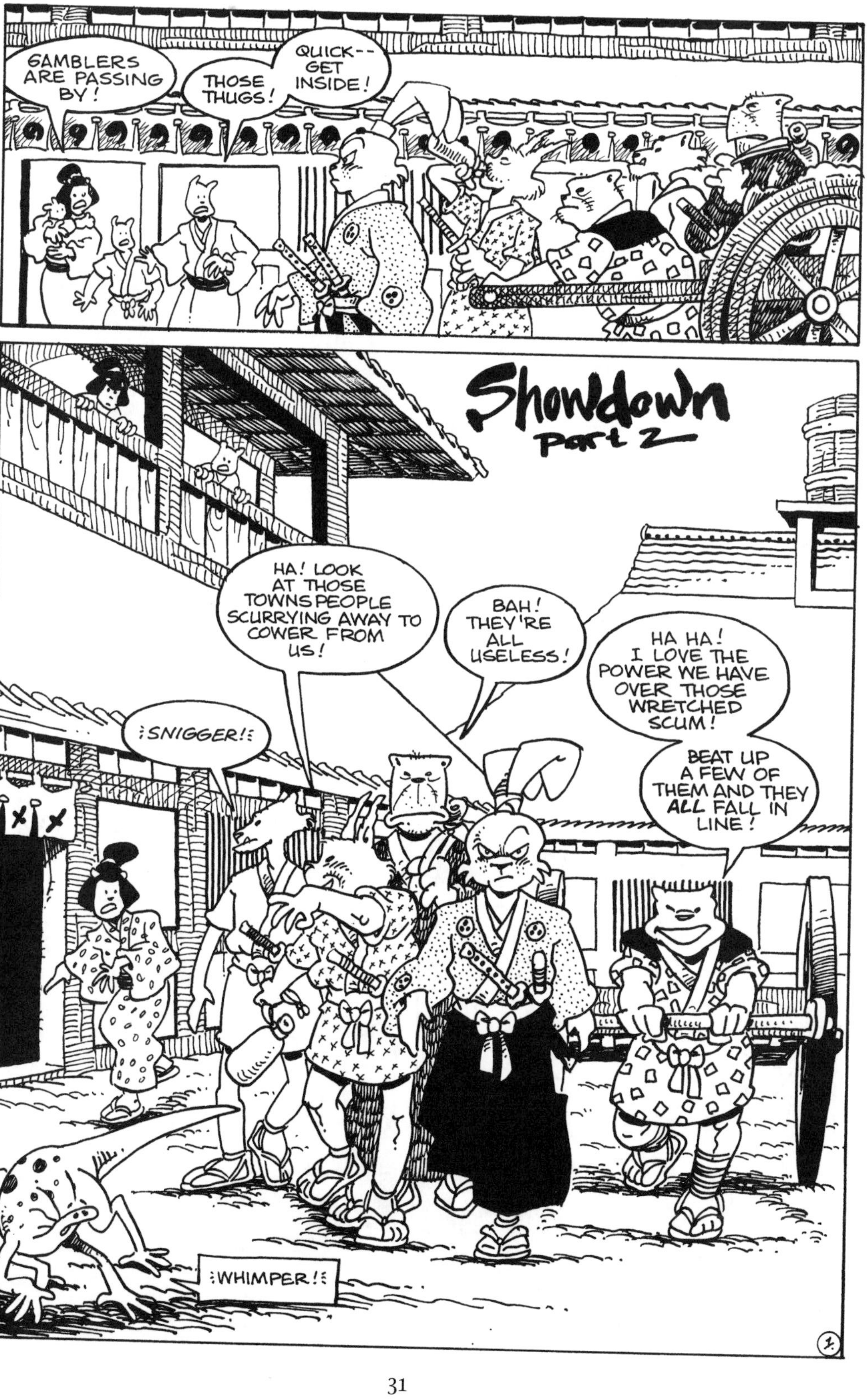
GAMBLERS ARE PASSING BY!
THOSE THUGS!
QUICK-- GET INSIDE!
Showdown
Part 2
HA! LOOK AT THOSE TOWNSPEOPLE SCURRYING AWAY TO COWER FROM US!
BAH! THEY'RE ALL USELESS!
HA HA! I LOVE THE POWER WE HAVE OVER THOSE WRETCHED SCUM!
BEAT UP A FEW OF THEM AND THEY ALL FALL IN LINE!
SNIGGER!
WHIMPER!
1

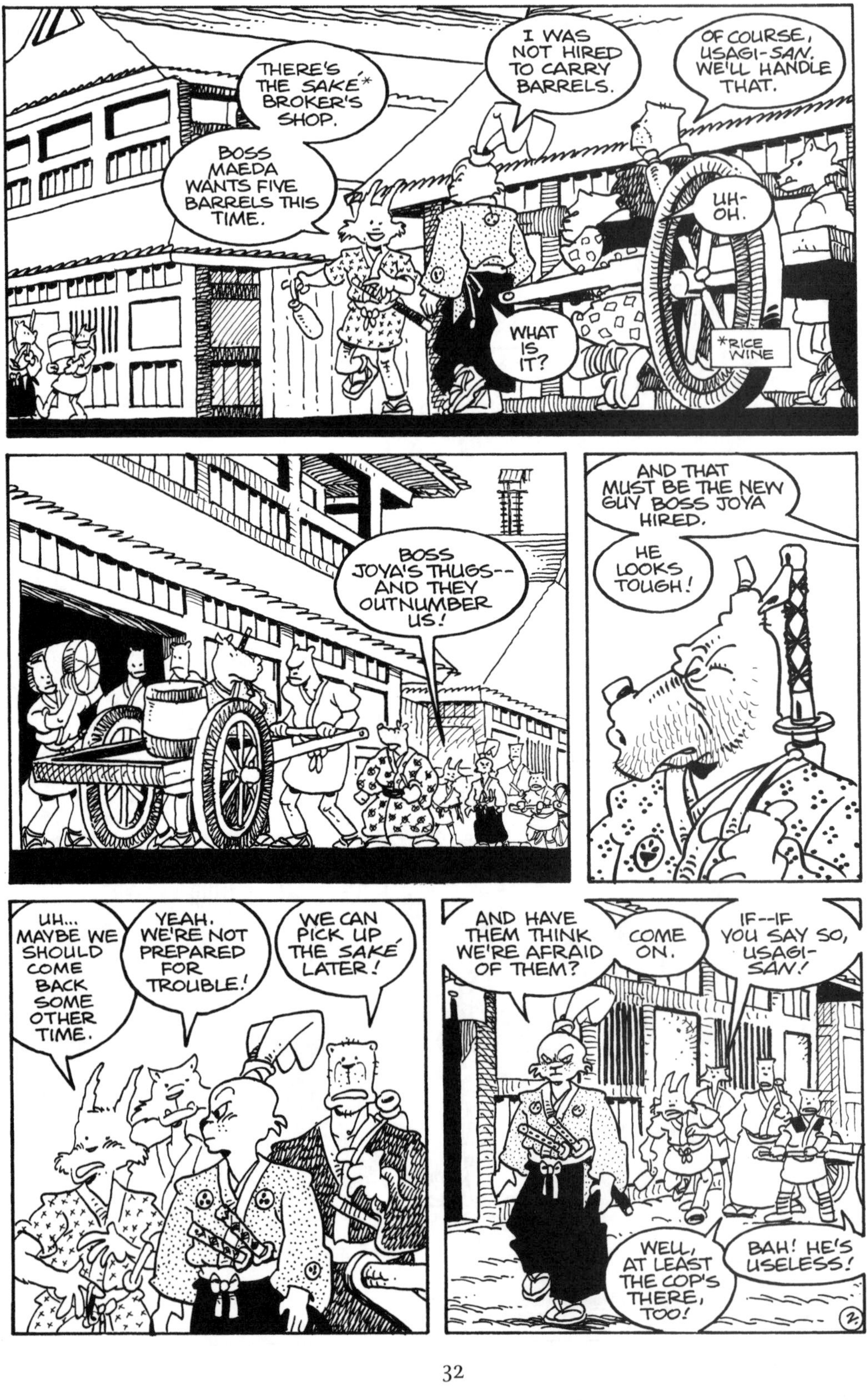
THERE'S THE SAKÉ* BROKER'S SHOP.
BOSS MAEDA WANTS FIVE BARRELS THIS TIME.
I WAS NOT HIRED TO CARRY BARRELS.
OF COURSE, USAGI-SAN. WE'LL HANDLE THAT.
UH-OH.
WHAT IS IT?
*RICE WINE
BOSS JOYA'S THUGS--AND THEY OUTNUMBER US!
AND THAT MUST BE THE NEW GUY BOSS JOYA HIRED.
HE LOOKS TOUGH!
UH... MAYBE WE SHOULD COME BACK SOME OTHER TIME.
YEAH. WE'RE NOT PREPARED FOR TROUBLE!
WE CAN PICK UP THE SAKÉ LATER!
AND HAVE THEM THINK WE'RE AFRAID OF THEM?
COME ON.
IF--IF YOU SAY SO, USAGI-SAN!
WELL, AT LEAST THE COP'S THERE, TOO!
BAH! HE'S USELESS!

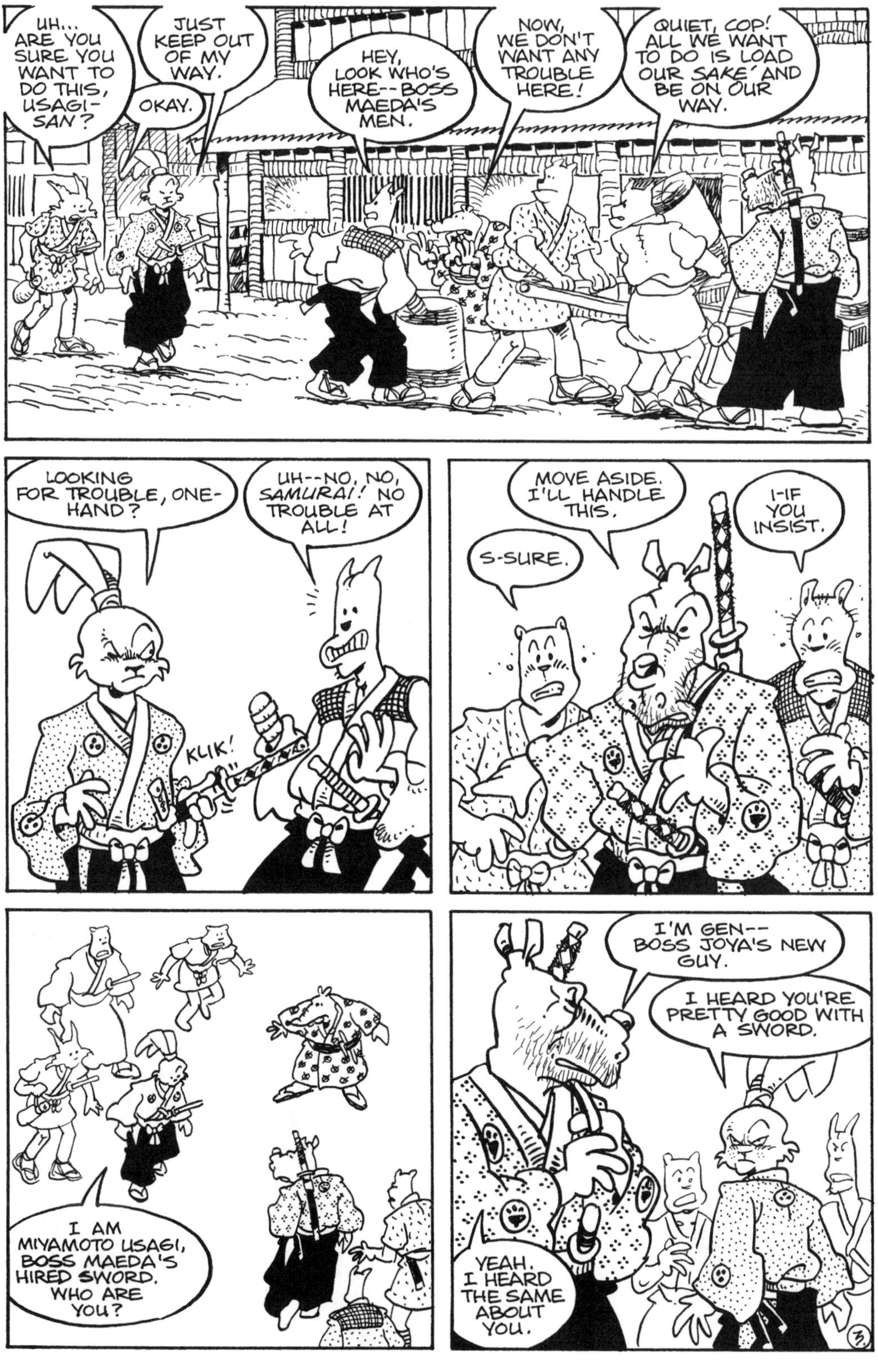
UH... ARE YOU SURE YOU WANT TO DO THIS, USAGI-SAN?
JUST KEEP OUT OF MY WAY.
OKAY.
HEY, LOOK WHO'S HERE--BOSS MAEDA'S MEN.
NOW, WE DON'T WANT ANY TROUBLE HERE!
QUIET, COP! ALL WE WANT TO DO IS LOAD OUR SAKÉ AND BE ON OUR WAY.
LOOKING FOR TROUBLE, ONE-HAND?
UH--NO, NO, SAMURAI! NO TROUBLE AT ALL!
KLIK!
MOVE ASIDE. I'LL HANDLE THIS.
S-SURE.
I-IF YOU INSIST.
I AM MIYAMOTO USAGI, BOSS MAEDA'S HIRED SWORD. WHO ARE YOU?
I'M GEN-- BOSS JOYA'S NEW GUY.
I HEARD YOU'RE PRETTY GOOD WITH A SWORD.
YEAH. I HEARD THE SAME ABOUT YOU.
3

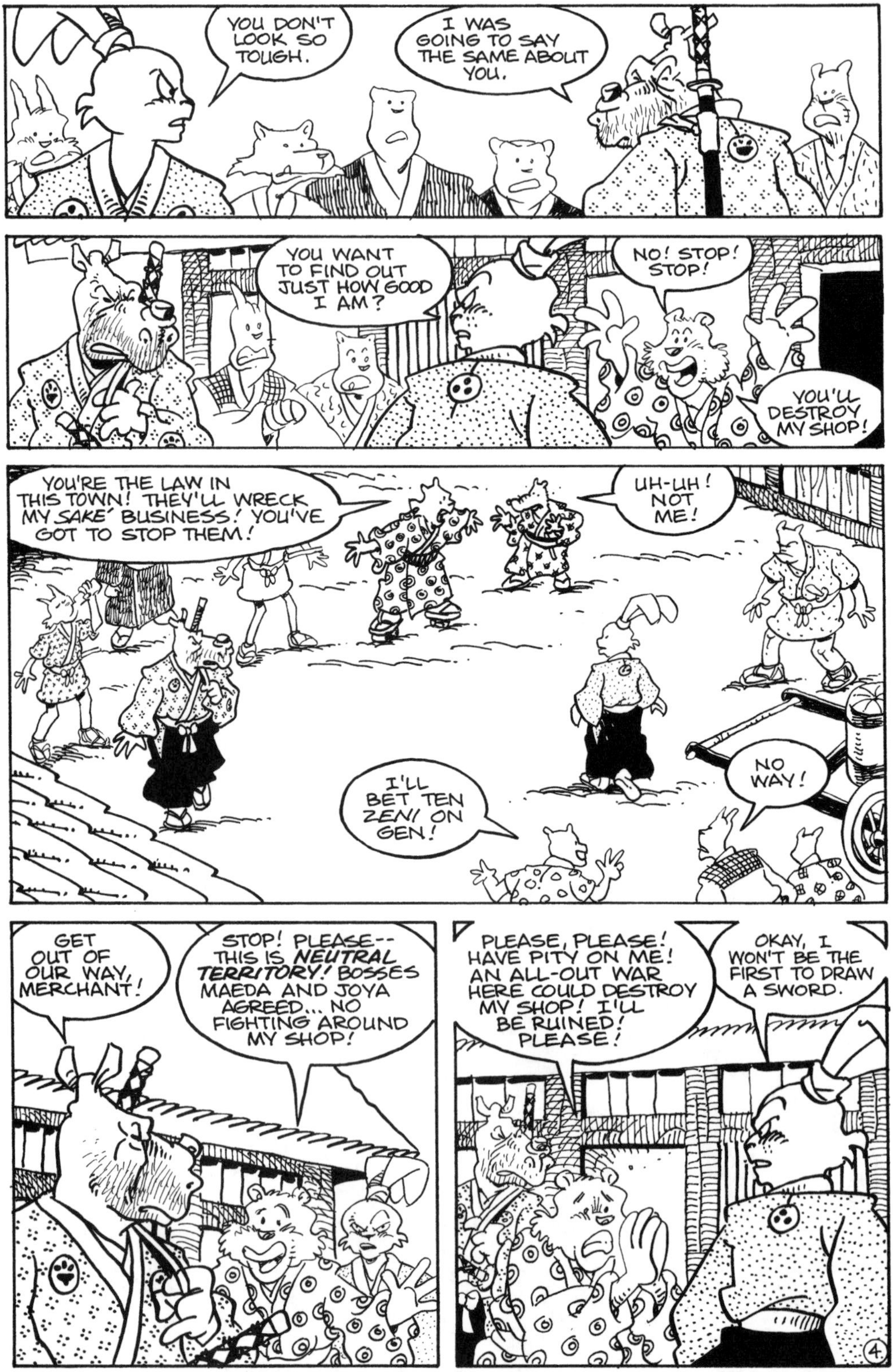
YOU DON'T LOOK SO TOUGH.
I WAS GOING TO SAY THE SAME ABOUT YOU.
YOU WANT TO FIND OUT JUST HOW GOOD I AM?
NO! STOP! STOP!
YOU'LL DESTROY MY SHOP!
YOU'RE THE LAW IN THIS TOWN! THEY'LL WRECK MY SAKE' BUSINESS! YOU'VE GOT TO STOP THEM!
UH-UH! NOT ME!
I'LL BET TEN ZENI ON GEN!
NO WAY!
GET OUT OF OUR WAY, MERCHANT!
STOP! PLEASE-- THIS IS NEUTRAL TERRITORY! BOSSES MAEDA AND JOYA AGREED... NO FIGHTING AROUND MY SHOP!
PLEASE, PLEASE! HAVE PITY ON ME! AN ALL-OUT WAR HERE COULD DESTROY MY SHOP! I'LL BE RUINED! PLEASE!
OKAY, I WON'T BE THE FIRST TO DRAW A SWORD.
4

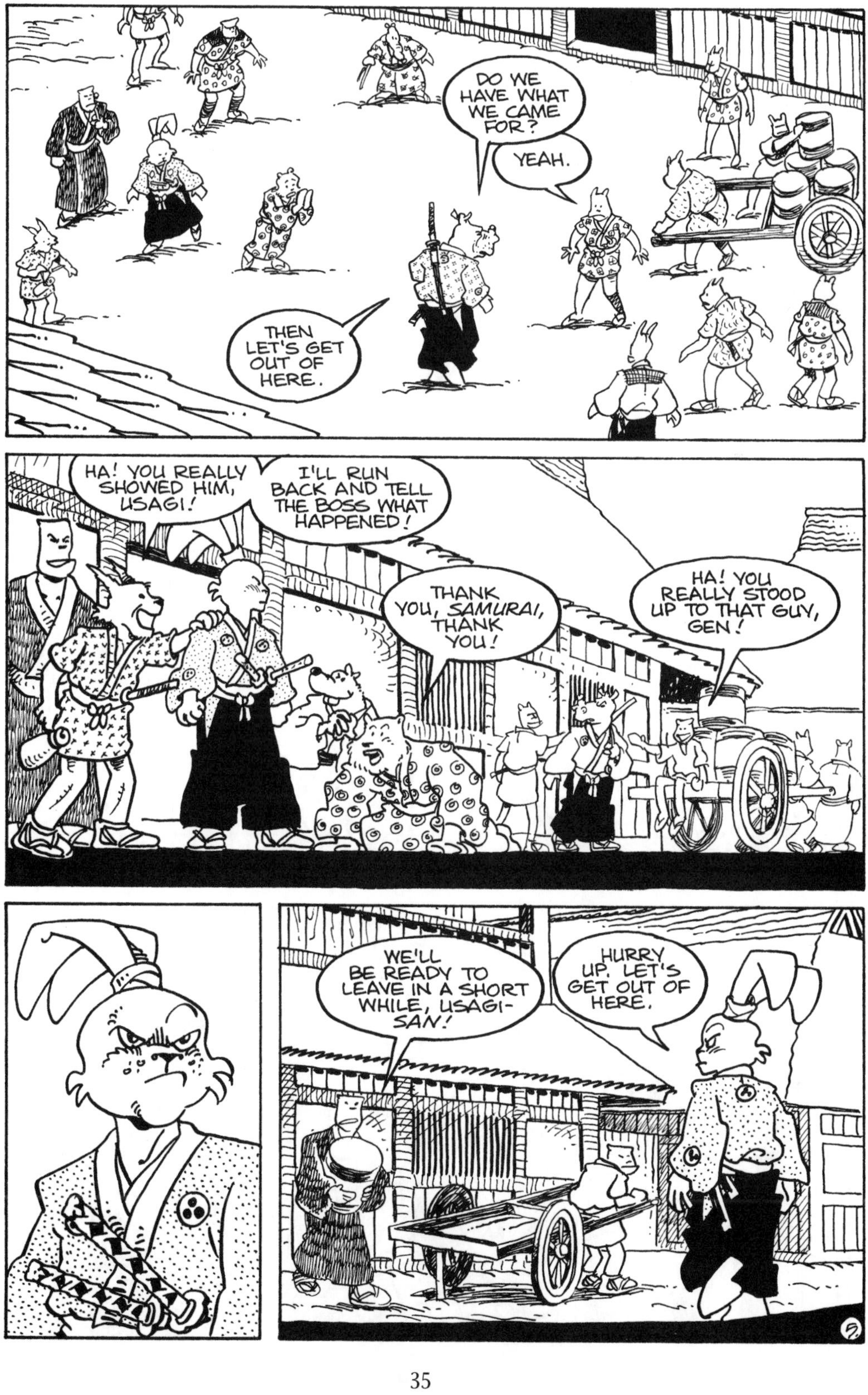
DO WE HAVE WHAT WE CAME FOR?
YEAH.
THEN LET'S GET OUT OF HERE.
HA! YOU REALLY SHOWED HIM, USAGI!
I'LL RUN BACK AND TELL THE BOSS WHAT HAPPENED!
THANK YOU, SAMURAI, THANK YOU!
HA! YOU REALLY STOOD UP TO THAT GUY, GEN!
WE'LL BE READY TO LEAVE IN A SHORT WHILE, USAGI-SAN!
HURRY UP. LET'S GET OUT OF HERE.

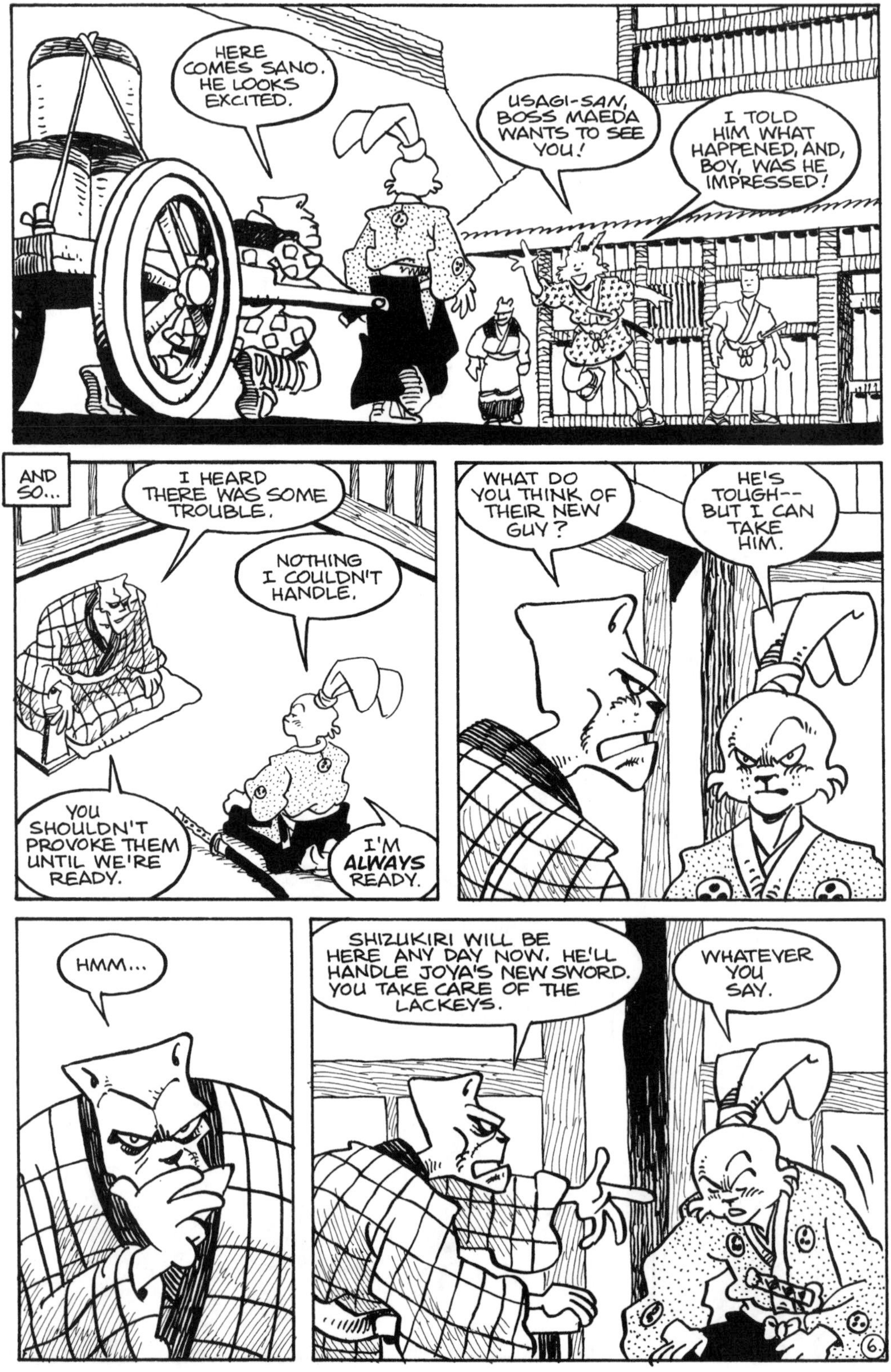
HERE COMES SANO. HE LOOKS EXCITED.
USAGI-SAN, BOSS MAEDA WANTS TO SEE YOU!
I TOLD HIM WHAT HAPPENED, AND, BOY, WAS HE IMPRESSED!
AND SO...
I HEARD THERE WAS SOME TROUBLE.
NOTHING I COULDN'T HANDLE.
YOU SHOULDN'T PROVOKE THEM UNTIL WE'RE READY.
I'M **ALWAYS** READY.
WHAT DO YOU THINK OF THEIR NEW GUY?
HE'S TOUGH-- BUT I CAN TAKE HIM.
HMM...
SHIZUKIRI WILL BE HERE ANY DAY NOW. HE'LL HANDLE JOYA'S NEW SWORD. YOU TAKE CARE OF THE LACKEYS.
WHATEVER YOU SAY.
6.

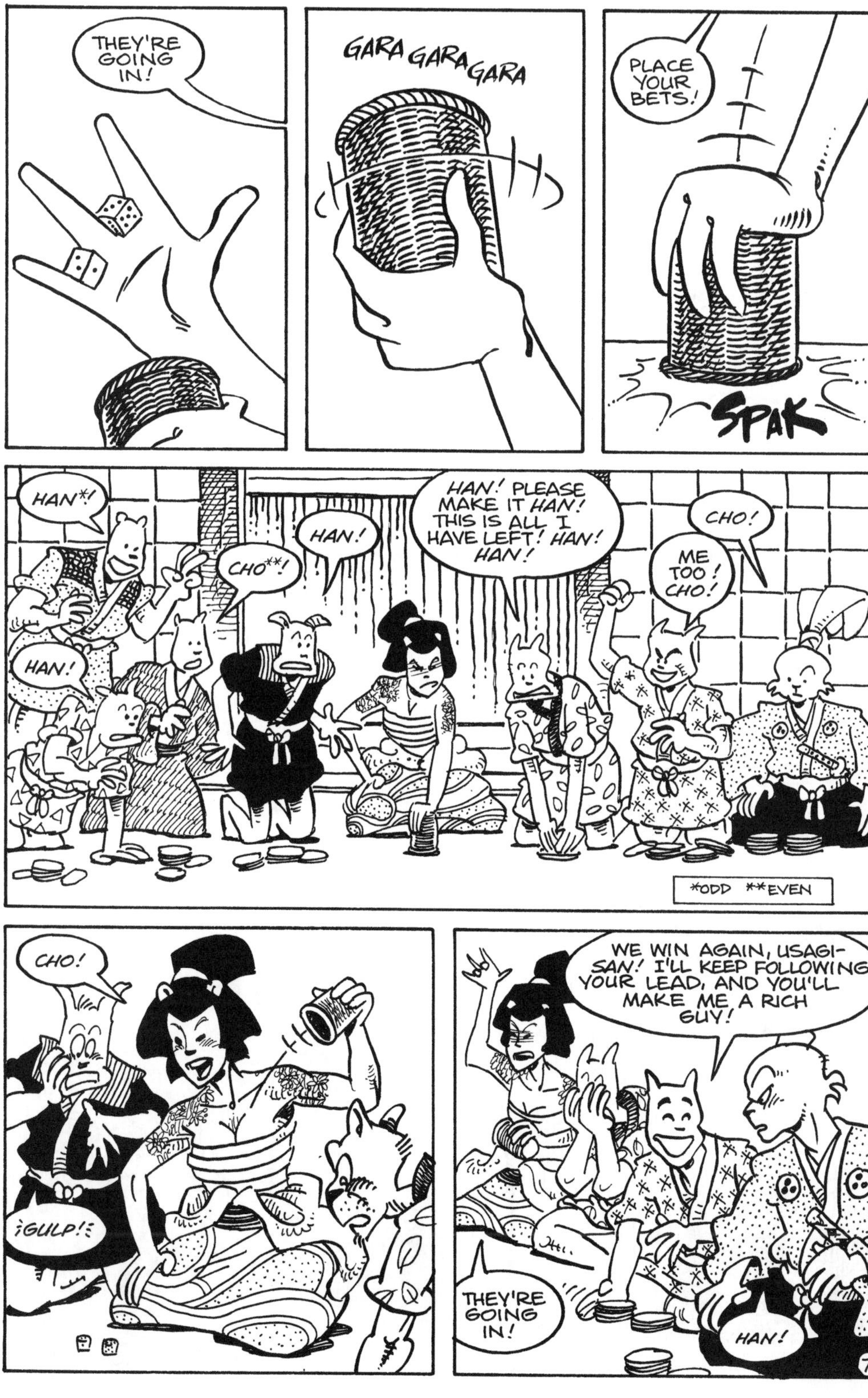

THEY'RE GOING IN!
GARA GARA GARA
PLACE YOUR BETS!
SPAK
HAN*!
HAN!
CHO**!
HAN!
HAN! PLEASE MAKE IT HAN! THIS IS ALL I HAVE LEFT! HAN! HAN!
CHO!
ME TOO! CHO!
*ODD **EVEN
CHO!
¡GULP!
WE WIN AGAIN, USAGI-SAN! I'LL KEEP FOLLOWING YOUR LEAD, AND YOU'LL MAKE ME A RICH GUY!
THEY'RE GOING IN!
HAN!
7.

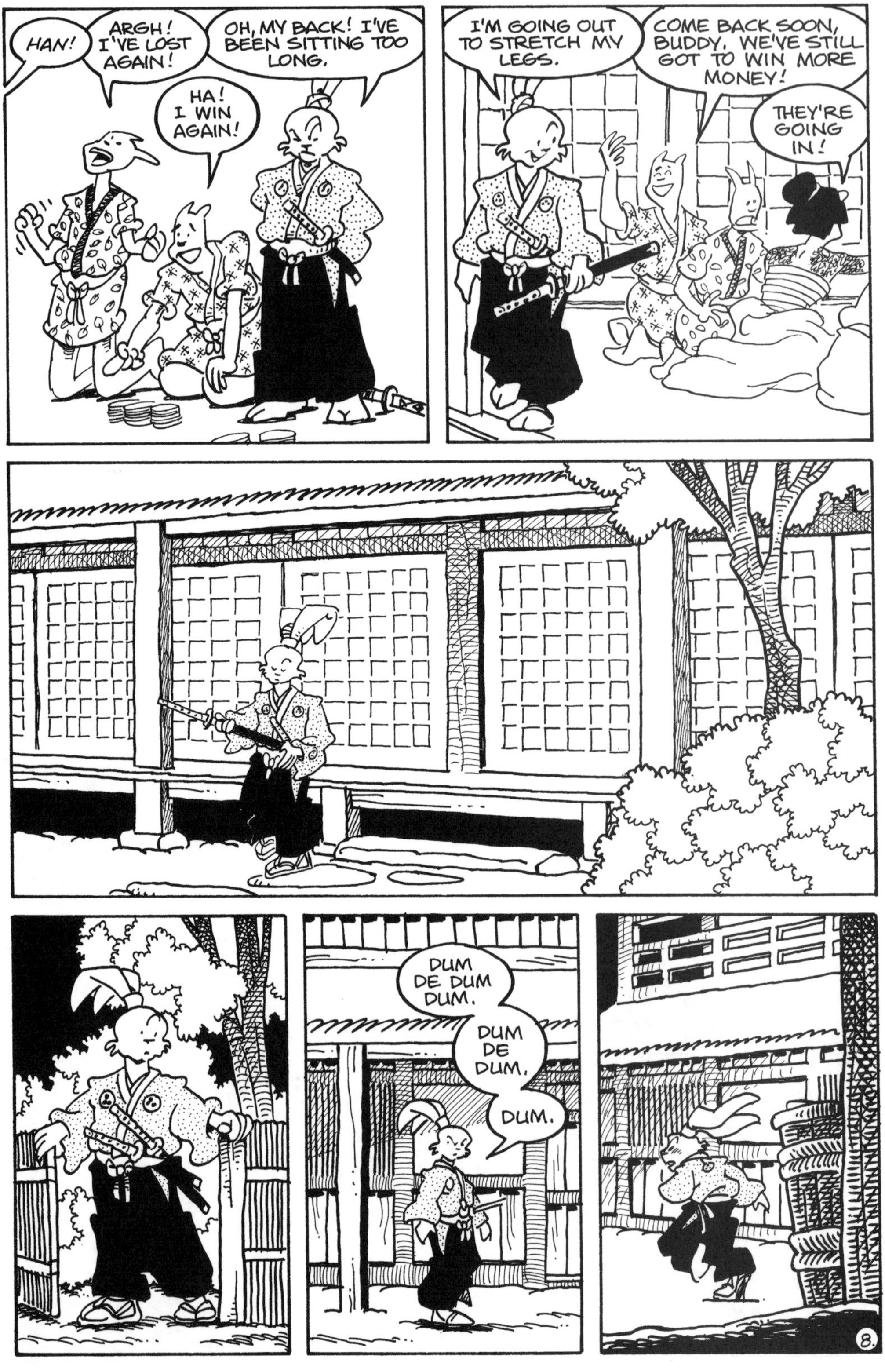
HAN!
ARGH! I'VE LOST AGAIN!
OH, MY BACK! I'VE BEEN SITTING TOO LONG.
HA! I WIN AGAIN!
I'M GOING OUT TO STRETCH MY LEGS.
COME BACK SOON, BUDDY. WE'VE STILL GOT TO WIN MORE MONEY!
THEY'RE GOING IN!
DUM DE DUM DUM.
DUM DE DUM.
DUM.
8.

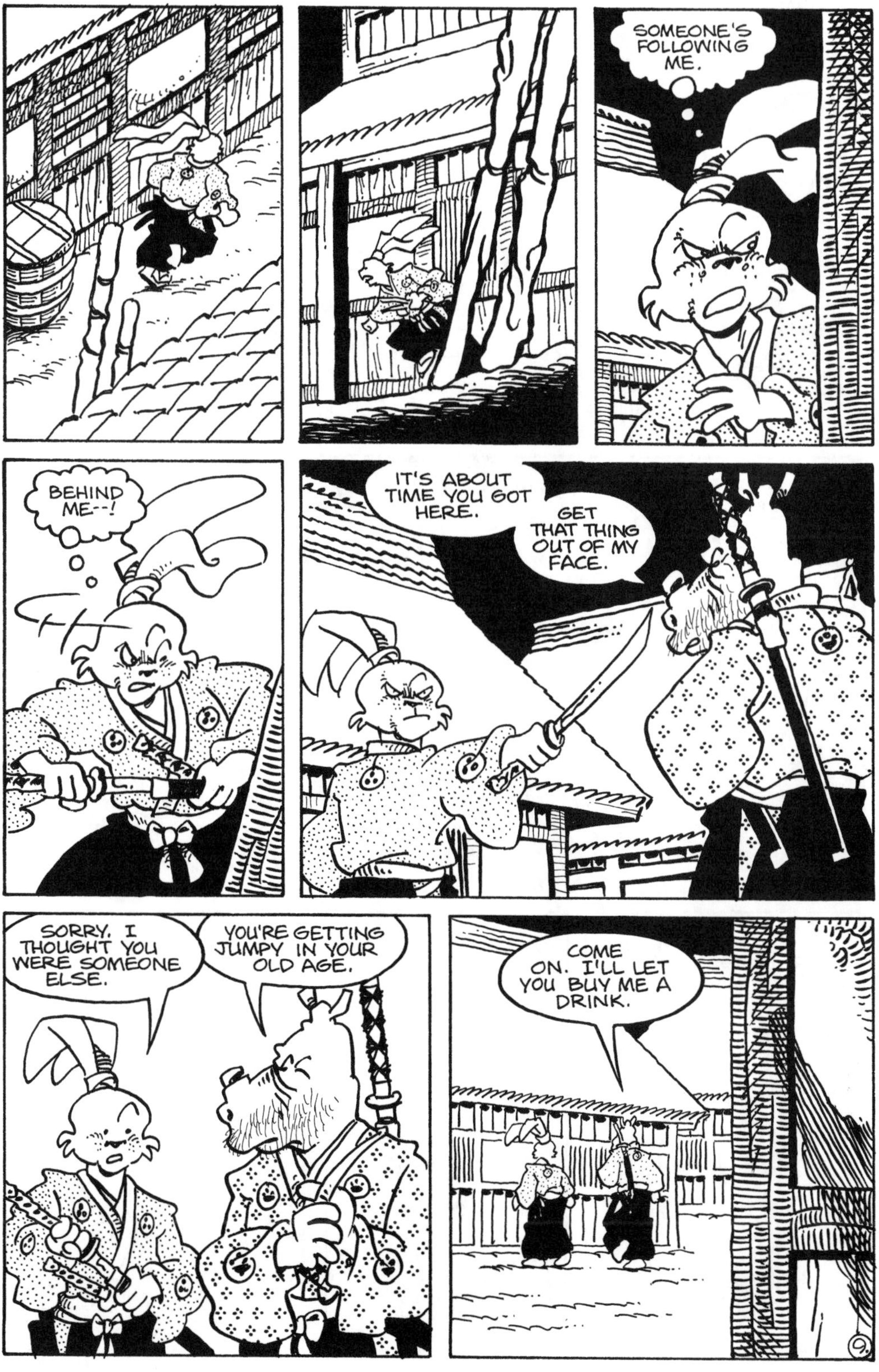
SOMEONE'S FOLLOWING ME.
BEHIND ME--!
IT'S ABOUT TIME YOU GOT HERE.
GET THAT THING OUT OF MY FACE.
SORRY. I THOUGHT YOU WERE SOMEONE ELSE.
YOU'RE GETTING JUMPY IN YOUR OLD AGE.
COME ON. I'LL LET YOU BUY ME A DRINK.
9

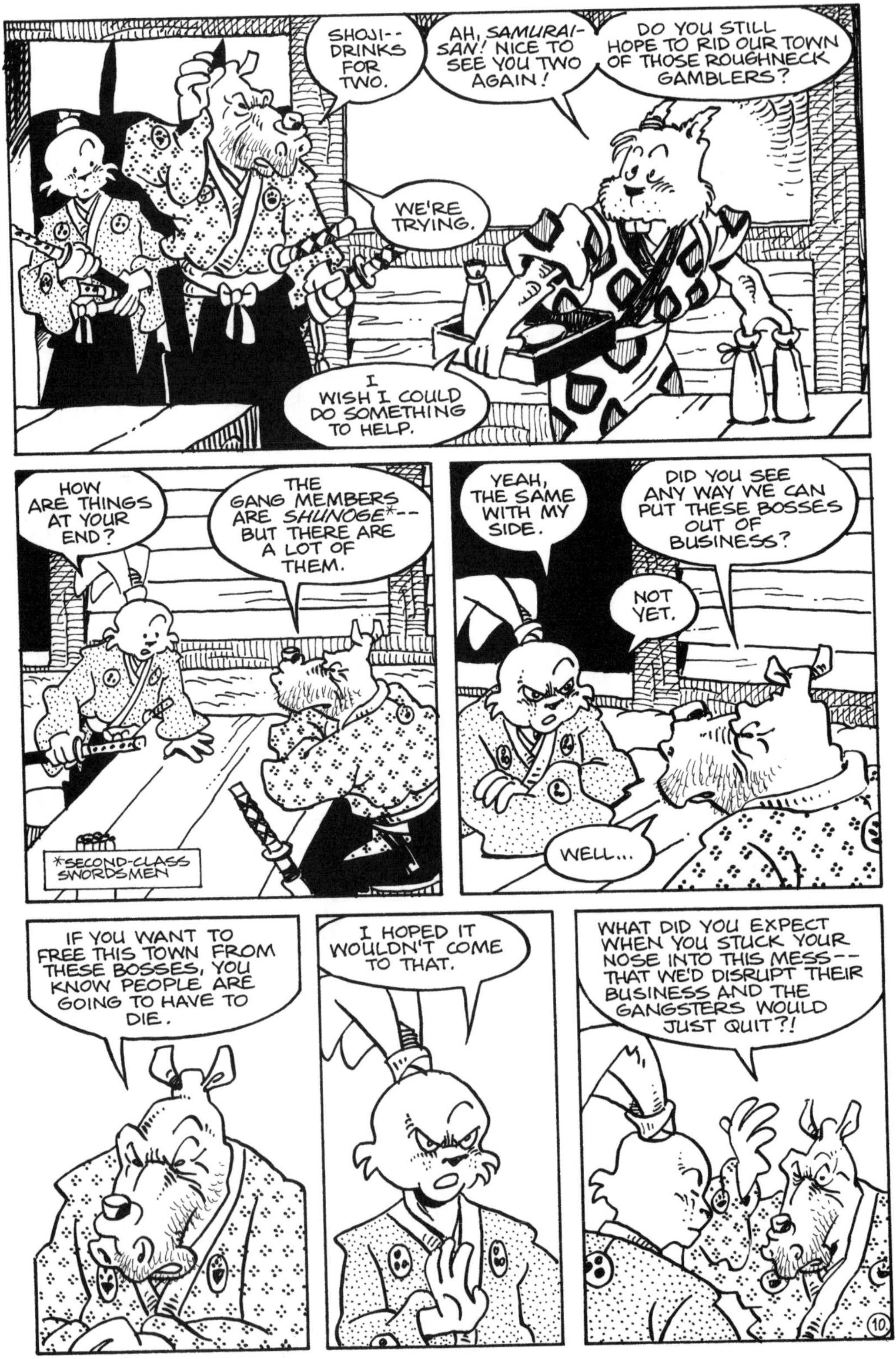
SHOJI-- DRINKS FOR TWO.
AH, SAMURAI-SAN! NICE TO SEE YOU TWO AGAIN!
DO YOU STILL HOPE TO RID OUR TOWN OF THOSE ROUGHNECK GAMBLERS?
WE'RE TRYING.
I WISH I COULD DO SOMETHING TO HELP.
HOW ARE THINGS AT YOUR END?
THE GANG MEMBERS ARE SHUNOGE*-- BUT THERE ARE A LOT OF THEM.
*SECOND-CLASS SWORDSMEN
YEAH, THE SAME WITH MY SIDE.
DID YOU SEE ANY WAY WE CAN PUT THESE BOSSES OUT OF BUSINESS?
NOT YET.
WELL...
IF YOU WANT TO FREE THIS TOWN FROM THESE BOSSES, YOU KNOW PEOPLE ARE GOING TO HAVE TO DIE.
I HOPED IT WOULDN'T COME TO THAT.
WHAT DID YOU EXPECT WHEN YOU STUCK YOUR NOSE INTO THIS MESS-- THAT WE'D DISRUPT THEIR BUSINESS AND THE GANGSTERS WOULD JUST QUIT?!
10

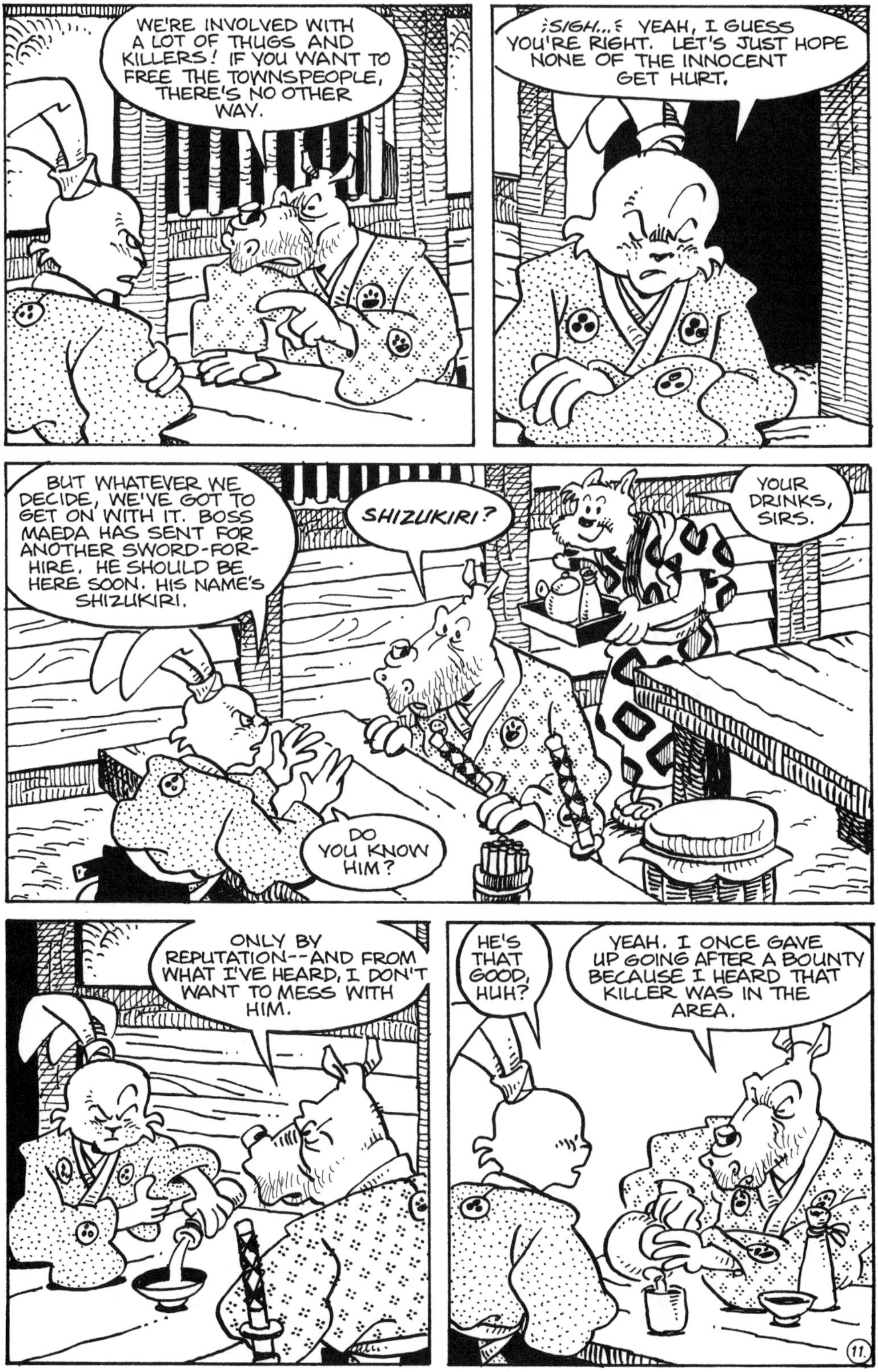
WE'RE INVOLVED WITH A LOT OF THUGS AND KILLERS! IF YOU WANT TO FREE THE TOWNSPEOPLE, THERE'S NO OTHER WAY.
SIGH... YEAH, I GUESS YOU'RE RIGHT. LET'S JUST HOPE NONE OF THE INNOCENT GET HURT.
BUT WHATEVER WE DECIDE, WE'VE GOT TO GET ON WITH IT. BOSS MAEDA HAS SENT FOR ANOTHER SWORD-FOR-HIRE. HE SHOULD BE HERE SOON. HIS NAME'S SHIZUKIRI.
SHIZUKIRI?
YOUR DRINKS, SIRS.
DO YOU KNOW HIM?
ONLY BY REPUTATION--AND FROM WHAT I'VE HEARD, I DON'T WANT TO MESS WITH HIM.
HE'S THAT GOOD, HUH?
YEAH. I ONCE GAVE UP GOING AFTER A BOUNTY BECAUSE I HEARD THAT KILLER WAS IN THE AREA.
11.

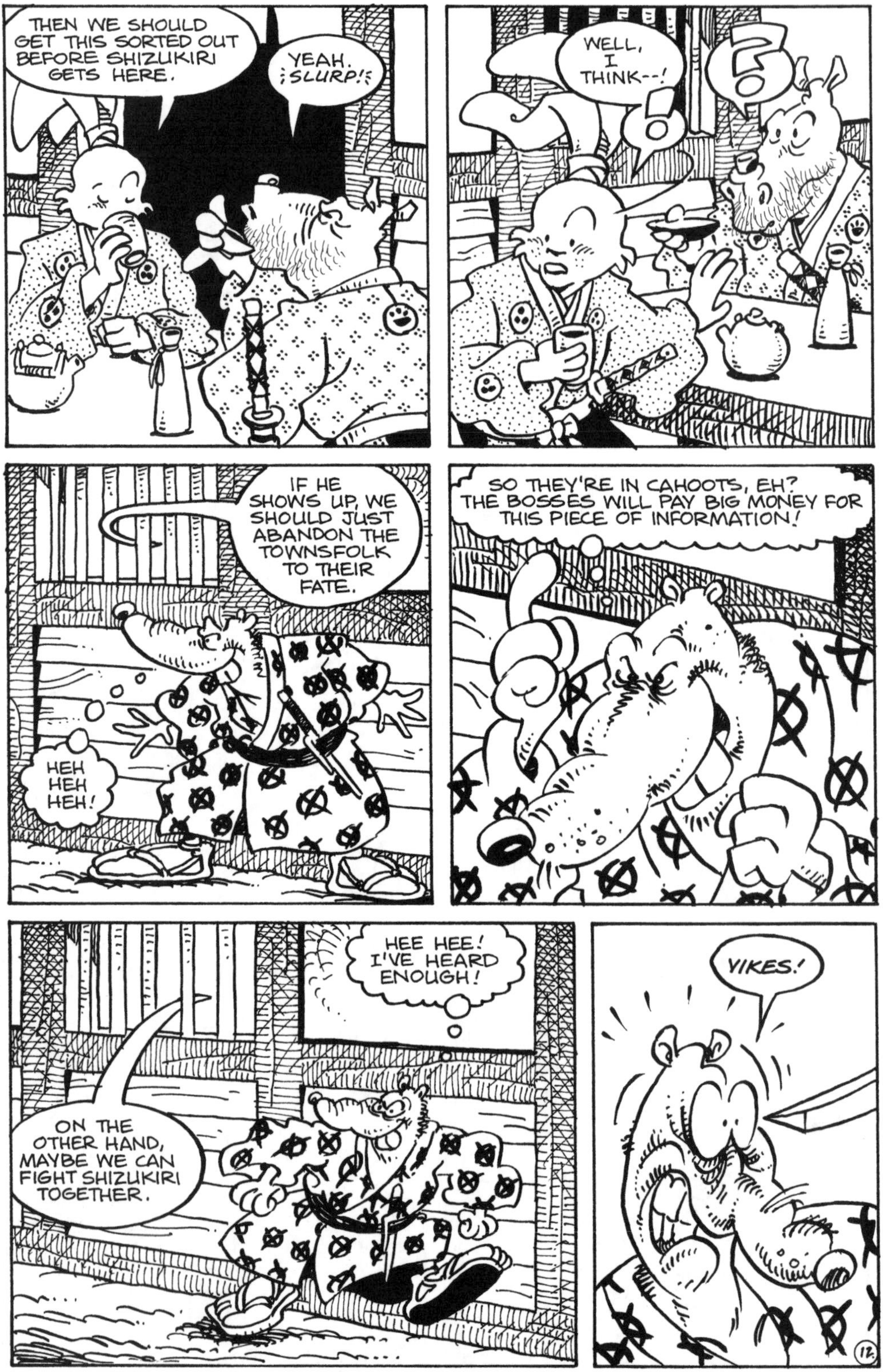
THEN WE SHOULD GET THIS SORTED OUT BEFORE SHIZUKIRI GETS HERE.
YEAH. ¡SLURP!¡
WELL, I THINK--!
!
?
IF HE SHOWS UP, WE SHOULD JUST ABANDON THE TOWNSFOLK TO THEIR FATE.
HEH HEH HEH!
SO THEY'RE IN CAHOOTS, EH? THE BOSSES WILL PAY BIG MONEY FOR THIS PIECE OF INFORMATION!
HEE HEE! I'VE HEARD ENOUGH!
ON THE OTHER HAND, MAYBE WE CAN FIGHT SHIZUKIRI TOGETHER.
YIKES!
12.

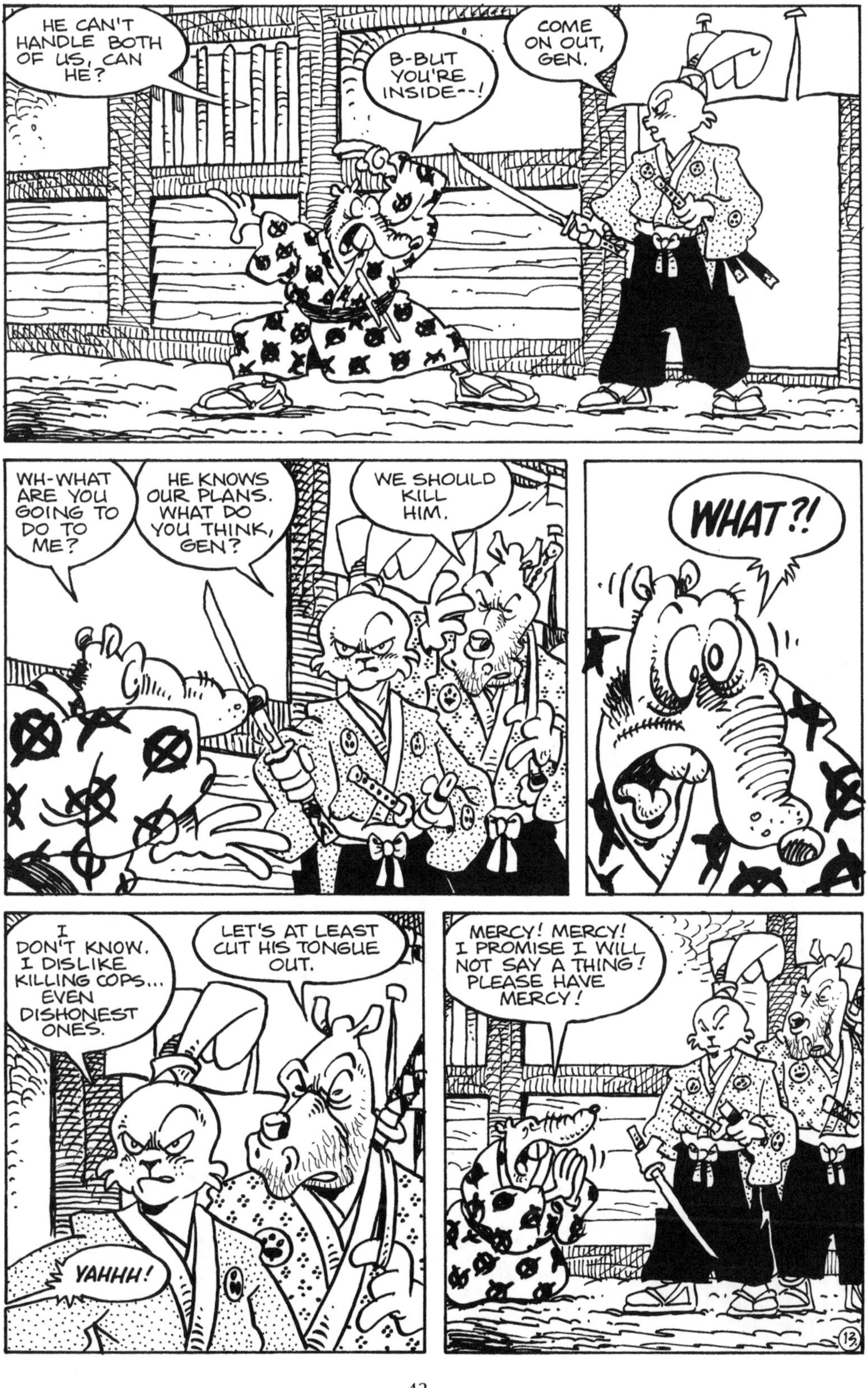
HE CAN'T HANDLE BOTH OF US, CAN HE?
B-BUT YOU'RE INSIDE--!
COME ON OUT, GEN.
WH-WHAT ARE YOU GOING TO DO TO ME?
HE KNOWS OUR PLANS. WHAT DO YOU THINK, GEN?
WE SHOULD KILL HIM.
WHAT?!
I DON'T KNOW. I DISLIKE KILLING COPS... EVEN DISHONEST ONES.
LET'S AT LEAST CUT HIS TONGUE OUT.
YAHHH!
MERCY! MERCY! I PROMISE I WILL NOT SAY A THING! PLEASE HAVE MERCY!
13

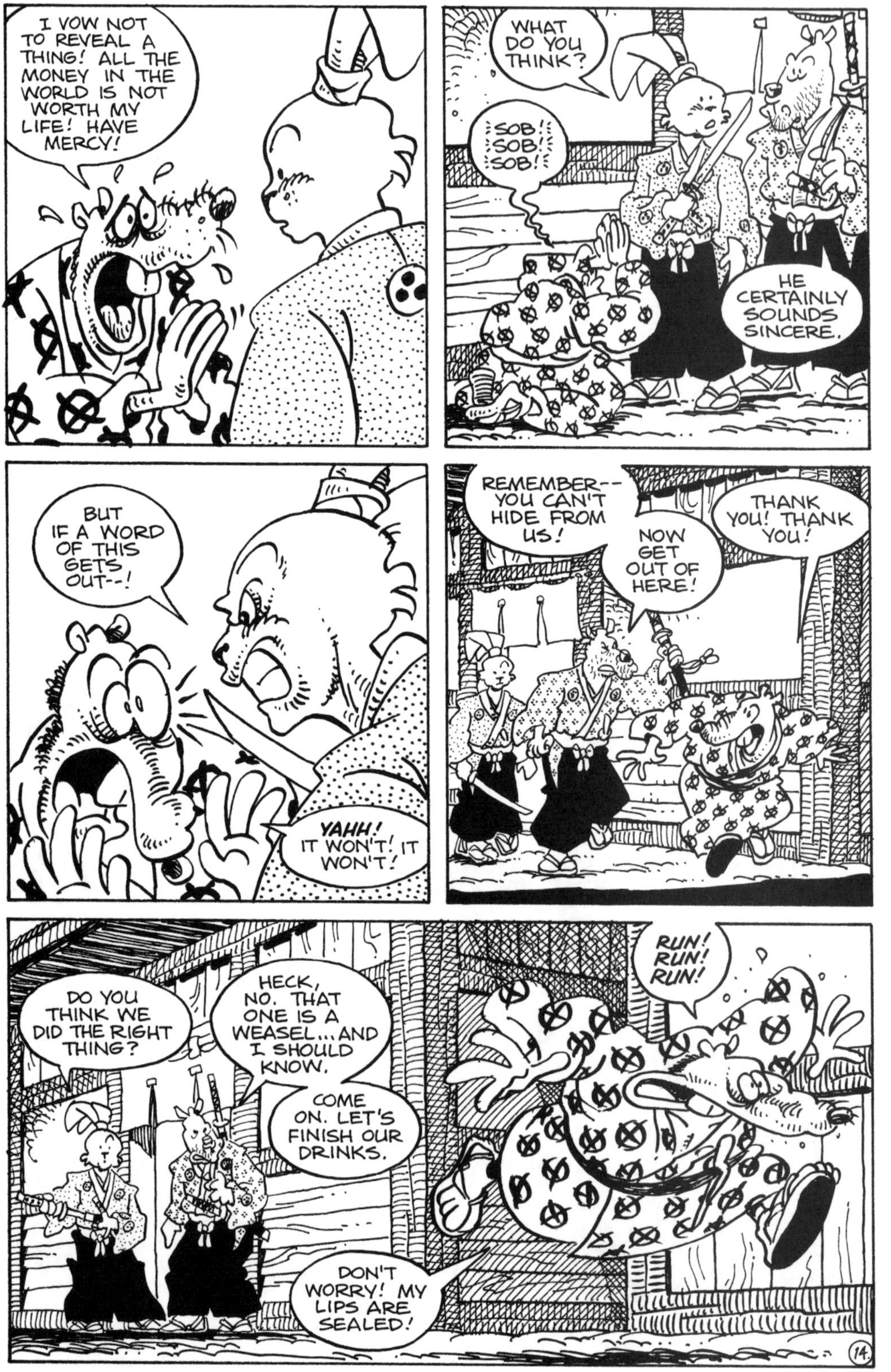
I VOW NOT TO REVEAL A THING! ALL THE MONEY IN THE WORLD IS NOT WORTH MY LIFE! HAVE MERCY!
WHAT DO YOU THINK?
SOB! SOB! SOB!
HE CERTAINLY SOUNDS SINCERE.
BUT IF A WORD OF THIS GETS OUT--!
YAHH! IT WON'T! IT WON'T!
REMEMBER-- YOU CAN'T HIDE FROM US!
NOW GET OUT OF HERE!
THANK YOU! THANK YOU!
DO YOU THINK WE DID THE RIGHT THING?
HECK, NO. THAT ONE IS A WEASEL...AND I SHOULD KNOW.
COME ON. LET'S FINISH OUR DRINKS.
RUN! RUN! RUN!
DON'T WORRY! MY LIPS ARE SEALED!
14.

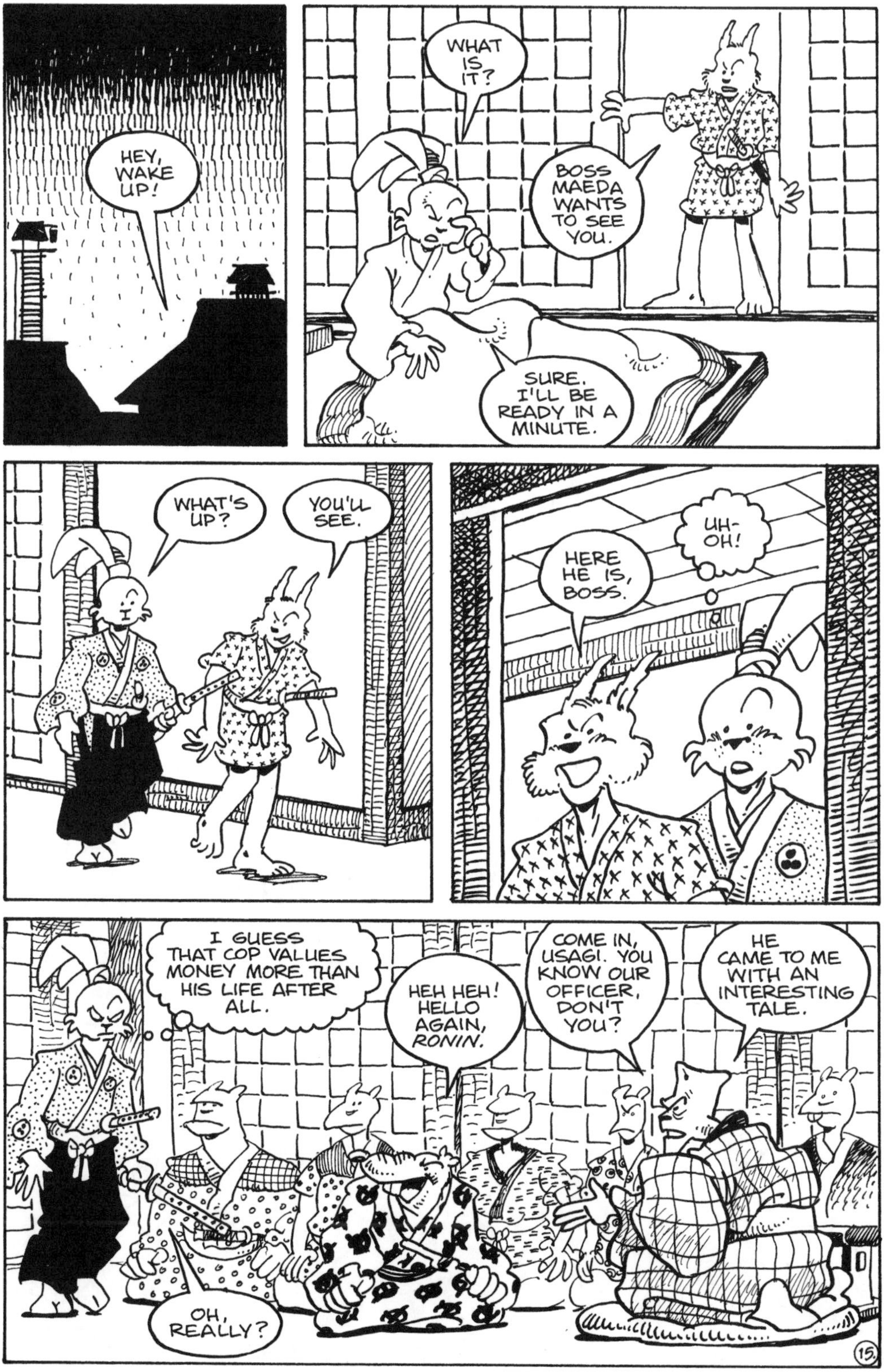
HEY, WAKE UP!
WHAT IS IT?
BOSS MAEDA WANTS TO SEE YOU.
SURE. I'LL BE READY IN A MINUTE.
WHAT'S UP?
YOU'LL SEE.
HERE HE IS, BOSS.
UH-OH!
I GUESS THAT COP VALUES MONEY MORE THAN HIS LIFE AFTER ALL.
HEH HEH! HELLO AGAIN, *RONIN.*
COME IN, USAGI. YOU KNOW OUR OFFICER, DON'T YOU?
HE CAME TO ME WITH AN INTERESTING TALE.
OH, REALLY?
15

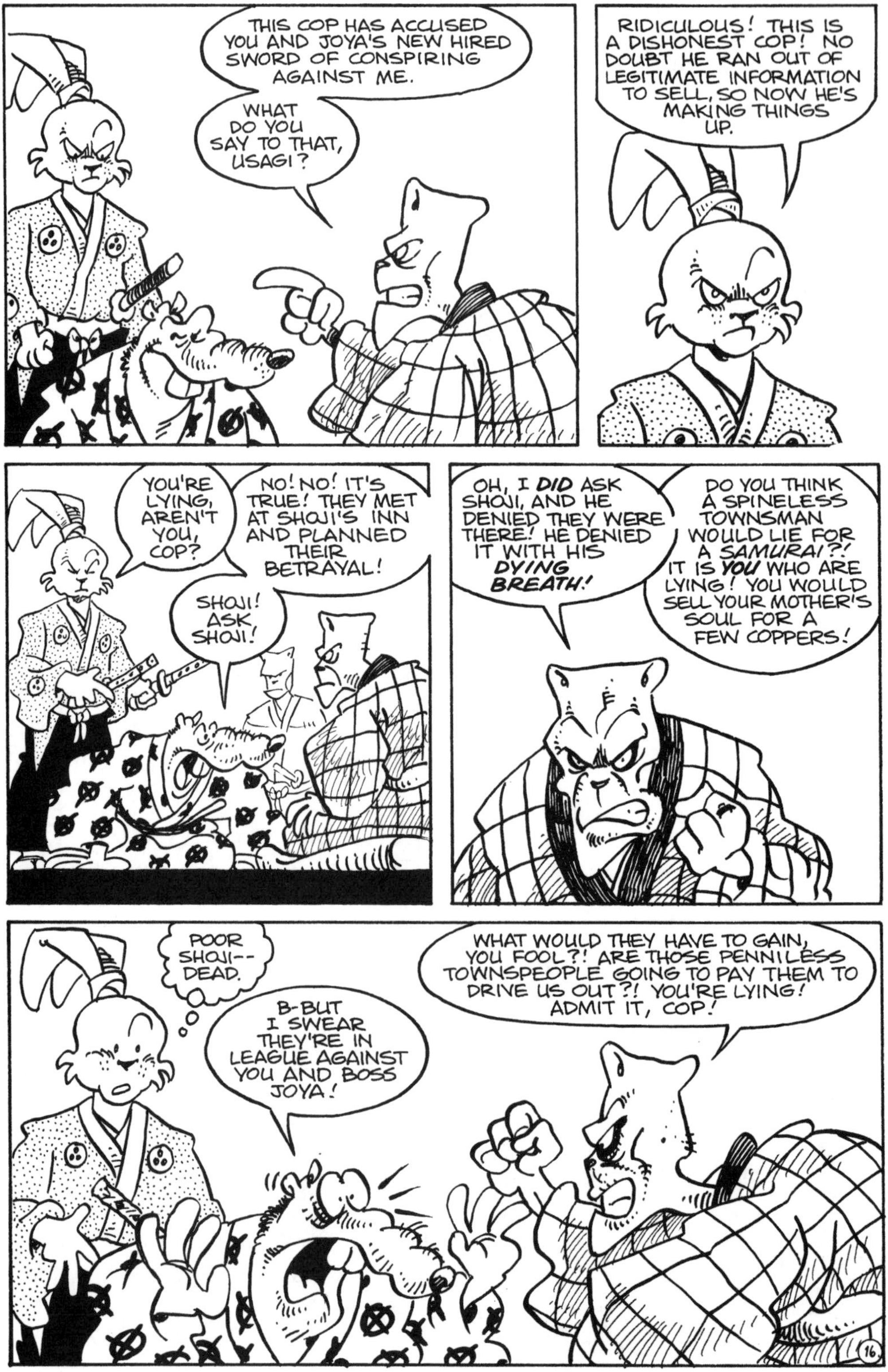
THIS COP HAS ACCUSED YOU AND JOYA'S NEW HIRED SWORD OF CONSPIRING AGAINST ME.
WHAT DO YOU SAY TO THAT, USAGI?
RIDICULOUS! THIS IS A DISHONEST COP! NO DOUBT HE RAN OUT OF LEGITIMATE INFORMATION TO SELL, SO NOW HE'S MAKING THINGS UP.
YOU'RE LYING, AREN'T YOU, COP?
NO! NO! IT'S TRUE! THEY MET AT SHOJI'S INN AND PLANNED THEIR BETRAYAL!
SHOJI! ASK SHOJI!
OH, I DID ASK SHOJI, AND HE DENIED THEY WERE THERE! HE DENIED IT WITH HIS DYING BREATH!
DO YOU THINK A SPINELESS TOWNSMAN WOULD LIE FOR A SAMURAI?! IT IS YOU WHO ARE LYING! YOU WOULD SELL YOUR MOTHER'S SOUL FOR A FEW COPPERS!
POOR SHOJI-- DEAD.
B-BUT I SWEAR THEY'RE IN LEAGUE AGAINST YOU AND BOSS JOYA!
WHAT WOULD THEY HAVE TO GAIN, YOU FOOL?! ARE THOSE PENNILESS TOWNSPEOPLE GOING TO PAY THEM TO DRIVE US OUT?! YOU'RE LYING! ADMIT IT, COP!
16

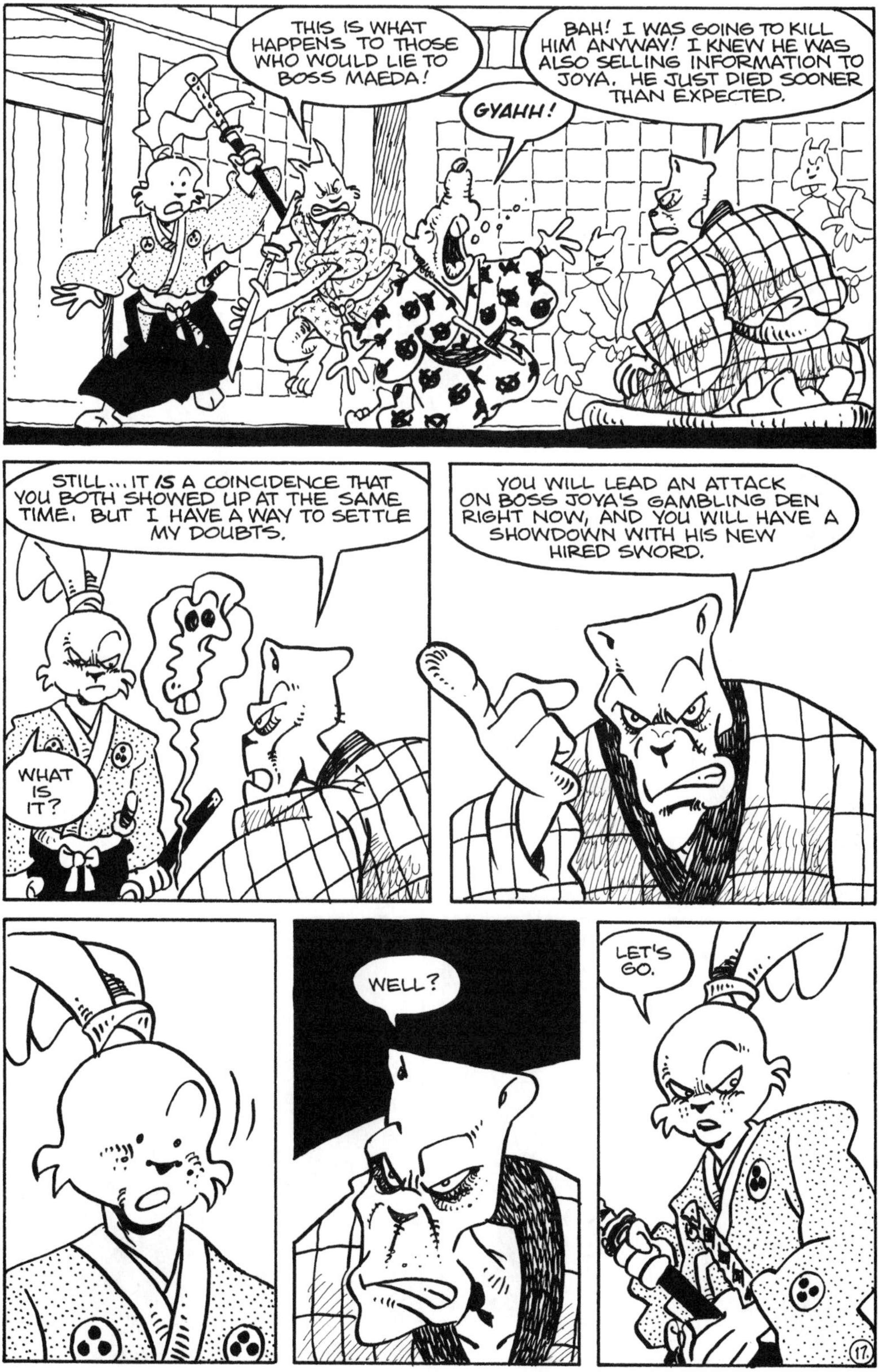
THIS IS WHAT HAPPENS TO THOSE WHO WOULD LIE TO BOSS MAEDA!
GYAHH!
BAH! I WAS GOING TO KILL HIM ANYWAY! I KNEW HE WAS ALSO SELLING INFORMATION TO JOYA. HE JUST DIED SOONER THAN EXPECTED.
STILL... IT IS A COINCIDENCE THAT YOU BOTH SHOWED UP AT THE SAME TIME. BUT I HAVE A WAY TO SETTLE MY DOUBTS.
WHAT IS IT?
YOU WILL LEAD AN ATTACK ON BOSS JOYA'S GAMBLING DEN RIGHT NOW, AND YOU WILL HAVE A SHOWDOWN WITH HIS NEW HIRED SWORD.
WELL?
LET'S GO.
17

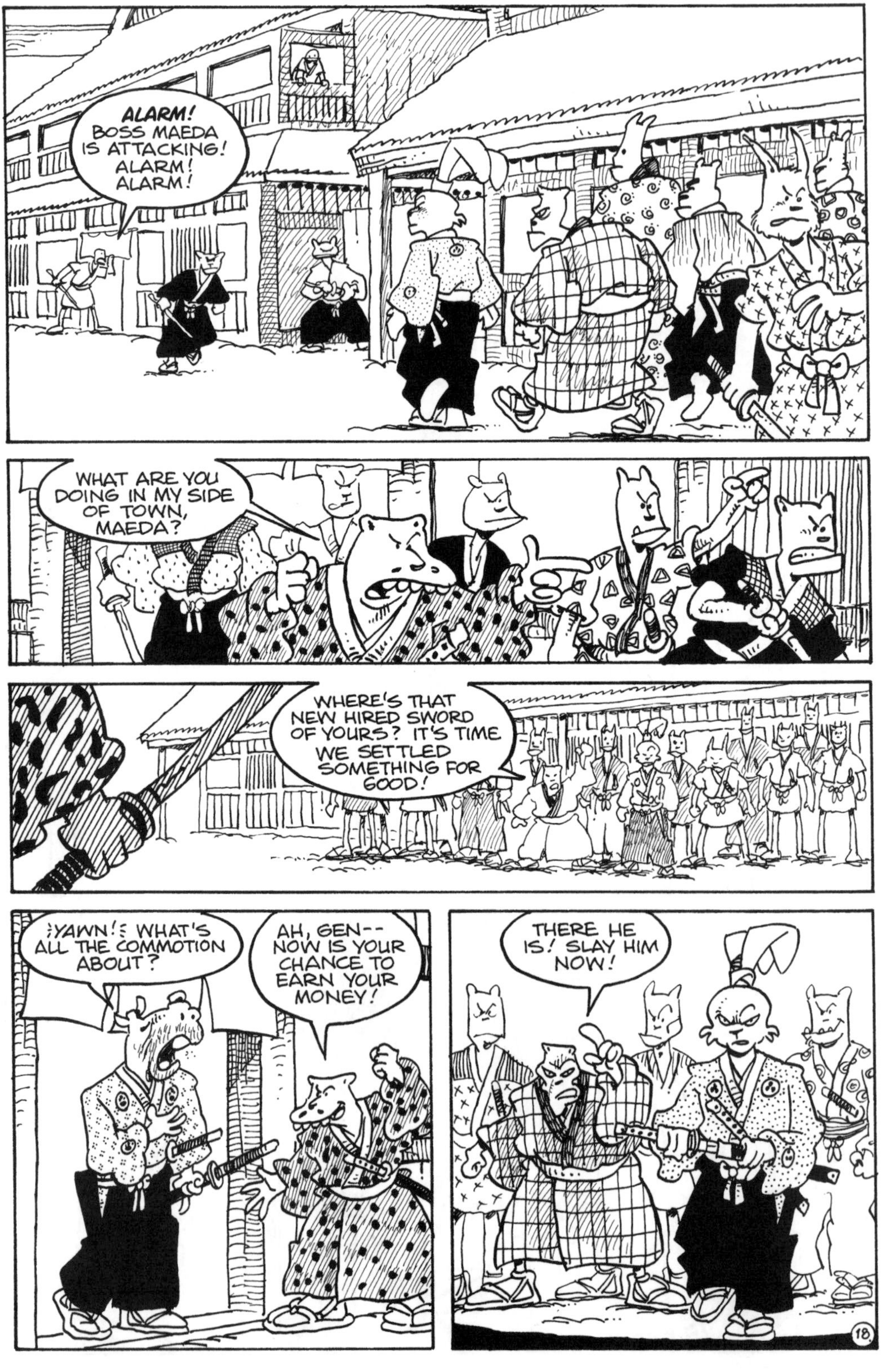
ALARM! BOSS MAEDA IS ATTACKING! ALARM! ALARM!
WHAT ARE YOU DOING IN MY SIDE OF TOWN, MAEDA?
WHERE'S THAT NEW HIRED SWORD OF YOURS? IT'S TIME WE SETTLED SOMETHING FOR GOOD!
≋YAWN!≋ WHAT'S ALL THE COMMOTION ABOUT?
AH, GEN-- NOW IS YOUR CHANCE TO EARN YOUR MONEY!
THERE HE IS! SLAY HIM NOW!
18

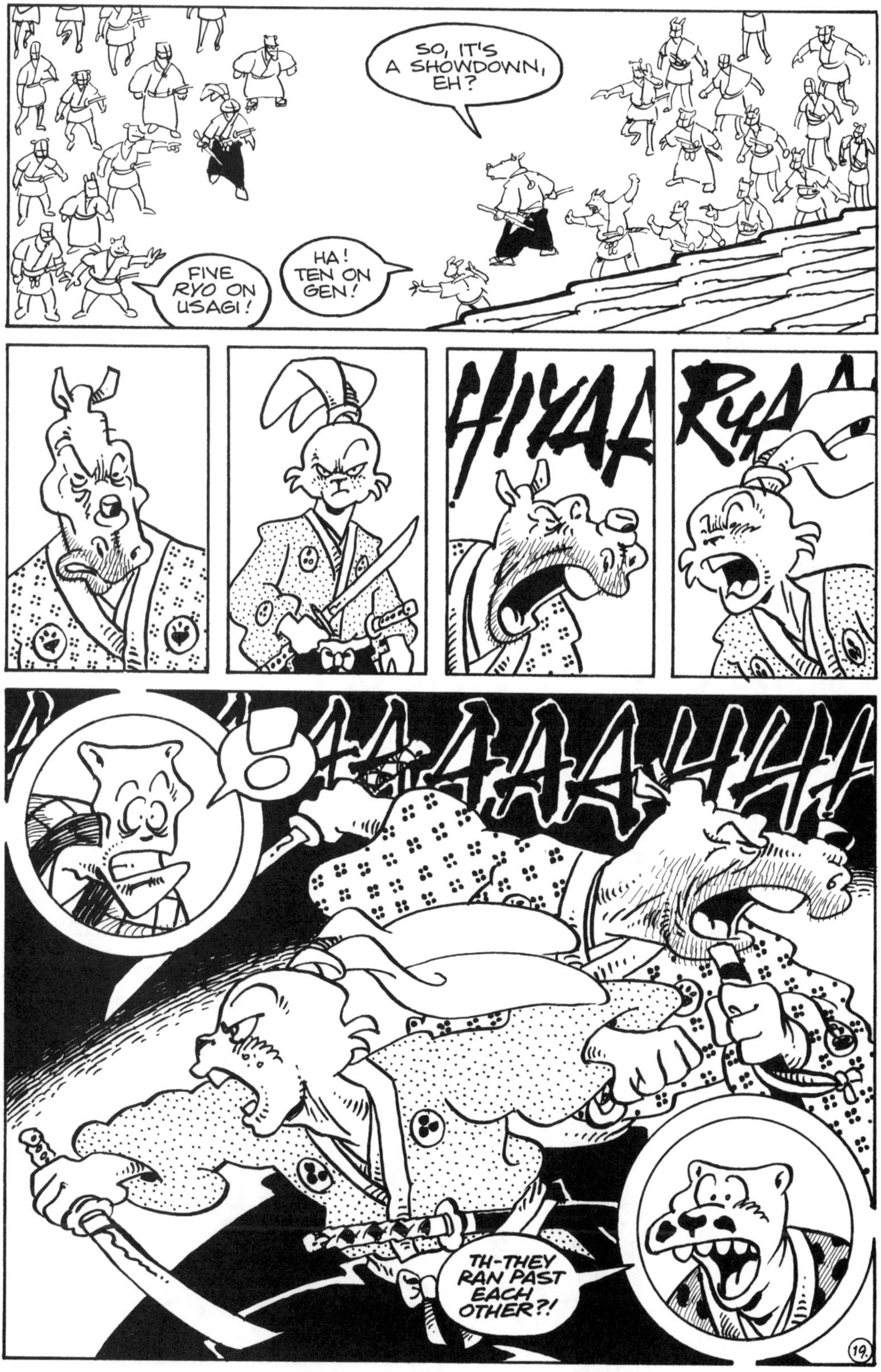
SO, IT'S A SHOWDOWN, EH?
FIVE RYO ON USAGI!
HA! TEN ON GEN!
HIYAA
RYA
AAAAAAAHH!
O
TH-THEY RAN PAST EACH OTHER?!
19.

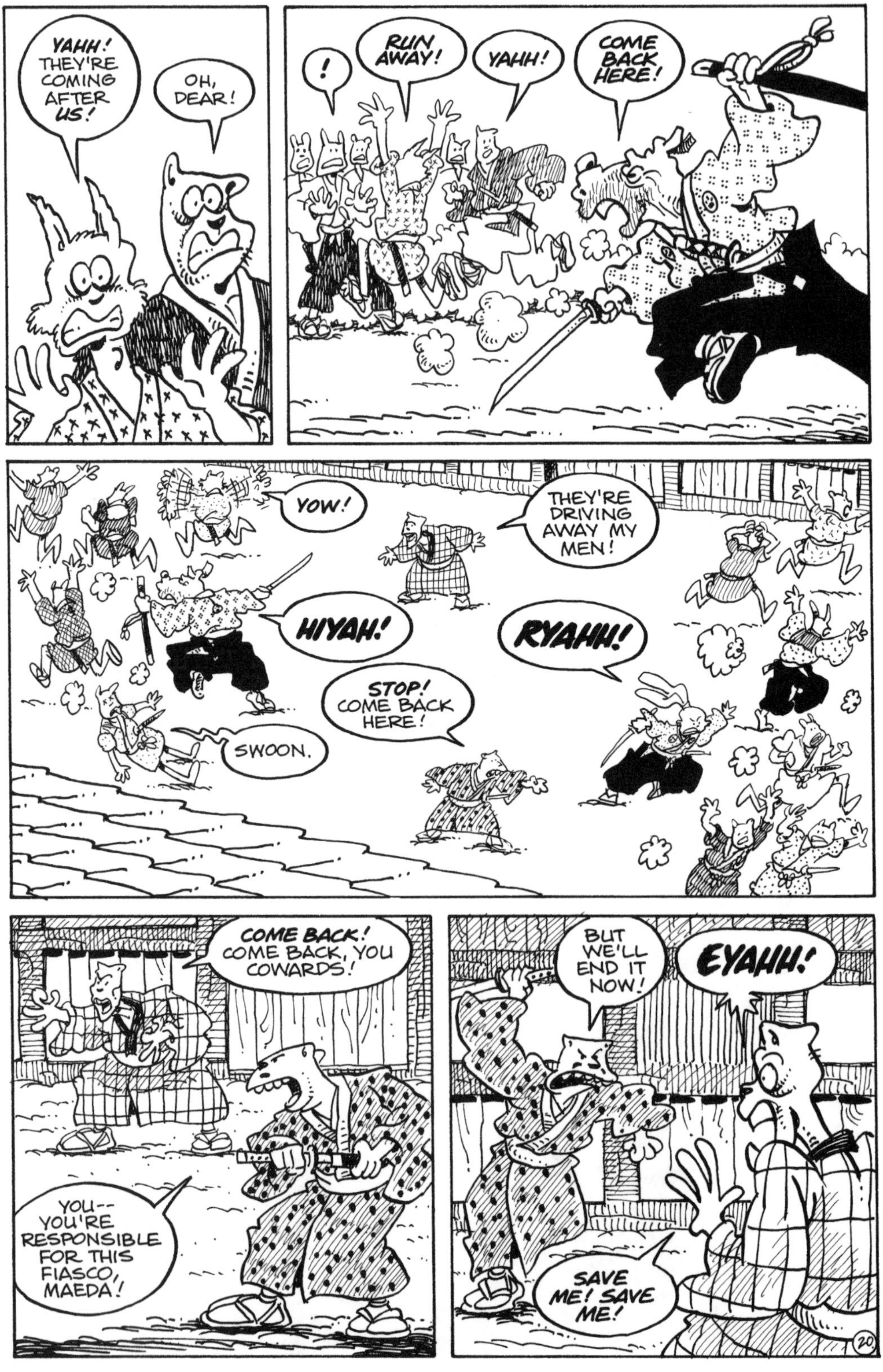
YAHH! THEY'RE COMING AFTER US!
OH, DEAR!
!
RUN AWAY!
YAHH!
COME BACK HERE!
YOW!
THEY'RE DRIVING AWAY MY MEN!
HIYAH!
RYAHH!
STOP! COME BACK HERE!
SWOON.
COME BACK! COME BACK, YOU COWARDS!
YOU-- YOU'RE RESPONSIBLE FOR THIS FIASCO, MAEDA!
BUT WE'LL END IT NOW!
EYAHH!
SAVE ME! SAVE ME!
20

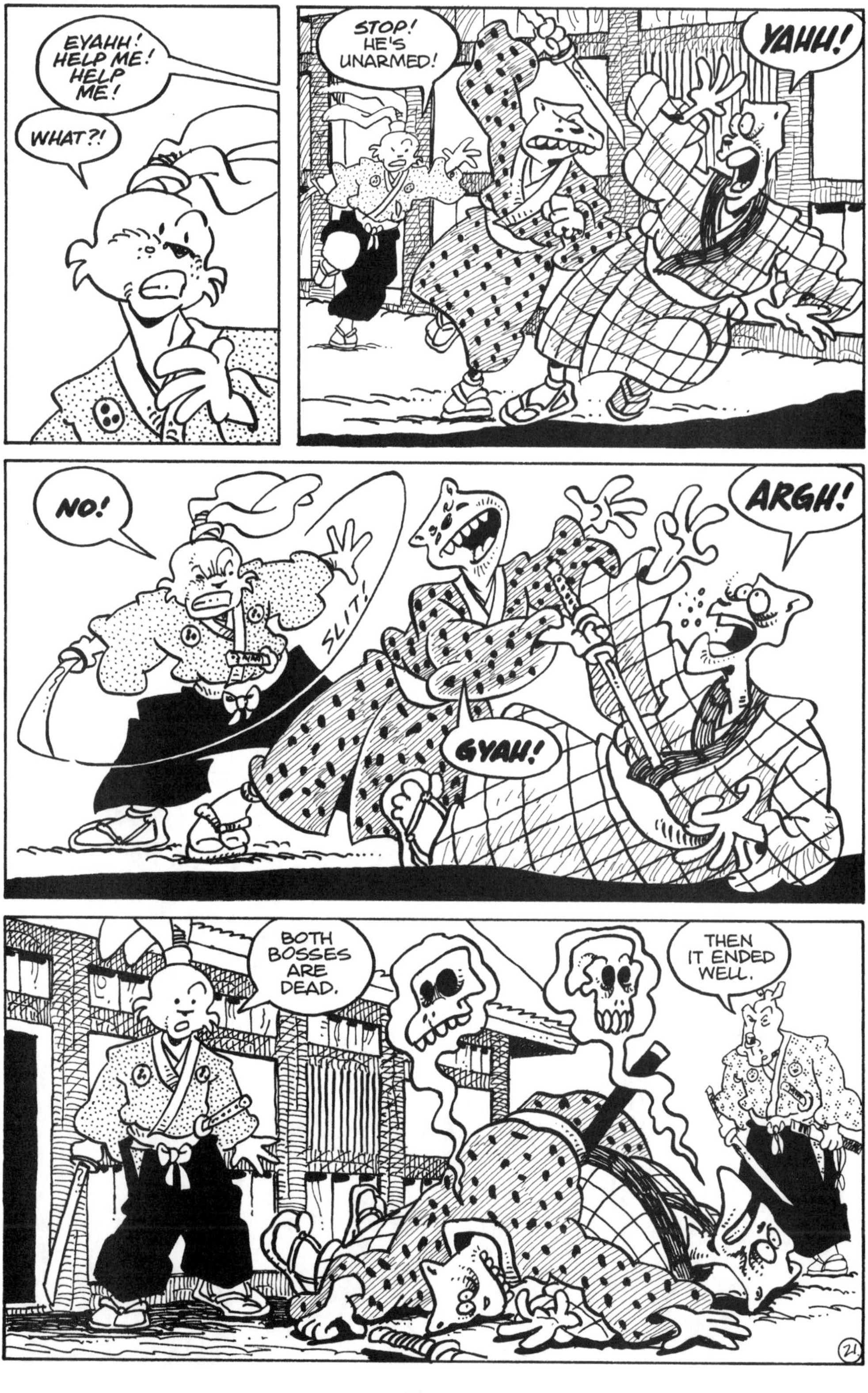
EYAHH! HELP ME! HELP ME!
WHAT?!
STOP! HE'S UNARMED!
YAHH!
NO!
SLIT!
ARGH!
GYAH!
BOTH BOSSES ARE DEAD.
THEN IT ENDED WELL.
21

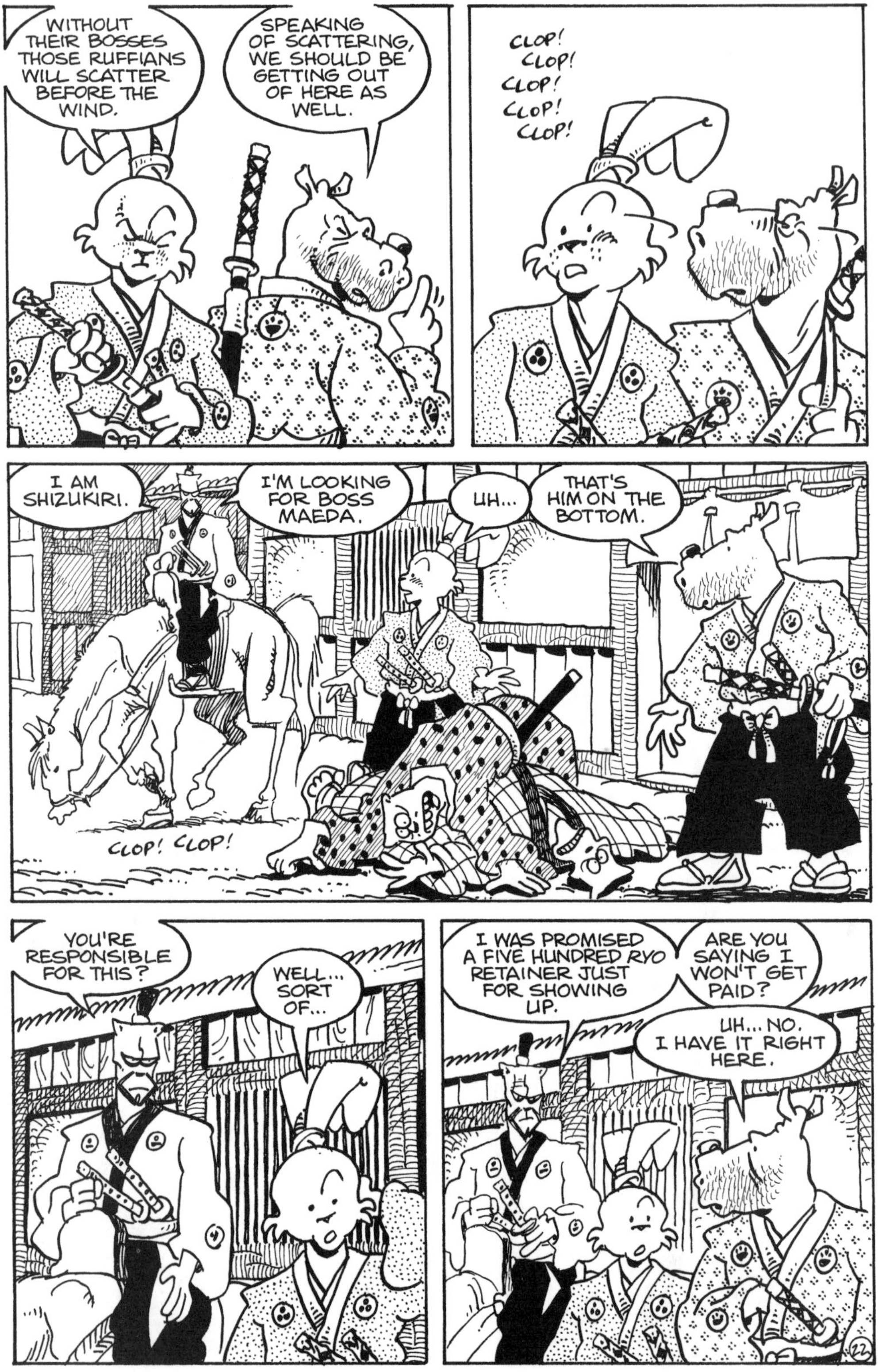
WITHOUT THEIR BOSSES THOSE RUFFIANS WILL SCATTER BEFORE THE WIND.
SPEAKING OF SCATTERING, WE SHOULD BE GETTING OUT OF HERE AS WELL.
CLOP! CLOP! CLOP! CLOP! CLOP!
I AM SHIZUKIRI.
I'M LOOKING FOR BOSS MAEDA.
UH...
THAT'S HIM ON THE BOTTOM.
CLOP! CLOP!
YOU'RE RESPONSIBLE FOR THIS?
WELL... SORT OF...
I WAS PROMISED A FIVE HUNDRED RYO RETAINER JUST FOR SHOWING UP.
ARE YOU SAYING I WON'T GET PAID?
UH... NO. I HAVE IT RIGHT HERE.
22

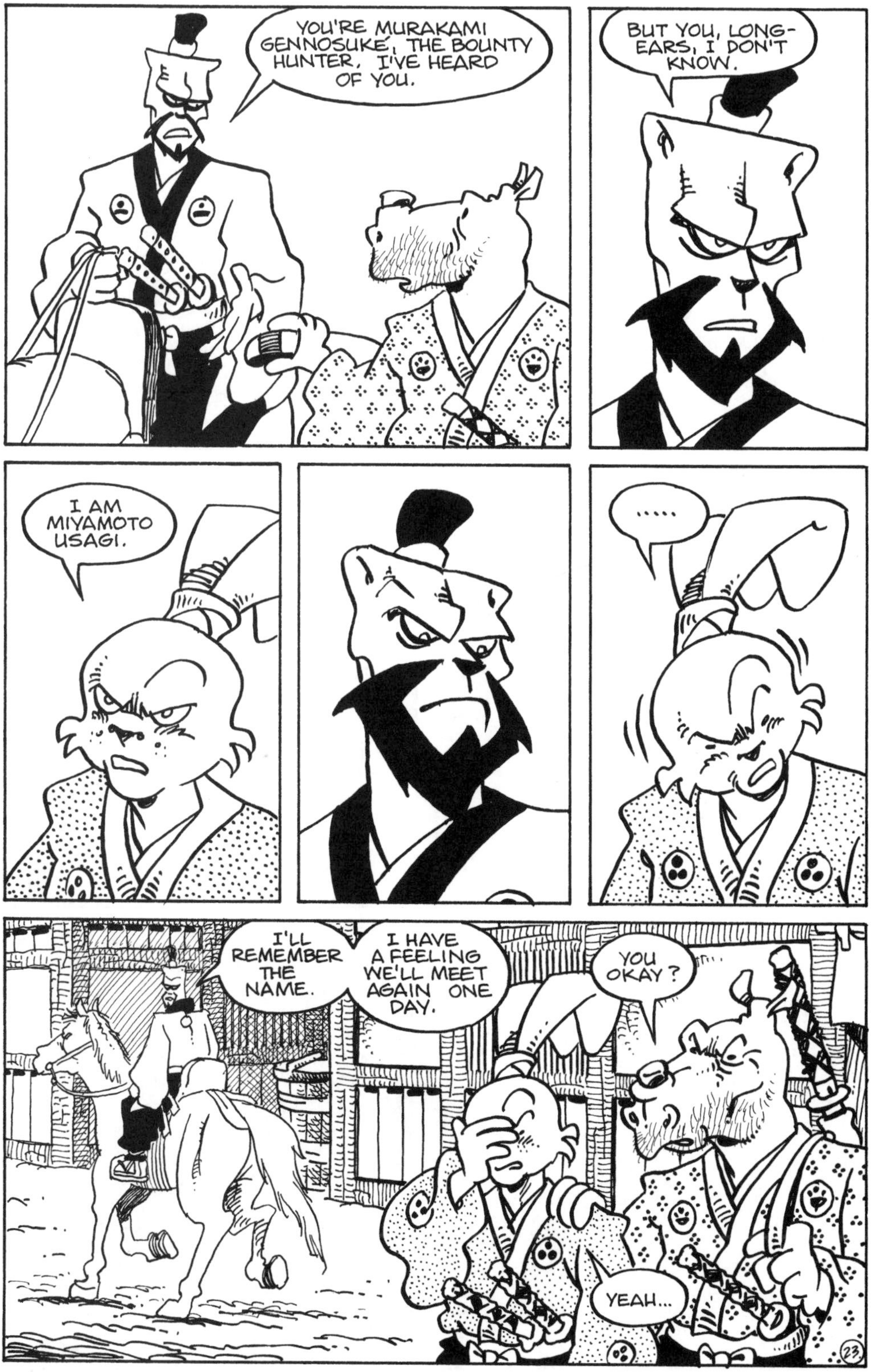
YOU'RE MURAKAMI GENNOSUKE, THE BOUNTY HUNTER. I'VE HEARD OF YOU.
BUT YOU, LONG-EARS, I DON'T KNOW.
I AM MIYAMOTO USAGI.
.....
I'LL REMEMBER THE NAME.
I HAVE A FEELING WE'LL MEET AGAIN ONE DAY.
YOU OKAY?
YEAH...
23

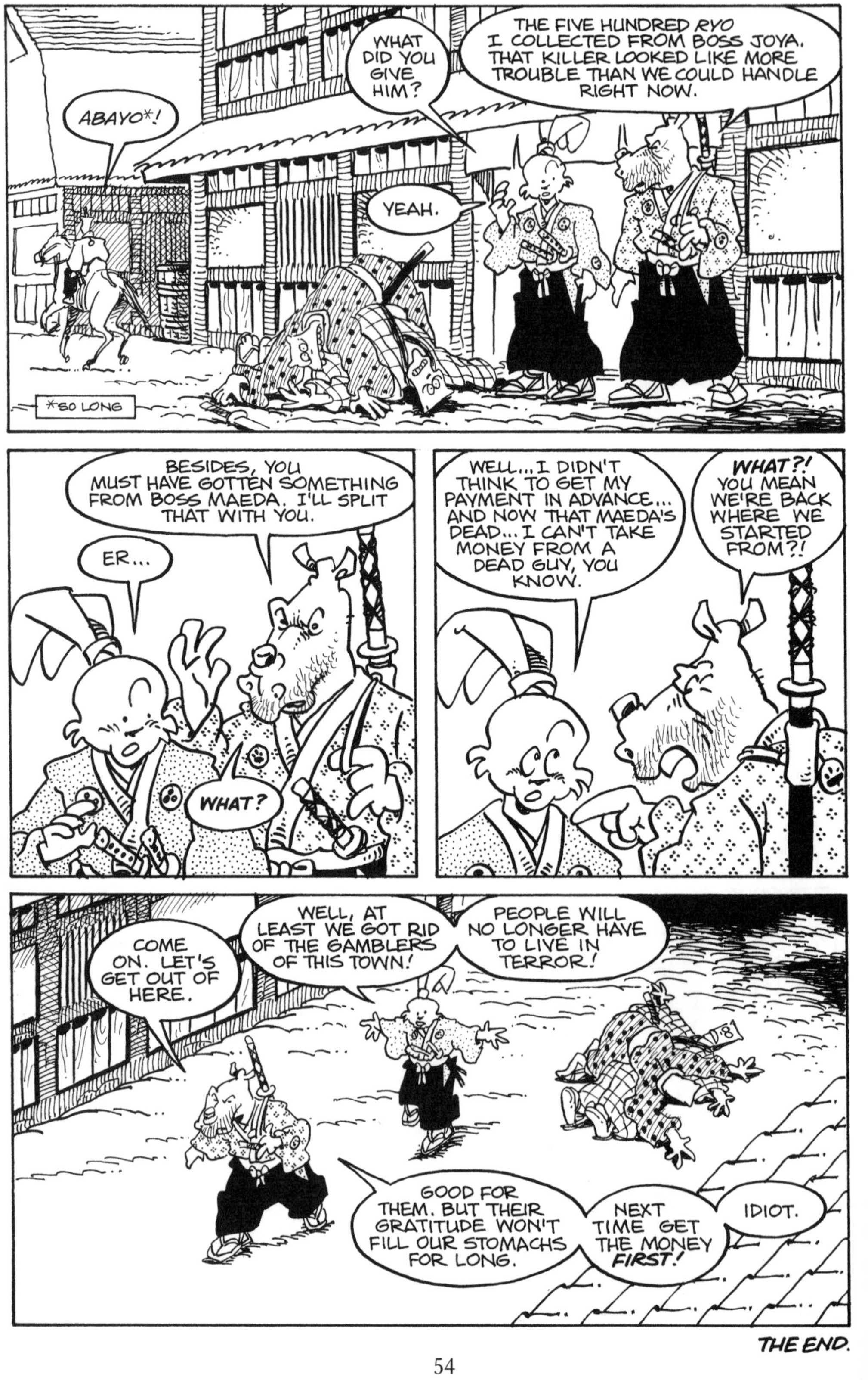
ABAYO*!
WHAT DID YOU GIVE HIM?
THE FIVE HUNDRED *RYO* I COLLECTED FROM BOSS JOYA. THAT KILLER LOOKED LIKE MORE TROUBLE THAN WE COULD HANDLE RIGHT NOW.
YEAH.
*SO LONG
BESIDES, YOU MUST HAVE GOTTEN SOMETHING FROM BOSS MAEDA. I'LL SPLIT THAT WITH YOU.
ER...
WHAT?
WELL... I DIDN'T THINK TO GET MY PAYMENT IN ADVANCE... AND NOW THAT MAEDA'S DEAD... I CAN'T TAKE MONEY FROM A DEAD GUY, YOU KNOW.
WHAT?! YOU MEAN WE'RE BACK WHERE WE STARTED FROM?!
COME ON. LET'S GET OUT OF HERE.
WELL, AT LEAST WE GOT RID OF THE GAMBLERS OF THIS TOWN!
PEOPLE WILL NO LONGER HAVE TO LIVE IN TERROR!
GOOD FOR THEM. BUT THEIR GRATITUDE WON'T FILL OUR STOMACHS FOR LONG.
NEXT TIME GET THE MONEY ***FIRST!***
IDIOT.

THE END.

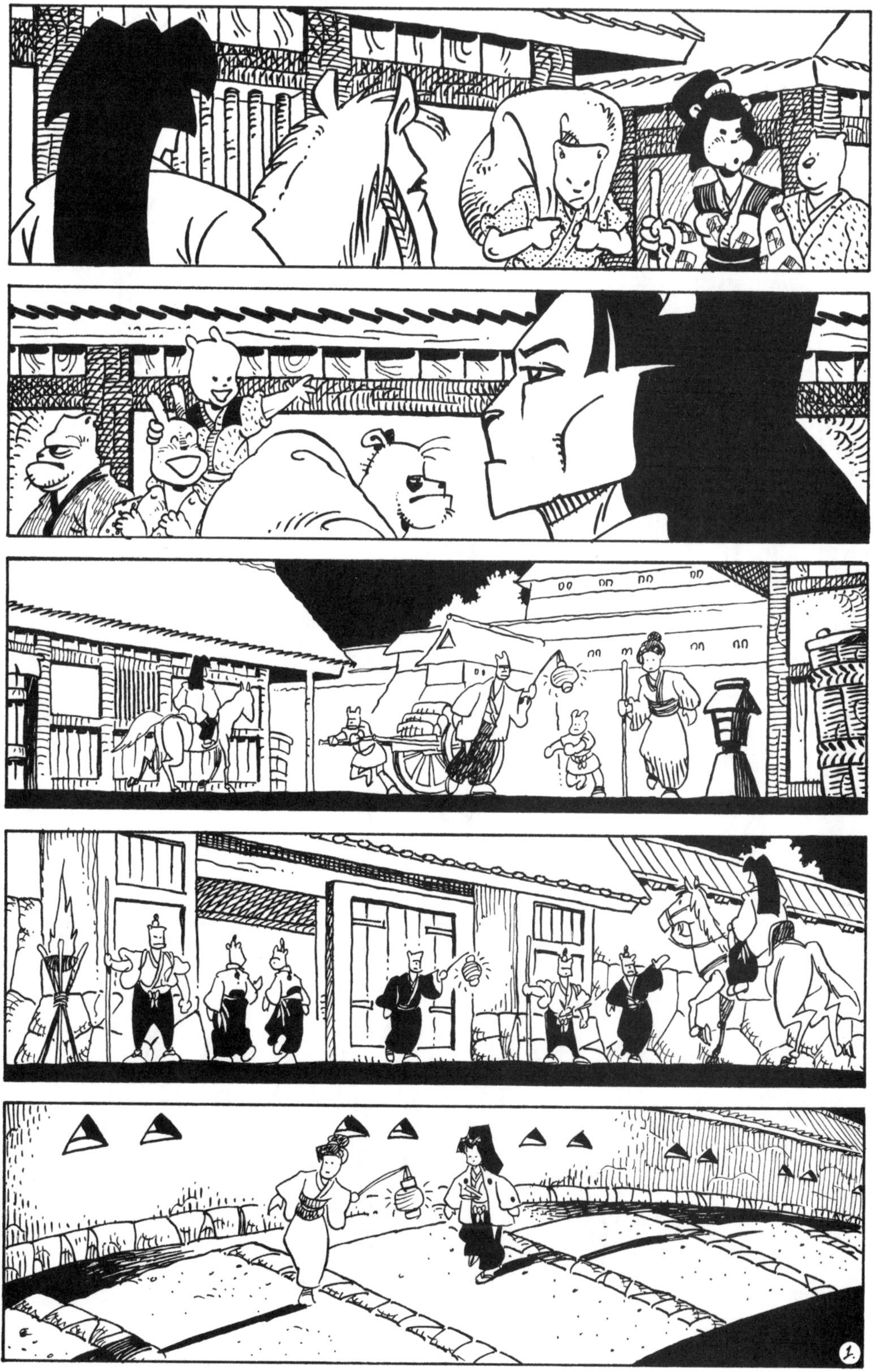

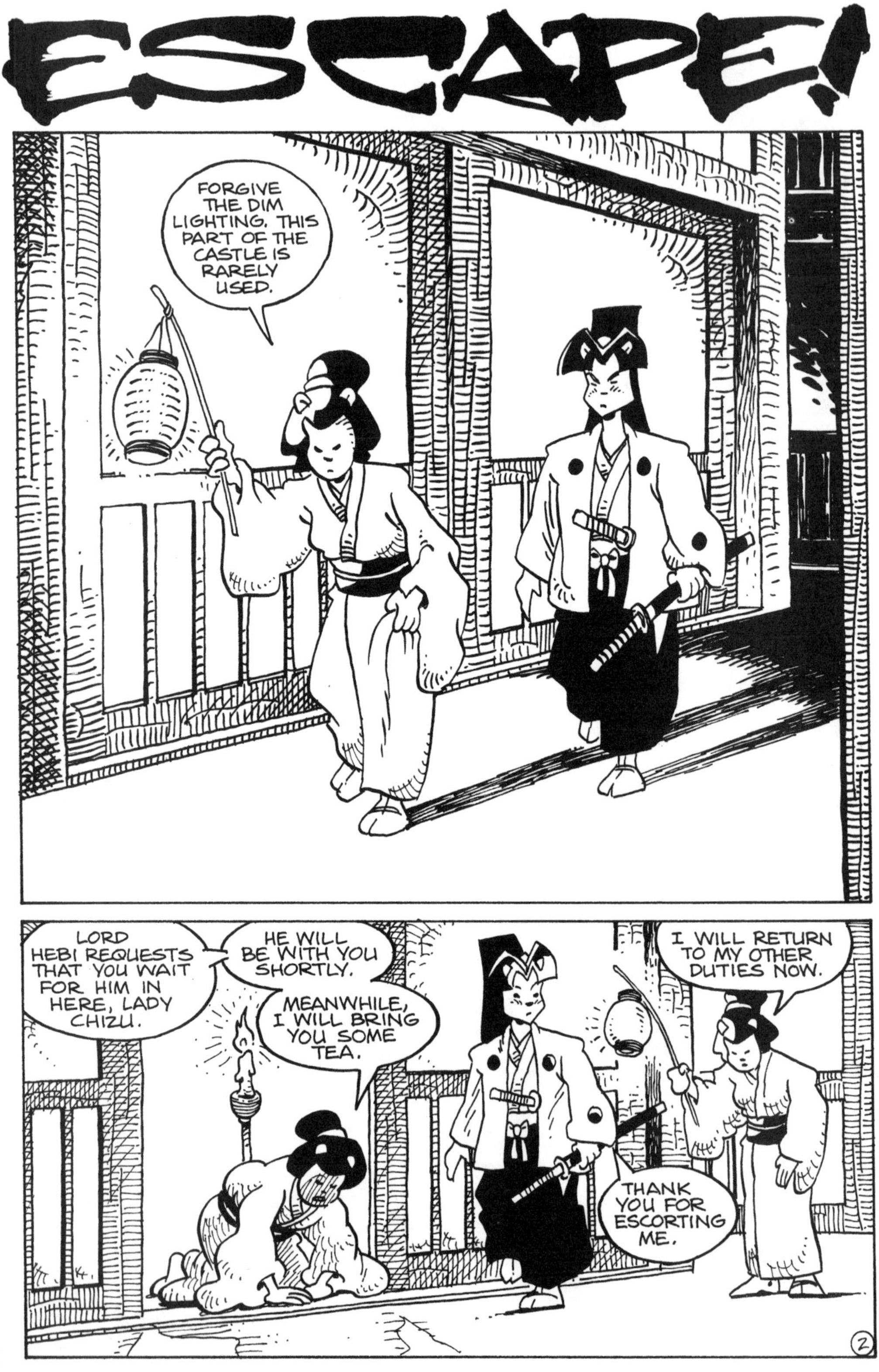
ESCAPE!
FORGIVE THE DIM LIGHTING. THIS PART OF THE CASTLE IS RARELY USED.
LORD HEBI REQUESTS THAT YOU WAIT FOR HIM IN HERE, LADY CHIZU.
HE WILL BE WITH YOU SHORTLY.
MEANWHILE, I WILL BRING YOU SOME TEA.
I WILL RETURN TO MY OTHER DUTIES NOW.
THANK YOU FOR ESCORTING ME.
2

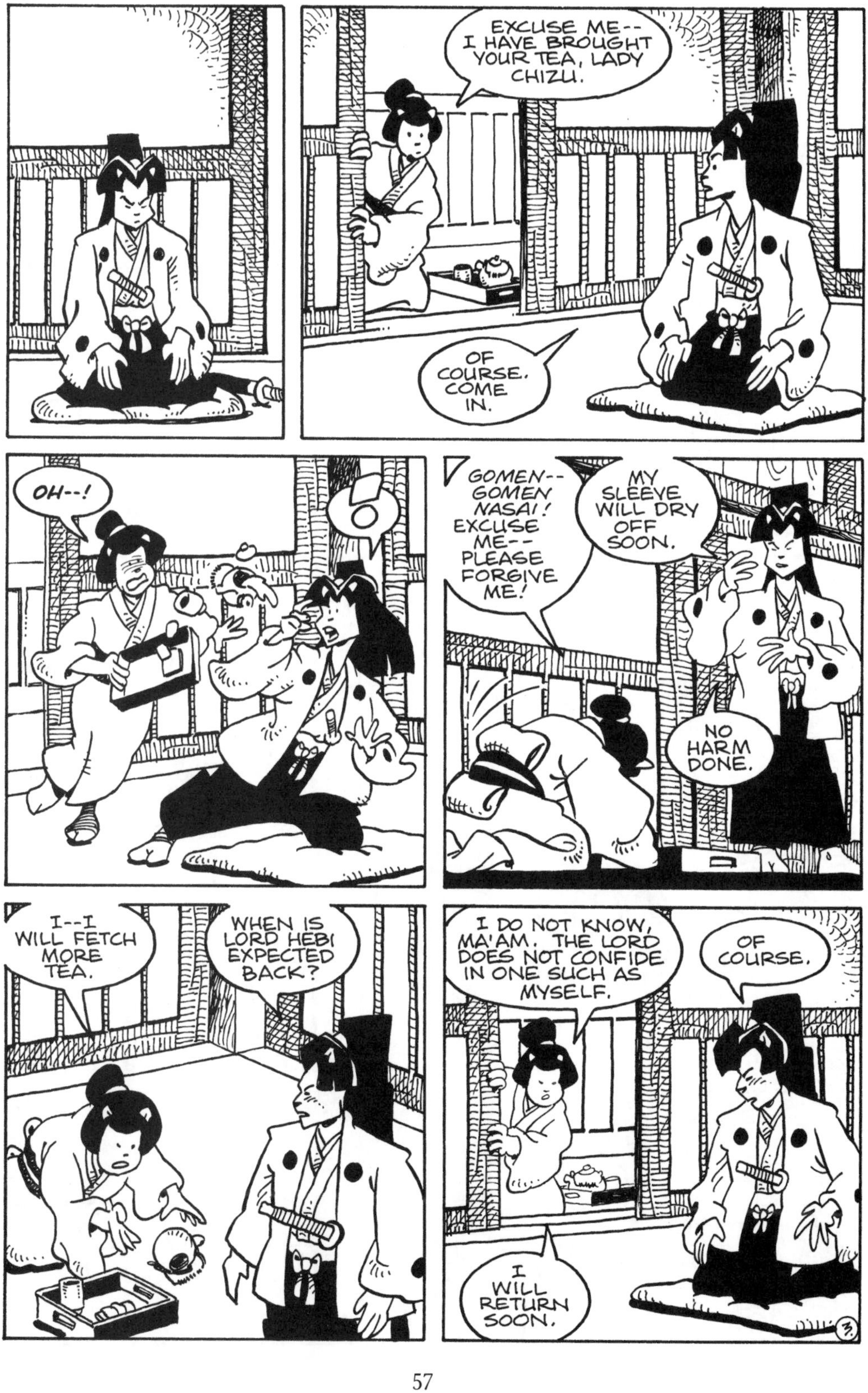
EXCUSE ME-- I HAVE BROUGHT YOUR TEA, LADY CHIZU.
OF COURSE. COME IN.
OH--!
!
GOMEN-- GOMEN NASAI! EXCUSE ME-- PLEASE FORGIVE ME!
MY SLEEVE WILL DRY OFF SOON.
NO HARM DONE.
I--I WILL FETCH MORE TEA.
WHEN IS LORD HEBI EXPECTED BACK?
I DO NOT KNOW, MA'AM. THE LORD DOES NOT CONFIDE IN ONE SUCH AS MYSELF.
OF COURSE.
I WILL RETURN SOON.
3.

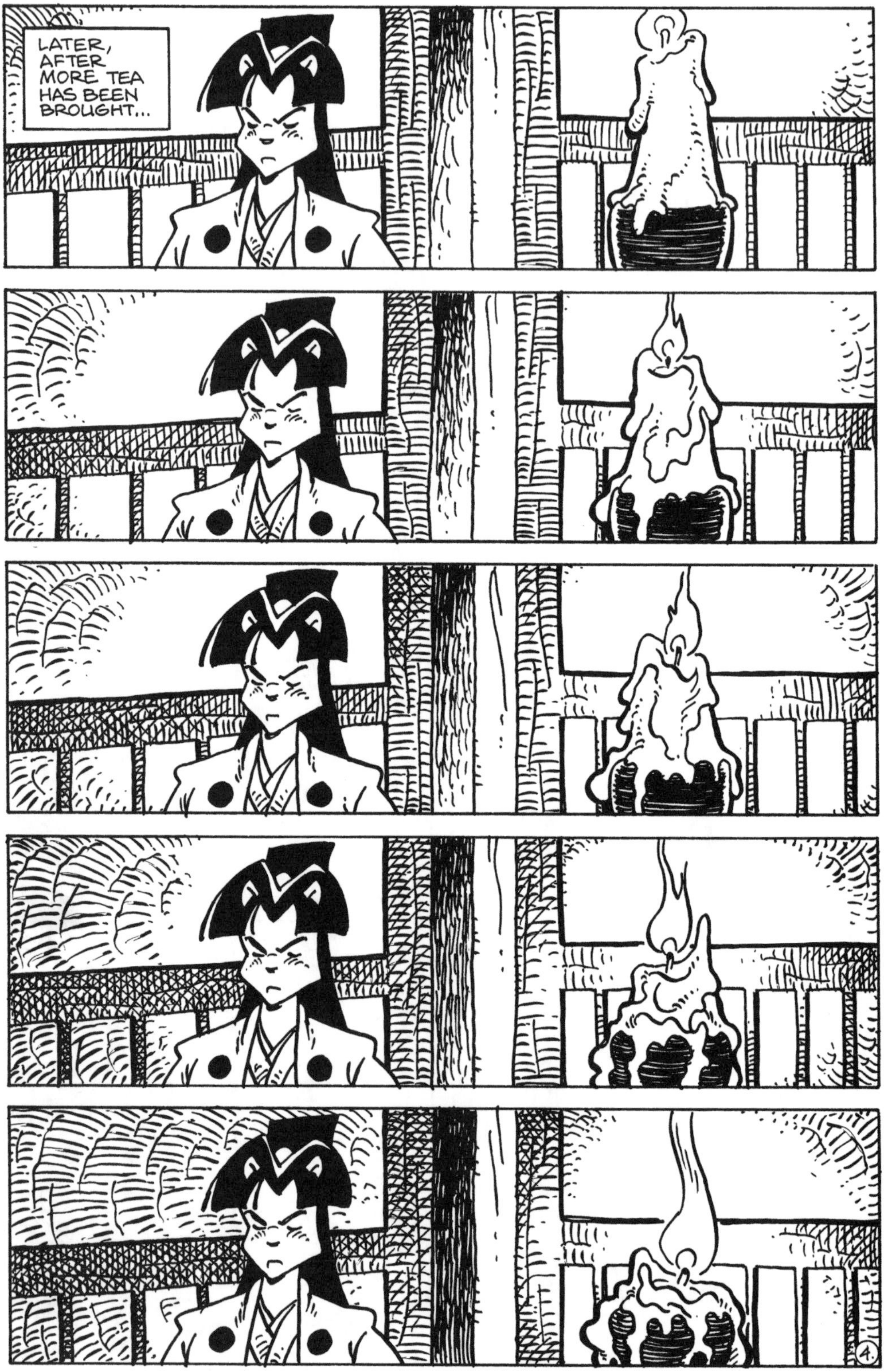
LATER, AFTER MORE TEA HAS BEEN BROUGHT...

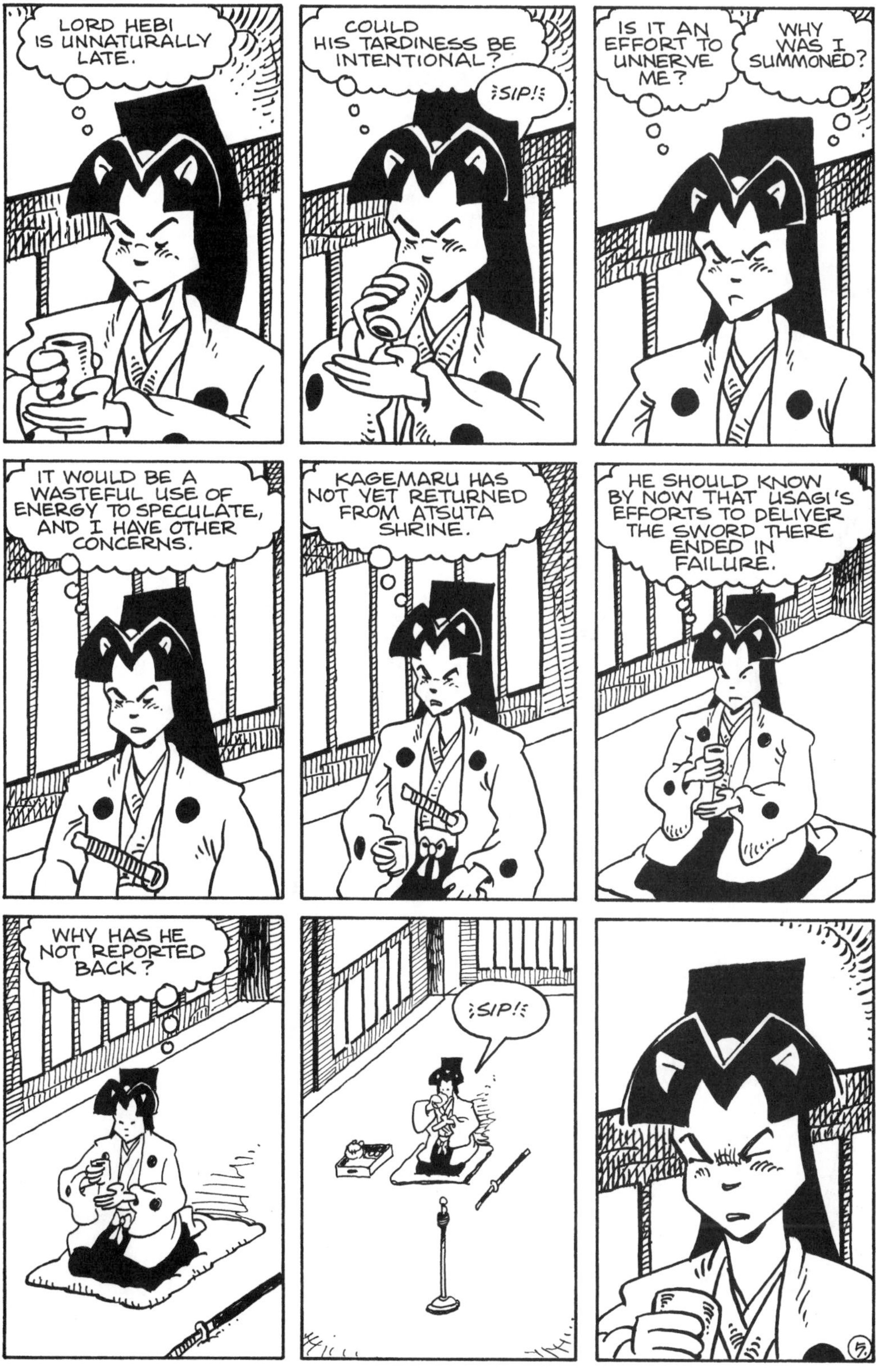
LORD HEBI IS UNNATURALLY LATE.
COULD HIS TARDINESS BE INTENTIONAL?
SIP!
IS IT AN EFFORT TO UNNERVE ME?
WHY WAS I SUMMONED?
IT WOULD BE A WASTEFUL USE OF ENERGY TO SPECULATE, AND I HAVE OTHER CONCERNS.
KAGEMARU HAS NOT YET RETURNED FROM ATSUTA SHRINE.
HE SHOULD KNOW BY NOW THAT USAGI'S EFFORTS TO DELIVER THE SWORD THERE ENDED IN FAILURE.
WHY HAS HE NOT REPORTED BACK?
SIP!
5

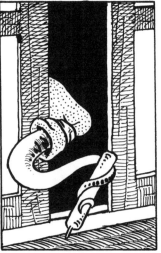

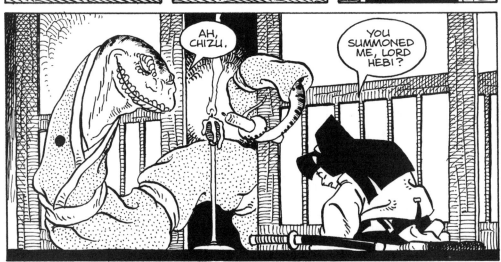

AH, CHIZU.

YOU SUMMONED ME, LORD HEBI?

I HAVE CONCERNS ABOUT YOUR PERFORMANCE OF LATE, *JONIN** OF THE NEKO NINJA CLAN.

......

*CHIEF

H-HOW HAVE I DISPLEASED YOU, MY LORD?

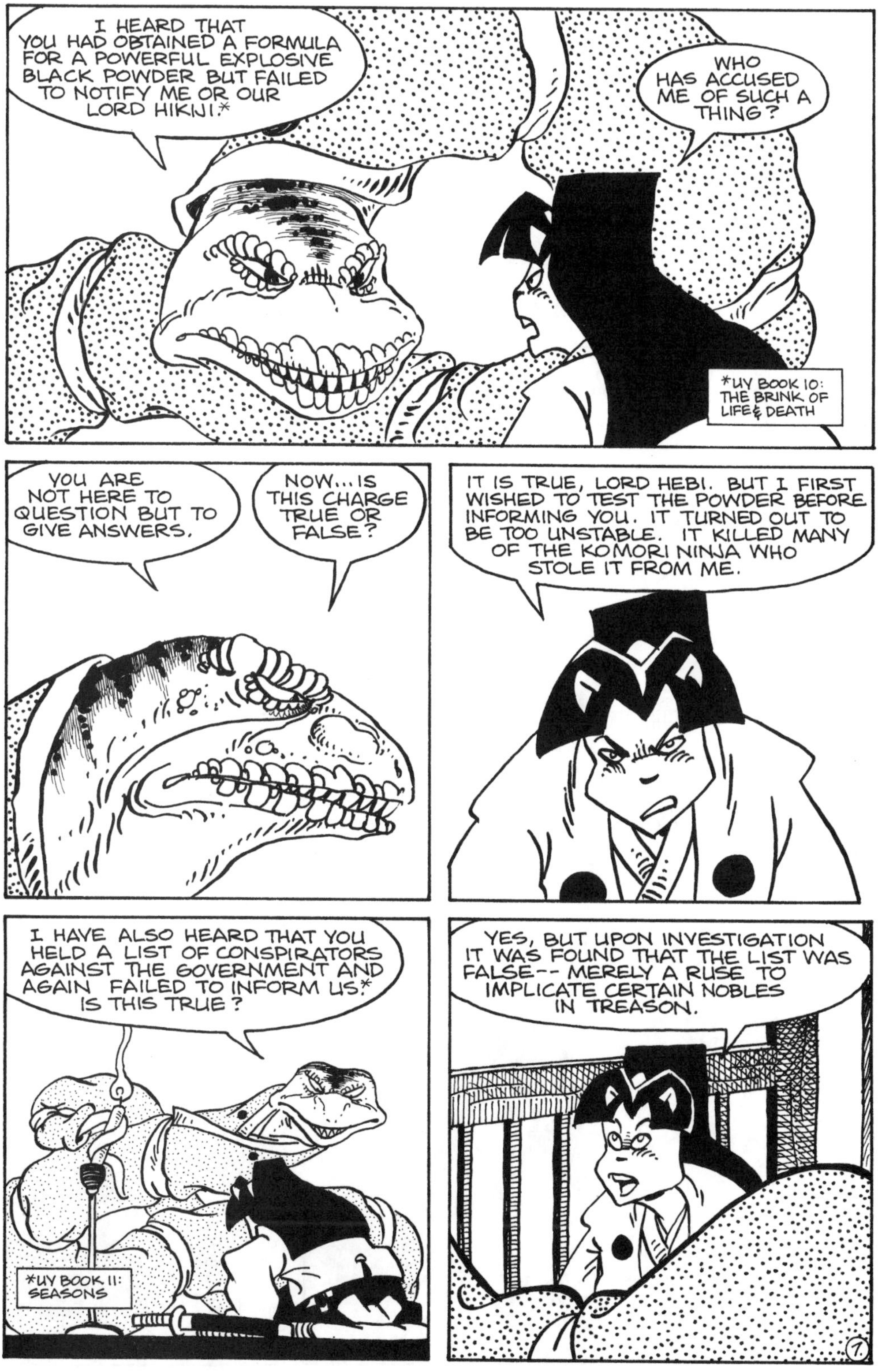
I HEARD THAT YOU HAD OBTAINED A FORMULA FOR A POWERFUL EXPLOSIVE BLACK POWDER BUT FAILED TO NOTIFY ME OR OUR LORD HIKIJI.*
WHO HAS ACCUSED ME OF SUCH A THING?
*UY BOOK 10: THE BRINK OF LIFE & DEATH
YOU ARE NOT HERE TO QUESTION BUT TO GIVE ANSWERS.
NOW...IS THIS CHARGE TRUE OR FALSE?
IT IS TRUE, LORD HEBI. BUT I FIRST WISHED TO TEST THE POWDER BEFORE INFORMING YOU. IT TURNED OUT TO BE TOO UNSTABLE. IT KILLED MANY OF THE KOMORI NINJA WHO STOLE IT FROM ME.
I HAVE ALSO HEARD THAT YOU HELD A LIST OF CONSPIRATORS AGAINST THE GOVERNMENT AND AGAIN FAILED TO INFORM US.* IS THIS TRUE?
*UY BOOK 11: SEASONS
YES, BUT UPON INVESTIGATION IT WAS FOUND THAT THE LIST WAS FALSE-- MERELY A RUSE TO IMPLICATE CERTAIN NOBLES IN TREASON.
7.

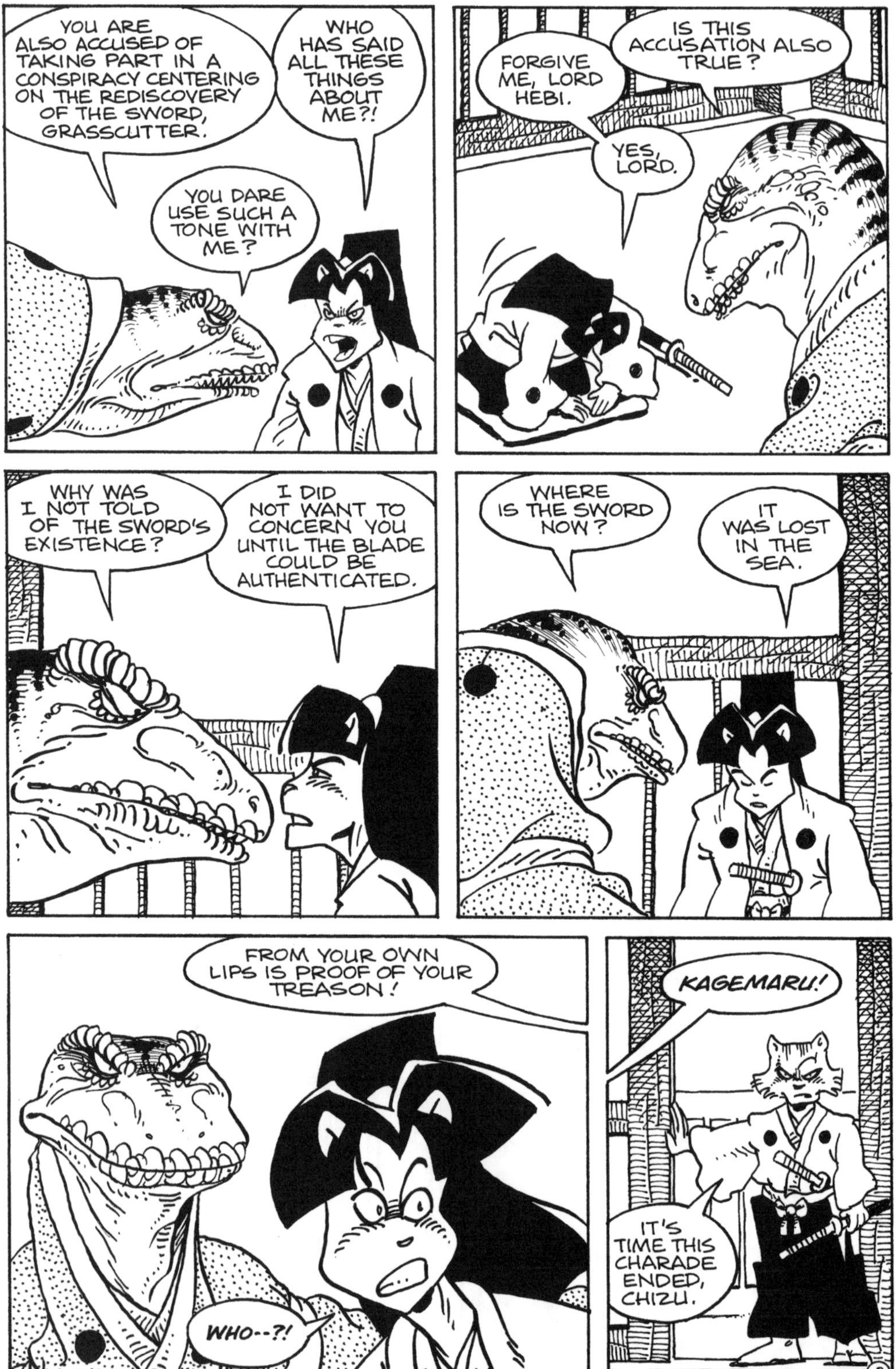
YOU ARE ALSO ACCUSED OF TAKING PART IN A CONSPIRACY CENTERING ON THE REDISCOVERY OF THE SWORD, GRASSCUTTER.
WHO HAS SAID ALL THESE THINGS ABOUT ME?!
YOU DARE USE SUCH A TONE WITH ME?
IS THIS ACCUSATION ALSO TRUE?
FORGIVE ME, LORD HEBI.
YES, LORD.
WHY WAS I NOT TOLD OF THE SWORD'S EXISTENCE?
I DID NOT WANT TO CONCERN YOU UNTIL THE BLADE COULD BE AUTHENTICATED.
WHERE IS THE SWORD NOW?
IT WAS LOST IN THE SEA.
FROM YOUR OWN LIPS IS PROOF OF YOUR TREASON!
WHO--?!
KAGEMARU!
IT'S TIME THIS CHARADE ENDED, CHIZU.
8.

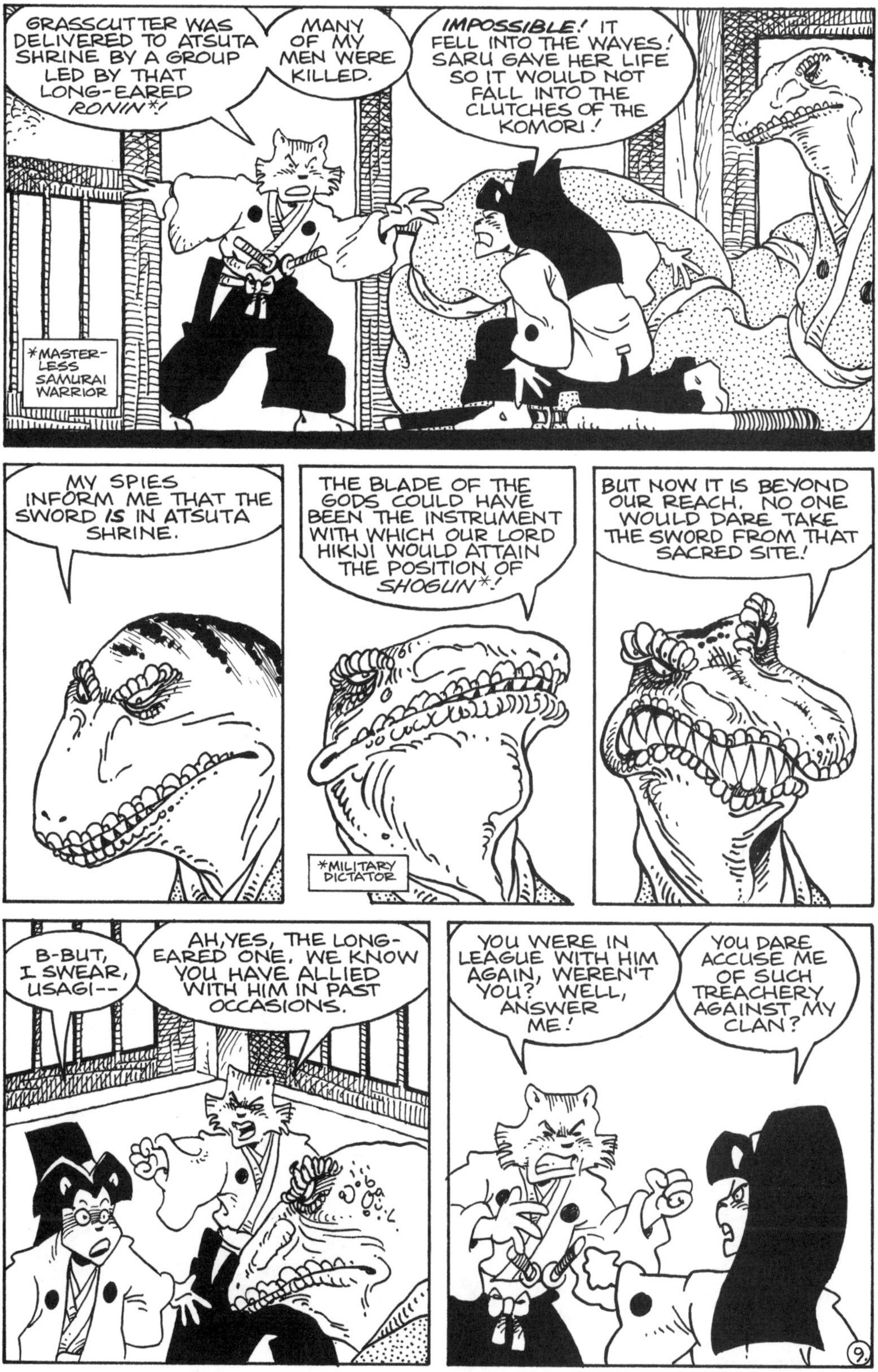
GRASSCUTTER WAS DELIVERED TO ATSUTA SHRINE BY A GROUP LED BY THAT LONG-EARED *RONIN**!
MANY OF MY MEN WERE KILLED.
IMPOSSIBLE! IT FELL INTO THE WAVES! SARU GAVE HER LIFE SO IT WOULD NOT FALL INTO THE CLUTCHES OF THE KOMORI!
*MASTER-LESS SAMURAI WARRIOR
MY SPIES INFORM ME THAT THE SWORD *IS* IN ATSUTA SHRINE.
THE BLADE OF THE GODS COULD HAVE BEEN THE INSTRUMENT WITH WHICH OUR LORD HIKIJI WOULD ATTAIN THE POSITION OF *SHOGUN**!
*MILITARY DICTATOR
BUT NOW IT IS BEYOND OUR REACH. NO ONE WOULD DARE TAKE THE SWORD FROM THAT SACRED SITE!
B-BUT, I SWEAR, USAGI--
AH, YES, THE LONG-EARED ONE. WE KNOW YOU HAVE ALLIED WITH HIM IN PAST OCCASIONS.
YOU WERE IN LEAGUE WITH HIM AGAIN, WEREN'T YOU? WELL, ANSWER ME!
YOU DARE ACCUSE ME OF SUCH TREACHERY AGAINST MY CLAN?
9.

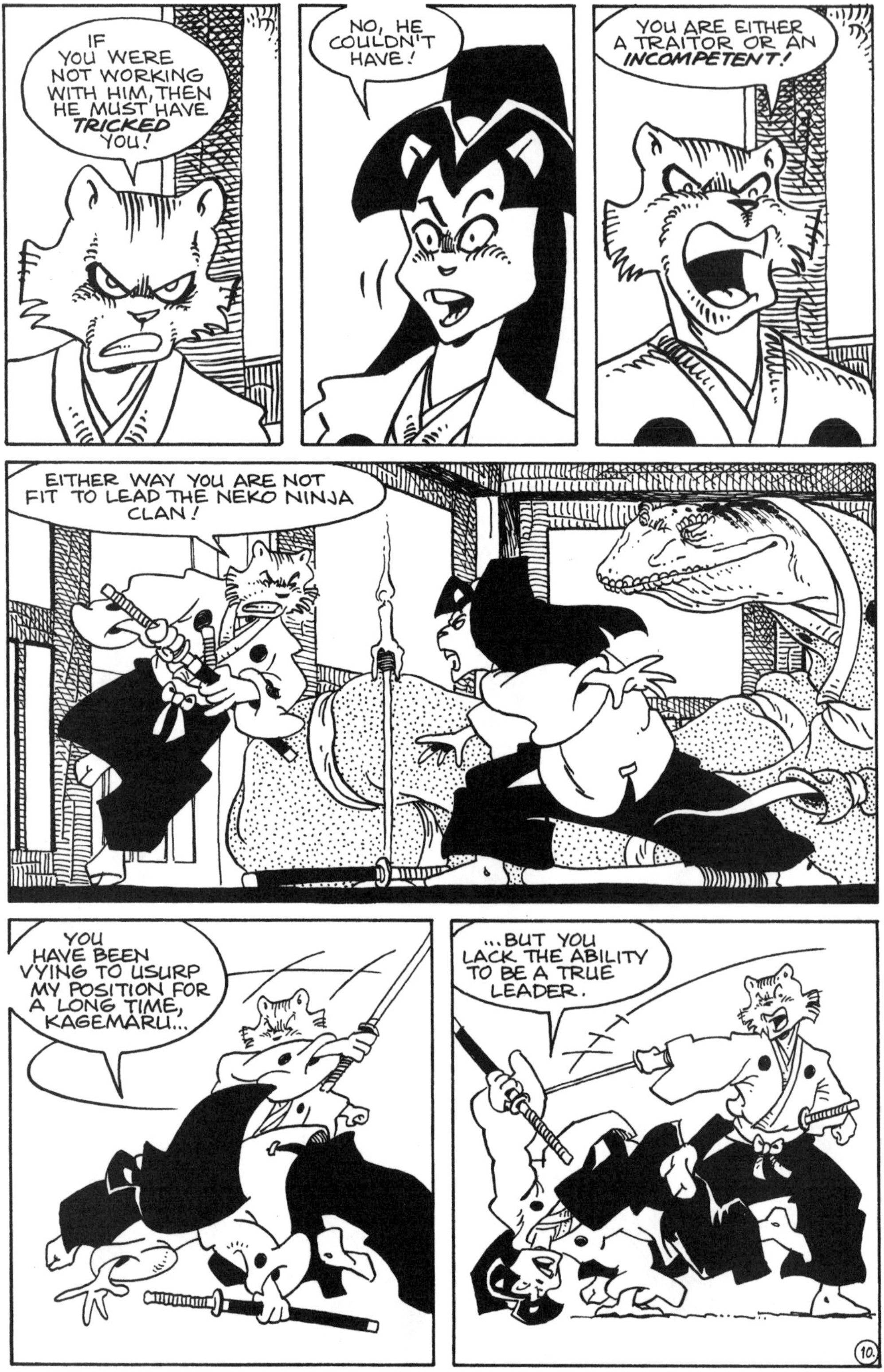
IF YOU WERE NOT WORKING WITH HIM, THEN HE MUST HAVE TRICKED YOU!
NO, HE COULDN'T HAVE!
YOU ARE EITHER A TRAITOR OR AN INCOMPETENT!
EITHER WAY YOU ARE NOT FIT TO LEAD THE NEKO NINJA CLAN!
YOU HAVE BEEN VYING TO USURP MY POSITION FOR A LONG TIME, KAGEMARU...
...BUT YOU LACK THE ABILITY TO BE A TRUE LEADER.
10.

WHY DON'T YOU JUST DIE WITH HONOR, CHIZU?!

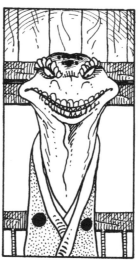

"HONOR"? YOU DON'T KNOW THE MEANING OF THE WORD!

NOW!

NOW!

WHAT?!

SLAM!

CRAK!

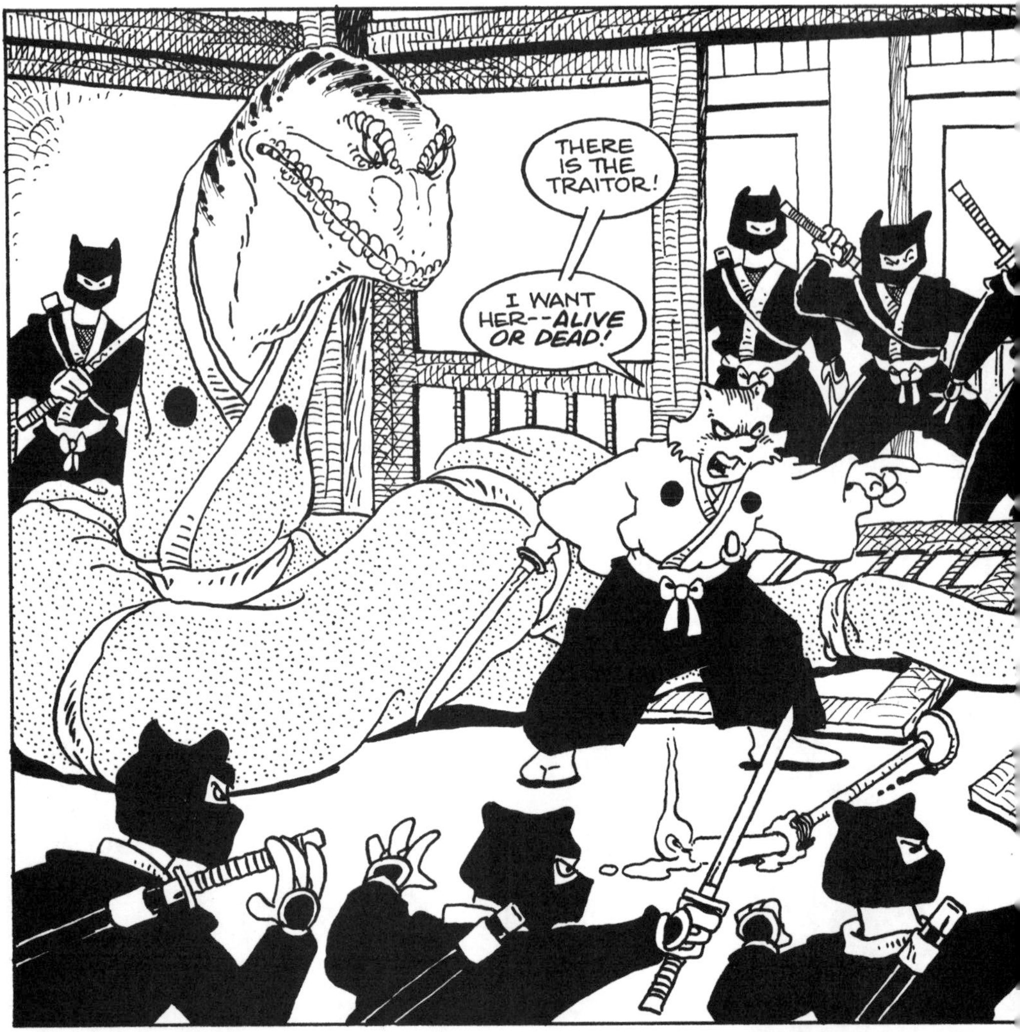
THERE IS THE TRAITOR!
I WANT HER--ALIVE OR DEAD!

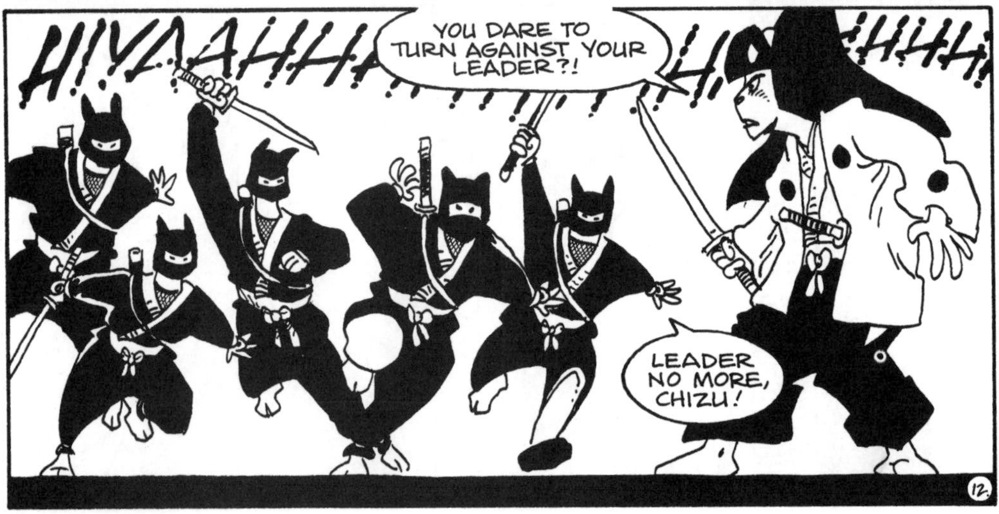
HIYAAHHH
YOU DARE TO TURN AGAINST YOUR LEADER?!
LEADER NO MORE, CHIZU!
12.

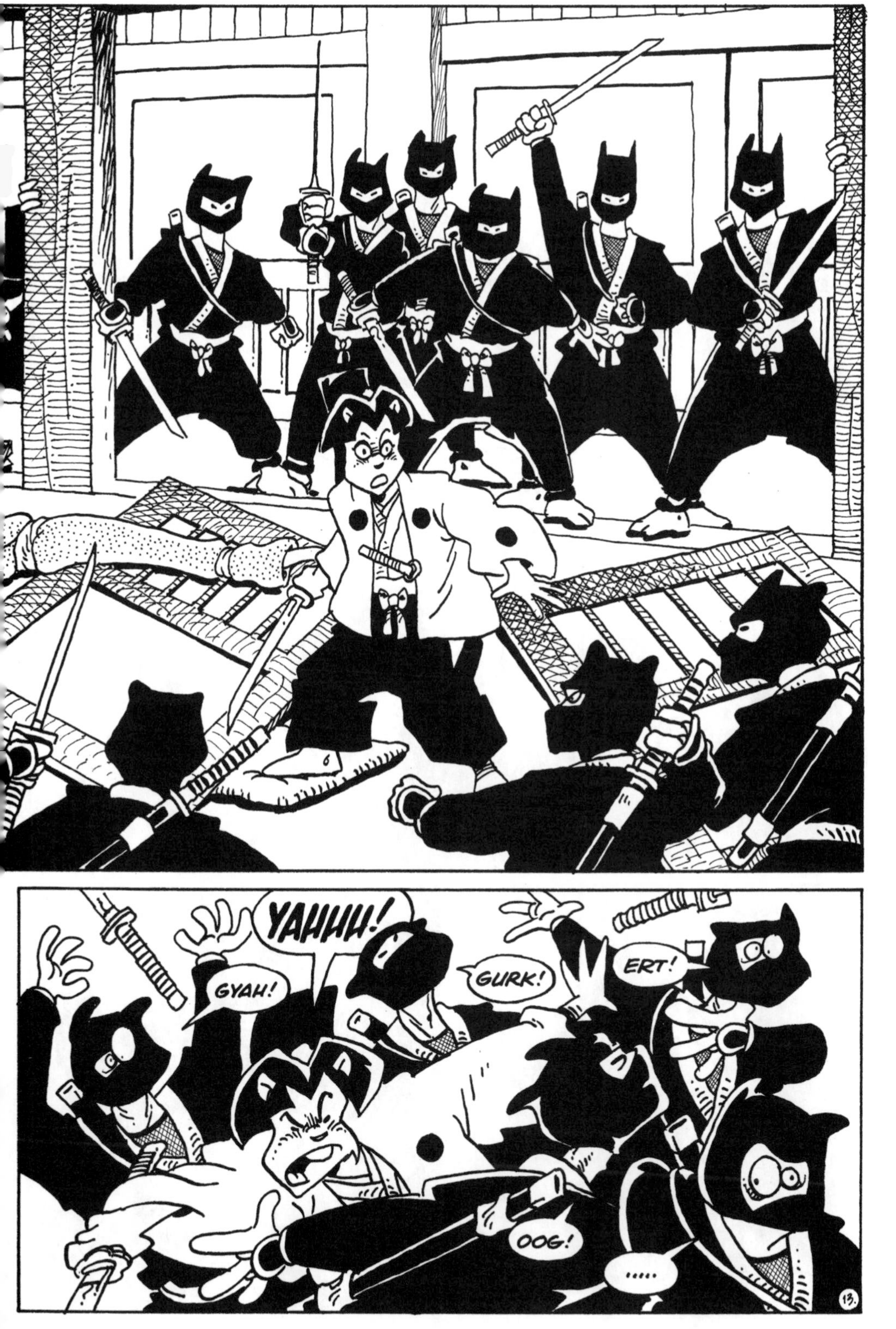
YAHHH!
GYAH!
GURK!
ERT!
OOG!
.....
13.

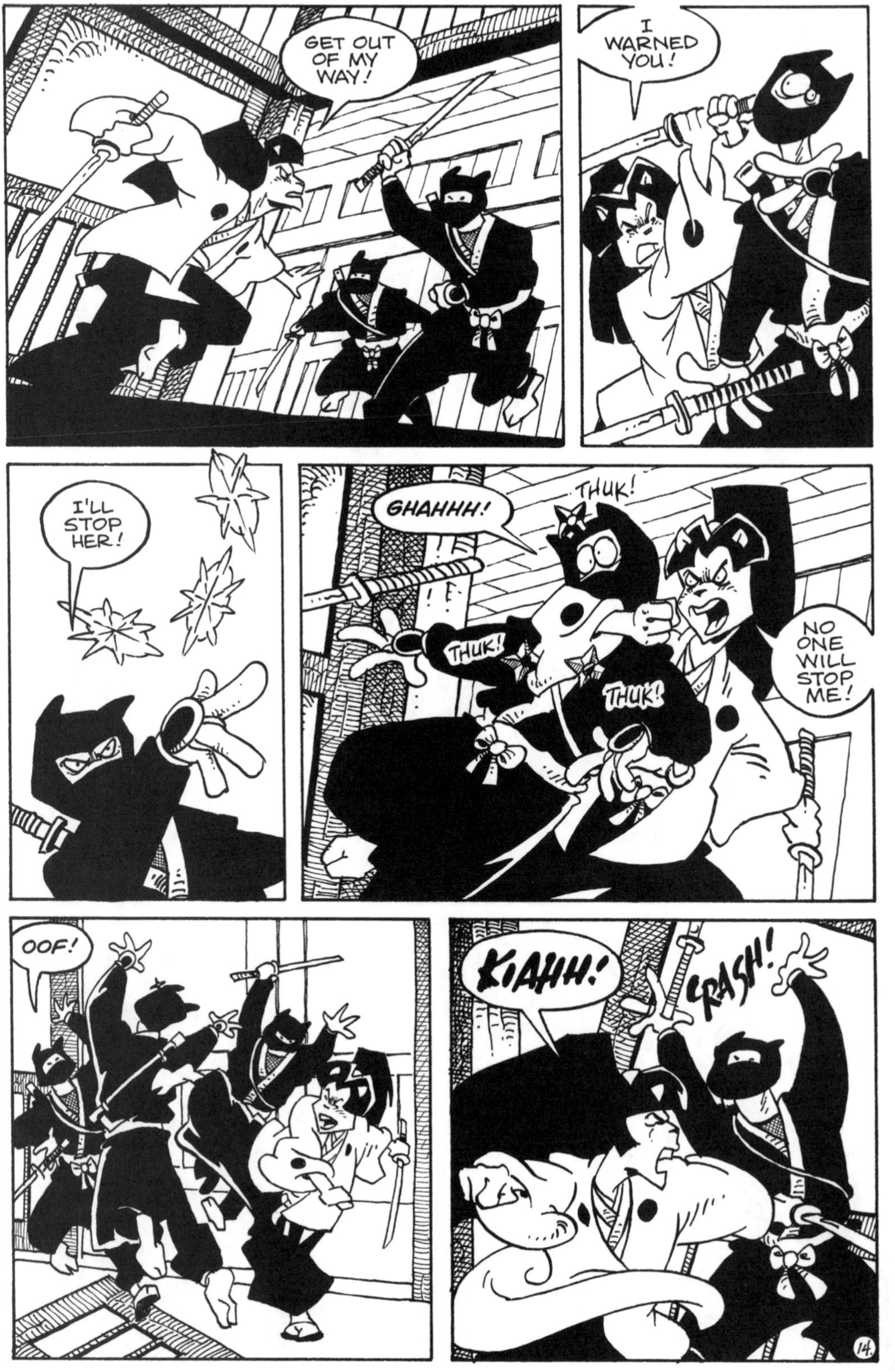
GET OUT OF MY WAY!
I WARNED YOU!
I'LL STOP HER!
GHAHHH!
THUK!
THUK!
THUK!
NO ONE WILL STOP ME!
OOF!
KIAHH!
CRASH!
14.

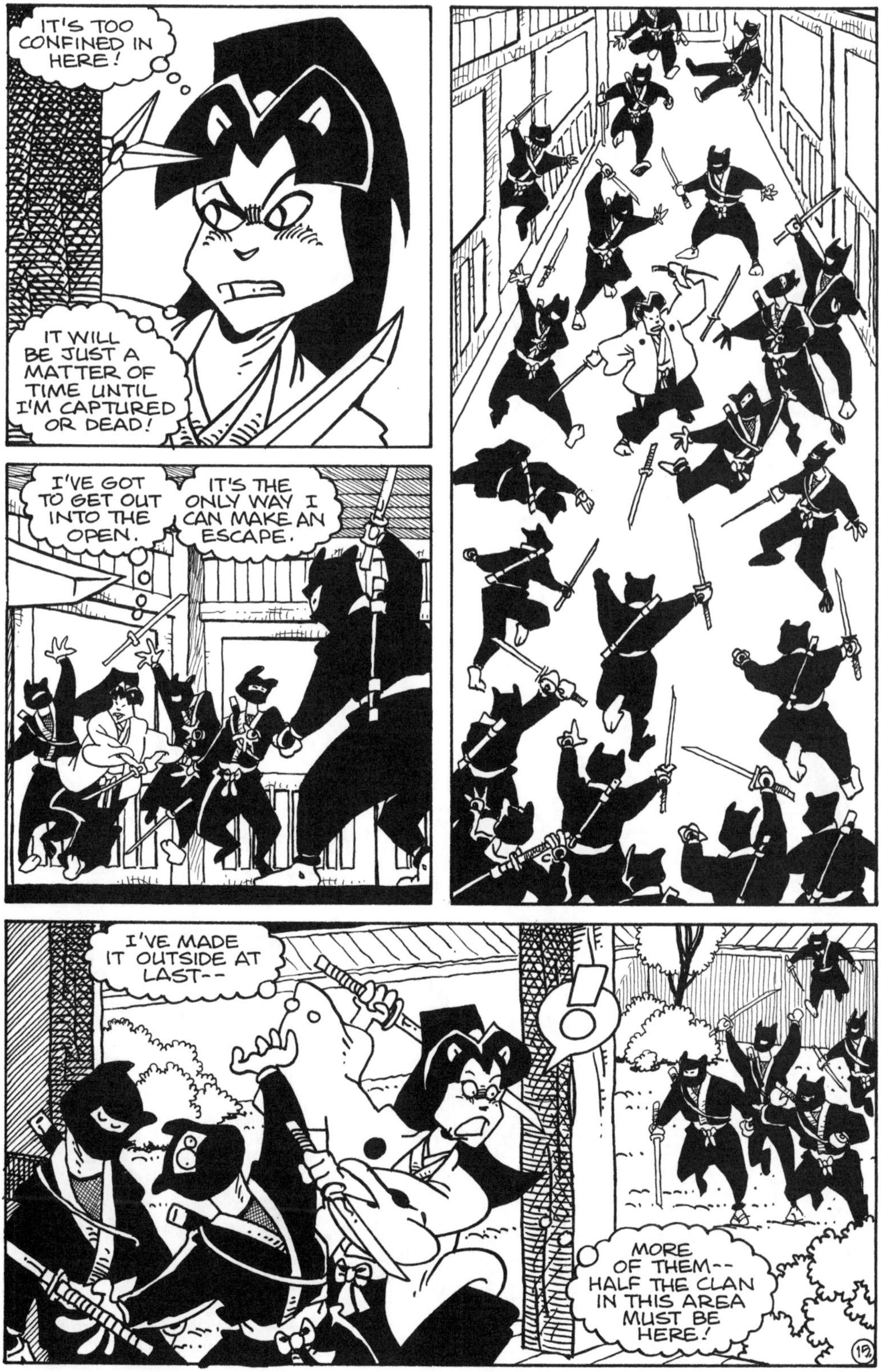
IT'S TOO CONFINED IN HERE!
IT WILL BE JUST A MATTER OF TIME UNTIL I'M CAPTURED OR DEAD!
I'VE GOT TO GET OUT INTO THE OPEN.
IT'S THE ONLY WAY I CAN MAKE AN ESCAPE.
I'VE MADE IT OUTSIDE AT LAST--
!
MORE OF THEM-- HALF THE CLAN IN THIS AREA MUST BE HERE!
13

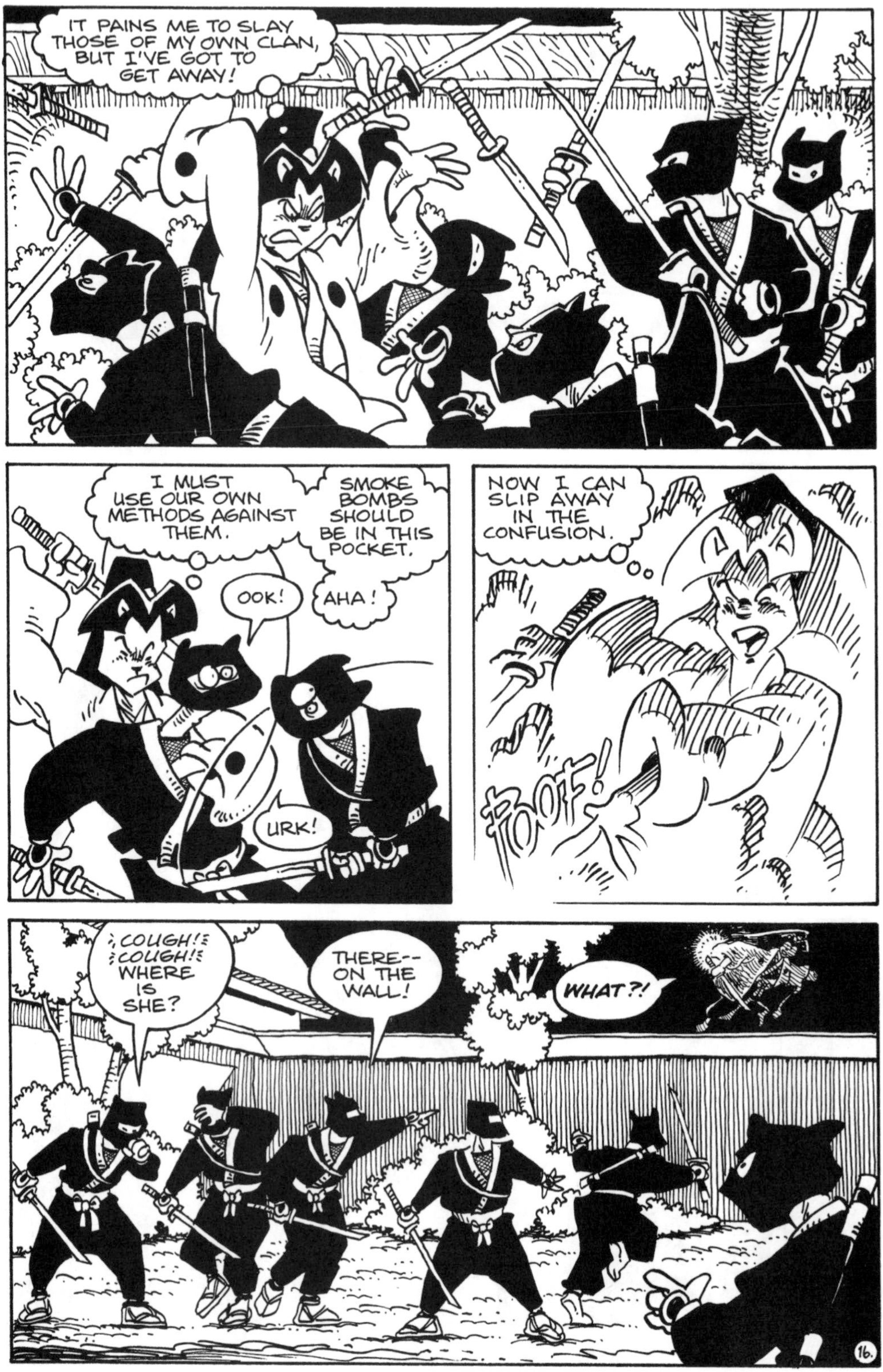
IT PAINS ME TO SLAY THOSE OF MY OWN CLAN, BUT I'VE GOT TO GET AWAY!
I MUST USE OUR OWN METHODS AGAINST THEM.
SMOKE BOMBS SHOULD BE IN THIS POCKET.
OOK!
AHA!
URK!
NOW I CAN SLIP AWAY IN THE CONFUSION.
POOF!
COUGH! COUGH! WHERE IS SHE?
THERE-- ON THE WALL!
WHAT?!
16.

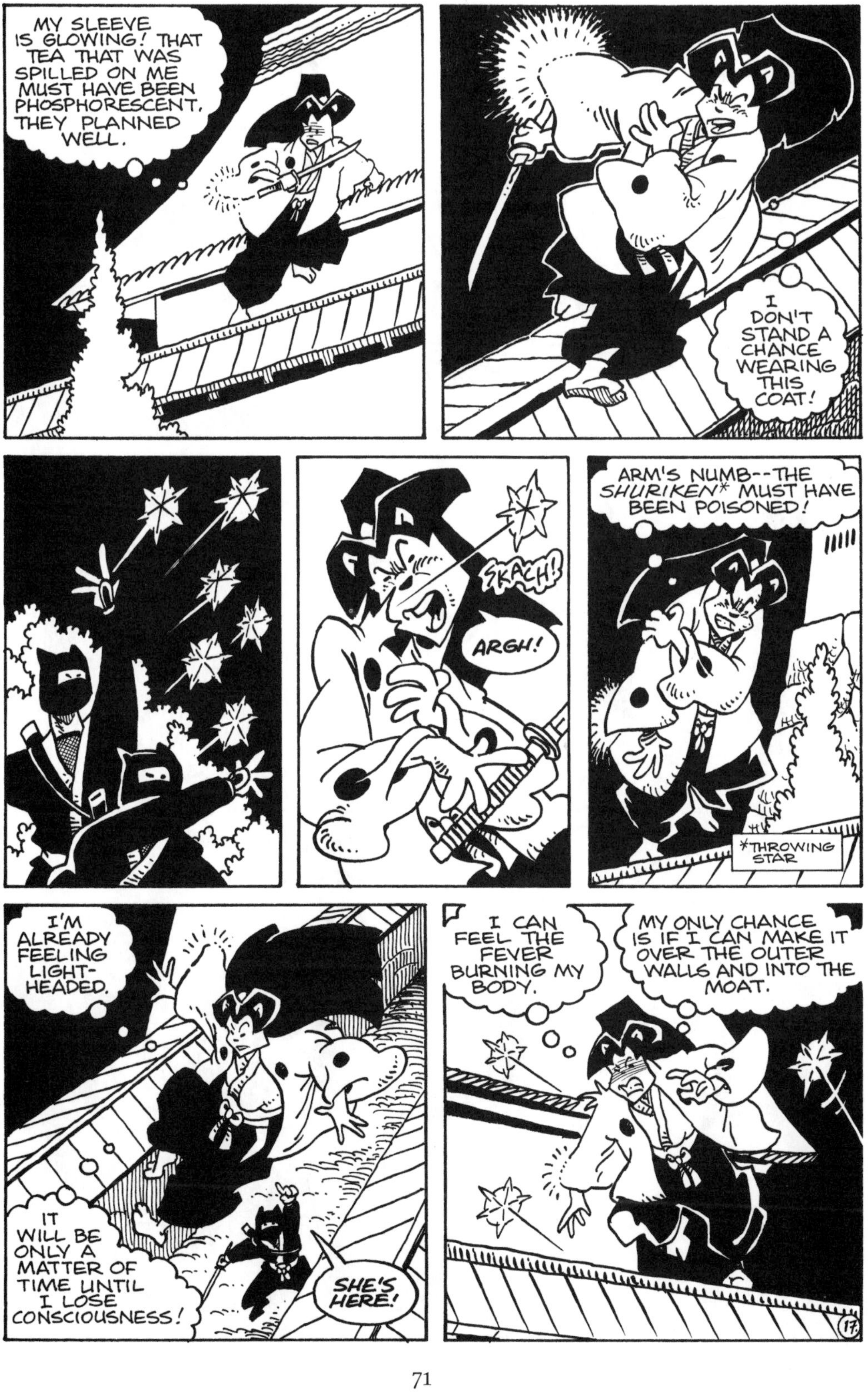
MY SLEEVE IS GLOWING! THAT TEA THAT WAS SPILLED ON ME MUST HAVE BEEN PHOSPHORESCENT. THEY PLANNED WELL.
I DON'T STAND A CHANCE WEARING THIS COAT!
SKACH!
ARGH!
ARM'S NUMB--THE SHURIKEN* MUST HAVE BEEN POISONED!
*THROWING STAR
I'M ALREADY FEELING LIGHT-HEADED.
IT WILL BE ONLY A MATTER OF TIME UNTIL I LOSE CONSCIOUSNESS!
SHE'S HERE!
I CAN FEEL THE FEVER BURNING MY BODY.
MY ONLY CHANCE IS IF I CAN MAKE IT OVER THE OUTER WALLS AND INTO THE MOAT.
17.

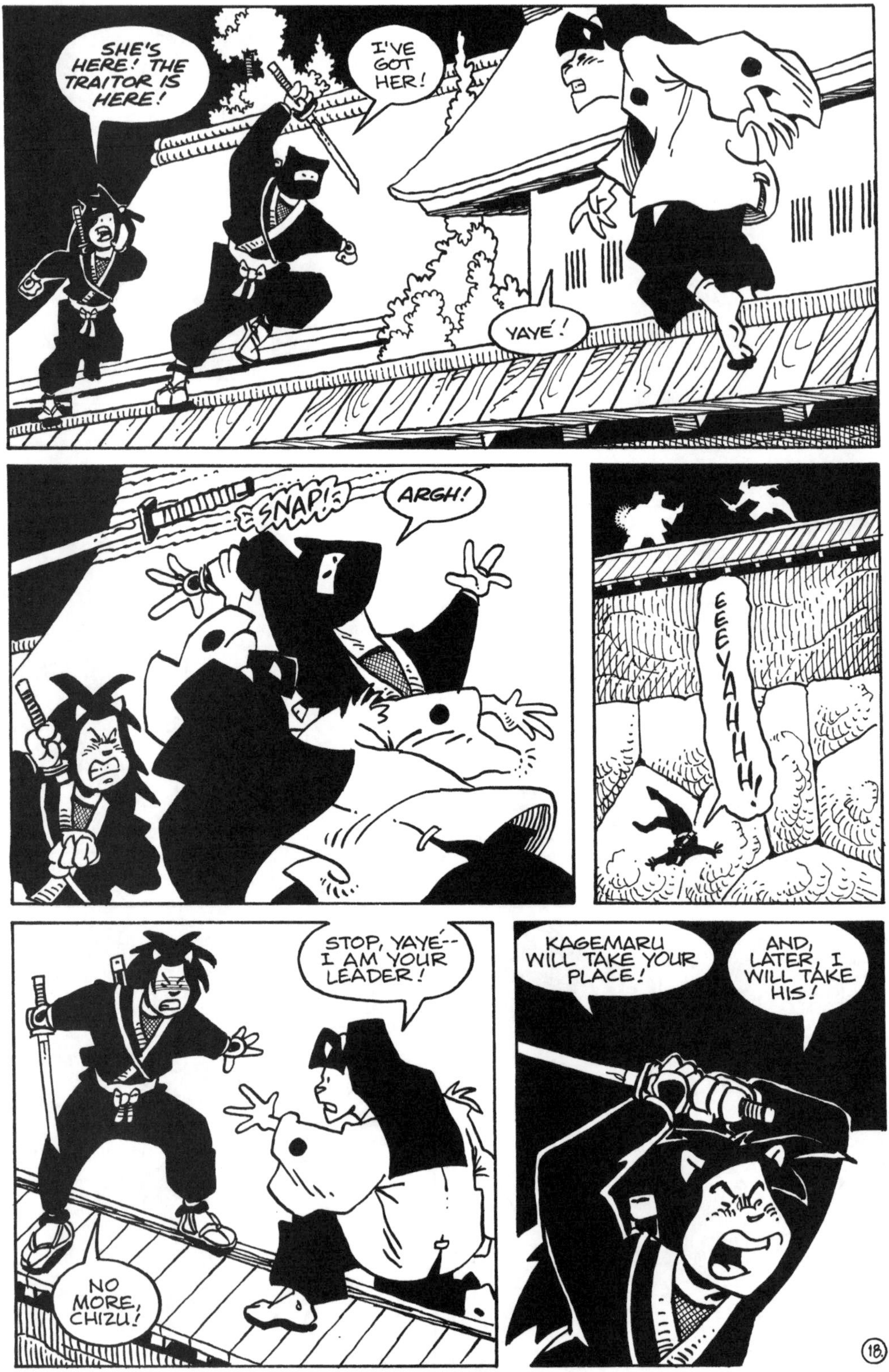
SHE'S HERE! THE TRAITOR IS HERE!
I'VE GOT HER!
YAYE!
SNAP!
ARGH!
EEEYAHHHH!
STOP, YAYE-- I AM YOUR LEADER!
NO MORE, CHIZU!
KAGEMARU WILL TAKE YOUR PLACE!
AND, LATER, I WILL TAKE HIS!
18.

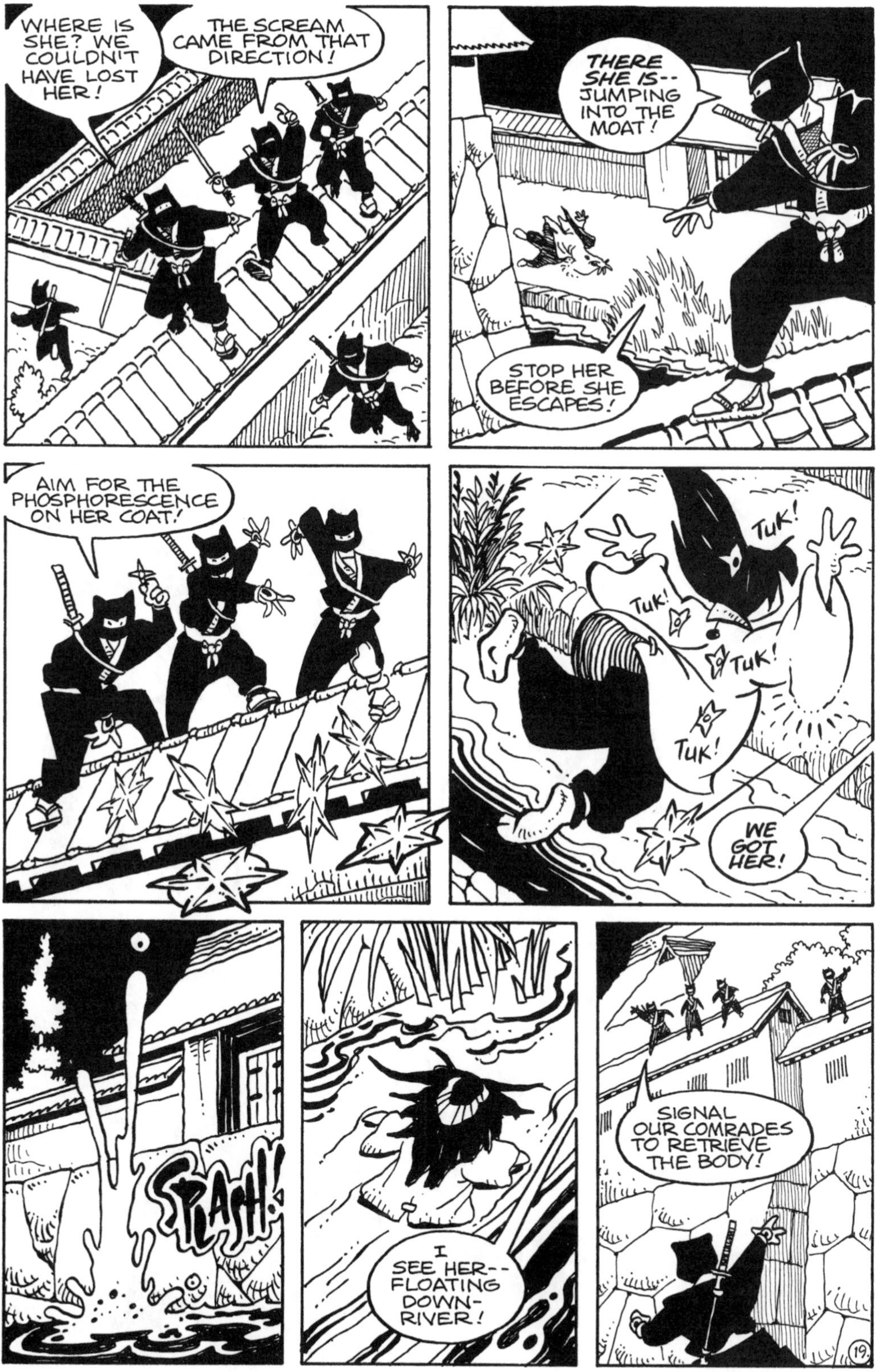
WHERE IS SHE? WE COULDN'T HAVE LOST HER!
THE SCREAM CAME FROM THAT DIRECTION!
THERE SHE IS-- JUMPING INTO THE MOAT!
STOP HER BEFORE SHE ESCAPES!
AIM FOR THE PHOSPHORESCENCE ON HER COAT!
TUK!
TUK!
TUK!
TUK!
WE GOT HER!
SPLASH!
I SEE HER-- FLOATING DOWN-RIVER!
SIGNAL OUR COMRADES TO RETRIEVE THE BODY!
19

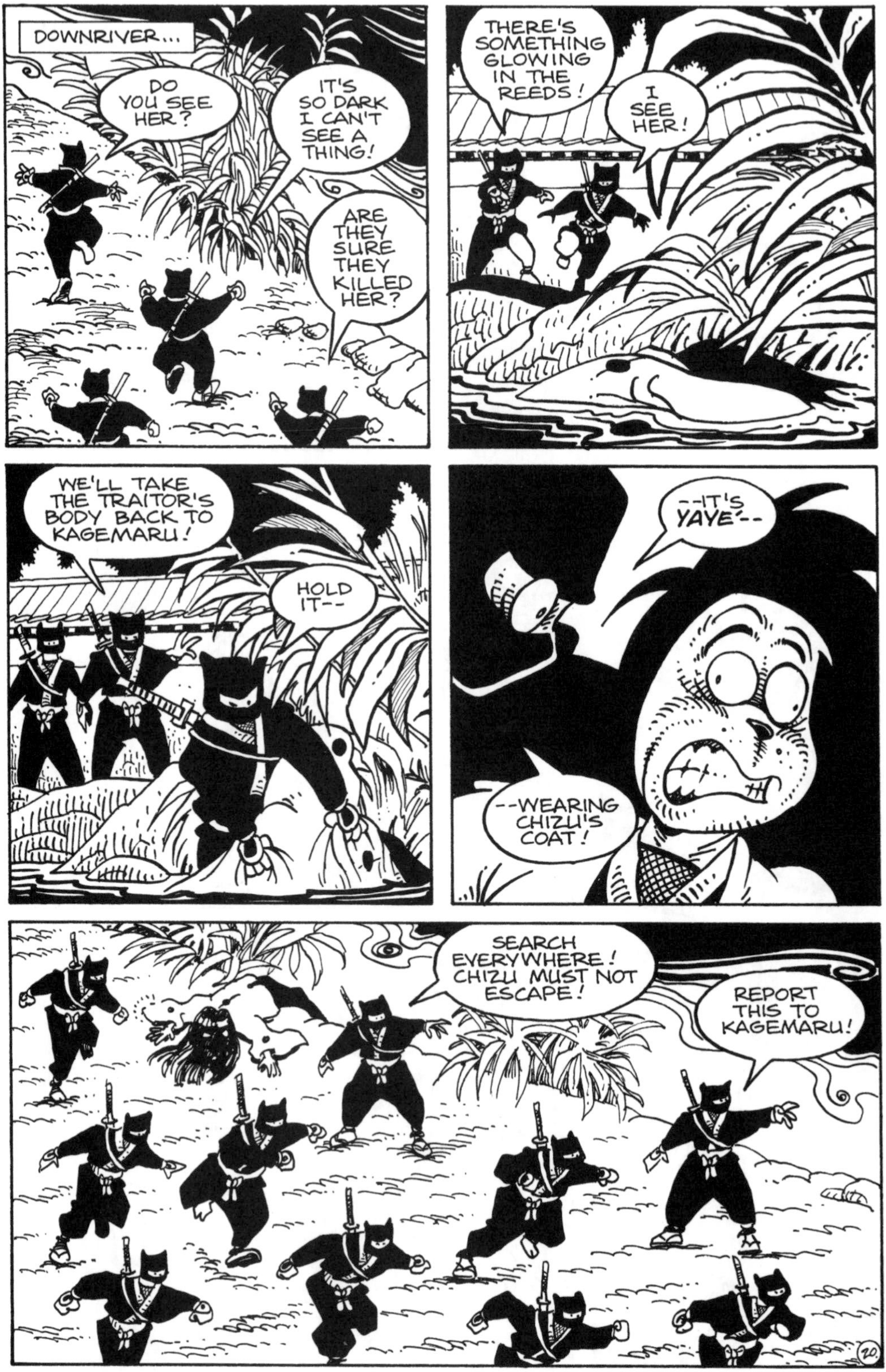
DOWNRIVER...
DO YOU SEE HER?
IT'S SO DARK I CAN'T SEE A THING!
ARE THEY SURE THEY KILLED HER?
THERE'S SOMETHING GLOWING IN THE REEDS!
I SEE HER!
WE'LL TAKE THE TRAITOR'S BODY BACK TO KAGEMARU!
HOLD IT--
--IT'S YAYE--
--WEARING CHIZU'S COAT!
SEARCH EVERYWHERE! CHIZU MUST NOT ESCAPE!
REPORT THIS TO KAGEMARU!
20.

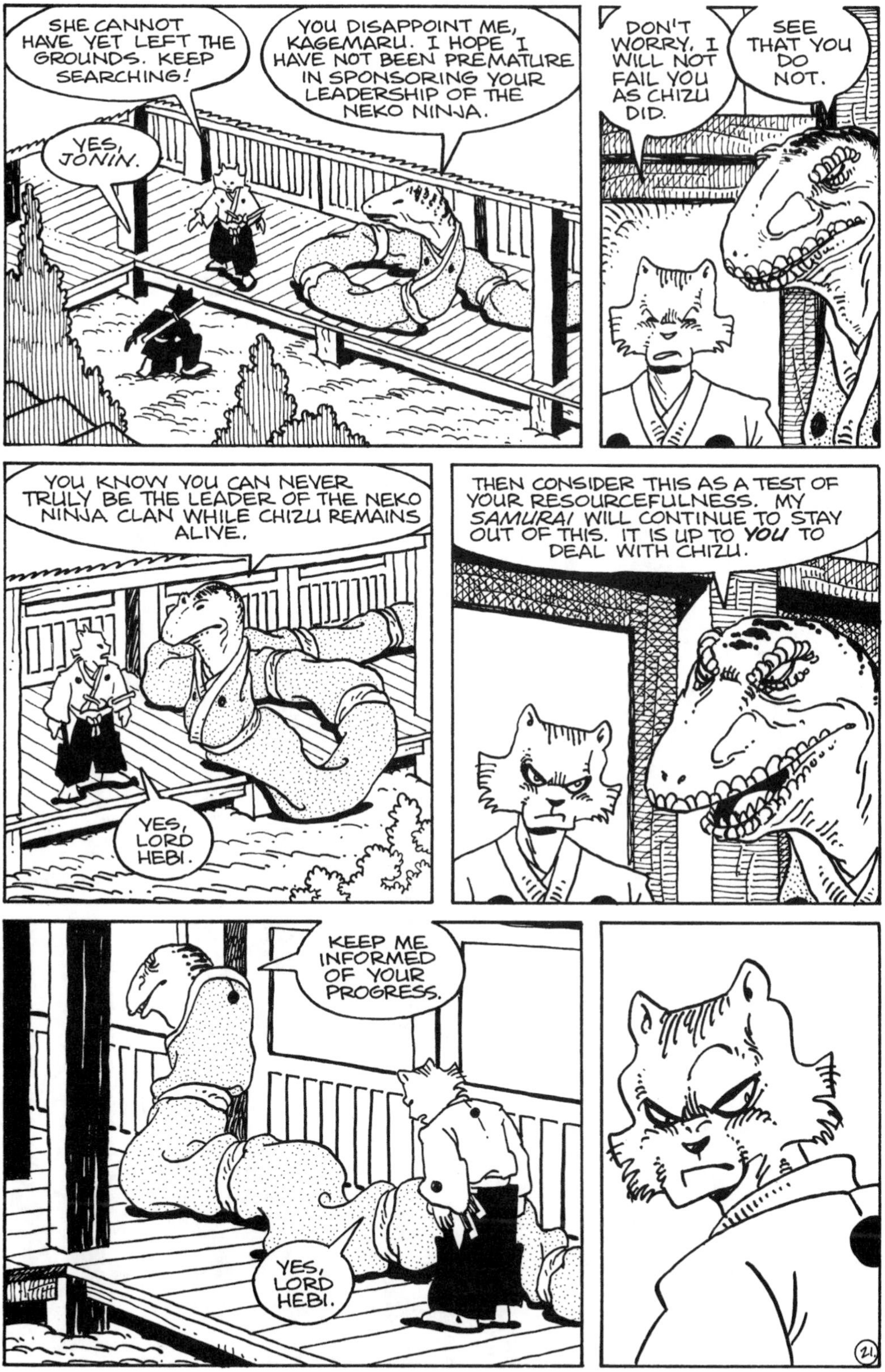
SHE CANNOT HAVE YET LEFT THE GROUNDS. KEEP SEARCHING!
YES, JONIN.
YOU DISAPPOINT ME, KAGEMARU. I HOPE I HAVE NOT BEEN PREMATURE IN SPONSORING YOUR LEADERSHIP OF THE NEKO NINJA.
DON'T WORRY. I WILL NOT FAIL YOU AS CHIZU DID.
SEE THAT YOU DO NOT.
YOU KNOW YOU CAN NEVER TRULY BE THE LEADER OF THE NEKO NINJA CLAN WHILE CHIZU REMAINS ALIVE.
YES, LORD HEBI.
THEN CONSIDER THIS AS A TEST OF YOUR RESOURCEFULNESS. MY SAMURAI WILL CONTINUE TO STAY OUT OF THIS. IT IS UP TO YOU TO DEAL WITH CHIZU.
KEEP ME INFORMED OF YOUR PROGRESS.
YES, LORD HEBI.
21

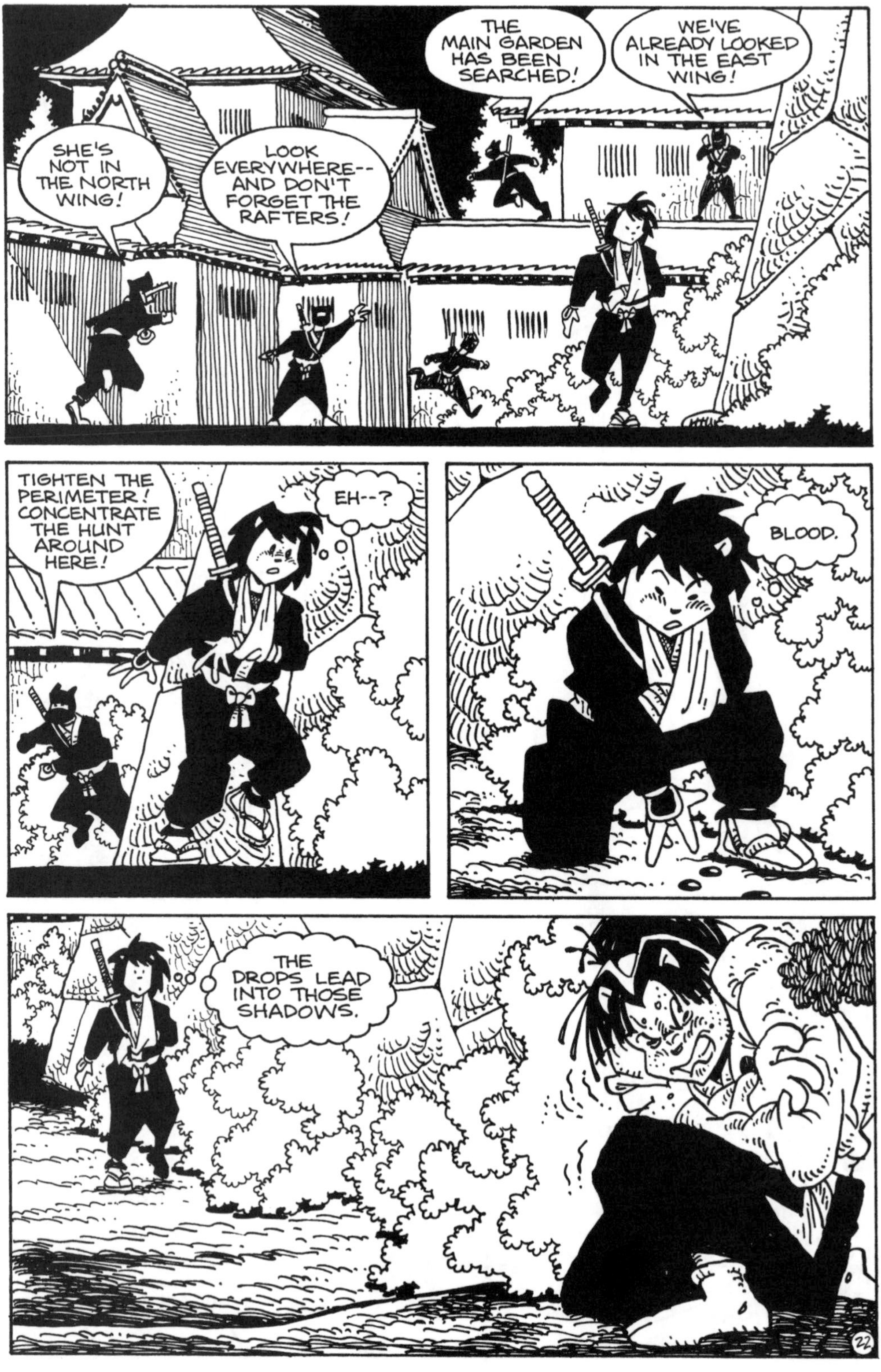
SHE'S NOT IN THE NORTH WING!
LOOK EVERYWHERE-- AND DON'T FORGET THE RAFTERS!
THE MAIN GARDEN HAS BEEN SEARCHED!
WE'VE ALREADY LOOKED IN THE EAST WING!
TIGHTEN THE PERIMETER! CONCENTRATE THE HUNT AROUND HERE!
EH--?
BLOOD.
THE DROPS LEAD INTO THOSE SHADOWS.
22

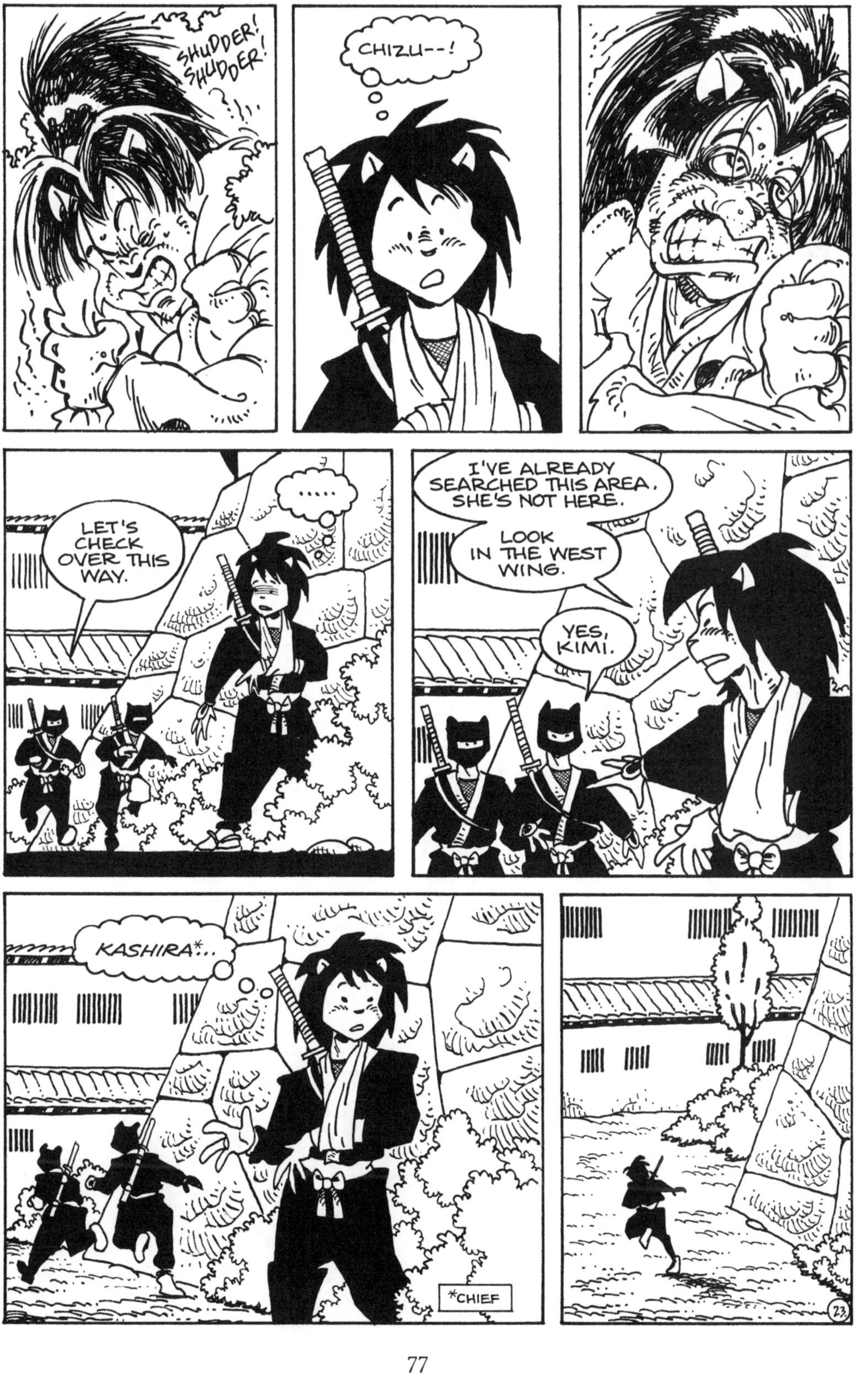
SHUDDER! SHUDDER!
CHIZU--!
LET'S CHECK OVER THIS WAY.
.....
I'VE ALREADY SEARCHED THIS AREA. SHE'S NOT HERE.
LOOK IN THE WEST WING.
YES, KIMI.
KASHIRA*...
*CHIEF
23

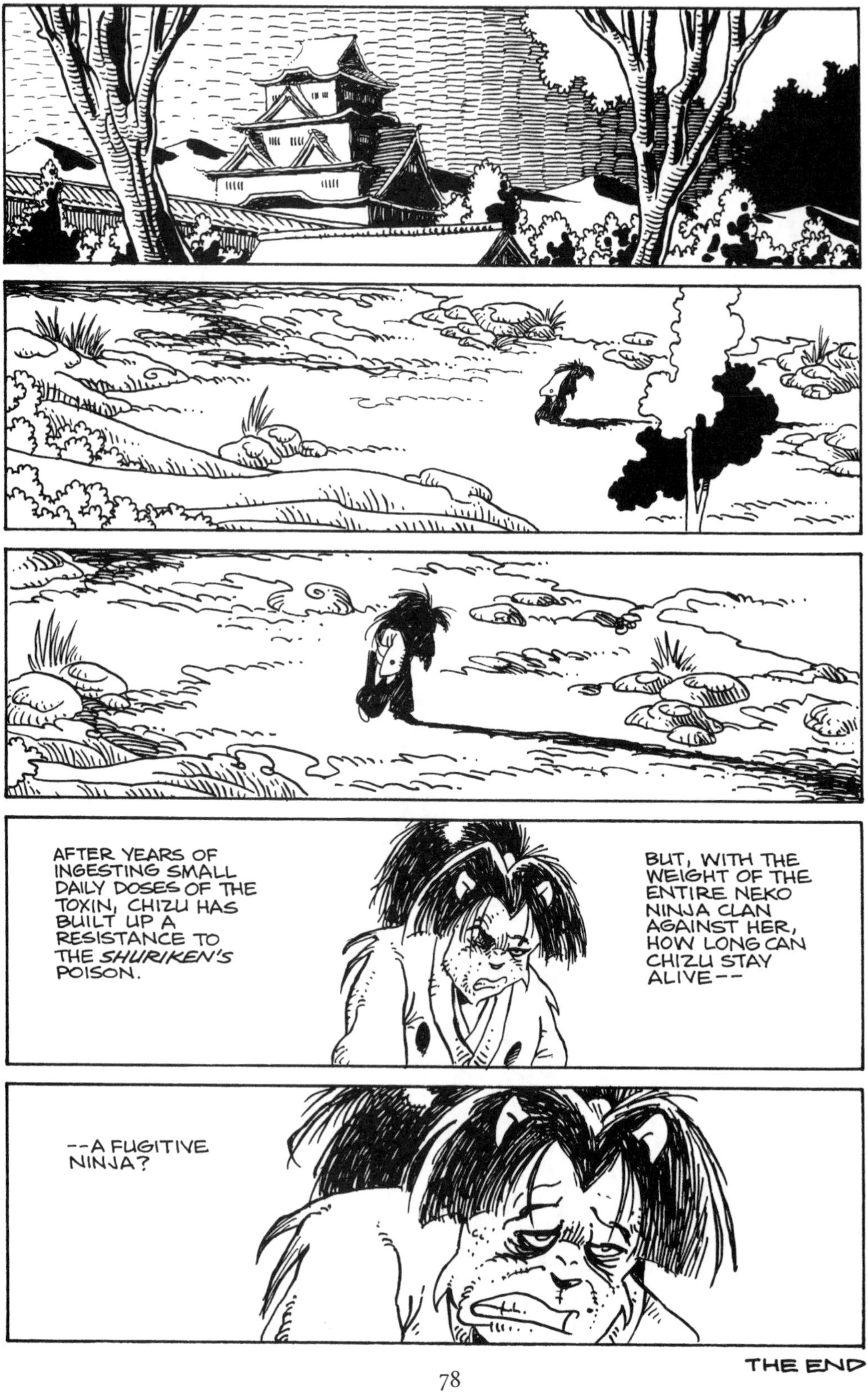
AFTER YEARS OF INGESTING SMALL DAILY DOSES OF THE TOXIN, CHIZU HAS BUILT UP A RESISTANCE TO THE *SHURIKEN'S* POISON.
BUT, WITH THE WEIGHT OF THE ENTIRE NEKO NINJA CLAN AGAINST HER, HOW LONG CAN CHIZU STAY ALIVE--
--A FUGITIVE NINJA?
THE END

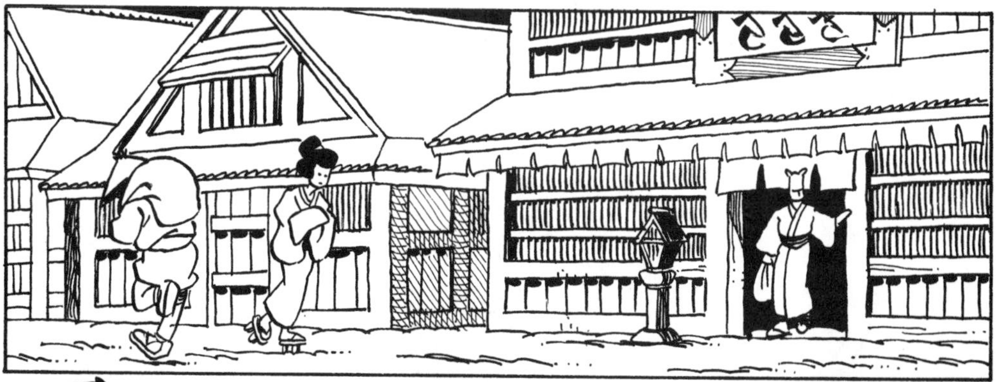

Three Seasons

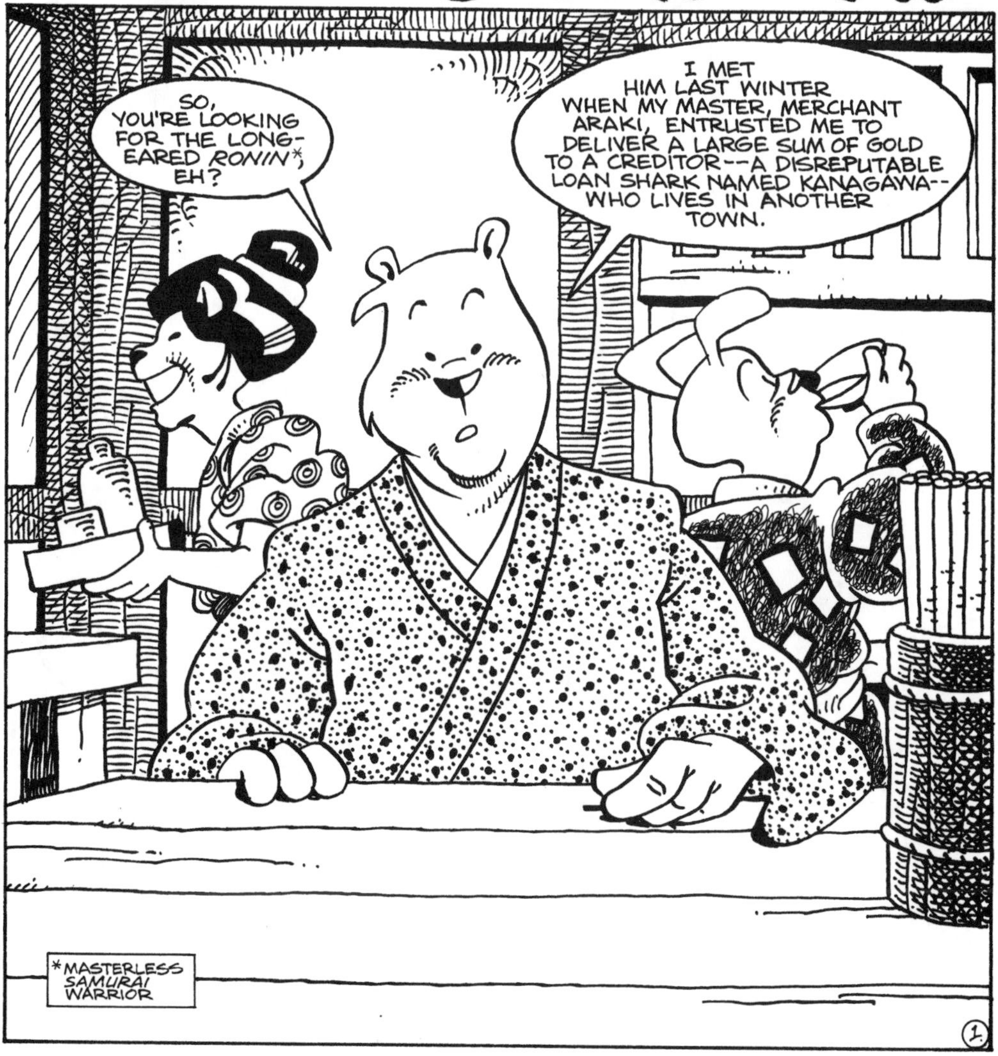

SO, YOU'RE LOOKING FOR THE LONG-EARED *RONIN**, EH?
I MET HIM LAST WINTER WHEN MY MASTER, MERCHANT ARAKI, ENTRUSTED ME TO DELIVER A LARGE SUM OF GOLD TO A CREDITOR--A DISREPUTABLE LOAN SHARK NAMED KANAGAWA--WHO LIVES IN ANOTHER TOWN.
*MASTERLESS SAMURAI WARRIOR

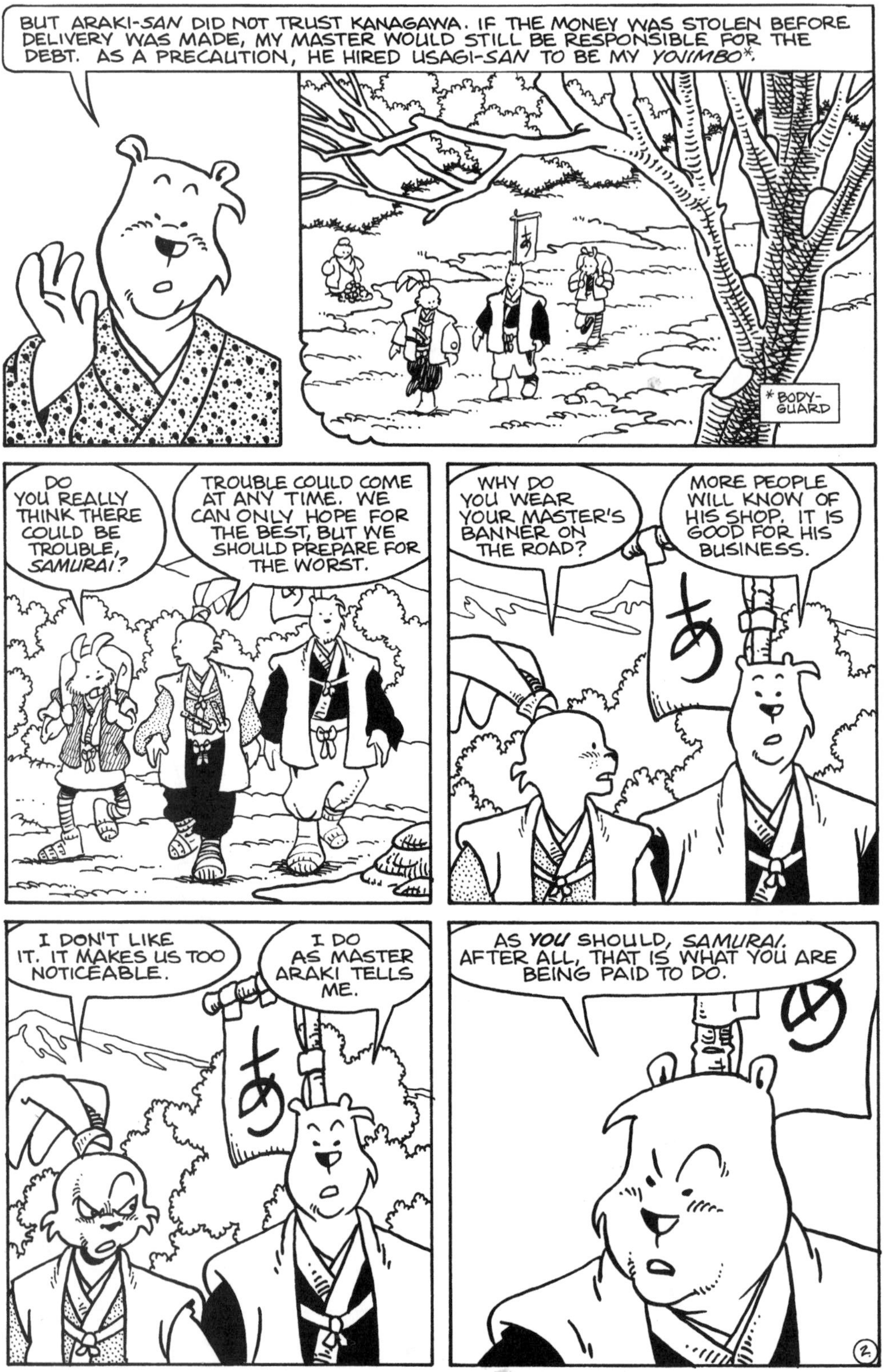
BUT ARAKI-SAN DID NOT TRUST KANAGAWA. IF THE MONEY WAS STOLEN BEFORE DELIVERY WAS MADE, MY MASTER WOULD STILL BE RESPONSIBLE FOR THE DEBT. AS A PRECAUTION, HE HIRED USAGI-SAN TO BE MY YOJIMBO*.
* BODY-GUARD
DO YOU REALLY THINK THERE COULD BE TROUBLE, SAMURAI?
TROUBLE COULD COME AT ANY TIME. WE CAN ONLY HOPE FOR THE BEST, BUT WE SHOULD PREPARE FOR THE WORST.
WHY DO YOU WEAR YOUR MASTER'S BANNER ON THE ROAD?
MORE PEOPLE WILL KNOW OF HIS SHOP. IT IS GOOD FOR HIS BUSINESS.
I DON'T LIKE IT. IT MAKES US TOO NOTICEABLE.
I DO AS MASTER ARAKI TELLS ME.
AS YOU SHOULD, SAMURAI. AFTER ALL, THAT IS WHAT YOU ARE BEING PAID TO DO.
2

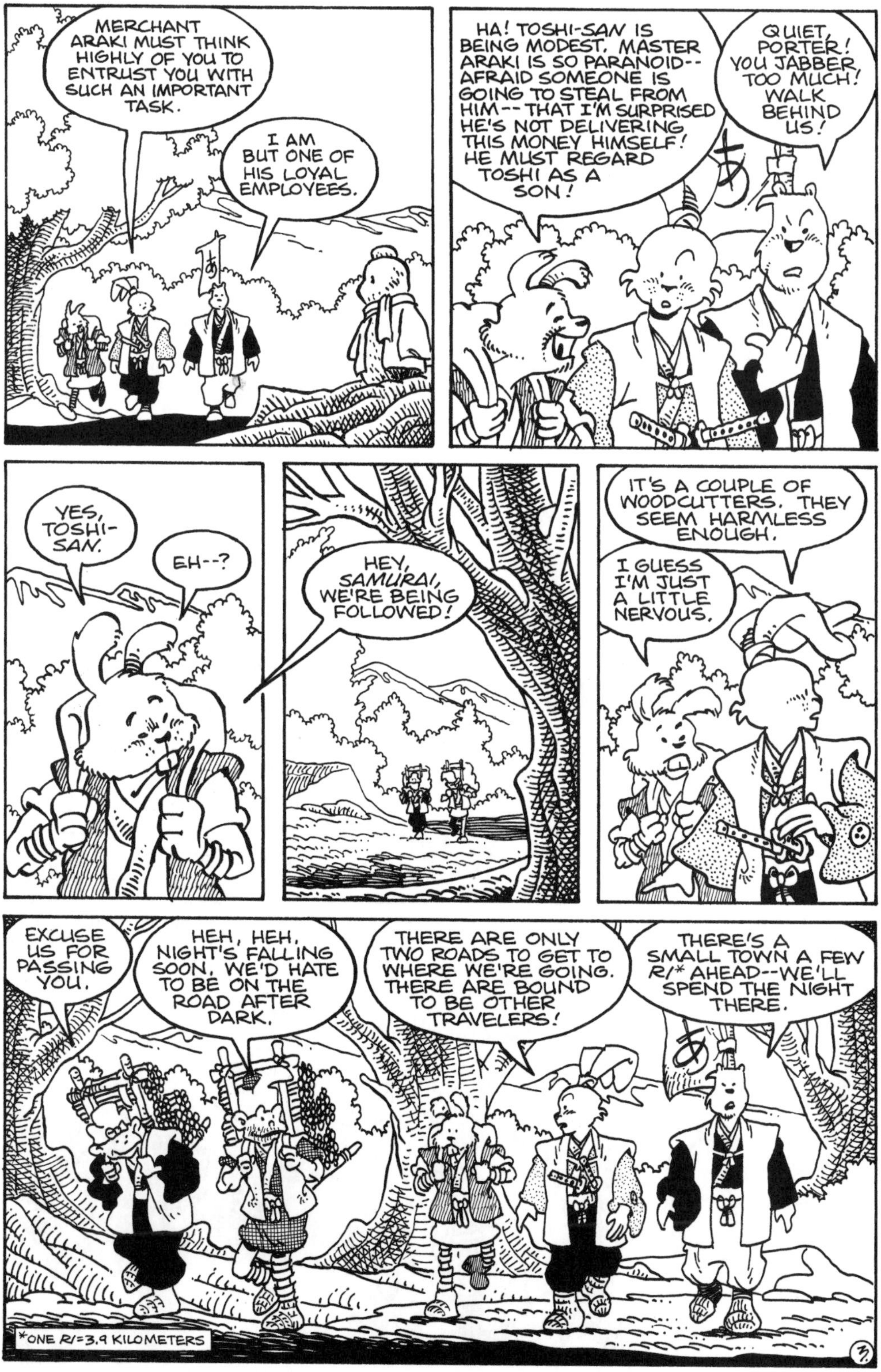
MERCHANT ARAKI MUST THINK HIGHLY OF YOU TO ENTRUST YOU WITH SUCH AN IMPORTANT TASK.
I AM BUT ONE OF HIS LOYAL EMPLOYEES.
HA! TOSHI-SAN IS BEING MODEST. MASTER ARAKI IS SO PARANOID-- AFRAID SOMEONE IS GOING TO STEAL FROM HIM-- THAT I'M SURPRISED HE'S NOT DELIVERING THIS MONEY HIMSELF! HE MUST REGARD TOSHI AS A SON!
QUIET, PORTER! YOU JABBER TOO MUCH! WALK BEHIND US!
YES, TOSHI-SAN.
EH--?
HEY, SAMURAI, WE'RE BEING FOLLOWED!
IT'S A COUPLE OF WOODCUTTERS. THEY SEEM HARMLESS ENOUGH.
I GUESS I'M JUST A LITTLE NERVOUS.
EXCUSE US FOR PASSING YOU.
HEH, HEH. NIGHT'S FALLING SOON. WE'D HATE TO BE ON THE ROAD AFTER DARK.
THERE ARE ONLY TWO ROADS TO GET TO WHERE WE'RE GOING. THERE ARE BOUND TO BE OTHER TRAVELERS!
THERE'S A SMALL TOWN A FEW RI* AHEAD--WE'LL SPEND THE NIGHT THERE.
*ONE RI=3.9 KILOMETERS
3.

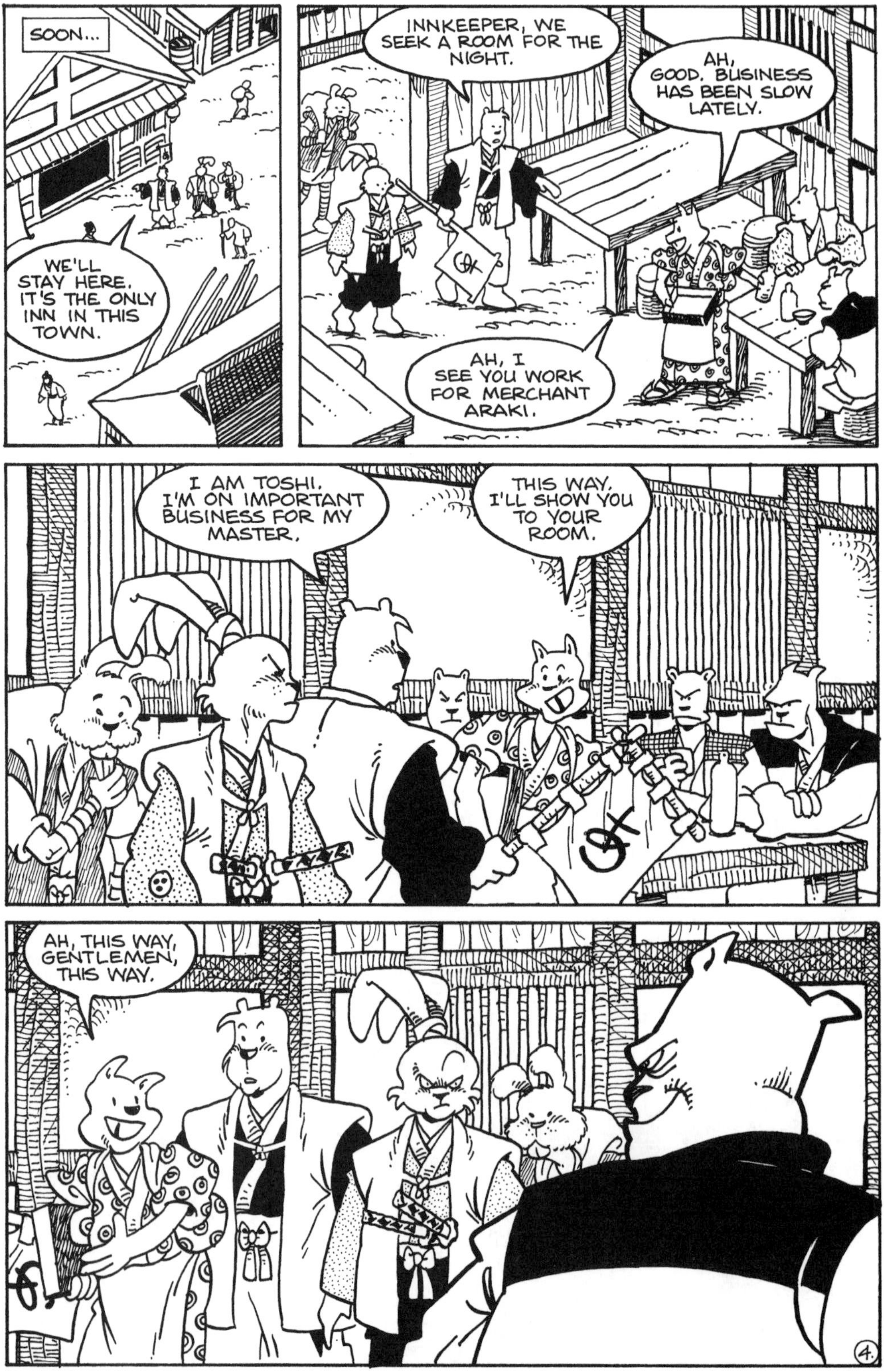
SOON...
WE'LL STAY HERE. IT'S THE ONLY INN IN THIS TOWN.
INNKEEPER, WE SEEK A ROOM FOR THE NIGHT.
AH, GOOD. BUSINESS HAS BEEN SLOW LATELY.
AH, I SEE YOU WORK FOR MERCHANT ARAKI.
I AM TOSHI. I'M ON IMPORTANT BUSINESS FOR MY MASTER.
THIS WAY. I'LL SHOW YOU TO YOUR ROOM.
AH, THIS WAY, GENTLEMEN, THIS WAY.
4.

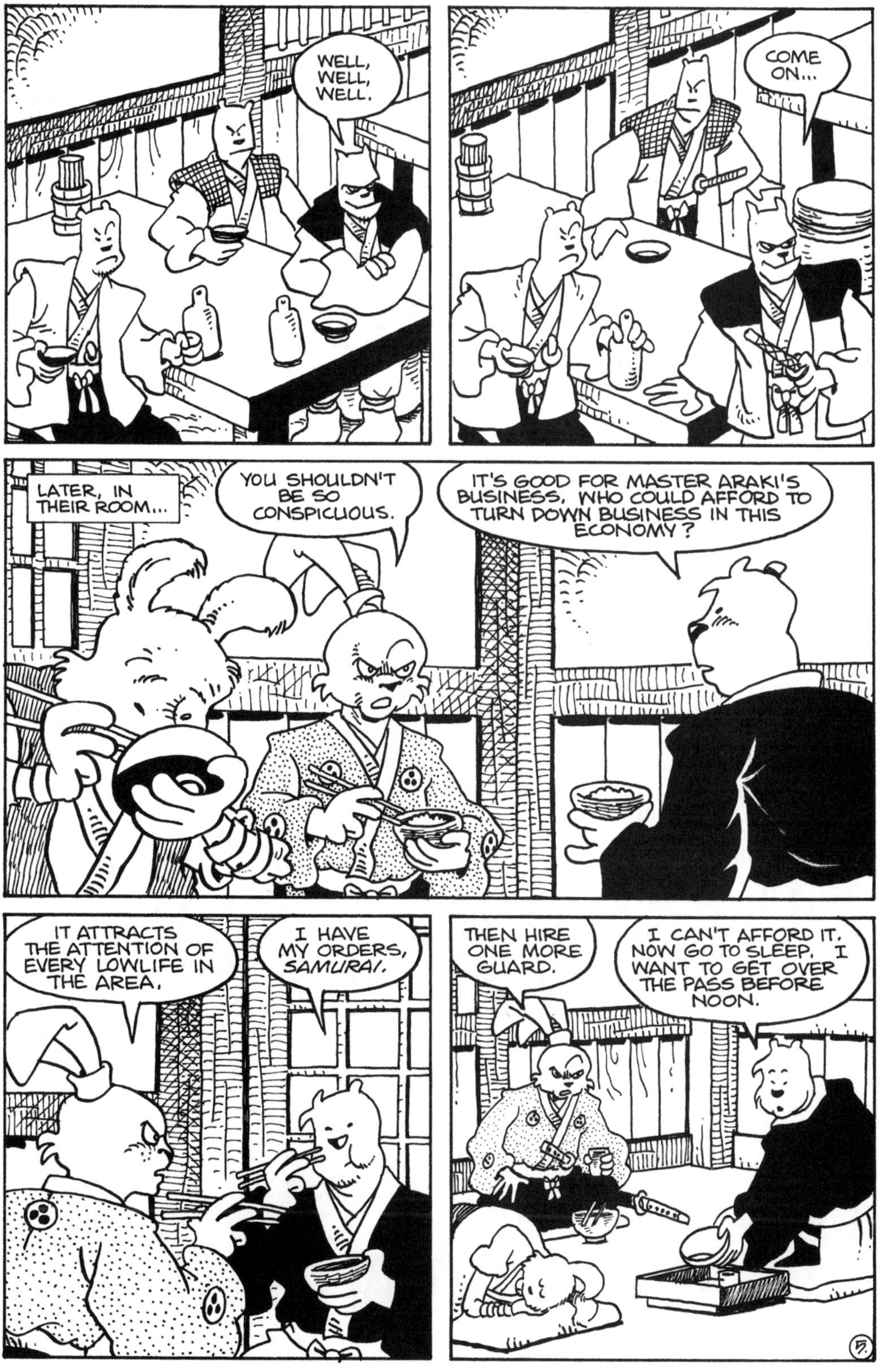
WELL, WELL, WELL.
COME ON...
LATER, IN THEIR ROOM...
YOU SHOULDN'T BE SO CONSPICUOUS.
IT'S GOOD FOR MASTER ARAKI'S BUSINESS. WHO COULD AFFORD TO TURN DOWN BUSINESS IN THIS ECONOMY?
IT ATTRACTS THE ATTENTION OF EVERY LOWLIFE IN THE AREA.
I HAVE MY ORDERS, *SAMURAI.*
THEN HIRE ONE MORE GUARD.
I CAN'T AFFORD IT. NOW GO TO SLEEP. I WANT TO GET OVER THE PASS BEFORE NOON.
5

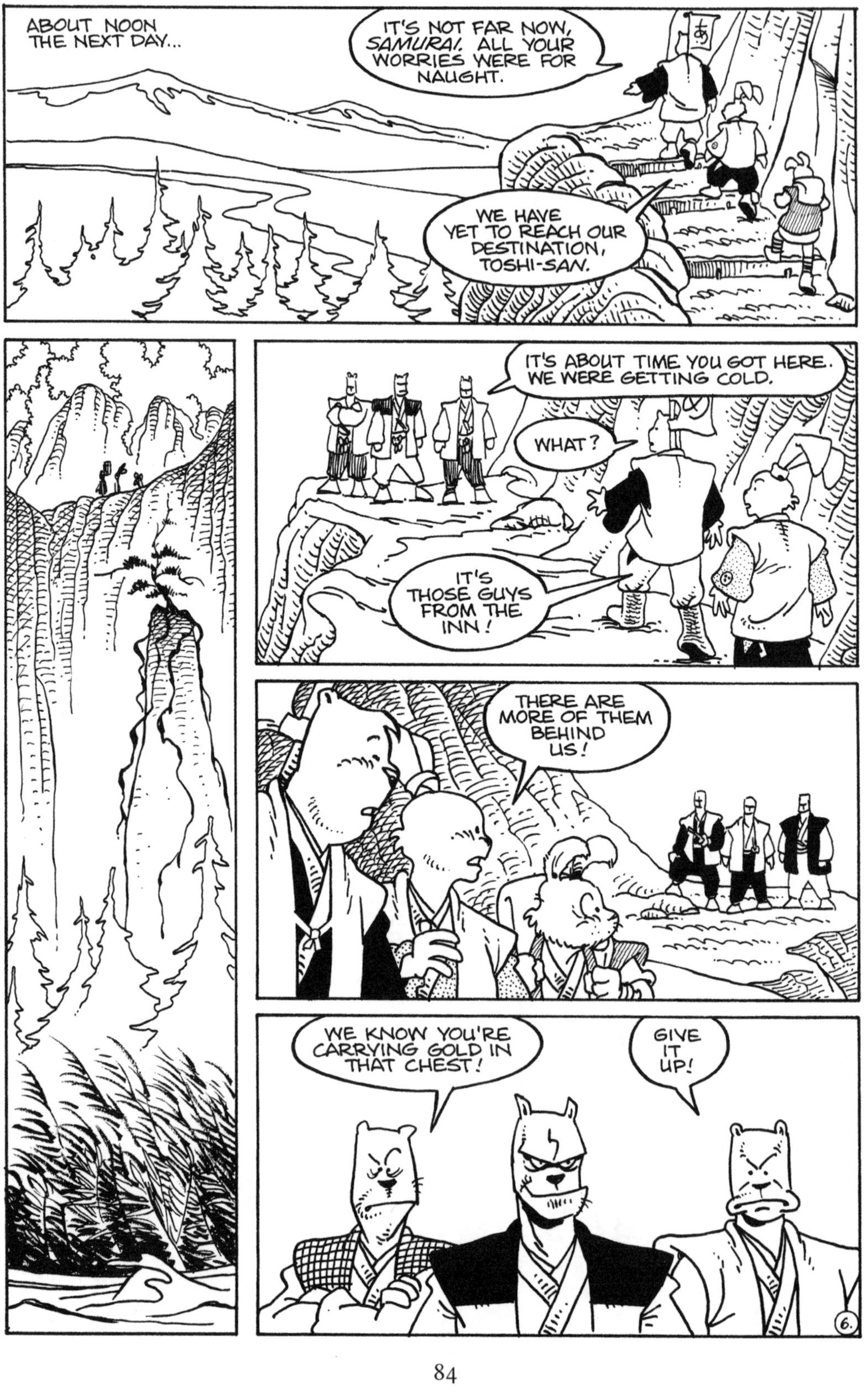
ABOUT NOON THE NEXT DAY...
IT'S NOT FAR NOW, SAMURAI! ALL YOUR WORRIES WERE FOR NAUGHT.
WE HAVE YET TO REACH OUR DESTINATION, TOSHI-SAN.
IT'S ABOUT TIME YOU GOT HERE. WE WERE GETTING COLD.
WHAT?
IT'S THOSE GUYS FROM THE INN!
THERE ARE MORE OF THEM BEHIND US!
WE KNOW YOU'RE CARRYING GOLD IN THAT CHEST!
GIVE IT UP!
6.

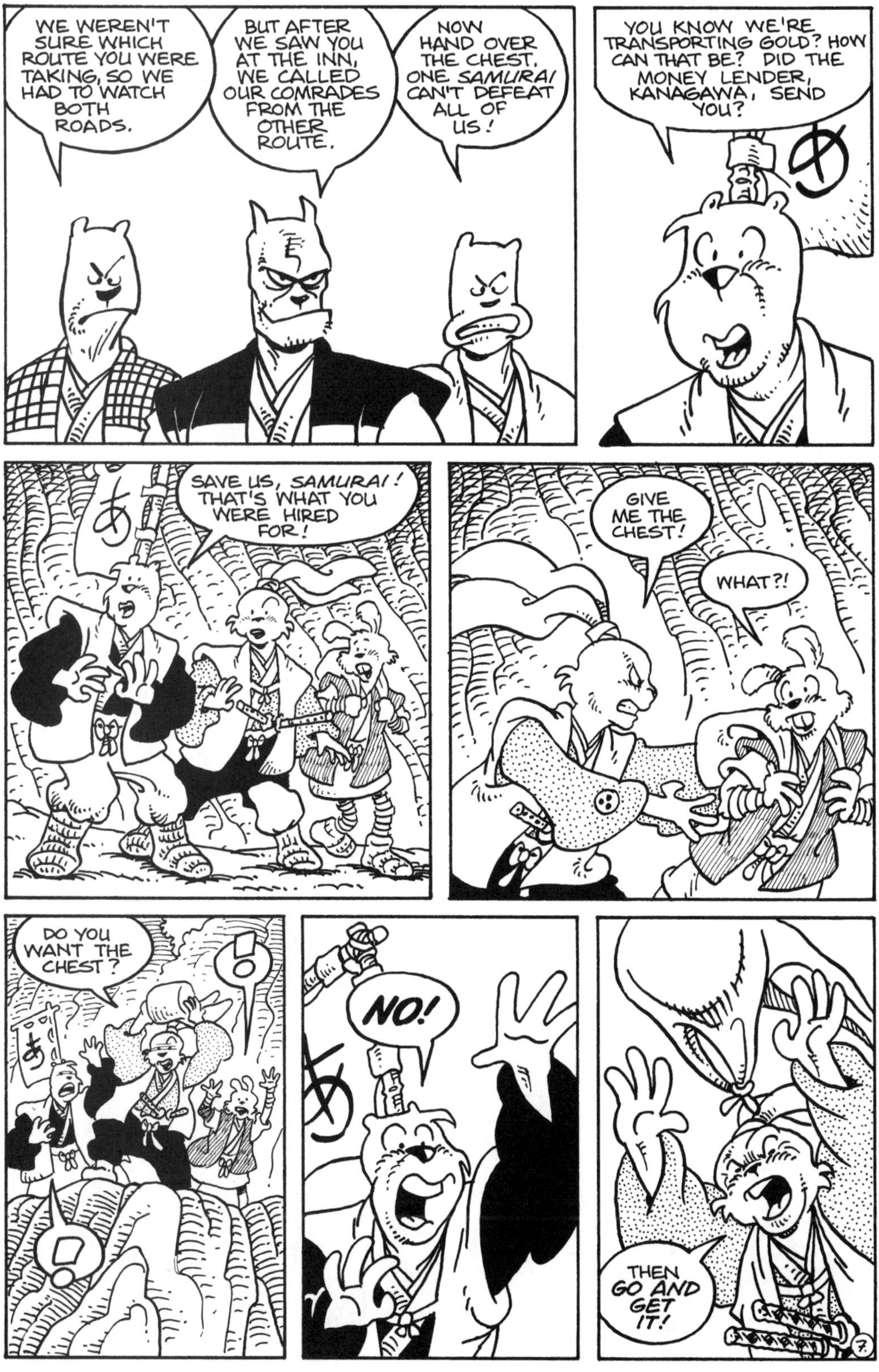
WE WEREN'T SURE WHICH ROUTE YOU WERE TAKING, SO WE HAD TO WATCH BOTH ROADS.
BUT AFTER WE SAW YOU AT THE INN, WE CALLED OUR COMRADES FROM THE OTHER ROUTE.
NOW HAND OVER THE CHEST. ONE *SAMURAI* CAN'T DEFEAT ALL OF US!
YOU KNOW WE'RE TRANSPORTING GOLD? HOW CAN THAT BE? DID THE MONEY LENDER, KANAGAWA, SEND YOU?
SAVE US, *SAMURAI*! THAT'S WHAT YOU WERE HIRED FOR!
GIVE ME THE CHEST!
WHAT?!
DO YOU WANT THE CHEST?
!
!
NO!
THEN GO AND GET IT!
7.

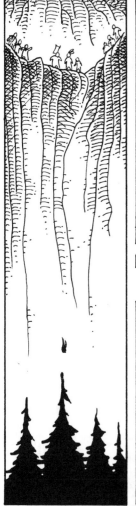

DOWN THE TRAIL--HURRY, BEFORE SOMEONE ELSE FINDS IT!

IMAGINE A *YOJIMBO* SO AFRAID, HE WOULD DISCARD THE TREASURE HE WAS GUARDING!

HURRY!

COWARD! MASTER ARAKI ENTRUSTED US WITH THAT CHEST!

WOULD IT HAVE BEEN BETTER IF THEY'D DISCOVERED THERE IS NO GOLD IN THAT CHEST?

WH-*WHAT?!*

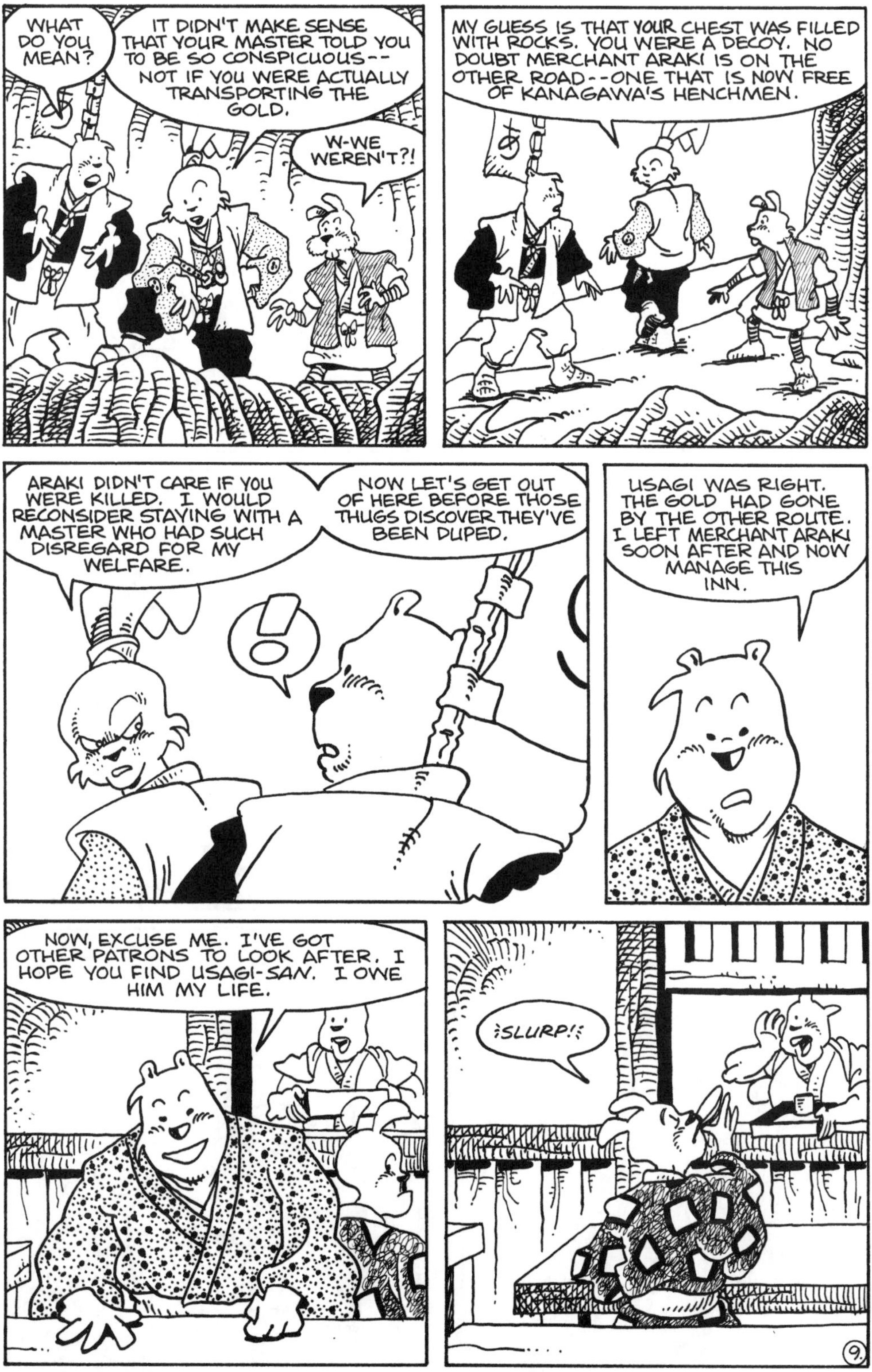
WHAT DO YOU MEAN?
IT DIDN'T MAKE SENSE THAT YOUR MASTER TOLD YOU TO BE SO CONSPICUOUS-- NOT IF YOU WERE ACTUALLY TRANSPORTING THE GOLD.
W-WE WEREN'T?!
MY GUESS IS THAT YOUR CHEST WAS FILLED WITH ROCKS. YOU WERE A DECOY. NO DOUBT MERCHANT ARAKI IS ON THE OTHER ROAD--ONE THAT IS NOW FREE OF KANAGAWA'S HENCHMEN.
ARAKI DIDN'T CARE IF YOU WERE KILLED. I WOULD RECONSIDER STAYING WITH A MASTER WHO HAD SUCH DISREGARD FOR MY WELFARE.
NOW LET'S GET OUT OF HERE BEFORE THOSE THUGS DISCOVER THEY'VE BEEN DUPED.
!
USAGI WAS RIGHT. THE GOLD HAD GONE BY THE OTHER ROUTE. I LEFT MERCHANT ARAKI SOON AFTER AND NOW MANAGE THIS INN.
NOW, EXCUSE ME. I'VE GOT OTHER PATRONS TO LOOK AFTER. I HOPE YOU FIND USAGI-SAN. I OWE HIM MY LIFE.
SLURP!
9.

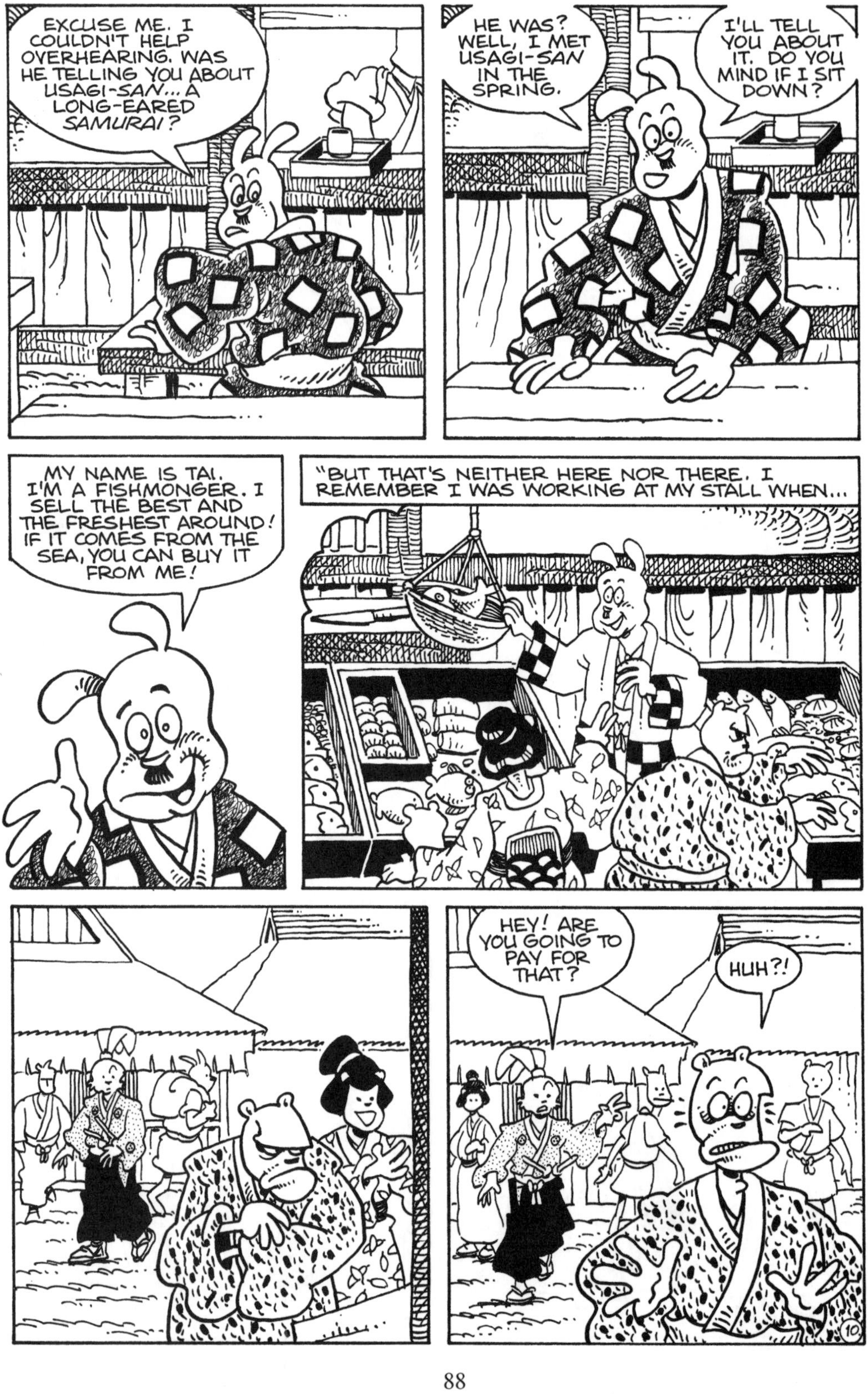
EXCUSE ME. I COULDN'T HELP OVERHEARING. WAS HE TELLING YOU ABOUT USAGI-SAN... A LONG-EARED SAMURAI?
HE WAS? WELL, I MET USAGI-SAN IN THE SPRING.
I'LL TELL YOU ABOUT IT. DO YOU MIND IF I SIT DOWN?
MY NAME IS TAI. I'M A FISHMONGER. I SELL THE BEST AND THE FRESHEST AROUND! IF IT COMES FROM THE SEA, YOU CAN BUY IT FROM ME!
"BUT THAT'S NEITHER HERE NOR THERE. I REMEMBER I WAS WORKING AT MY STALL WHEN...
HEY! ARE YOU GOING TO PAY FOR THAT?
HUH?!
10

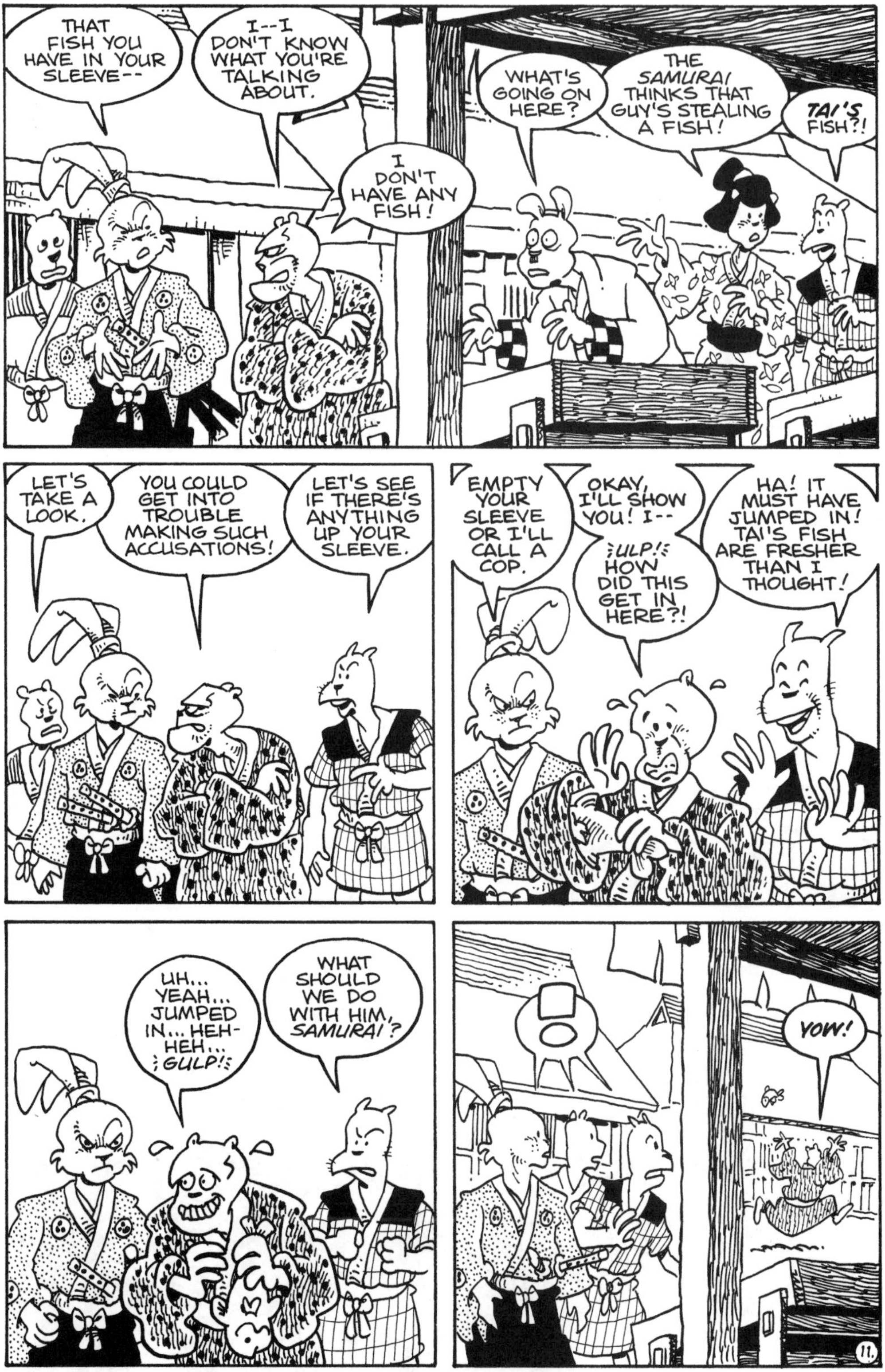
THAT FISH YOU HAVE IN YOUR SLEEVE--
I--I DON'T KNOW WHAT YOU'RE TALKING ABOUT.
I DON'T HAVE ANY FISH!
WHAT'S GOING ON HERE?
THE SAMURAI THINKS THAT GUY'S STEALING A FISH!
TAI'S FISH?!
LET'S TAKE A LOOK.
YOU COULD GET INTO TROUBLE MAKING SUCH ACCUSATIONS!
LET'S SEE IF THERE'S ANYTHING UP YOUR SLEEVE.
EMPTY YOUR SLEEVE OR I'LL CALL A COP.
OKAY, I'LL SHOW YOU! I--
ULP! HOW DID THIS GET IN HERE?!
HA! IT MUST HAVE JUMPED IN! TAI'S FISH ARE FRESHER THAN I THOUGHT!
UH... YEAH... JUMPED IN... HEH-HEH... GULP!
WHAT SHOULD WE DO WITH HIM, SAMURAI?
YOW!
11.

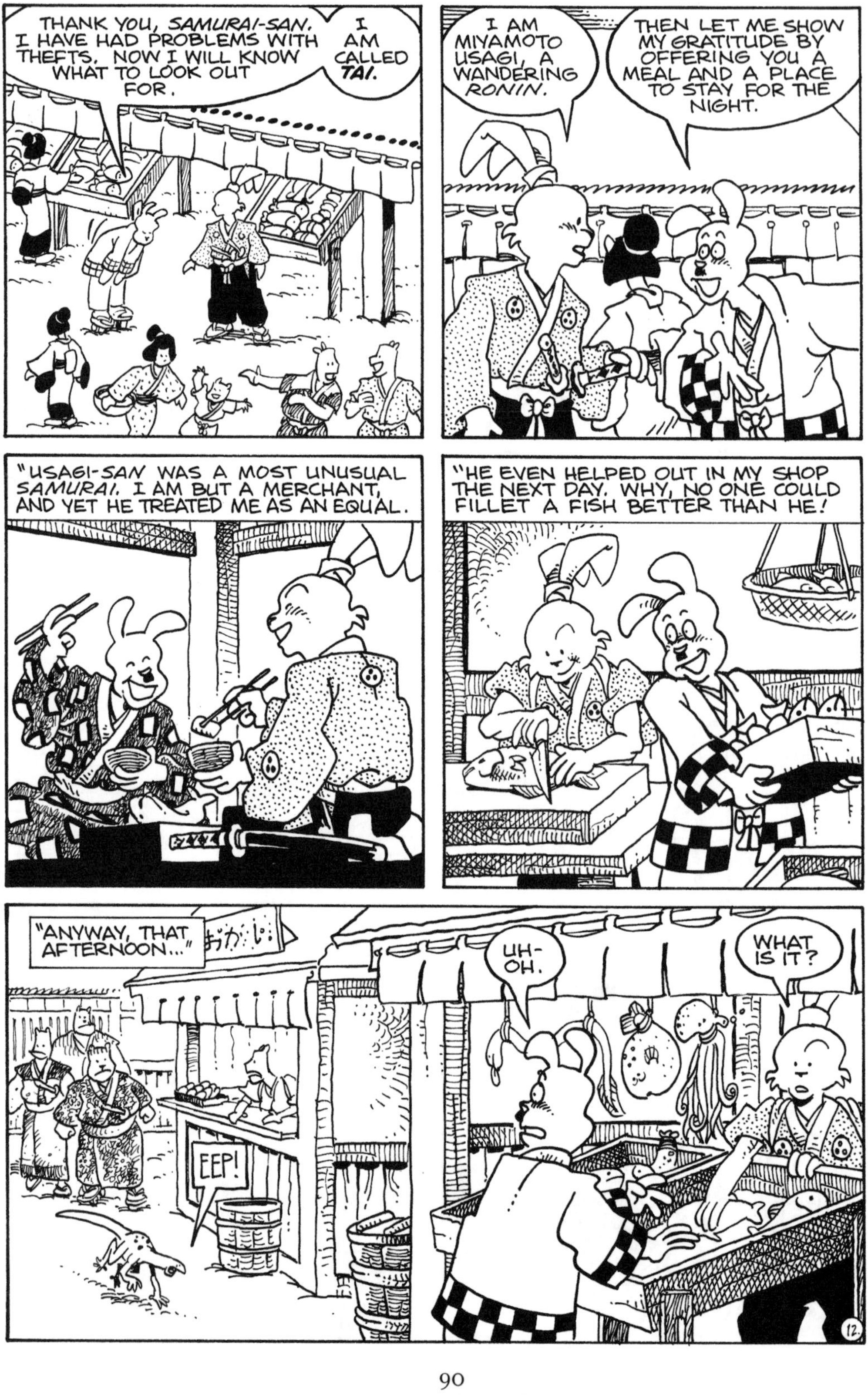
THANK YOU, SAMURAI-SAN. I HAVE HAD PROBLEMS WITH THEFTS. NOW I WILL KNOW WHAT TO LOOK OUT FOR.
I AM CALLED TAI.
I AM MIYAMOTO USAGI, A WANDERING RONIN.
THEN LET ME SHOW MY GRATITUDE BY OFFERING YOU A MEAL AND A PLACE TO STAY FOR THE NIGHT.
"USAGI-SAN WAS A MOST UNUSUAL SAMURAI. I AM BUT A MERCHANT, AND YET HE TREATED ME AS AN EQUAL.
"HE EVEN HELPED OUT IN MY SHOP THE NEXT DAY. WHY, NO ONE COULD FILLET A FISH BETTER THAN HE!
"ANYWAY, THAT AFTERNOON..."
おかし
EEP!
UH-OH.
WHAT IS IT?
12.

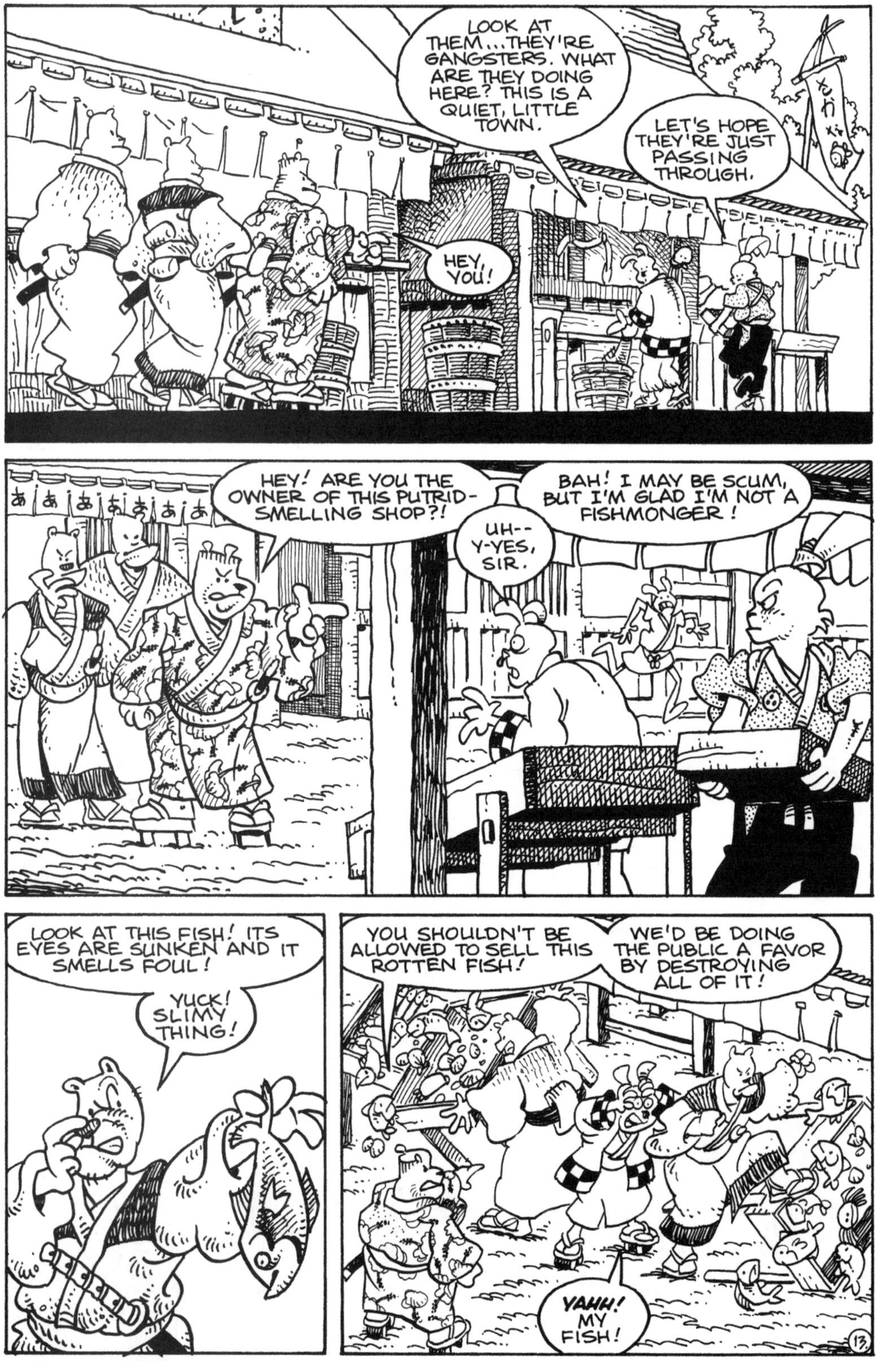
LOOK AT THEM...THEY'RE GANGSTERS. WHAT ARE THEY DOING HERE? THIS IS A QUIET, LITTLE TOWN.
LET'S HOPE THEY'RE JUST PASSING THROUGH.
HEY, YOU!
HEY! ARE YOU THE OWNER OF THIS PUTRID-SMELLING SHOP?!
UH-- Y-YES, SIR.
BAH! I MAY BE SCUM, BUT I'M GLAD I'M NOT A FISHMONGER!
LOOK AT THIS FISH! ITS EYES ARE SUNKEN AND IT SMELLS FOUL!
YUCK! SLIMY THING!
YOU SHOULDN'T BE ALLOWED TO SELL THIS ROTTEN FISH!
WE'D BE DOING THE PUBLIC A FAVOR BY DESTROYING ALL OF IT!
YAHH! MY FISH!
13

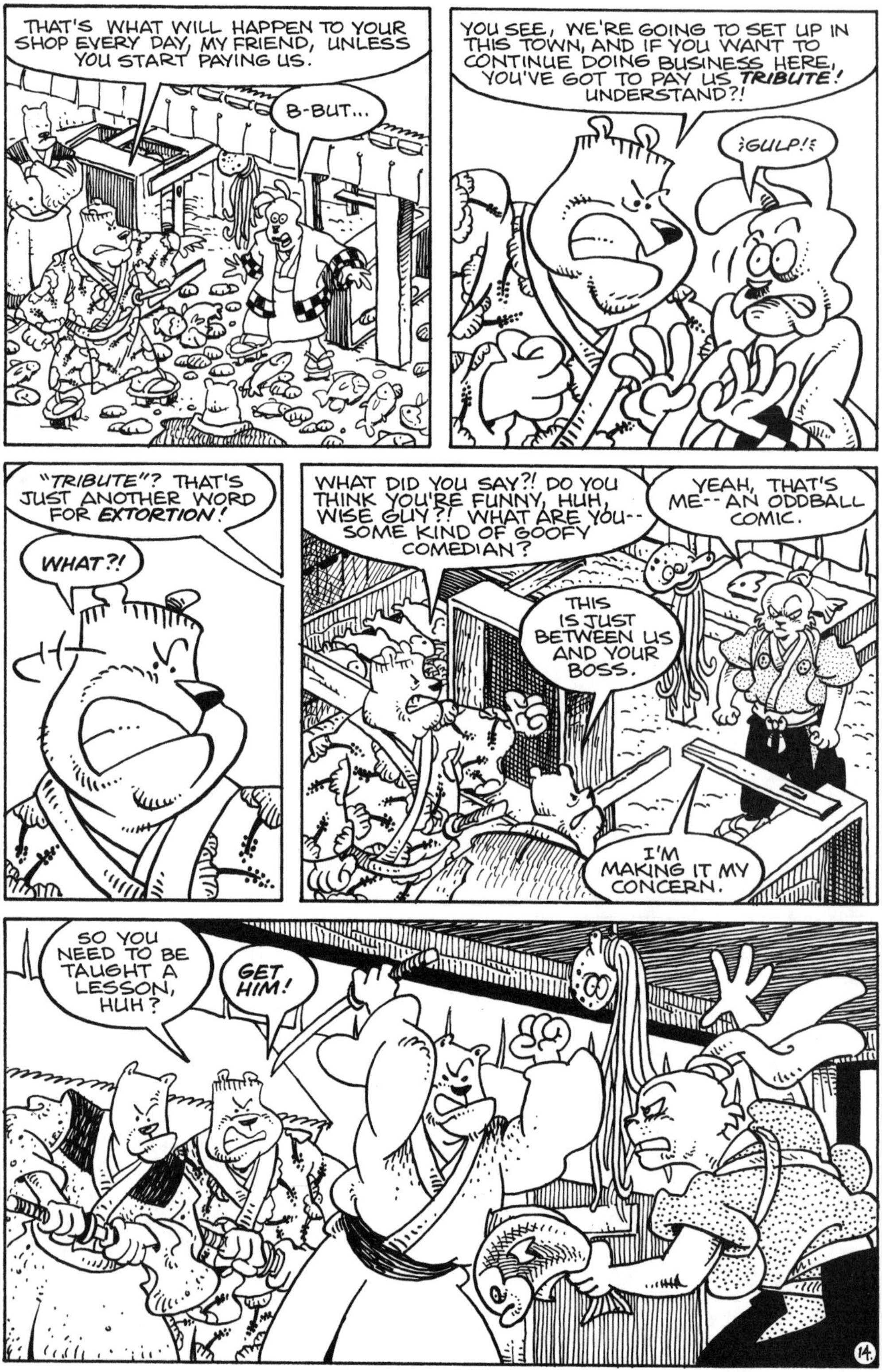
THAT'S WHAT WILL HAPPEN TO YOUR SHOP EVERY DAY, MY FRIEND, UNLESS YOU START PAYING US.
B-BUT...
YOU SEE, WE'RE GOING TO SET UP IN THIS TOWN, AND IF YOU WANT TO CONTINUE DOING BUSINESS HERE, YOU'VE GOT TO PAY US TRIBUTE! UNDERSTAND?!
GULP!
"TRIBUTE"? THAT'S JUST ANOTHER WORD FOR EXTORTION!
WHAT?!
WHAT DID YOU SAY?! DO YOU THINK YOU'RE FUNNY, HUH, WISE GUY?! WHAT ARE YOU-- SOME KIND OF GOOFY COMEDIAN?
YEAH, THAT'S ME-- AN ODDBALL COMIC.
THIS IS JUST BETWEEN US AND YOUR BOSS.
I'M MAKING IT MY CONCERN.
SO YOU NEED TO BE TAUGHT A LESSON, HUH?
GET HIM!
14.

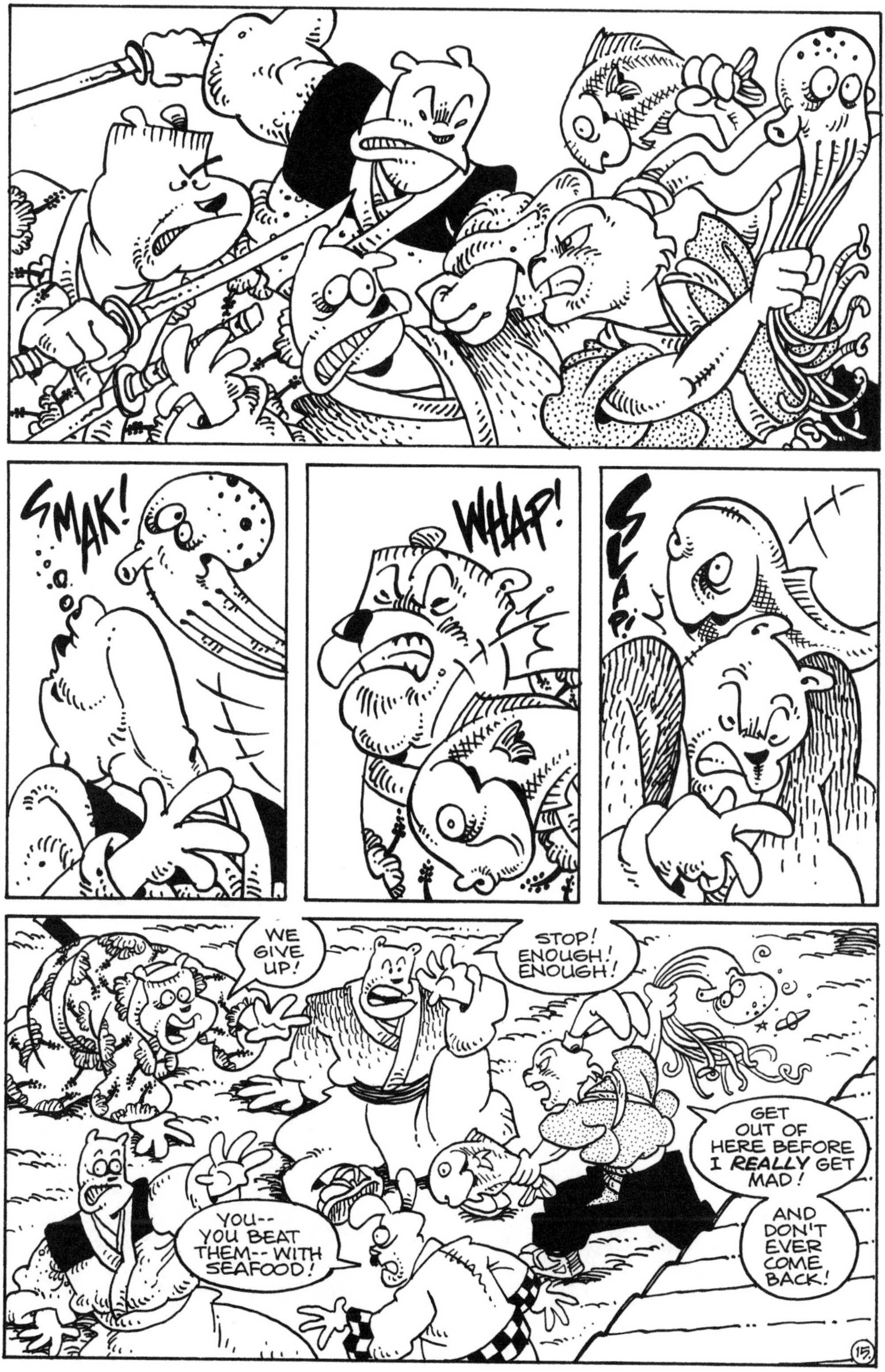
SMAK!
WHAP!
SLAP!
WE GIVE UP!
STOP! ENOUGH! ENOUGH!
GET OUT OF HERE BEFORE I *REALLY* GET MAD!
AND DON'T EVER COME BACK!
YOU-- YOU BEAT THEM-- WITH SEAFOOD!
15

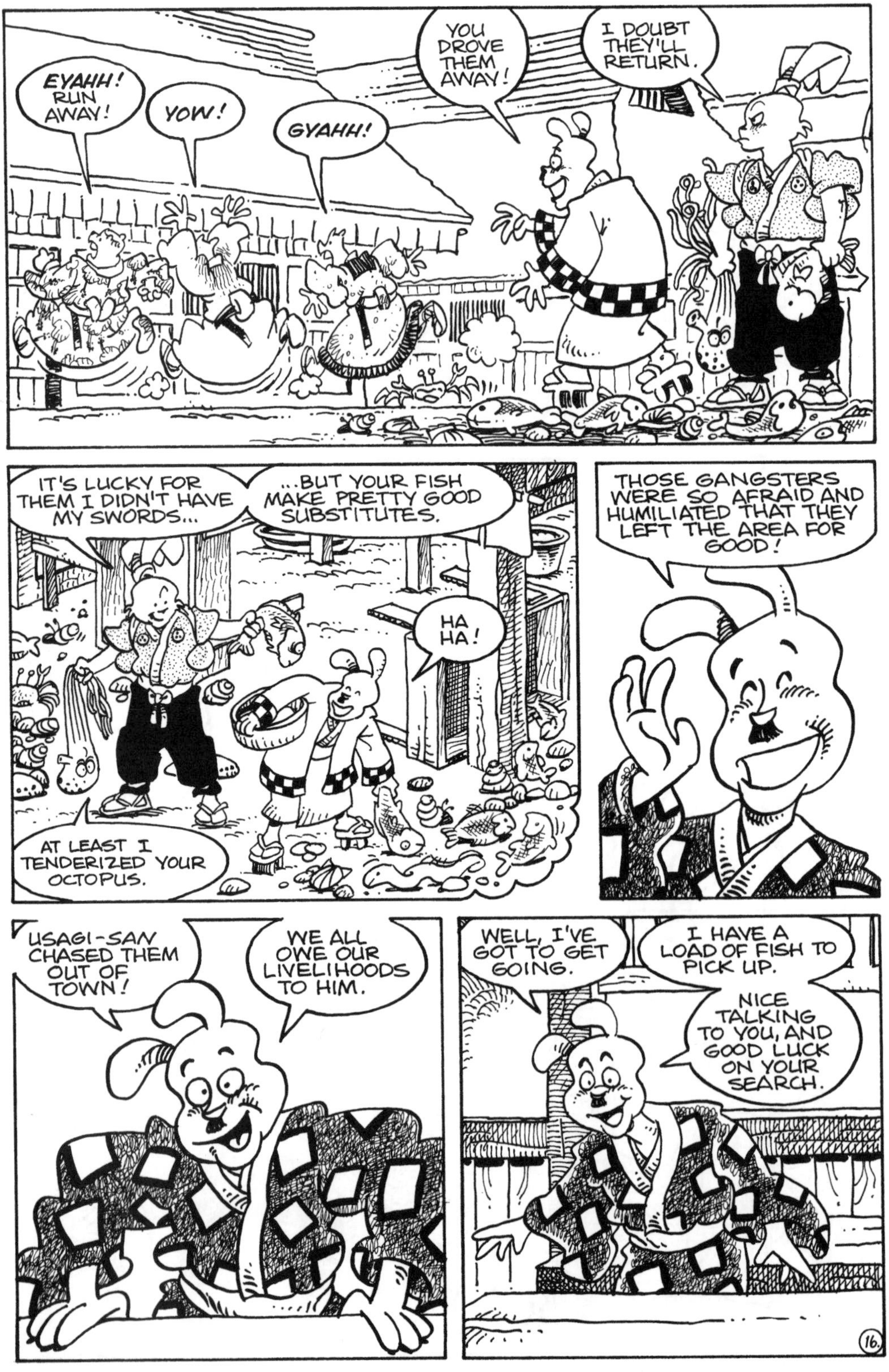
EYAHH! RUN AWAY!
YOW!
GYAHH!
YOU DROVE THEM AWAY!
I DOUBT THEY'LL RETURN.
IT'S LUCKY FOR THEM I DIDN'T HAVE MY SWORDS...
...BUT YOUR FISH MAKE PRETTY GOOD SUBSTITUTES.
HA HA!
AT LEAST I TENDERIZED YOUR OCTOPUS.
THOSE GANGSTERS WERE SO AFRAID AND HUMILIATED THAT THEY LEFT THE AREA FOR GOOD!
USAGI-SAN CHASED THEM OUT OF TOWN!
WE ALL OWE OUR LIVELIHOODS TO HIM.
WELL, I'VE GOT TO GET GOING.
I HAVE A LOAD OF FISH TO PICK UP.
NICE TALKING TO YOU, AND GOOD LUCK ON YOUR SEARCH.
16.

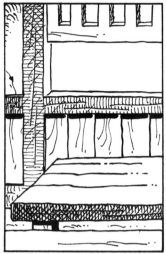

UH...

OKAY IF I SIT DOWN?

I HEARD YOU WERE ASKING ABOUT THAT LONG-EARED SAMURAI. I--I MET HIM JUST A FEW DAYS AGO.

I SHOULDN'T BE TELLING YOU THIS, BUT I'VE GOT TO TELL SOMEONE. YOU KNOW HOW IT IS. BESIDES, YOU DON'T LOOK LIKE THE TYPE OF PERSON WHO WOULD TURN ME IN. HEH-HEH. I'M REFORMED NOW, ANYWAY.

I DON'T WANT TO TELL YOU MY NAME, BUT MY FATHER IS A POOR FARMER LIVING IN THE NEXT PROVINCE.

"BUT THAT KIND OF DIRTY LIFE, WORKING HARD IN THE FIELDS, WAS NOT FOR ME.

SPLAT!

17

95

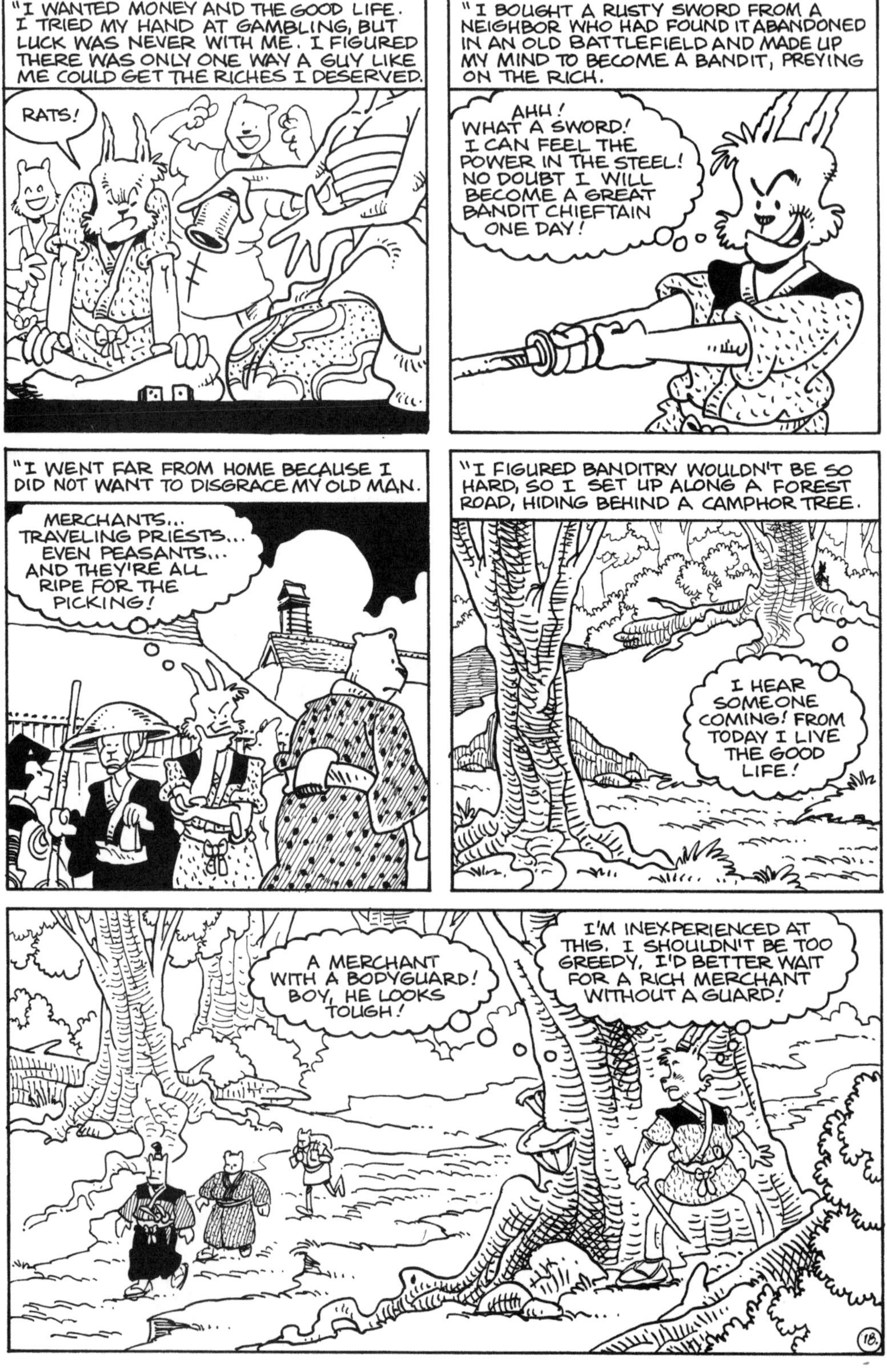
"I WANTED MONEY AND THE GOOD LIFE. I TRIED MY HAND AT GAMBLING, BUT LUCK WAS NEVER WITH ME. I FIGURED THERE WAS ONLY ONE WAY A GUY LIKE ME COULD GET THE RICHES I DESERVED.
RATS!
"I BOUGHT A RUSTY SWORD FROM A NEIGHBOR WHO HAD FOUND IT ABANDONED IN AN OLD BATTLEFIELD AND MADE UP MY MIND TO BECOME A BANDIT, PREYING ON THE RICH.
AHH! WHAT A SWORD! I CAN FEEL THE POWER IN THE STEEL! NO DOUBT I WILL BECOME A GREAT BANDIT CHIEFTAIN ONE DAY!
"I WENT FAR FROM HOME BECAUSE I DID NOT WANT TO DISGRACE MY OLD MAN.
MERCHANTS... TRAVELING PRIESTS... EVEN PEASANTS... AND THEY'RE ALL RIPE FOR THE PICKING!
"I FIGURED BANDITRY WOULDN'T BE SO HARD, SO I SET UP ALONG A FOREST ROAD, HIDING BEHIND A CAMPHOR TREE.
I HEAR SOMEONE COMING! FROM TODAY I LIVE THE GOOD LIFE!
A MERCHANT WITH A BODYGUARD! BOY, HE LOOKS TOUGH!
I'M INEXPERIENCED AT THIS. I SHOULDN'T BE TOO GREEDY. I'D BETTER WAIT FOR A RICH MERCHANT WITHOUT A GUARD!
18.

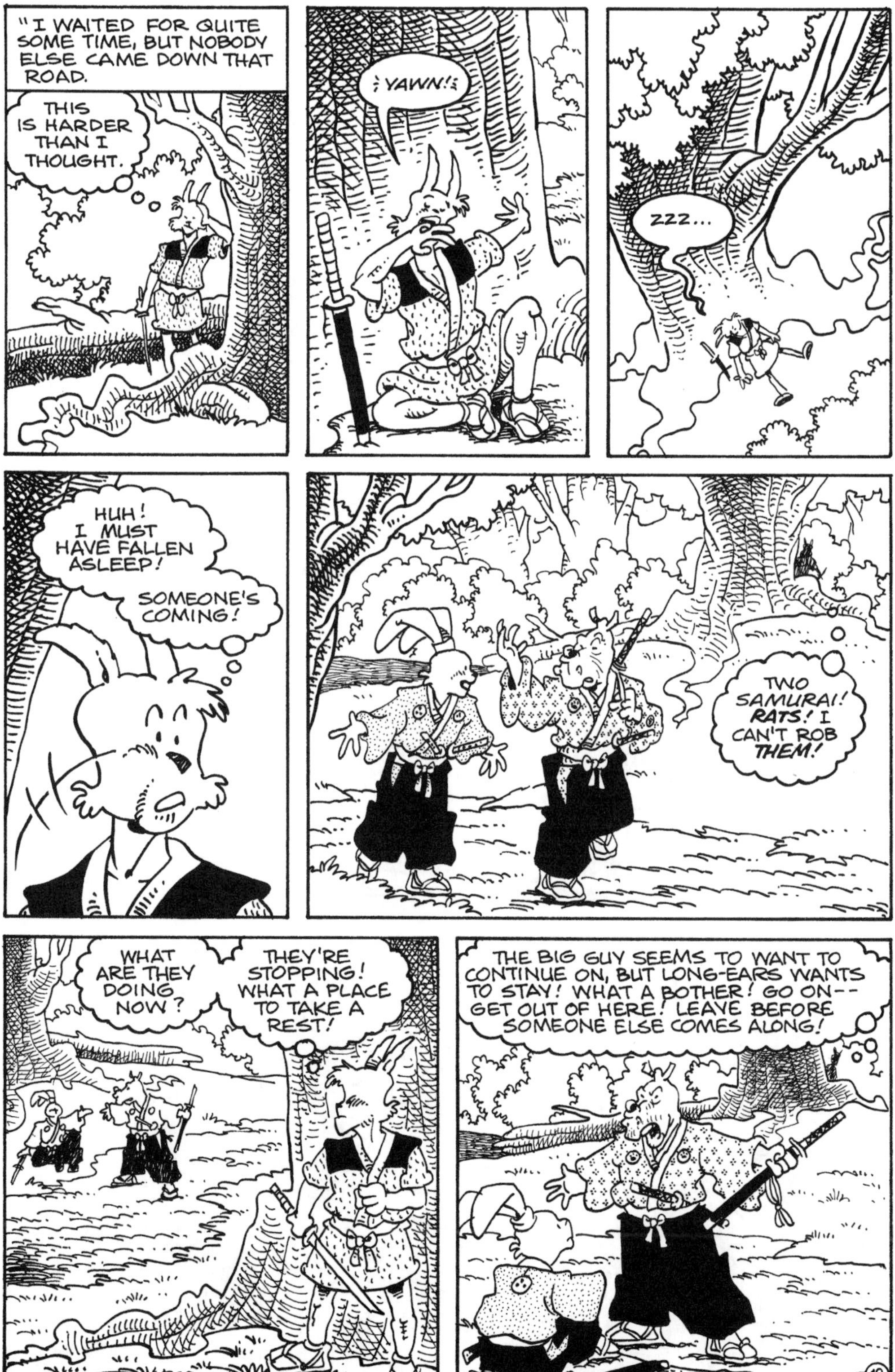
"I WAITED FOR QUITE SOME TIME, BUT NOBODY ELSE CAME DOWN THAT ROAD.
THIS IS HARDER THAN I THOUGHT.
YAWN!
ZZZ...
HUH! I MUST HAVE FALLEN ASLEEP!
SOMEONE'S COMING!
TWO SAMURAI! RATS! I CAN'T ROB THEM!
WHAT ARE THEY DOING NOW?
THEY'RE STOPPING! WHAT A PLACE TO TAKE A REST!
THE BIG GUY SEEMS TO WANT TO CONTINUE ON, BUT LONG-EARS WANTS TO STAY! WHAT A BOTHER! GO ON--GET OUT OF HERE! LEAVE BEFORE SOMEONE ELSE COMES ALONG!
19.

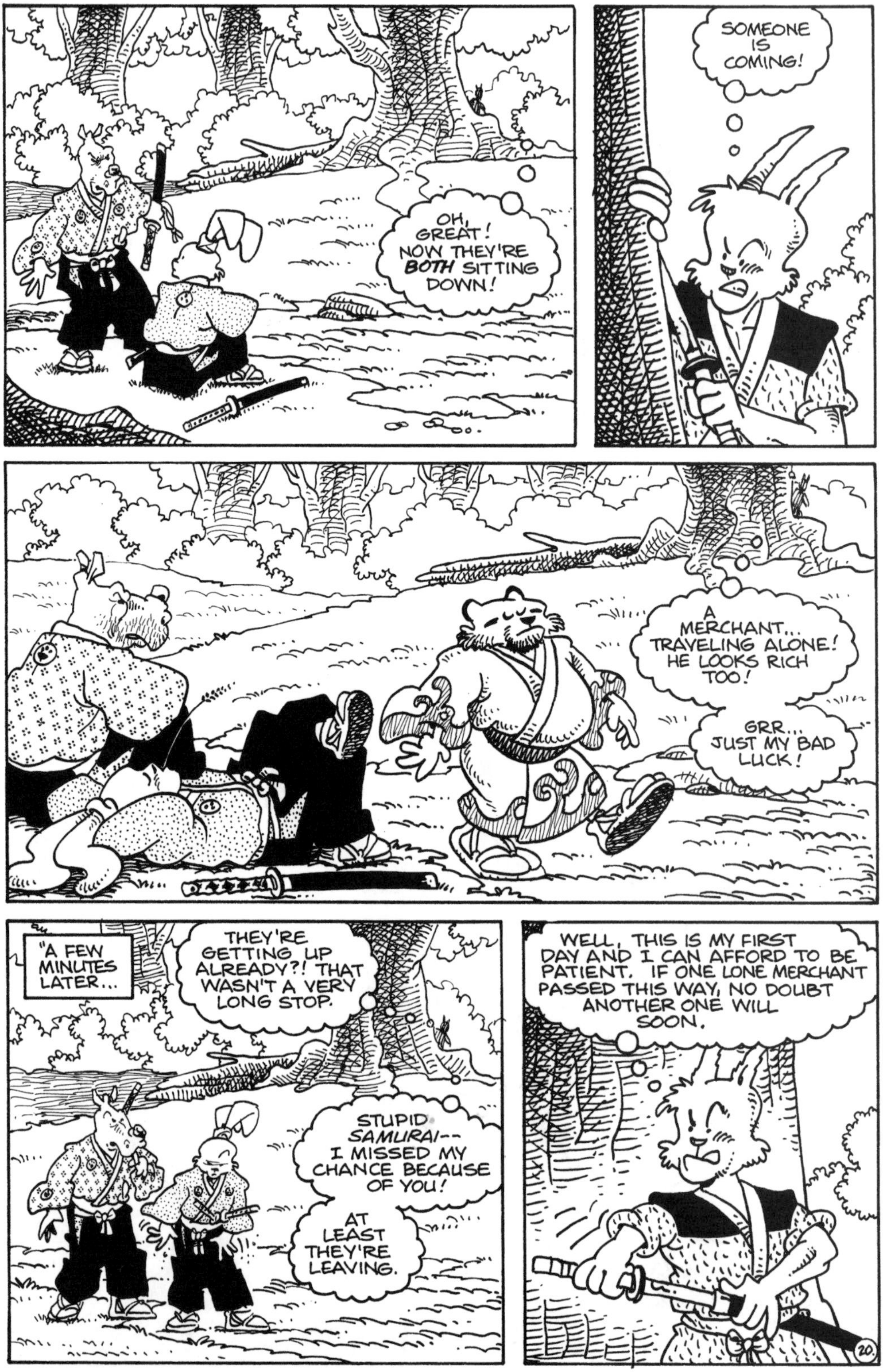
OH, GREAT! NOW THEY'RE BOTH SITTING DOWN!
SOMEONE IS COMING!
A MERCHANT... TRAVELING ALONE! HE LOOKS RICH TOO!
GRR... JUST MY BAD LUCK!
A FEW MINUTES LATER...
THEY'RE GETTING UP ALREADY?! THAT WASN'T A VERY LONG STOP.
STUPID SAMURAI-- I MISSED MY CHANCE BECAUSE OF YOU!
AT LEAST THEY'RE LEAVING.
WELL, THIS IS MY FIRST DAY AND I CAN AFFORD TO BE PATIENT. IF ONE LONE MERCHANT PASSED THIS WAY, NO DOUBT ANOTHER ONE WILL SOON.
20.

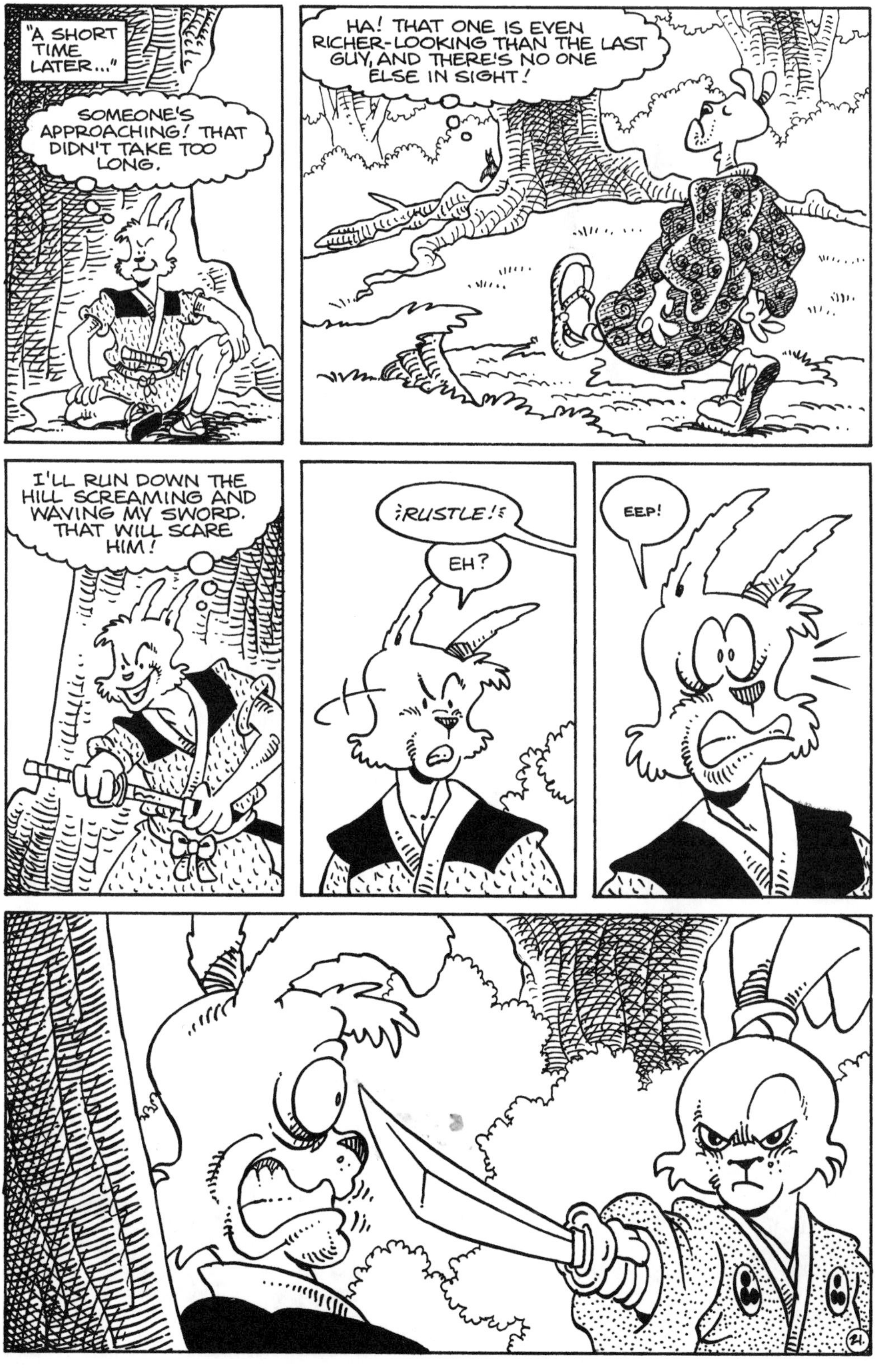
"A SHORT TIME LATER..."
SOMEONE'S APPROACHING! THAT DIDN'T TAKE TOO LONG.
HA! THAT ONE IS EVEN RICHER-LOOKING THAN THE LAST GUY, AND THERE'S NO ONE ELSE IN SIGHT!
I'LL RUN DOWN THE HILL SCREAMING AND WAVING MY SWORD. THAT WILL SCARE HIM!
¡RUSTLE!¡
EH?
EEP!
21.

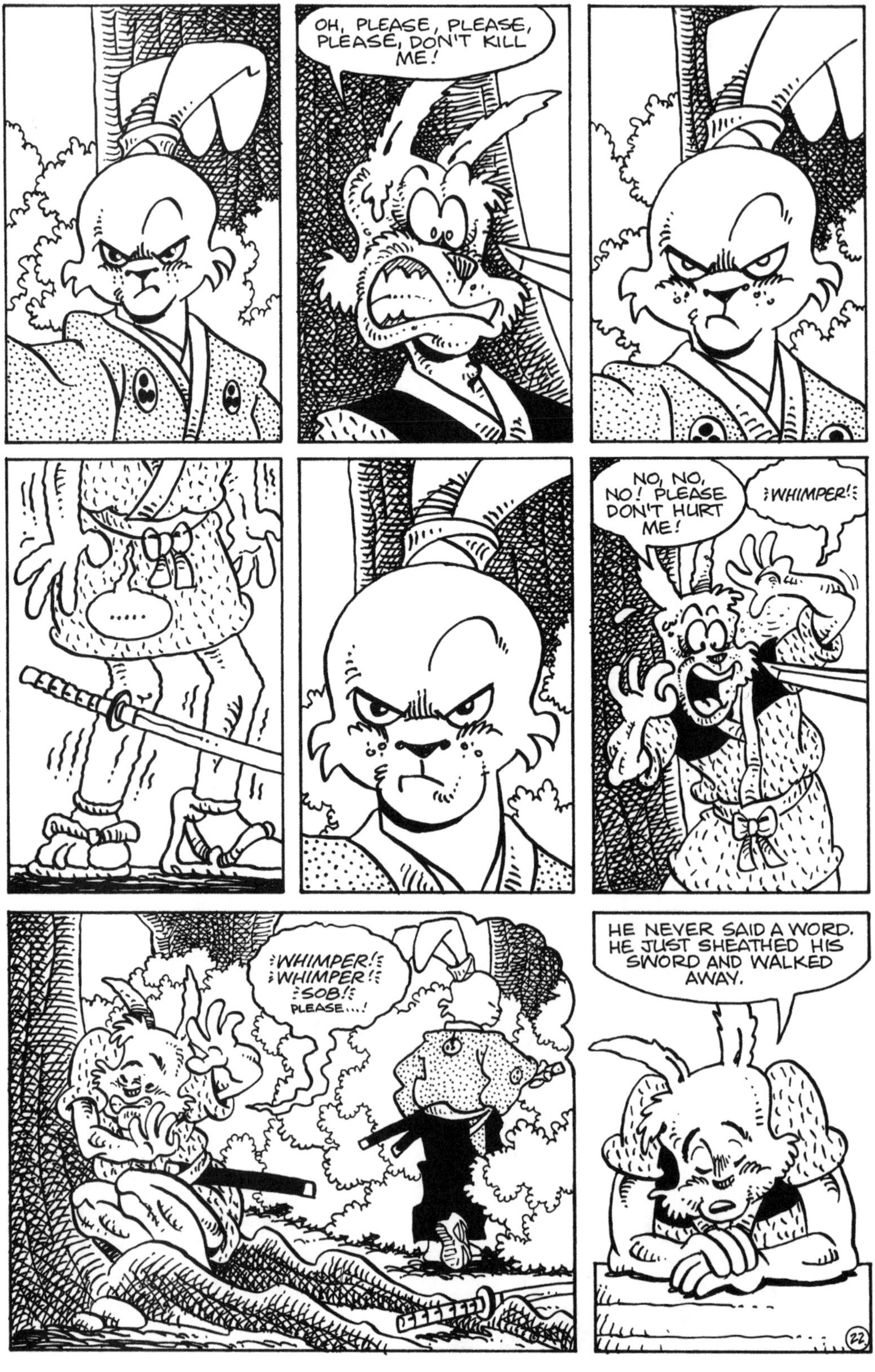

OH, PLEASE, PLEASE, PLEASE, DON'T KILL ME!
.....
NO, NO, NO! PLEASE DON'T HURT ME!
WHIMPER!
WHIMPER! WHIMPER! SOB! PLEASE...!
HE NEVER SAID A WORD. HE JUST SHEATHED HIS SWORD AND WALKED AWAY.
22

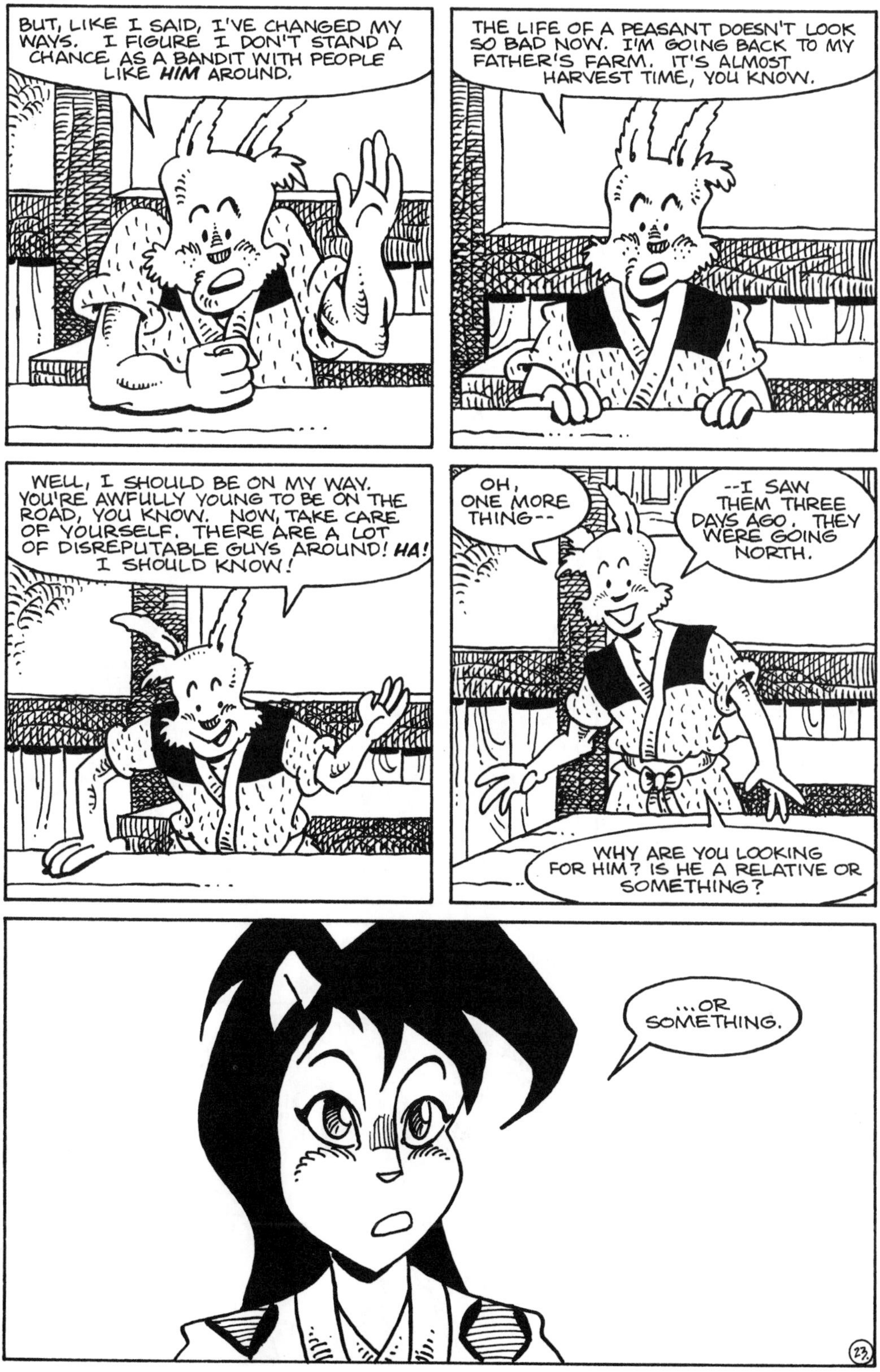
BUT, LIKE I SAID, I'VE CHANGED MY WAYS. I FIGURE I DON'T STAND A CHANCE AS A BANDIT WITH PEOPLE LIKE *HIM* AROUND.
THE LIFE OF A PEASANT DOESN'T LOOK SO BAD NOW. I'M GOING BACK TO MY FATHER'S FARM. IT'S ALMOST HARVEST TIME, YOU KNOW.
WELL, I SHOULD BE ON MY WAY. YOU'RE AWFULLY YOUNG TO BE ON THE ROAD, YOU KNOW. NOW, TAKE CARE OF YOURSELF. THERE ARE A LOT OF DISREPUTABLE GUYS AROUND! *HA!* I SHOULD KNOW!
OH, ONE MORE THING--
--I SAW THEM THREE DAYS AGO. THEY WERE GOING NORTH.
WHY ARE YOU LOOKING FOR HIM? IS HE A RELATIVE OR SOMETHING?
...OR SOMETHING.
23

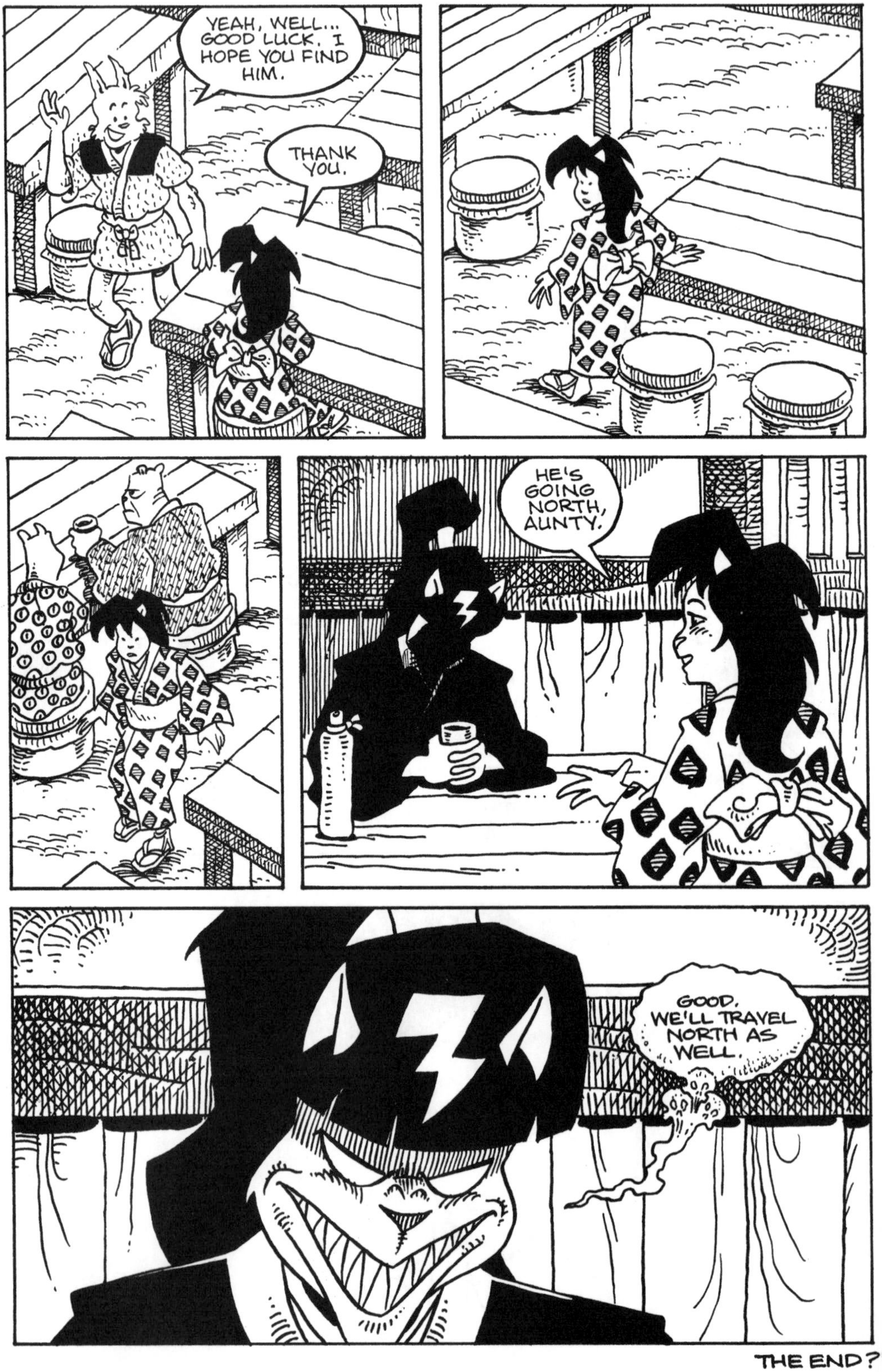
YEAH, WELL... GOOD LUCK. I HOPE YOU FIND HIM.
THANK YOU.
HE'S GOING NORTH, AUNTY.
GOOD, WE'LL TRAVEL NORTH AS WELL.
THE END?

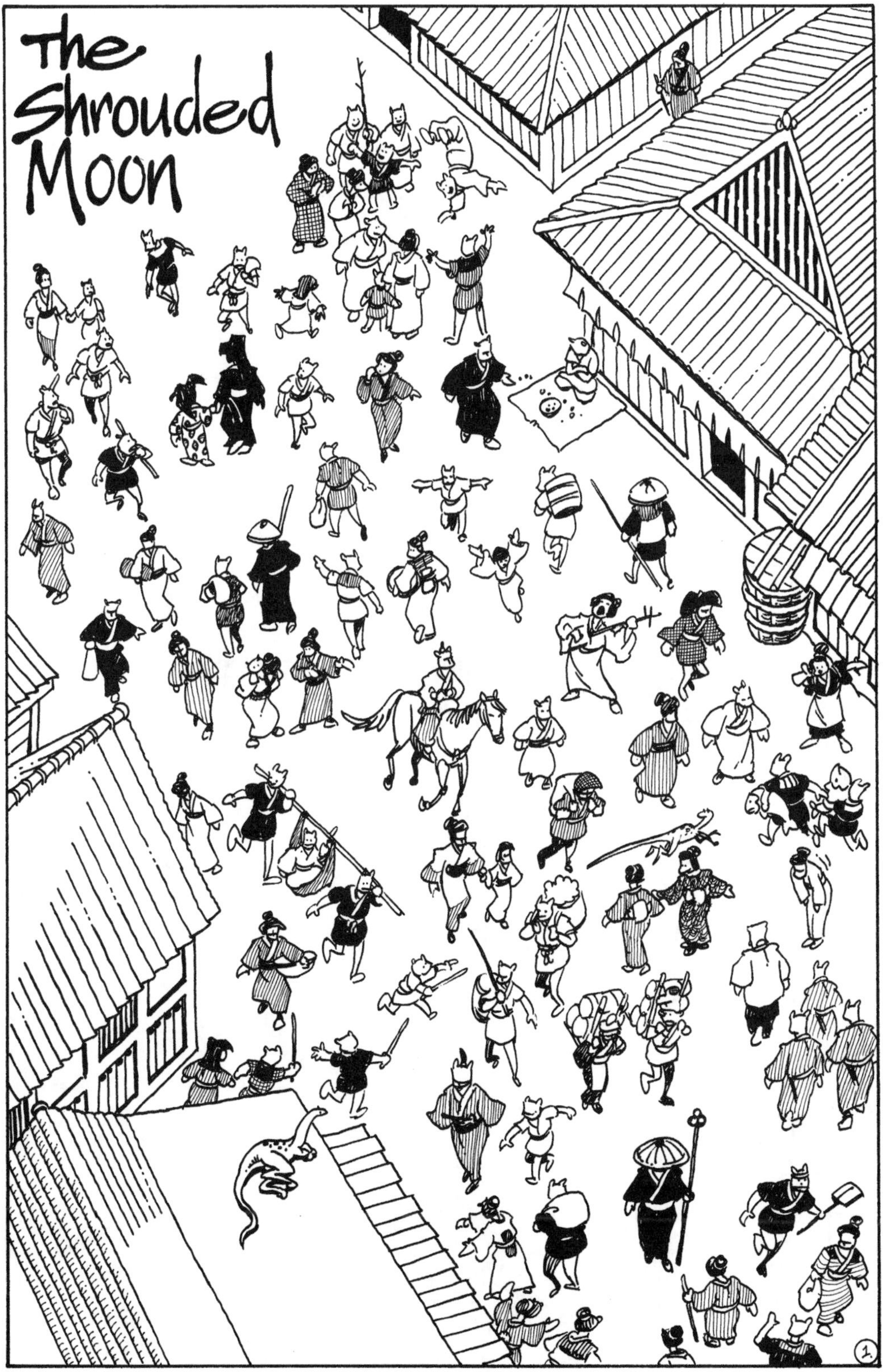
The Shrouded Moon
1

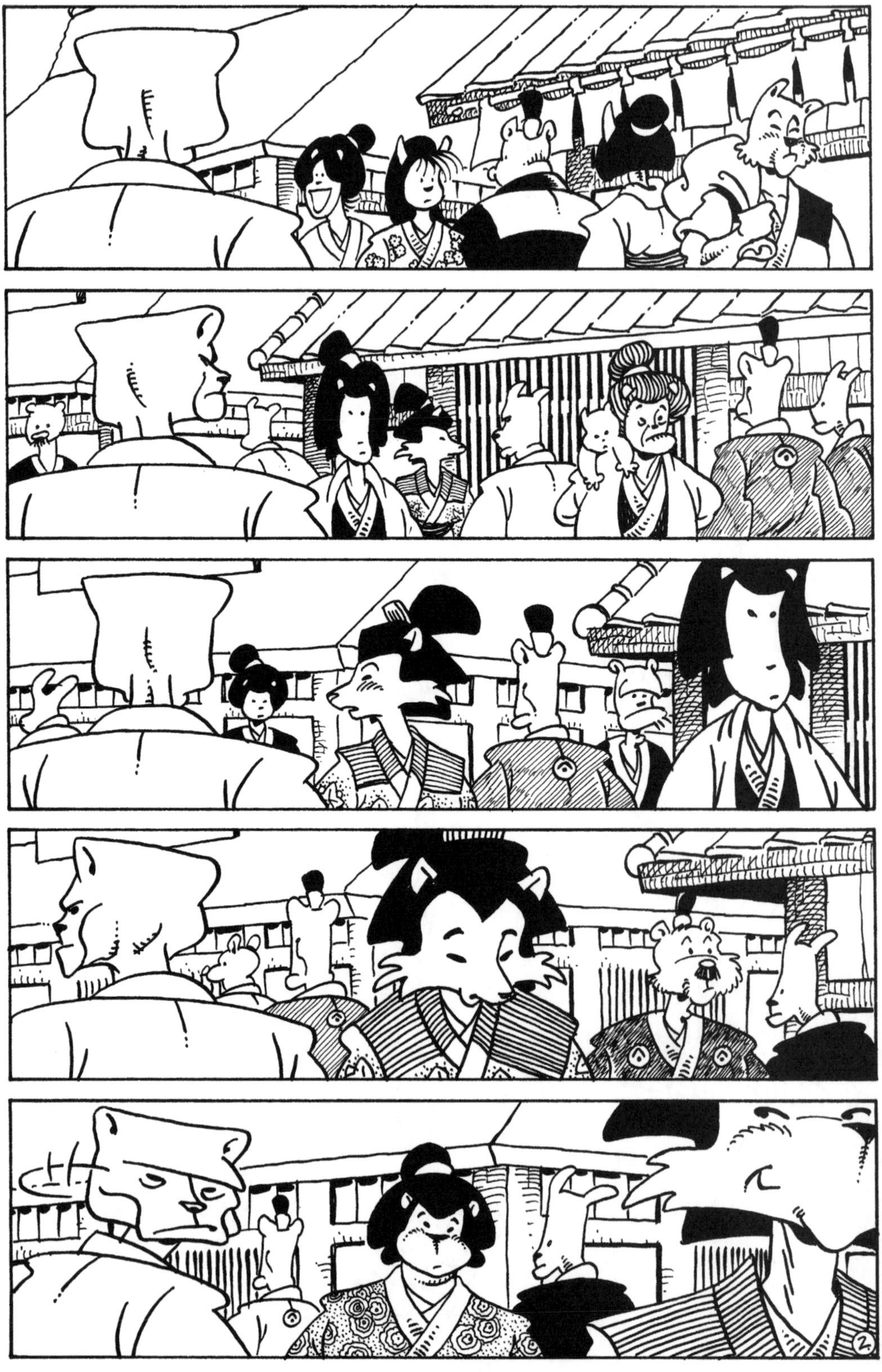

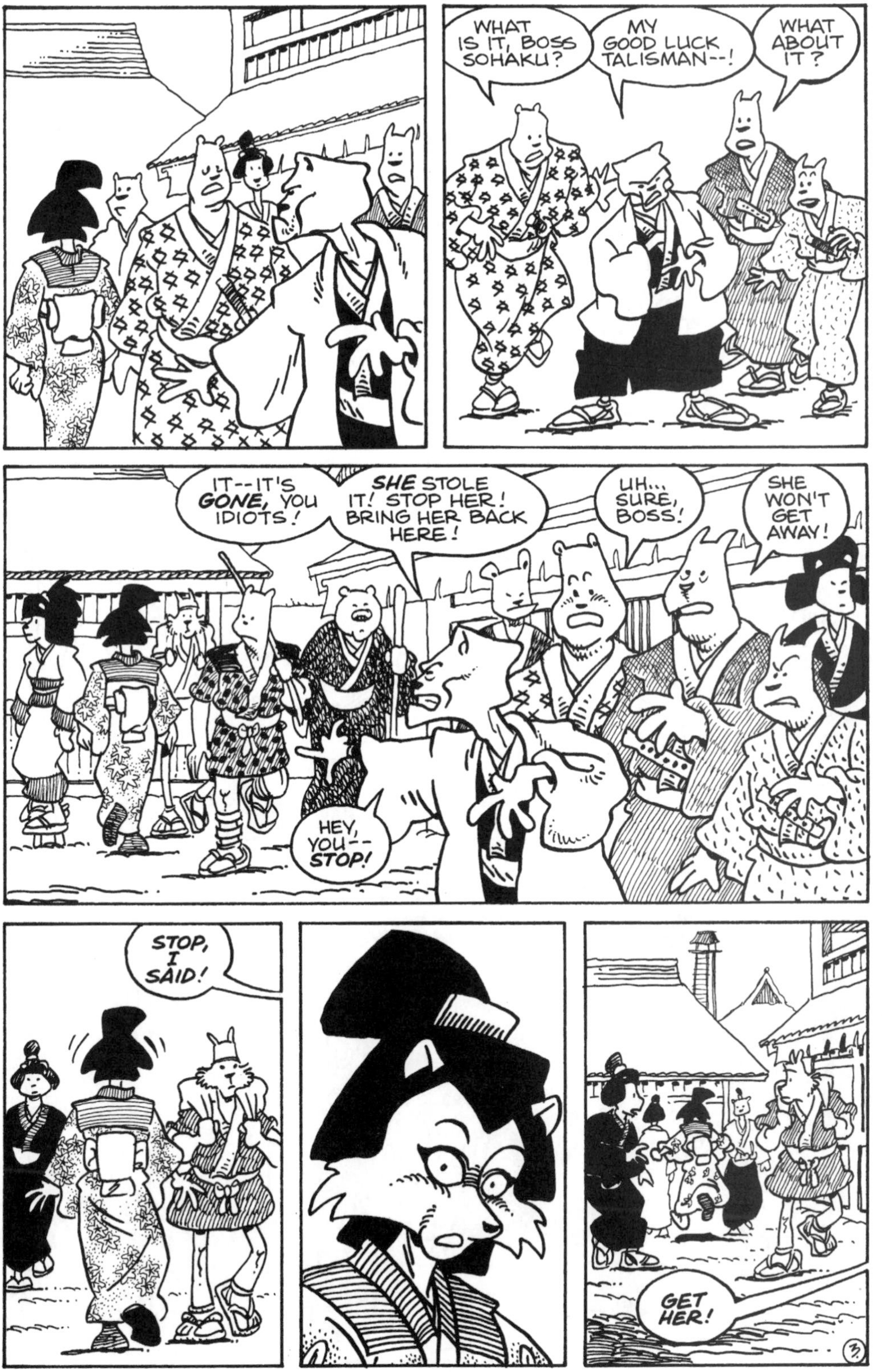
WHAT IS IT, BOSS SOHAKU?
MY GOOD LUCK TALISMAN--!
WHAT ABOUT IT?
IT--IT'S **GONE**, YOU IDIOTS!
SHE STOLE IT! STOP HER! BRING HER BACK HERE!
UH... SURE, BOSS!
SHE WON'T GET AWAY!
HEY, YOU--**STOP!**
STOP, I SAID!
GET HER!
3

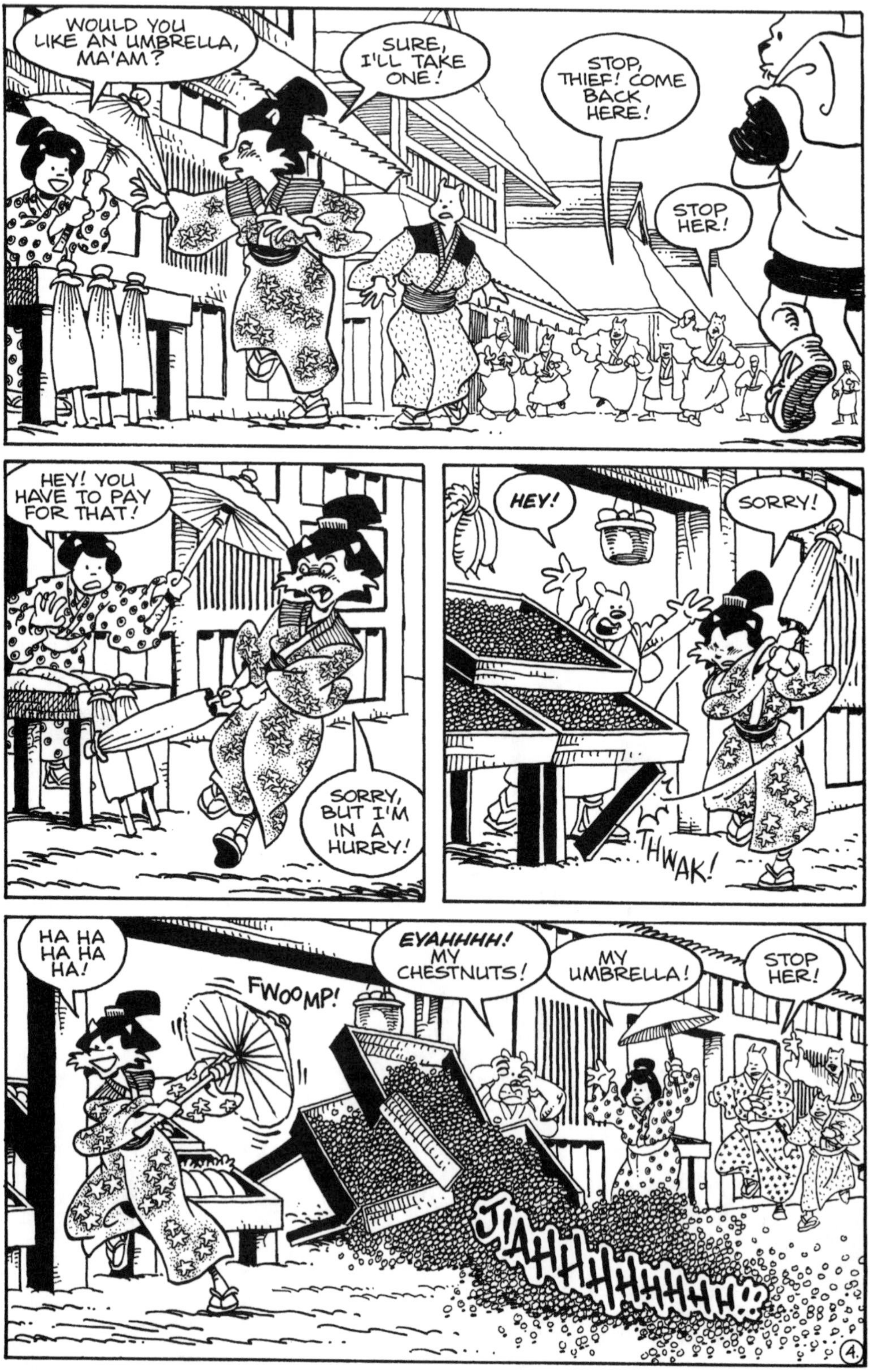

WOULD YOU LIKE AN UMBRELLA, MA'AM?
SURE, I'LL TAKE ONE!
STOP, THIEF! COME BACK HERE!
STOP HER!
HEY! YOU HAVE TO PAY FOR THAT!
SORRY, BUT I'M IN A HURRY!
HEY!
SORRY!
THWAK!
HA HA HA HA HA!
FWOOMP!
EYAHHHH! MY CHESTNUTS!
MY UMBRELLA!
STOP HER!
JIAHHHHHHHHH!!
4.

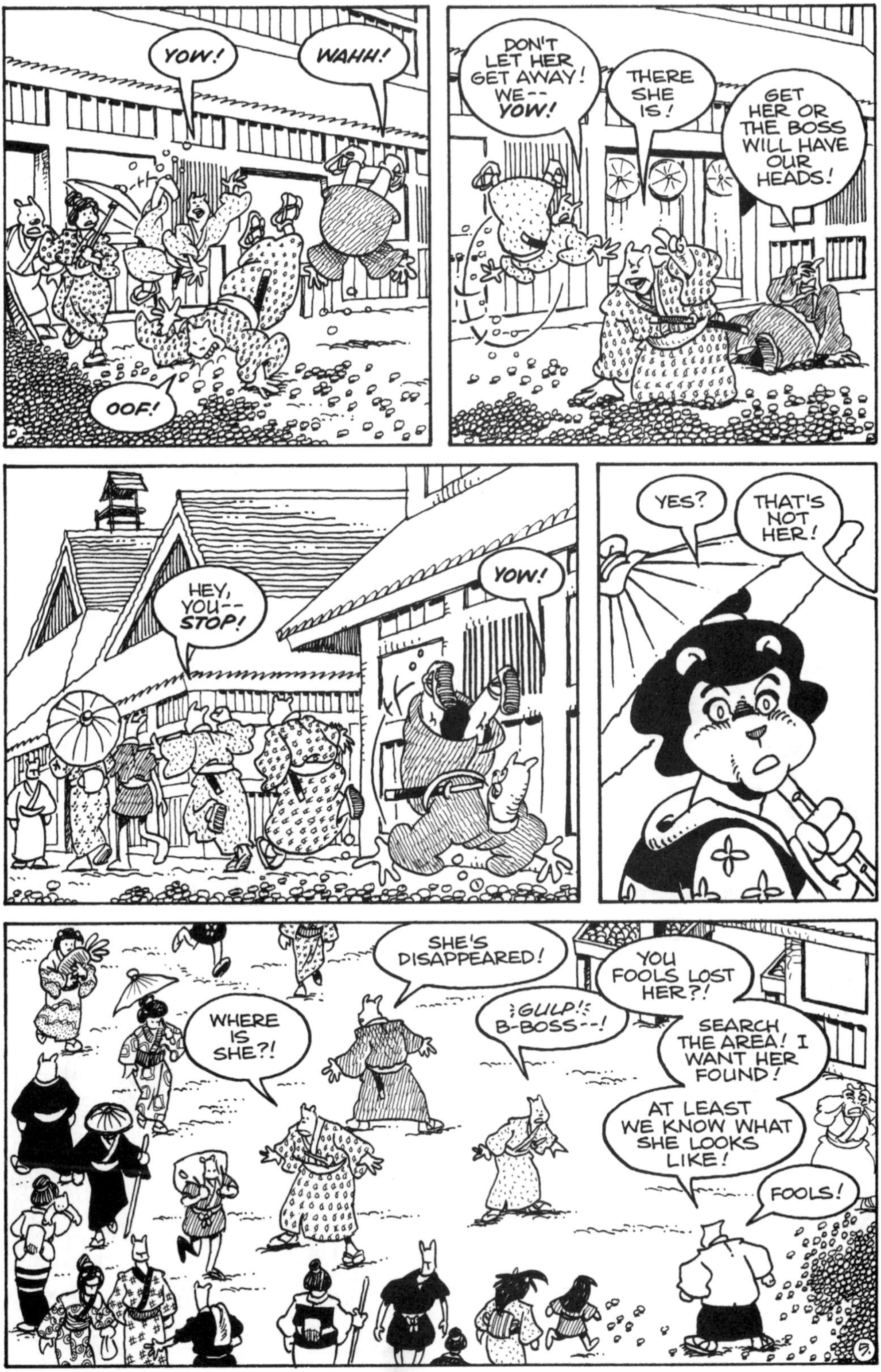
YOW!
WAHH!
OOF!
DON'T LET HER GET AWAY! WE-- YOW!
THERE SHE IS!
GET HER OR THE BOSS WILL HAVE OUR HEADS!
HEY, YOU-- STOP!
YOW!
YES?
THAT'S NOT HER!
WHERE IS SHE?!
SHE'S DISAPPEARED!
GULP! B-BOSS--!
YOU FOOLS LOST HER?!
SEARCH THE AREA! I WANT HER FOUND!
AT LEAST WE KNOW WHAT SHE LOOKS LIKE!
FOOLS!

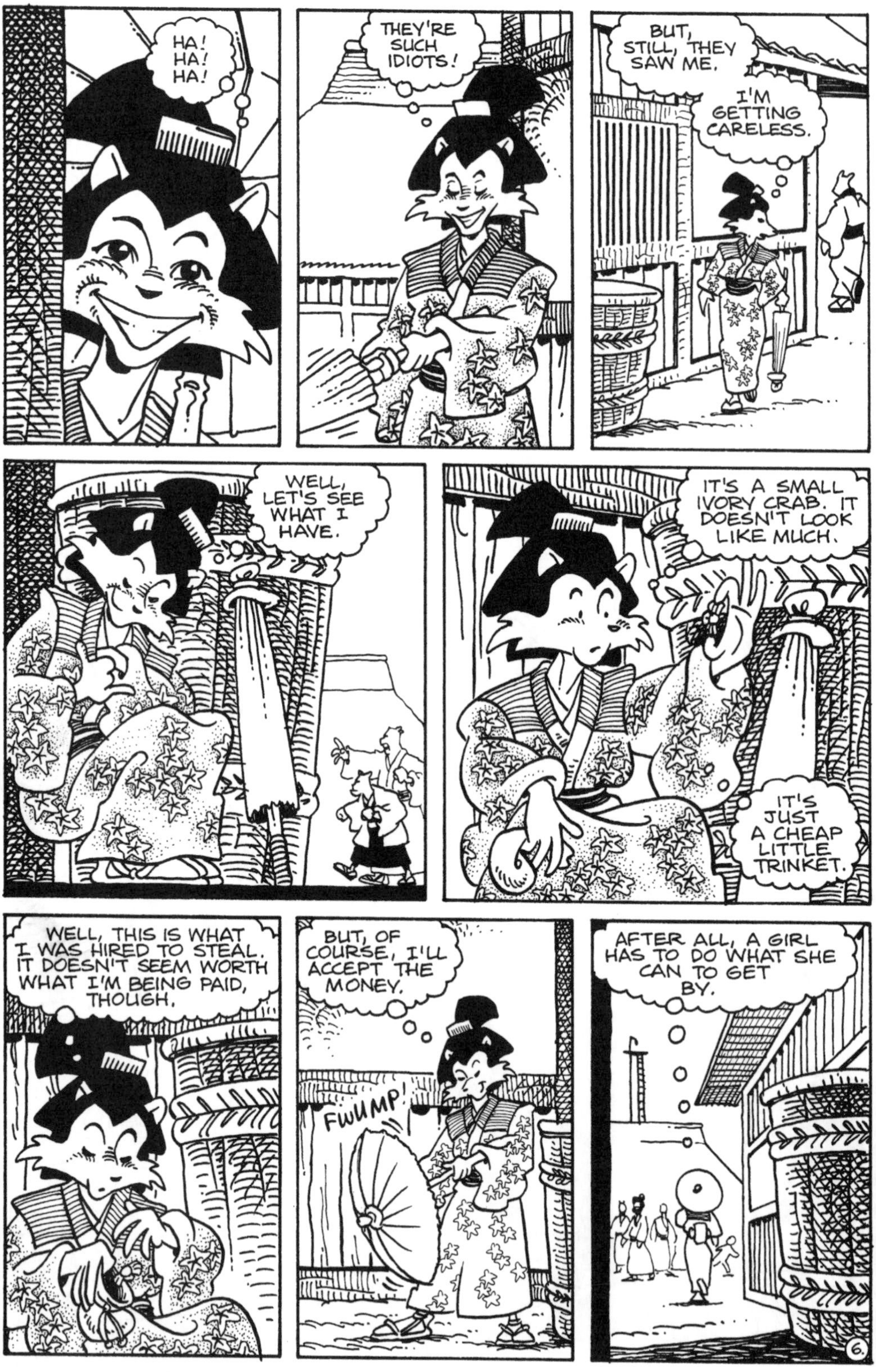
HA! HA! HA!
THEY'RE SUCH IDIOTS!
BUT, STILL, THEY SAW ME.
I'M GETTING CARELESS.
WELL, LET'S SEE WHAT I HAVE.
IT'S A SMALL IVORY CRAB. IT DOESN'T LOOK LIKE MUCH.
IT'S JUST A CHEAP LITTLE TRINKET.
WELL, THIS IS WHAT I WAS HIRED TO STEAL. IT DOESN'T SEEM WORTH WHAT I'M BEING PAID, THOUGH.
BUT, OF COURSE, I'LL ACCEPT THE MONEY.
FWUMP!
AFTER ALL, A GIRL HAS TO DO WHAT SHE CAN TO GET BY.
6.

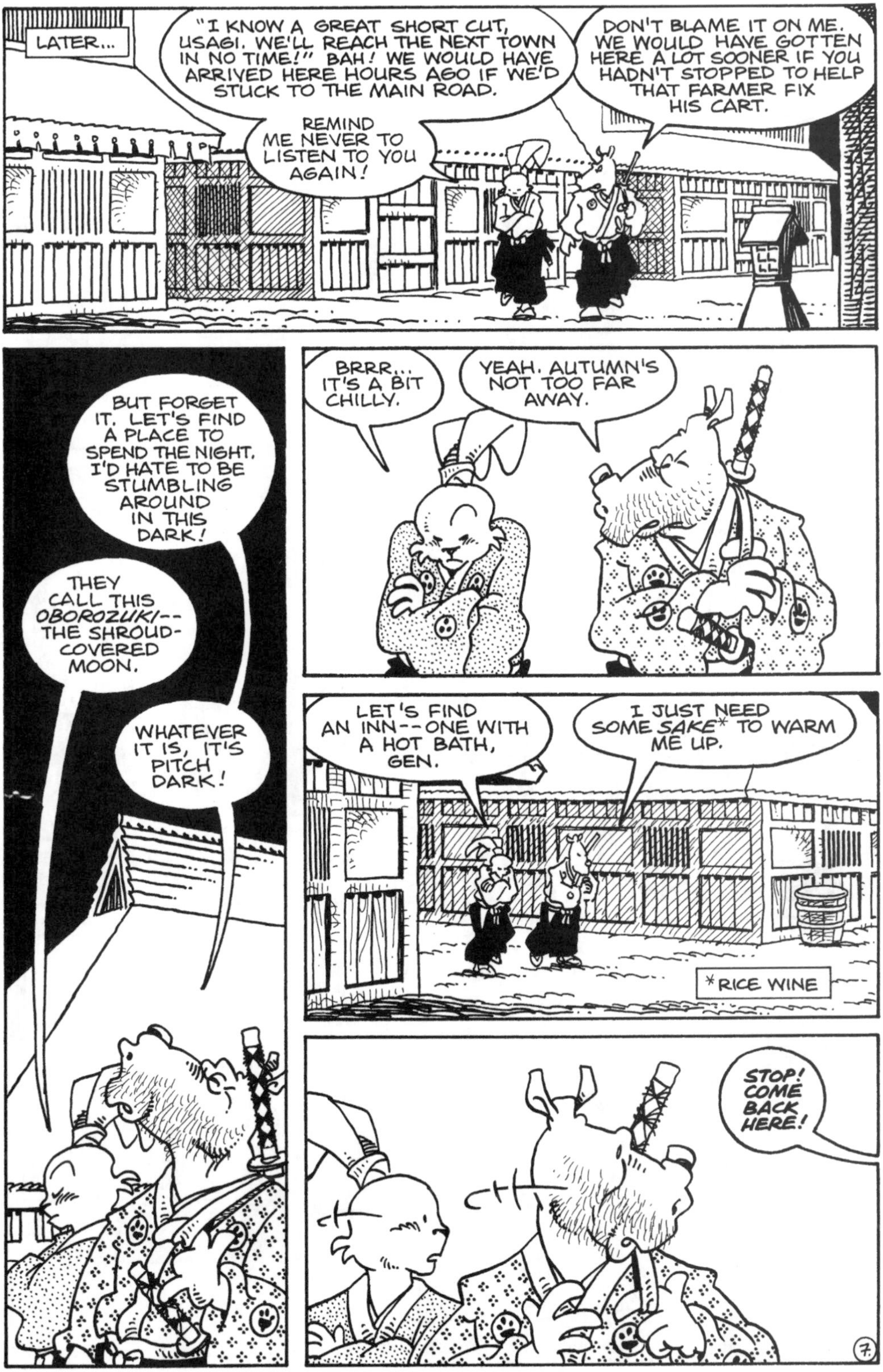
LATER...
"I KNOW A GREAT SHORT CUT, USAGI. WE'LL REACH THE NEXT TOWN IN NO TIME!" BAH! WE WOULD HAVE ARRIVED HERE HOURS AGO IF WE'D STUCK TO THE MAIN ROAD.
REMIND ME NEVER TO LISTEN TO YOU AGAIN!
DON'T BLAME IT ON ME. WE WOULD HAVE GOTTEN HERE A LOT SOONER IF YOU HADN'T STOPPED TO HELP THAT FARMER FIX HIS CART.
BUT FORGET IT. LET'S FIND A PLACE TO SPEND THE NIGHT. I'D HATE TO BE STUMBLING AROUND IN THIS DARK!
THEY CALL THIS *OBOROZUKI*--THE SHROUD-COVERED MOON.
WHATEVER IT IS, IT'S PITCH DARK!
BRRR... IT'S A BIT CHILLY.
YEAH. AUTUMN'S NOT TOO FAR AWAY.
LET'S FIND AN INN--ONE WITH A HOT BATH, GEN.
I JUST NEED SOME *SAKE** TO WARM ME UP.
*RICE WINE
STOP! COME BACK HERE!
7

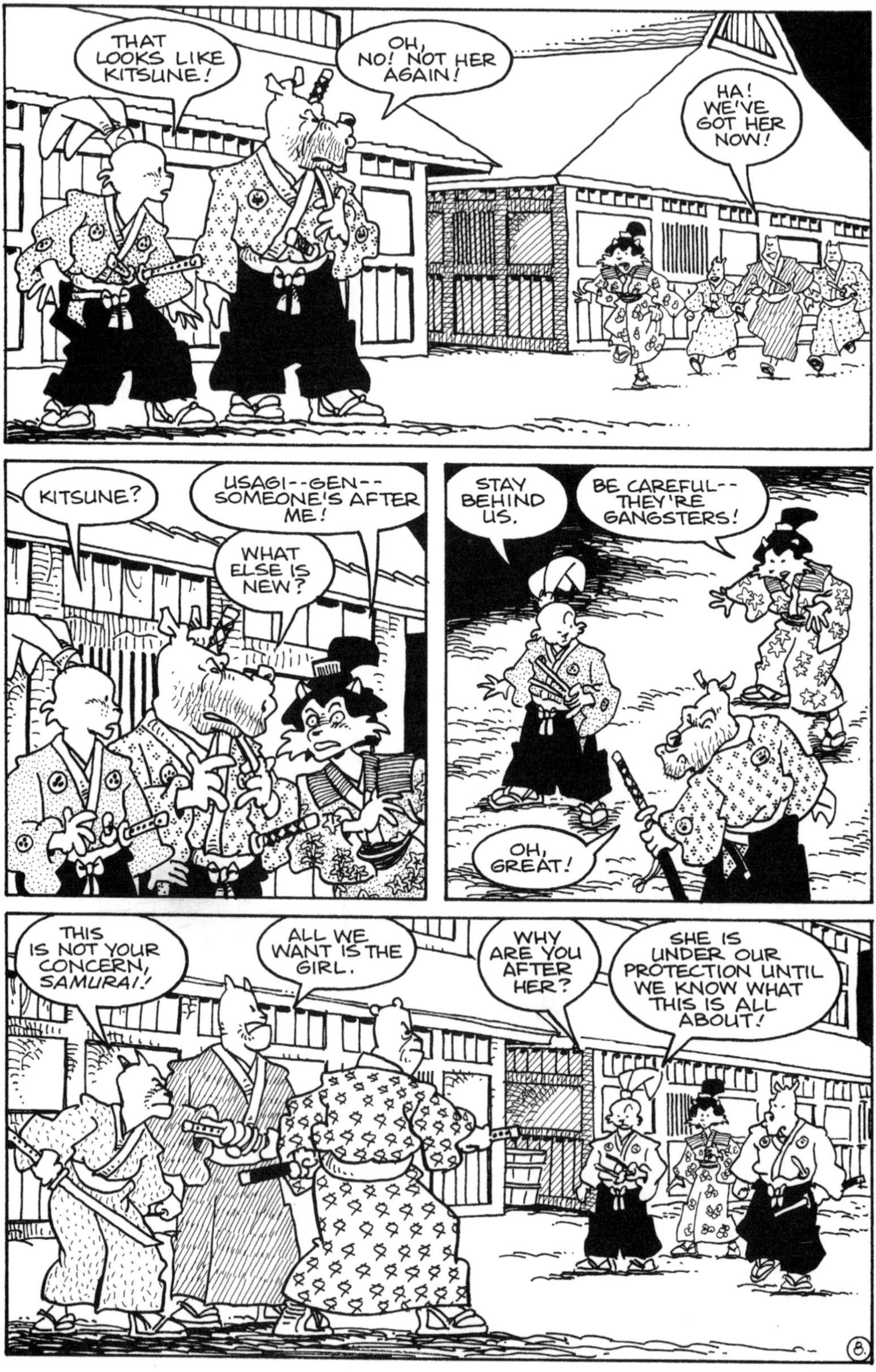
THAT LOOKS LIKE KITSUNE!
OH, NO! NOT HER AGAIN!
HA! WE'VE GOT HER NOW!
KITSUNE?
USAGI--GEN--SOMEONE'S AFTER ME!
WHAT ELSE IS NEW?
STAY BEHIND US.
BE CAREFUL--THEY'RE GANGSTERS!
OH, GREAT!
THIS IS NOT YOUR CONCERN, SAMURAI!
ALL WE WANT IS THE GIRL.
WHY ARE YOU AFTER HER?
SHE IS UNDER OUR PROTECTION UNTIL WE KNOW WHAT THIS IS ALL ABOUT!
8.

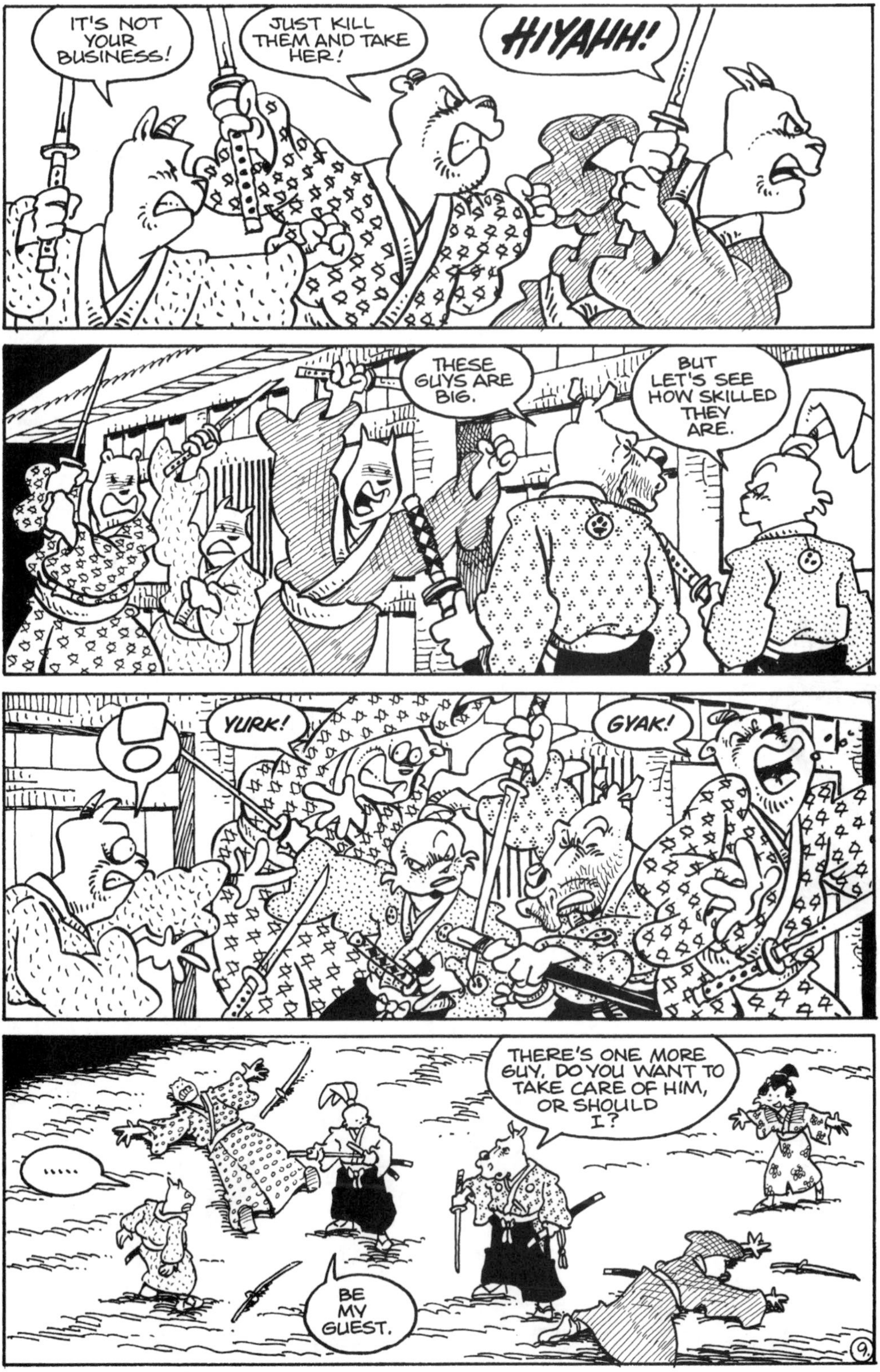
IT'S NOT YOUR BUSINESS!
JUST KILL THEM AND TAKE HER!
HIYAHH!
THESE GUYS ARE BIG.
BUT LET'S SEE HOW SKILLED THEY ARE.
YURK!
GYAK!
THERE'S ONE MORE GUY, DO YOU WANT TO TAKE CARE OF HIM, OR SHOULD I?
.....
BE MY GUEST.
9.

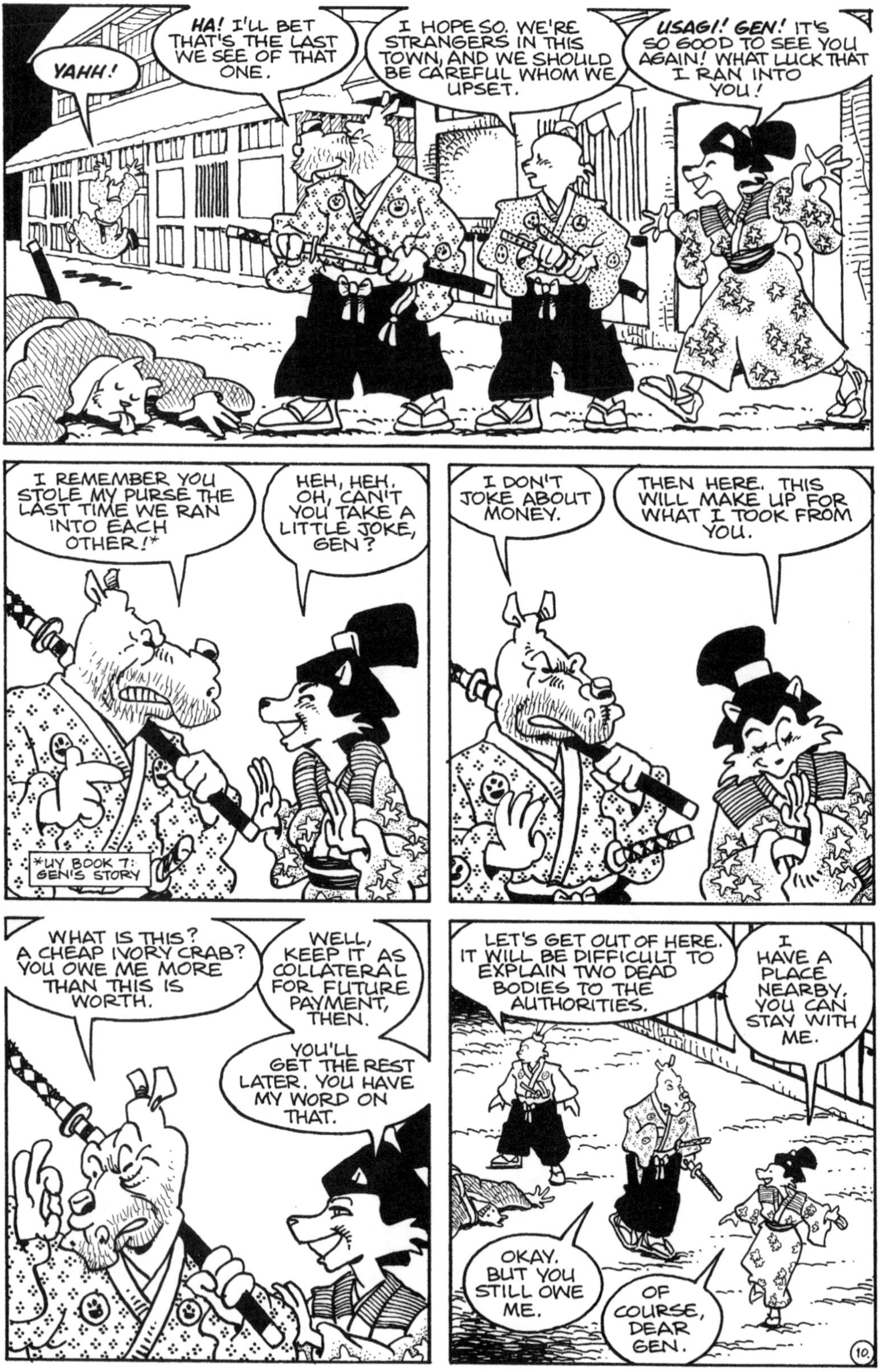
YAHH!
HA! I'LL BET THAT'S THE LAST WE SEE OF THAT ONE.
I HOPE SO. WE'RE STRANGERS IN THIS TOWN, AND WE SHOULD BE CAREFUL WHOM WE UPSET.
USAGI! GEN! IT'S SO GOOD TO SEE YOU AGAIN! WHAT LUCK THAT I RAN INTO YOU!
I REMEMBER YOU STOLE MY PURSE THE LAST TIME WE RAN INTO EACH OTHER!*
HEH, HEH. OH, CAN'T YOU TAKE A LITTLE JOKE, GEN?
*UY BOOK 7: GEN'S STORY
I DON'T JOKE ABOUT MONEY.
THEN HERE. THIS WILL MAKE UP FOR WHAT I TOOK FROM YOU.
WHAT IS THIS? A CHEAP IVORY CRAB? YOU OWE ME MORE THAN THIS IS WORTH.
WELL, KEEP IT AS COLLATERAL FOR FUTURE PAYMENT, THEN.
YOU'LL GET THE REST LATER. YOU HAVE MY WORD ON THAT.
LET'S GET OUT OF HERE. IT WILL BE DIFFICULT TO EXPLAIN TWO DEAD BODIES TO THE AUTHORITIES.
I HAVE A PLACE NEARBY. YOU CAN STAY WITH ME.
OKAY. BUT YOU STILL OWE ME.
OF COURSE, DEAR GEN.
10.

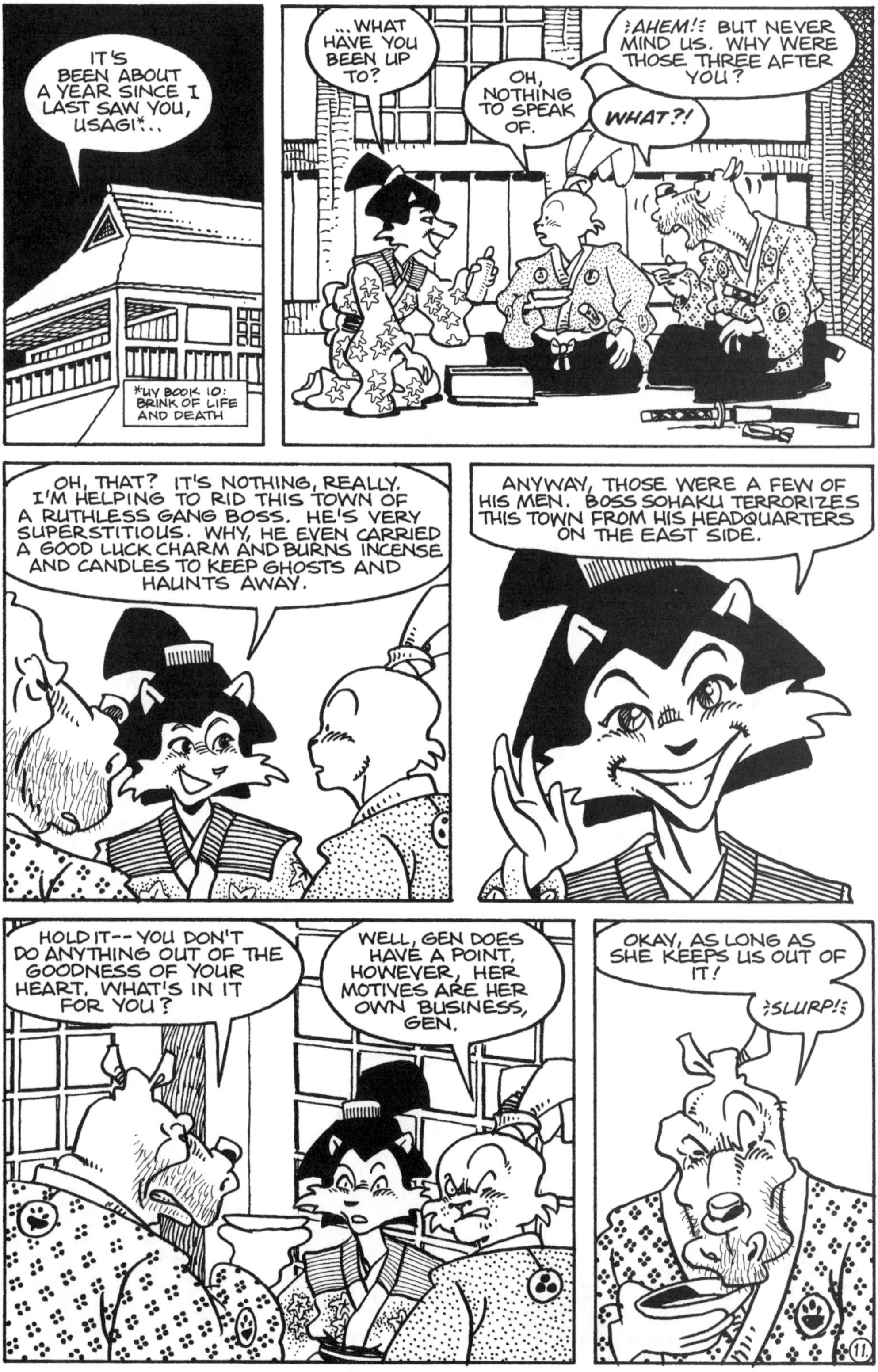

IT'S BEEN ABOUT A YEAR SINCE I LAST SAW YOU, USAGI*...
*UY BOOK 10: BRINK OF LIFE AND DEATH
...WHAT HAVE YOU BEEN UP TO?
OH, NOTHING TO SPEAK OF.
AHEM! BUT NEVER MIND US. WHY WERE THOSE THREE AFTER YOU?
WHAT?!
OH, THAT? IT'S NOTHING, REALLY. I'M HELPING TO RID THIS TOWN OF A RUTHLESS GANG BOSS. HE'S VERY SUPERSTITIOUS. WHY, HE EVEN CARRIED A GOOD LUCK CHARM AND BURNS INCENSE AND CANDLES TO KEEP GHOSTS AND HAUNTS AWAY.
ANYWAY, THOSE WERE A FEW OF HIS MEN. BOSS SOHAKU TERRORIZES THIS TOWN FROM HIS HEADQUARTERS ON THE EAST SIDE.
HOLD IT-- YOU DON'T DO ANYTHING OUT OF THE GOODNESS OF YOUR HEART. WHAT'S IN IT FOR YOU?
WELL, GEN DOES HAVE A POINT. HOWEVER, HER MOTIVES ARE HER OWN BUSINESS, GEN.
OKAY, AS LONG AS SHE KEEPS US OUT OF IT!
SLURP!
11

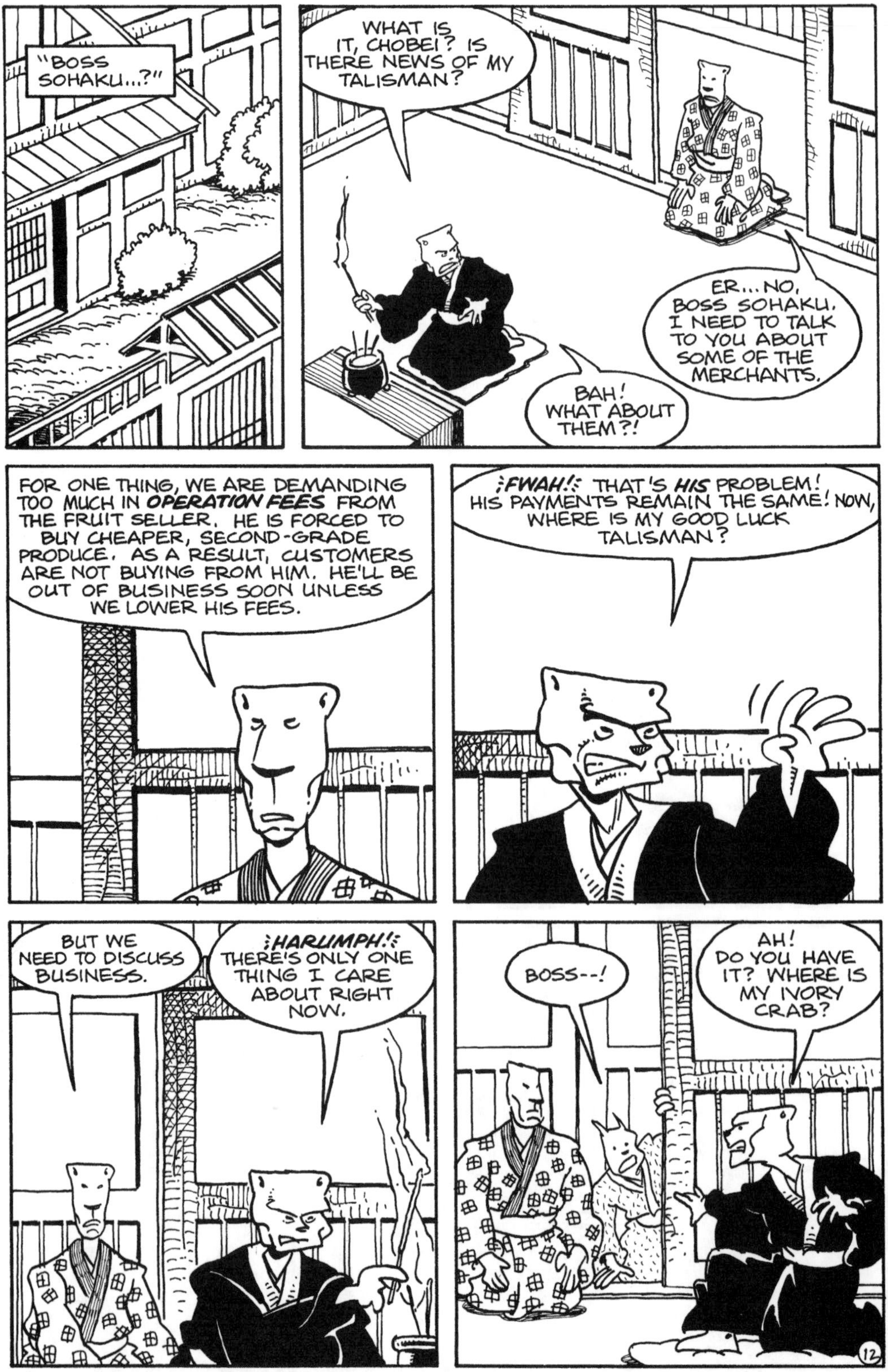
"BOSS SOHAKU...?"
WHAT IS IT, CHOBEI? IS THERE NEWS OF MY TALISMAN?
ER...NO, BOSS SOHAKU. I NEED TO TALK TO YOU ABOUT SOME OF THE MERCHANTS.
BAH! WHAT ABOUT THEM?!
FOR ONE THING, WE ARE DEMANDING TOO MUCH IN OPERATION FEES FROM THE FRUIT SELLER. HE IS FORCED TO BUY CHEAPER, SECOND-GRADE PRODUCE. AS A RESULT, CUSTOMERS ARE NOT BUYING FROM HIM. HE'LL BE OUT OF BUSINESS SOON UNLESS WE LOWER HIS FEES.
FWAH! THAT'S HIS PROBLEM! HIS PAYMENTS REMAIN THE SAME! NOW, WHERE IS MY GOOD LUCK TALISMAN?
BUT WE NEED TO DISCUSS BUSINESS.
HARUMPH! THERE'S ONLY ONE THING I CARE ABOUT RIGHT NOW.
BOSS--!
AH! DO YOU HAVE IT? WHERE IS MY IVORY CRAB?
12

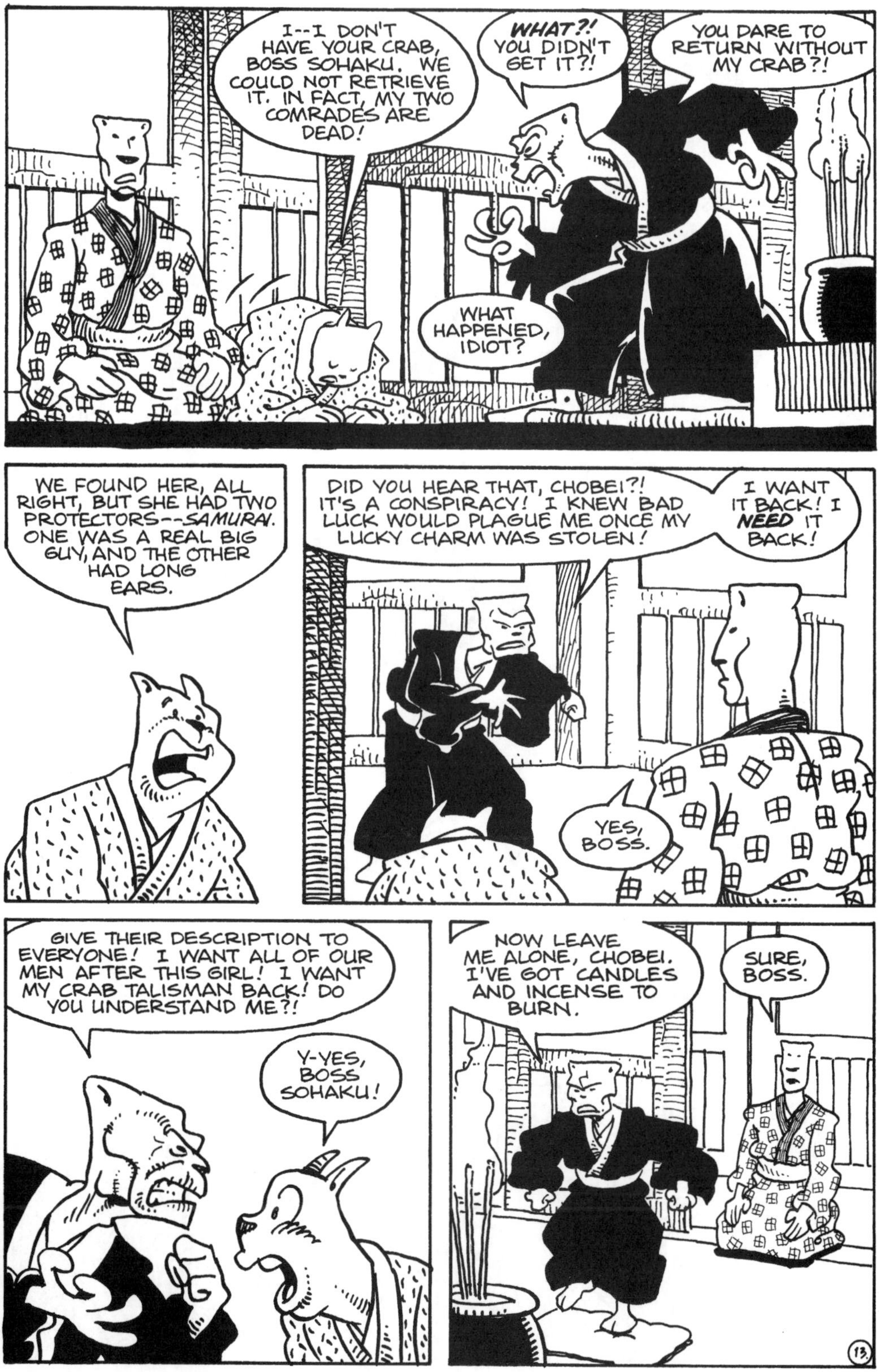
I--I DON'T HAVE YOUR CRAB, BOSS SOHAKU. WE COULD NOT RETRIEVE IT. IN FACT, MY TWO COMRADES ARE DEAD!
WHAT?! YOU DIDN'T GET IT?!
YOU DARE TO RETURN WITHOUT MY CRAB?!
WHAT HAPPENED, IDIOT?
WE FOUND HER, ALL RIGHT, BUT SHE HAD TWO PROTECTORS--SAMURAI. ONE WAS A REAL BIG GUY, AND THE OTHER HAD LONG EARS.
DID YOU HEAR THAT, CHOBEI?! IT'S A CONSPIRACY! I KNEW BAD LUCK WOULD PLAGUE ME ONCE MY LUCKY CHARM WAS STOLEN!
I WANT IT BACK! I NEED IT BACK!
YES, BOSS.
GIVE THEIR DESCRIPTION TO EVERYONE! I WANT ALL OF OUR MEN AFTER THIS GIRL! I WANT MY CRAB TALISMAN BACK! DO YOU UNDERSTAND ME?!
Y-YES, BOSS SOHAKU!
NOW LEAVE ME ALONE, CHOBEI. I'VE GOT CANDLES AND INCENSE TO BURN.
SURE, BOSS.
13

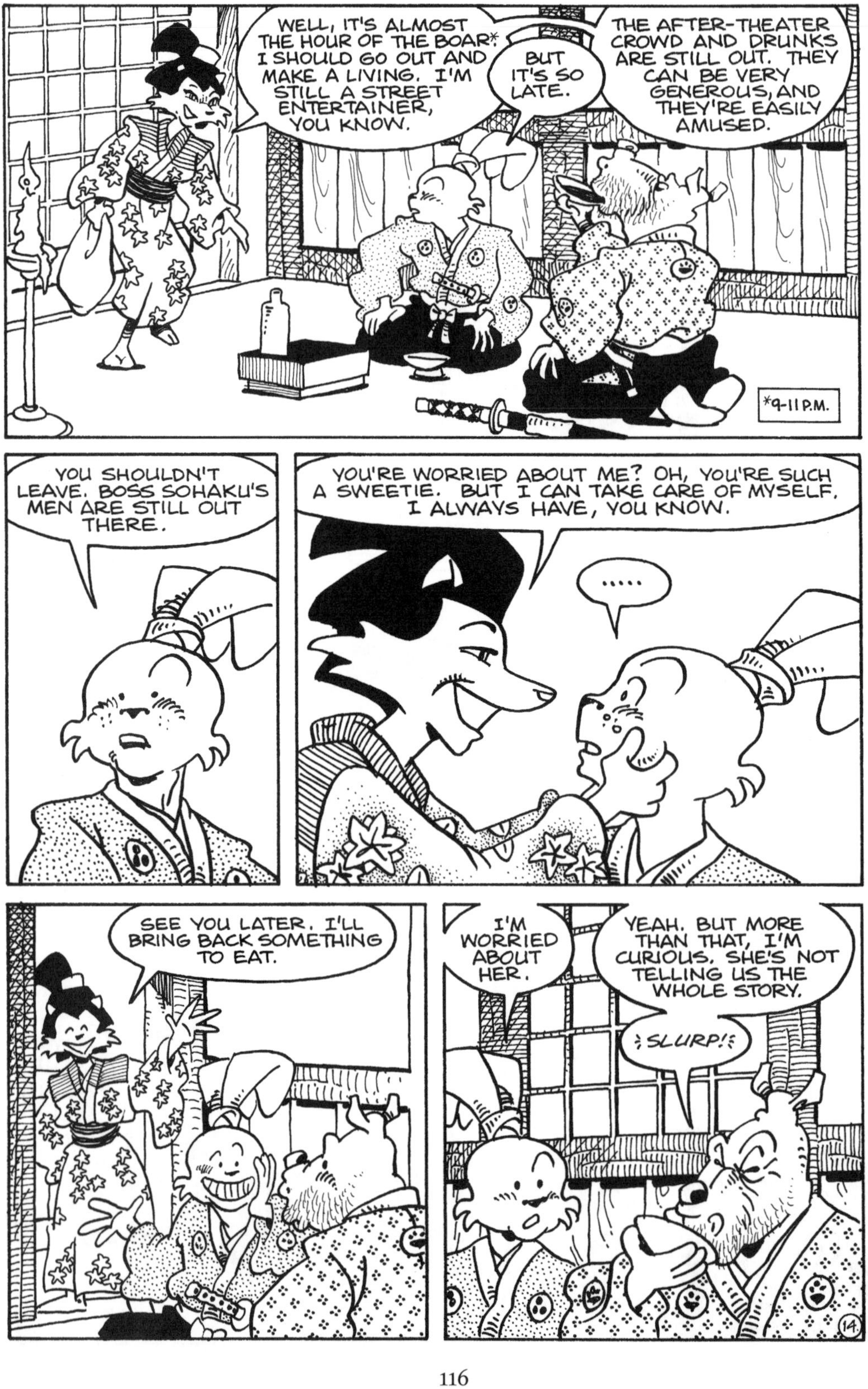
WELL, IT'S ALMOST THE HOUR OF THE BOAR* I SHOULD GO OUT AND MAKE A LIVING. I'M STILL A STREET ENTERTAINER, YOU KNOW.
BUT IT'S SO LATE.
THE AFTER-THEATER CROWD AND DRUNKS ARE STILL OUT. THEY CAN BE VERY GENEROUS, AND THEY'RE EASILY AMUSED.
*9-11 P.M.
YOU SHOULDN'T LEAVE. BOSS SOHAKU'S MEN ARE STILL OUT THERE.
YOU'RE WORRIED ABOUT ME? OH, YOU'RE SUCH A SWEETIE. BUT I CAN TAKE CARE OF MYSELF. I ALWAYS HAVE, YOU KNOW.
.....
SEE YOU LATER. I'LL BRING BACK SOMETHING TO EAT.
I'M WORRIED ABOUT HER.
YEAH. BUT MORE THAN THAT, I'M CURIOUS. SHE'S NOT TELLING US THE WHOLE STORY.
SLURP!
14

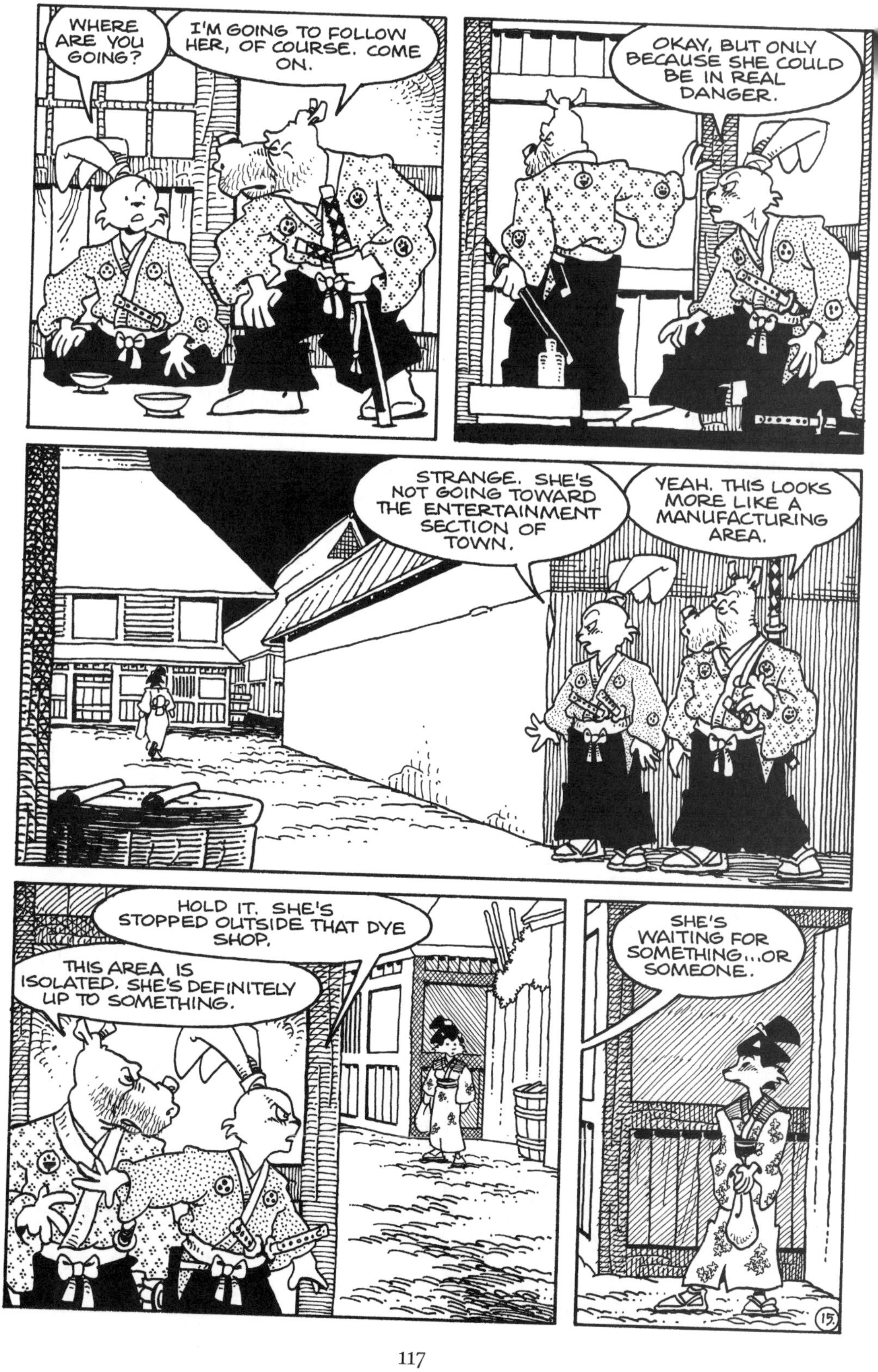
WHERE ARE YOU GOING?
I'M GOING TO FOLLOW HER, OF COURSE. COME ON.
OKAY, BUT ONLY BECAUSE SHE COULD BE IN REAL DANGER.
STRANGE. SHE'S NOT GOING TOWARD THE ENTERTAINMENT SECTION OF TOWN.
YEAH. THIS LOOKS MORE LIKE A MANUFACTURING AREA.
HOLD IT. SHE'S STOPPED OUTSIDE THAT DYE SHOP.
THIS AREA IS ISOLATED. SHE'S DEFINITELY UP TO SOMETHING.
SHE'S WAITING FOR SOMETHING...OR SOMEONE.
15

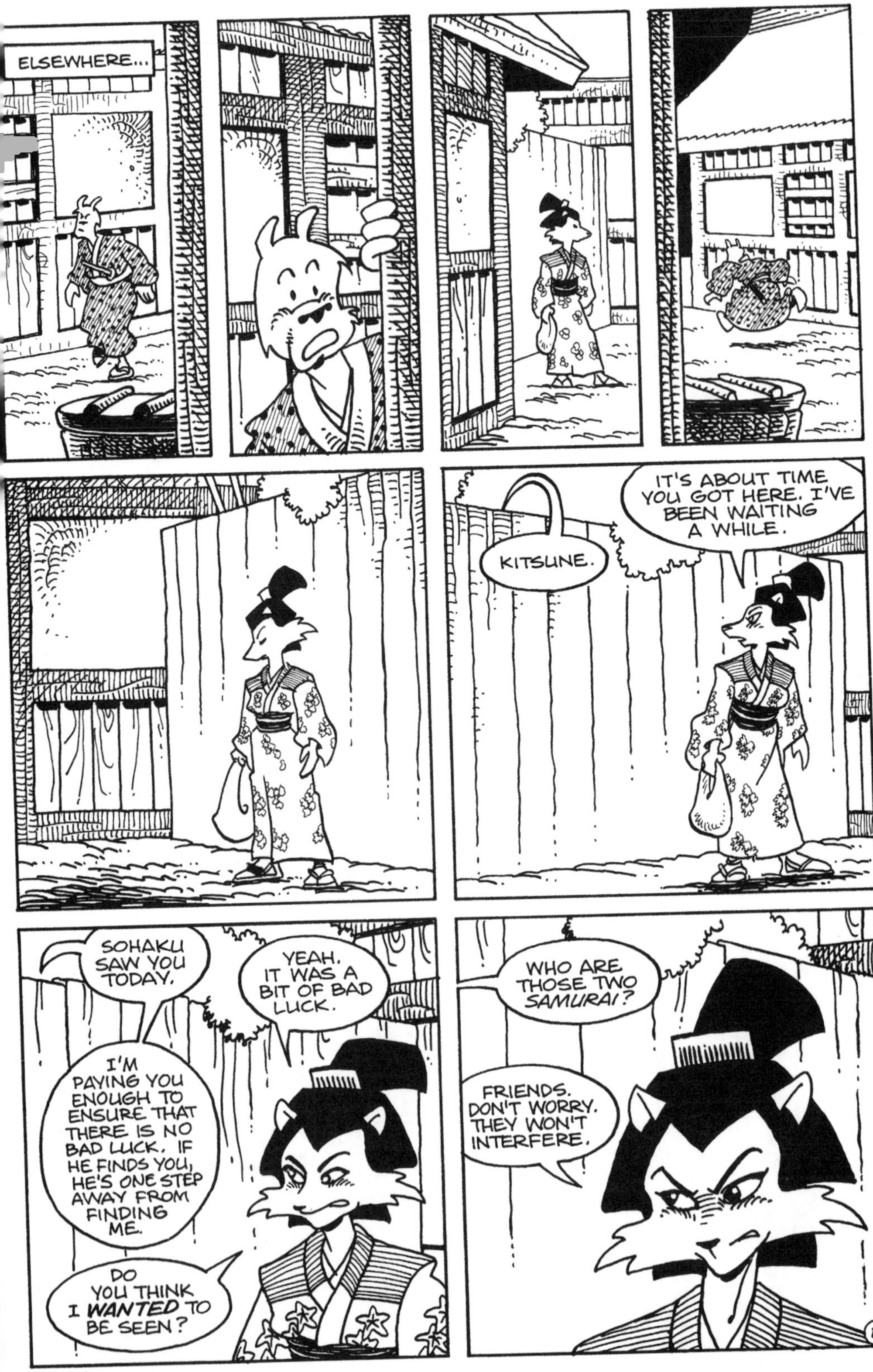

ELSEWHERE...
KITSUNE.
IT'S ABOUT TIME YOU GOT HERE. I'VE BEEN WAITING A WHILE.
SOHAKU SAW YOU TODAY.
YEAH. IT WAS A BIT OF BAD LUCK.
I'M PAYING YOU ENOUGH TO ENSURE THAT THERE IS NO BAD LUCK. IF HE FINDS YOU, HE'S ONE STEP AWAY FROM FINDING ME.
DO YOU THINK I WANTED TO BE SEEN?
WHO ARE THOSE TWO SAMURAI?
FRIENDS. DON'T WORRY. THEY WON'T INTERFERE.
16

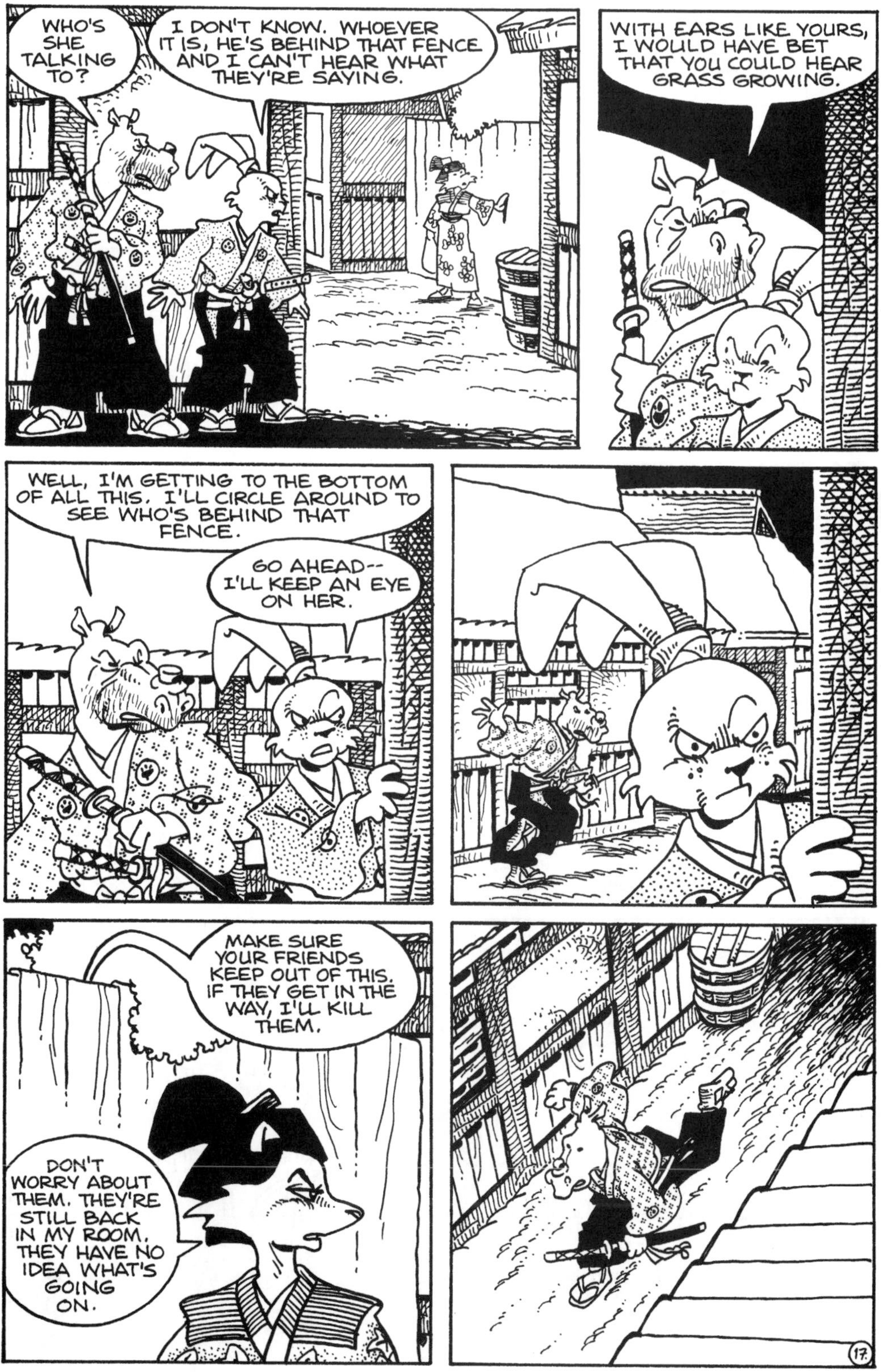
WHO'S SHE TALKING TO?
I DON'T KNOW. WHOEVER IT IS, HE'S BEHIND THAT FENCE AND I CAN'T HEAR WHAT THEY'RE SAYING.
WITH EARS LIKE YOURS, I WOULD HAVE BET THAT YOU COULD HEAR GRASS GROWING.
WELL, I'M GETTING TO THE BOTTOM OF ALL THIS. I'LL CIRCLE AROUND TO SEE WHO'S BEHIND THAT FENCE.
GO AHEAD-- I'LL KEEP AN EYE ON HER.
MAKE SURE YOUR FRIENDS KEEP OUT OF THIS. IF THEY GET IN THE WAY, I'LL KILL THEM.
DON'T WORRY ABOUT THEM. THEY'RE STILL BACK IN MY ROOM. THEY HAVE NO IDEA WHAT'S GOING ON.
17

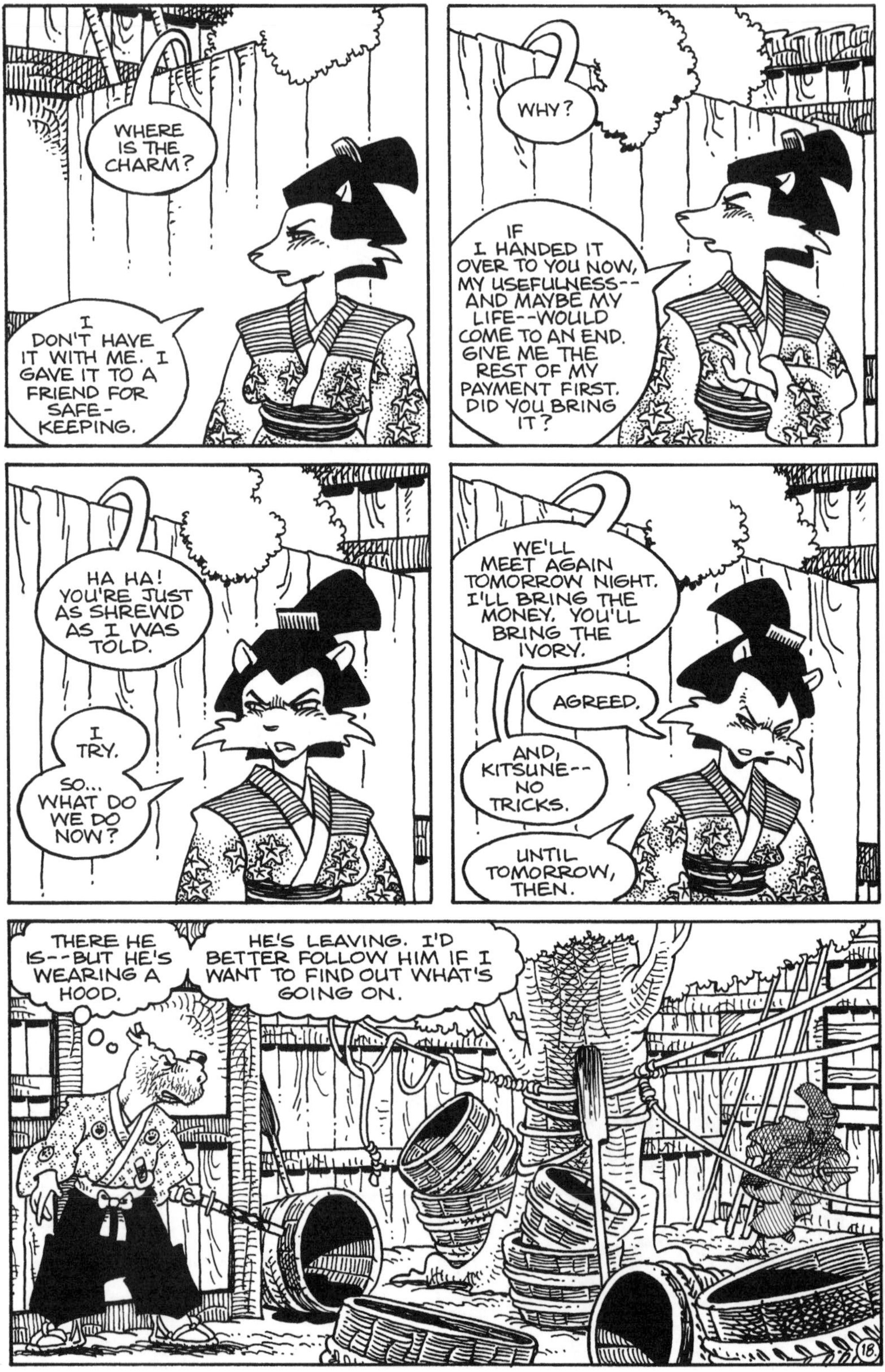
WHERE IS THE CHARM?
I DON'T HAVE IT WITH ME. I GAVE IT TO A FRIEND FOR SAFE-KEEPING.
WHY?
IF I HANDED IT OVER TO YOU NOW, MY USEFULNESS--AND MAYBE MY LIFE--WOULD COME TO AN END. GIVE ME THE REST OF MY PAYMENT FIRST. DID YOU BRING IT?
HA HA! YOU'RE JUST AS SHREWD AS I WAS TOLD.
I TRY.
SO... WHAT DO WE DO NOW?
WE'LL MEET AGAIN TOMORROW NIGHT. I'LL BRING THE MONEY. YOU'LL BRING THE IVORY.
AGREED.
AND, KITSUNE--NO TRICKS.
UNTIL TOMORROW, THEN.
THERE HE IS--BUT HE'S WEARING A HOOD.
HE'S LEAVING. I'D BETTER FOLLOW HIM IF I WANT TO FIND OUT WHAT'S GOING ON.
18.

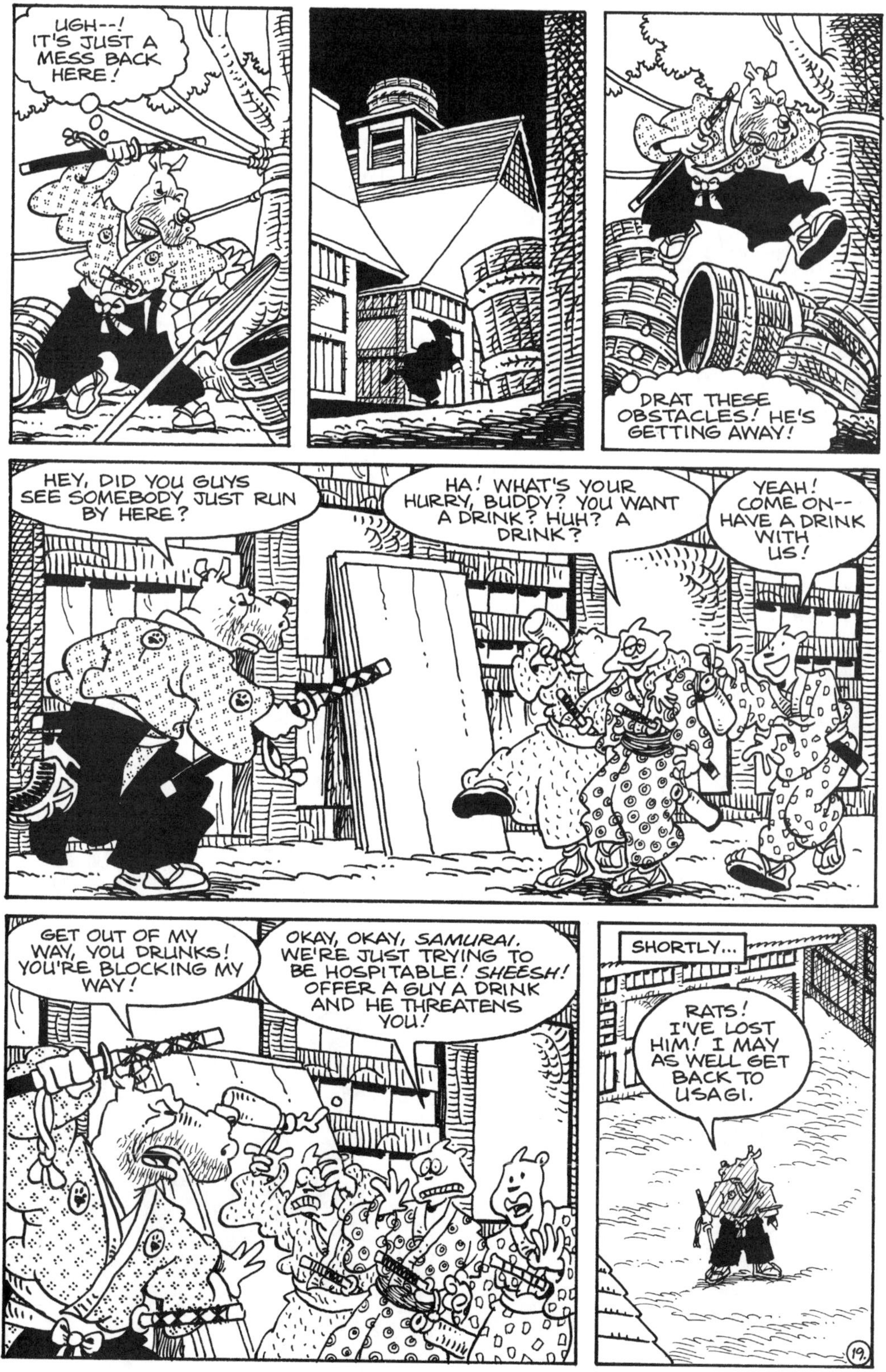
UGH--! IT'S JUST A MESS BACK HERE!
DRAT THESE OBSTACLES! HE'S GETTING AWAY!
HEY, DID YOU GUYS SEE SOMEBODY JUST RUN BY HERE?
HA! WHAT'S YOUR HURRY, BUDDY? YOU WANT A DRINK? HUH? A DRINK?
YEAH! COME ON-- HAVE A DRINK WITH US!
GET OUT OF MY WAY, YOU DRUNKS! YOU'RE BLOCKING MY WAY!
OKAY, OKAY, *SAMURAI*. WE'RE JUST TRYING TO BE HOSPITABLE! *SHEESH!* OFFER A GUY A DRINK AND HE THREATENS YOU!
SHORTLY...
RATS! I'VE LOST HIM! I MAY AS WELL GET BACK TO USAGI.
19.

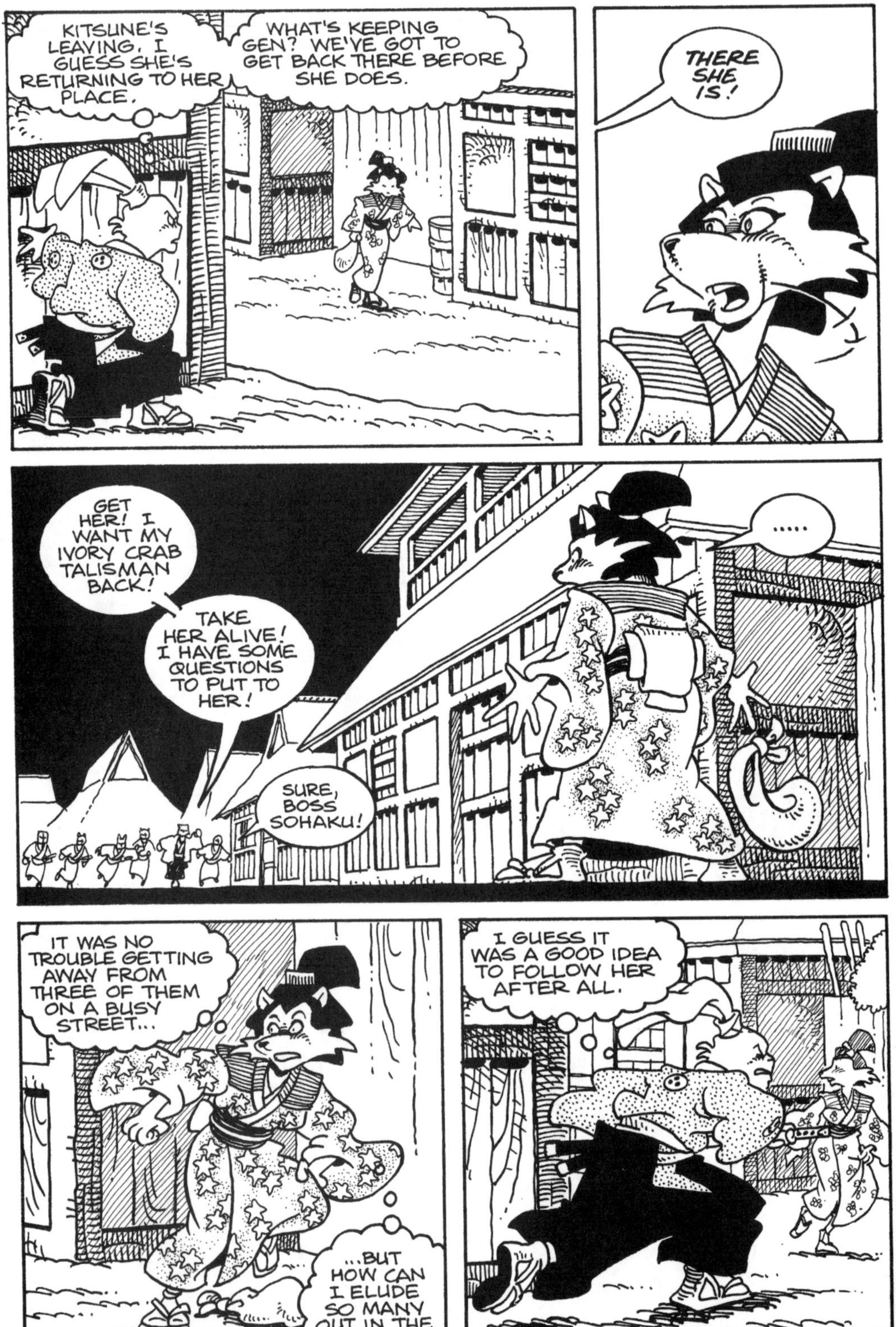
KITSUNE'S LEAVING. I GUESS SHE'S RETURNING TO HER PLACE.
WHAT'S KEEPING GEN? WE'VE GOT TO GET BACK THERE BEFORE SHE DOES.
THERE SHE IS!
GET HER! I WANT MY IVORY CRAB TALISMAN BACK!
TAKE HER ALIVE! I HAVE SOME QUESTIONS TO PUT TO HER!
SURE, BOSS SOHAKU!
.....
IT WAS NO TROUBLE GETTING AWAY FROM THREE OF THEM ON A BUSY STREET...
...BUT HOW CAN I ELUDE SO MANY OUT IN THE OPEN?
I GUESS IT WAS A GOOD IDEA TO FOLLOW HER AFTER ALL.
20.

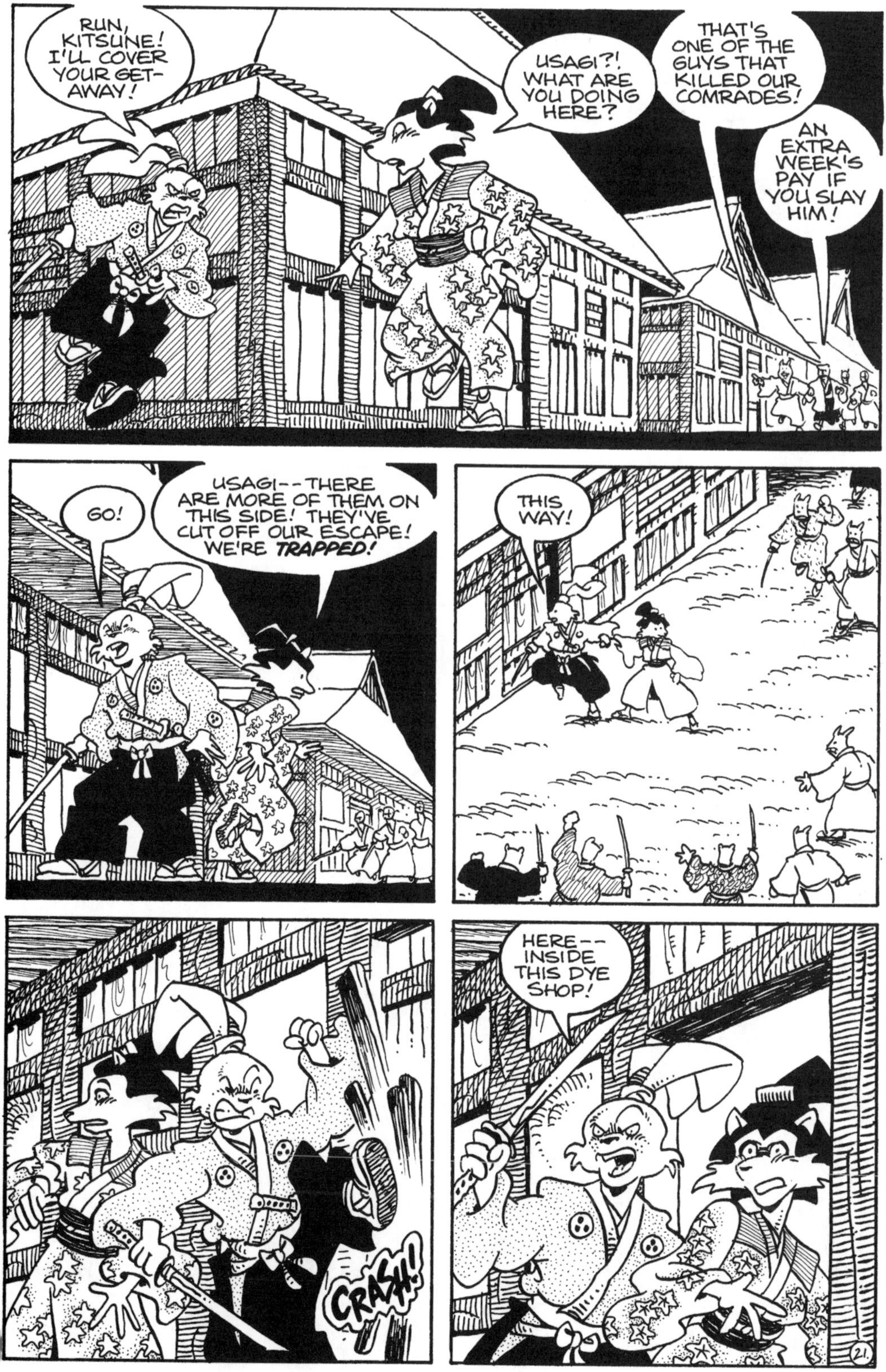
RUN, KITSUNE! I'LL COVER YOUR GET-AWAY!
USAGI?! WHAT ARE YOU DOING HERE?
THAT'S ONE OF THE GUYS THAT KILLED OUR COMRADES!
AN EXTRA WEEK'S PAY IF YOU SLAY HIM!
GO!
USAGI--THERE ARE MORE OF THEM ON THIS SIDE! THEY'VE CUT OFF OUR ESCAPE! WE'RE TRAPPED!
THIS WAY!
CRASH!
HERE--INSIDE THIS DYE SHOP!
21.

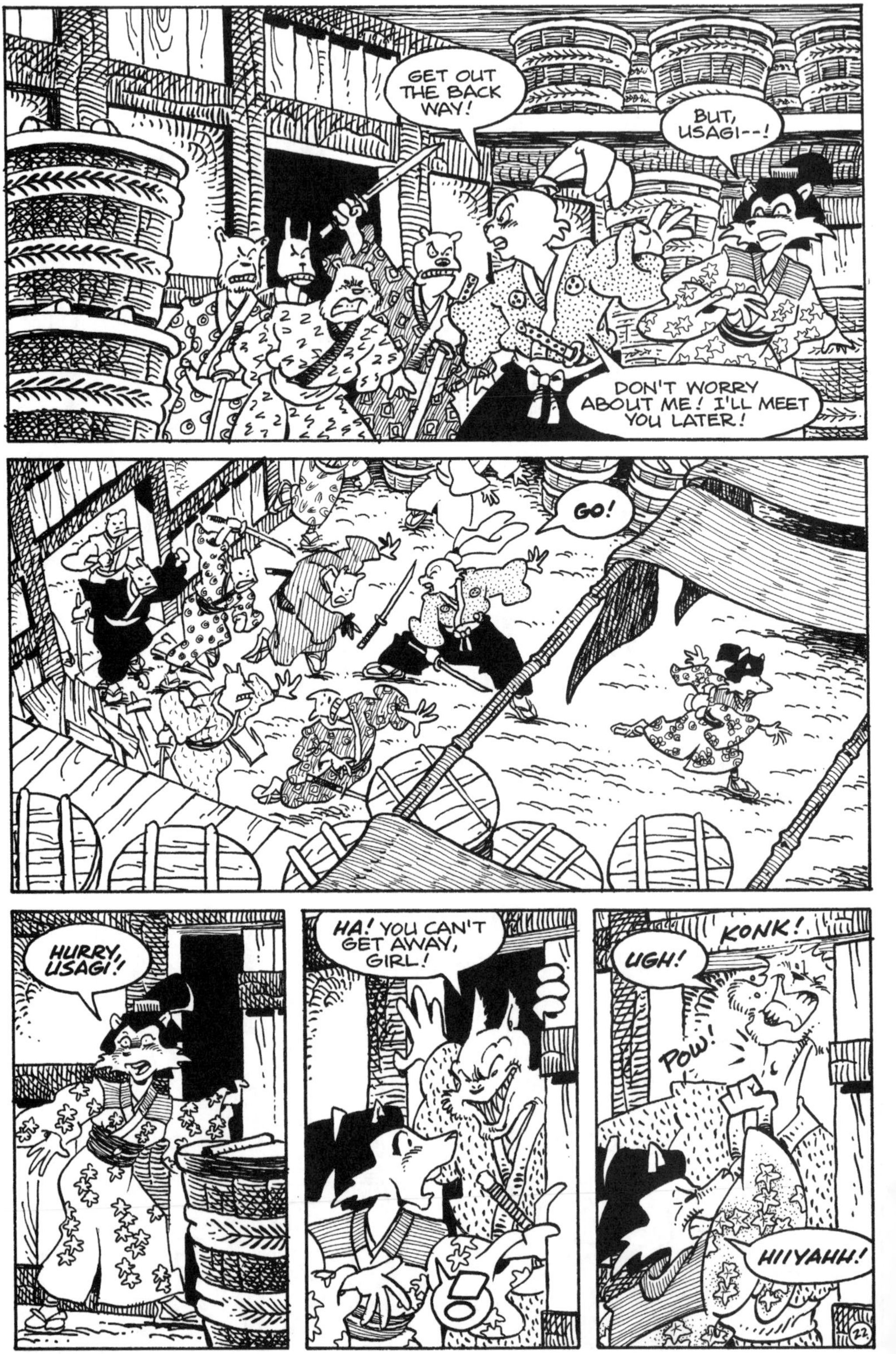
GET OUT THE BACK WAY!
BUT, USAGI--!
DON'T WORRY ABOUT ME! I'LL MEET YOU LATER!
GO!
HURRY, USAGI!
HA! YOU CAN'T GET AWAY, GIRL!
KONK!
UGH!
POW!
HIIYAHH!
22

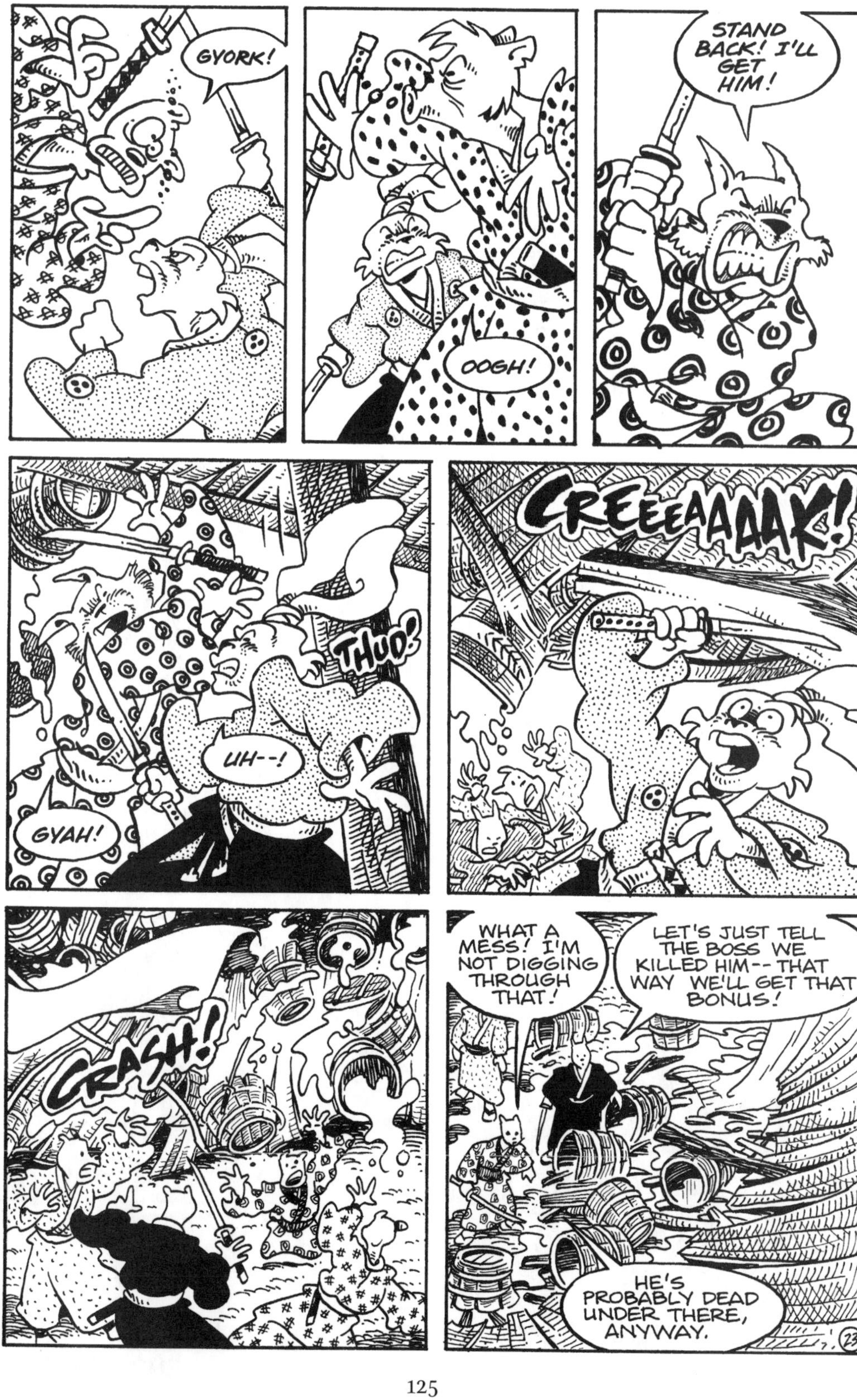
GYORK!
OOGH!
STAND BACK! I'LL GET HIM!
THUD!
UH--!
GYAH!
CREEEEAAAAK!
GRASH!
WHAT A MESS! I'M NOT DIGGING THROUGH THAT!
LET'S JUST TELL THE BOSS WE KILLED HIM-- THAT WAY WE'LL GET THAT BONUS!
HE'S PROBABLY DEAD UNDER THERE, ANYWAY.
23

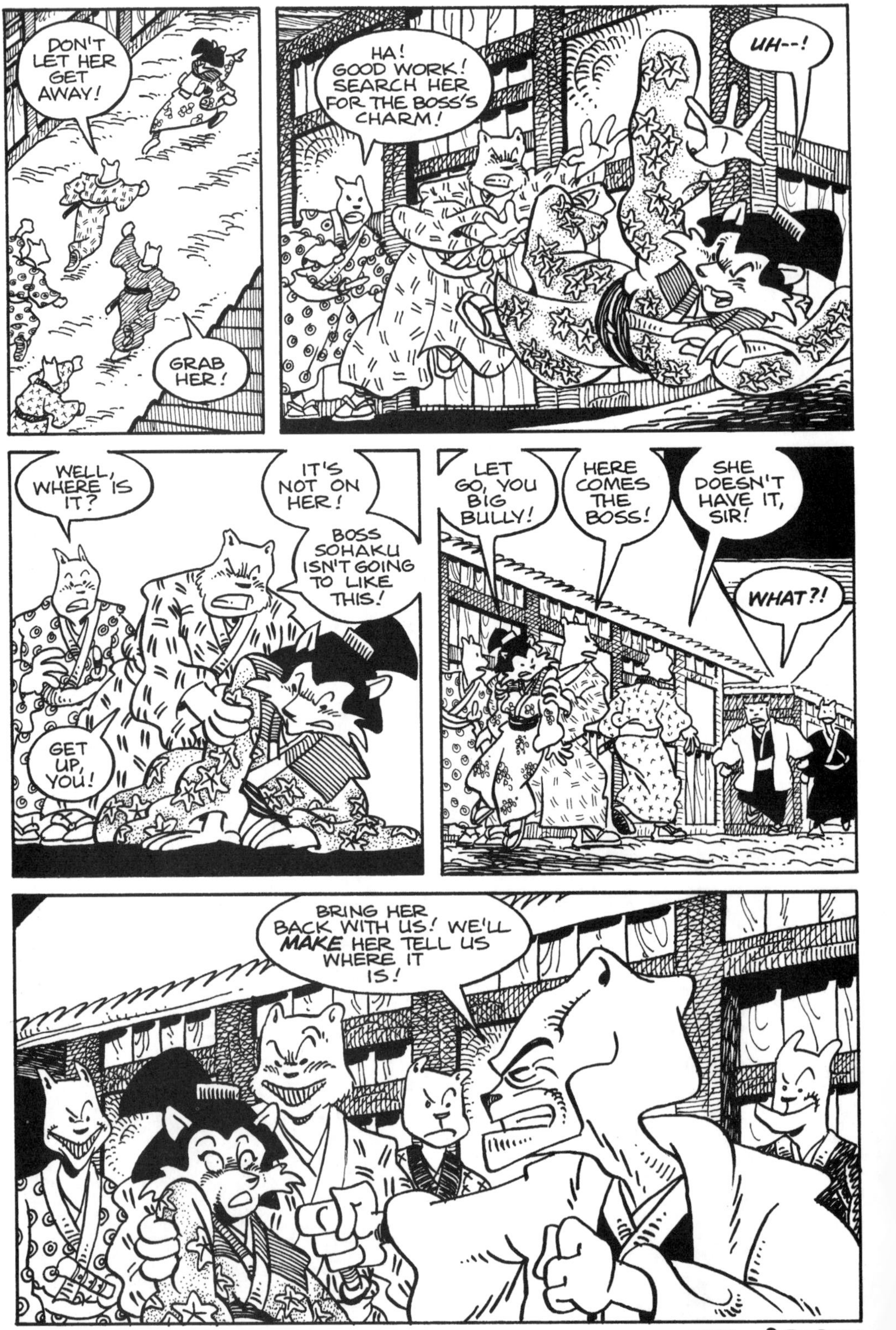
DON'T LET HER GET AWAY!
GRAB HER!
HA! GOOD WORK! SEARCH HER FOR THE BOSS'S CHARM!
UH--!
WELL, WHERE IS IT?
GET UP, YOU!
IT'S NOT ON HER!
BOSS SOHAKU ISN'T GOING TO LIKE THIS!
LET GO, YOU BIG BULLY!
HERE COMES THE BOSS!
SHE DOESN'T HAVE IT, SIR!
WHAT?!
BRING HER BACK WITH US! WE'LL *MAKE* HER TELL US WHERE IT IS!

END of PART 1

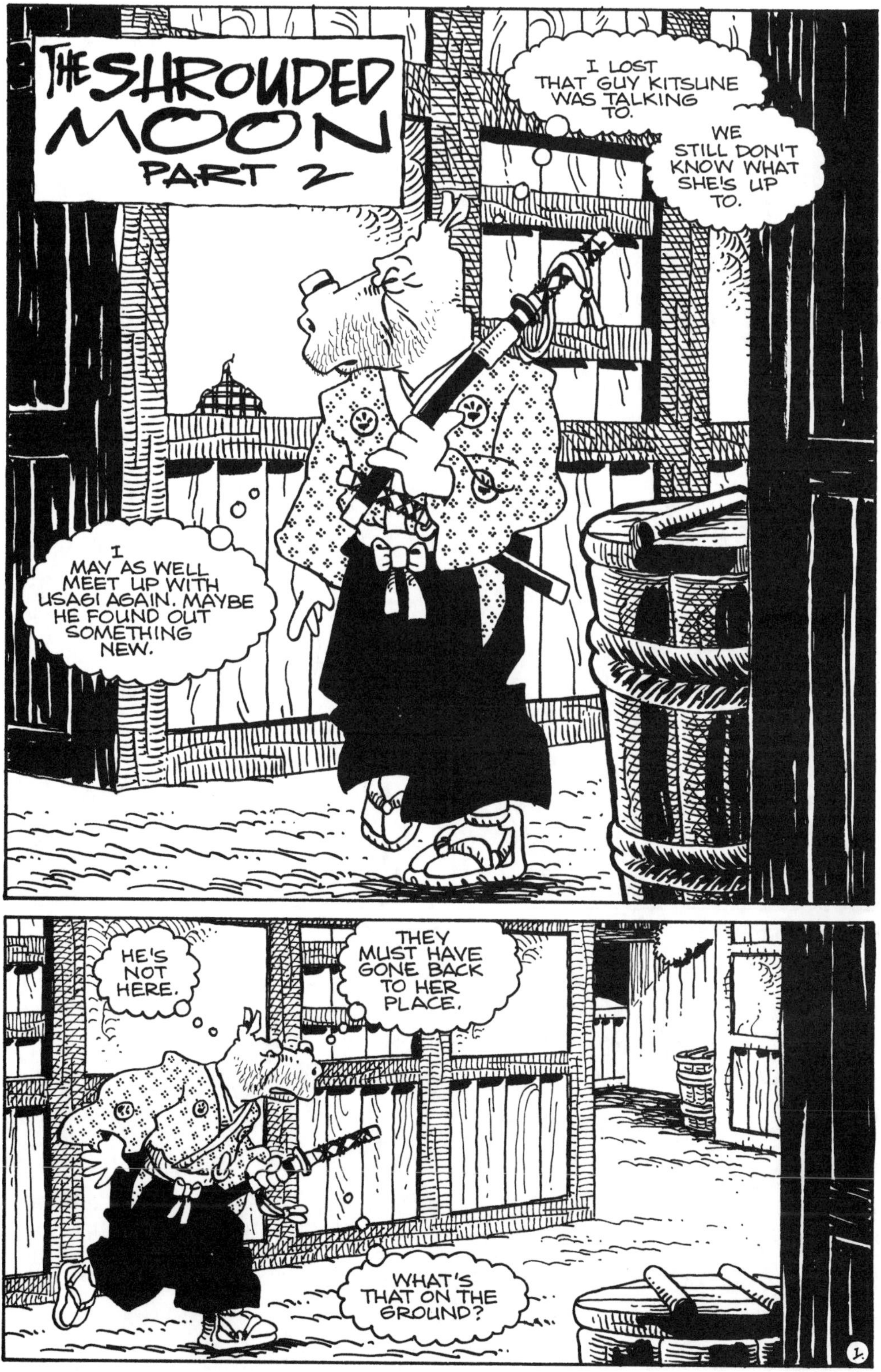
THE SHROUDED MOON
PART 2
I LOST THAT GUY KITSUNE WAS TALKING TO.
WE STILL DON'T KNOW WHAT SHE'S UP TO.
I MAY AS WELL MEET UP WITH USAGI AGAIN. MAYBE HE FOUND OUT SOMETHING NEW.
HE'S NOT HERE.
THEY MUST HAVE GONE BACK TO HER PLACE.
WHAT'S THAT ON THE GROUND?
1.

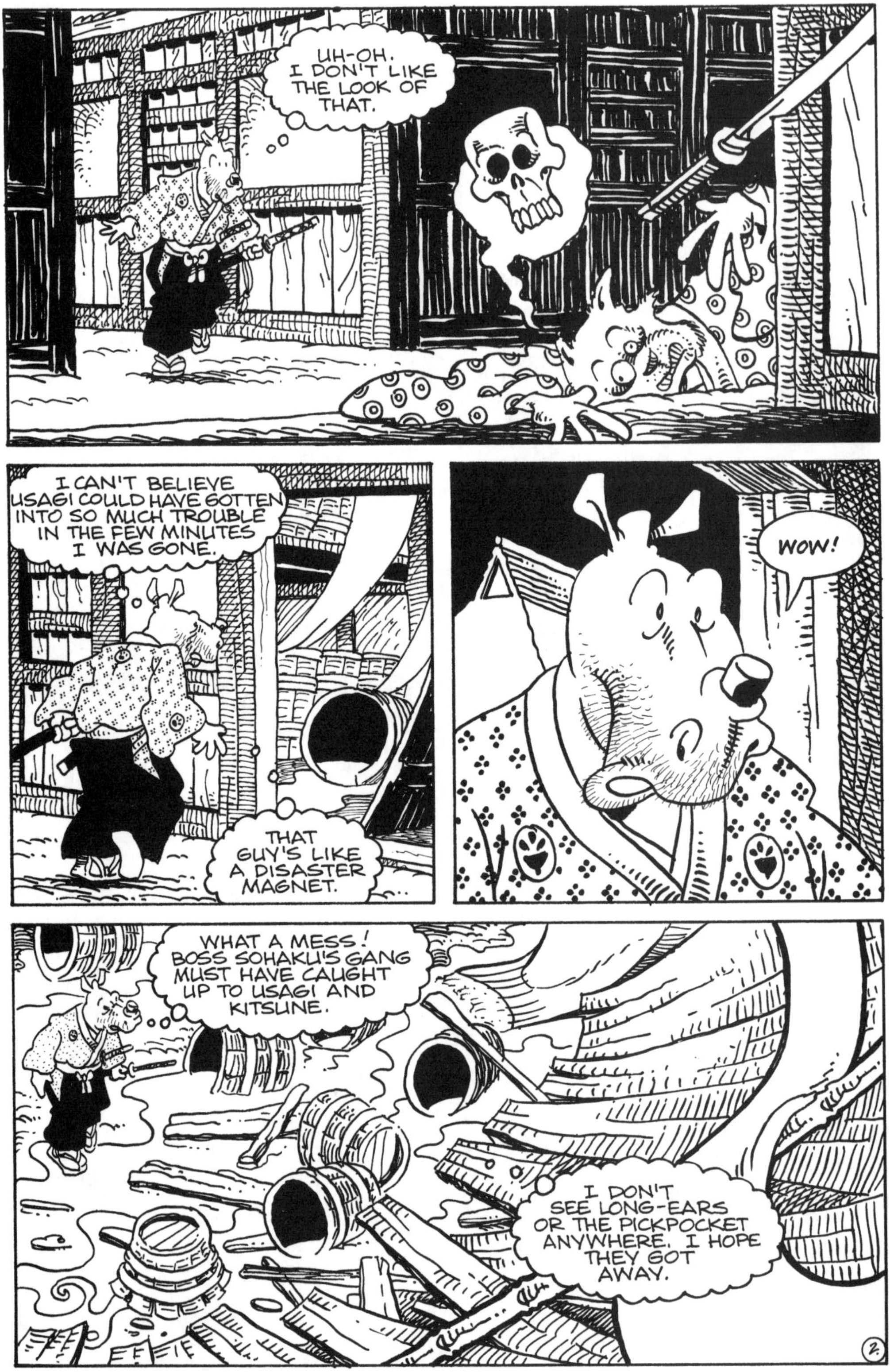
UH-OH. I DON'T LIKE THE LOOK OF THAT.
I CAN'T BELIEVE USAGI COULD HAVE GOTTEN INTO SO MUCH TROUBLE IN THE FEW MINUTES I WAS GONE.
THAT GUY'S LIKE A DISASTER MAGNET.
WOW!
WHAT A MESS! BOSS SOHAKU'S GANG MUST HAVE CAUGHT UP TO USAGI AND KITSUNE.
I DON'T SEE LONG-EARS OR THE PICKPOCKET ANYWHERE. I HOPE THEY GOT AWAY.
2.

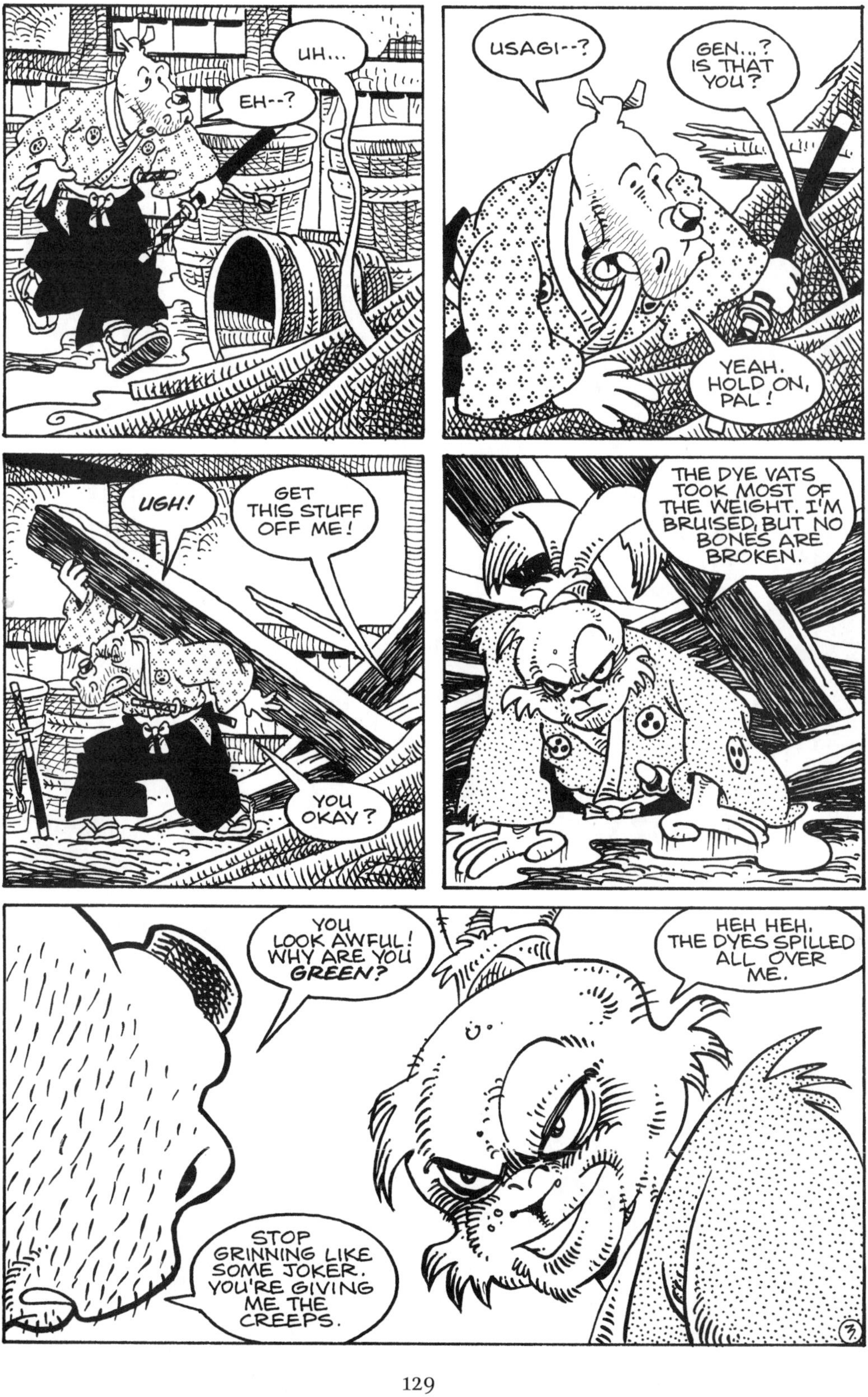
UH...
EH--?
USAGI--?
GEN...? IS THAT YOU?
YEAH. HOLD ON, PAL!
UGH!
GET THIS STUFF OFF ME!
YOU OKAY?
THE DYE VATS TOOK MOST OF THE WEIGHT. I'M BRUISED, BUT NO BONES ARE BROKEN.
YOU LOOK AWFUL! WHY ARE YOU GREEN?
HEH HEH. THE DYES SPILLED ALL OVER ME.
STOP GRINNING LIKE SOME JOKER. YOU'RE GIVING ME THE CREEPS.
3.

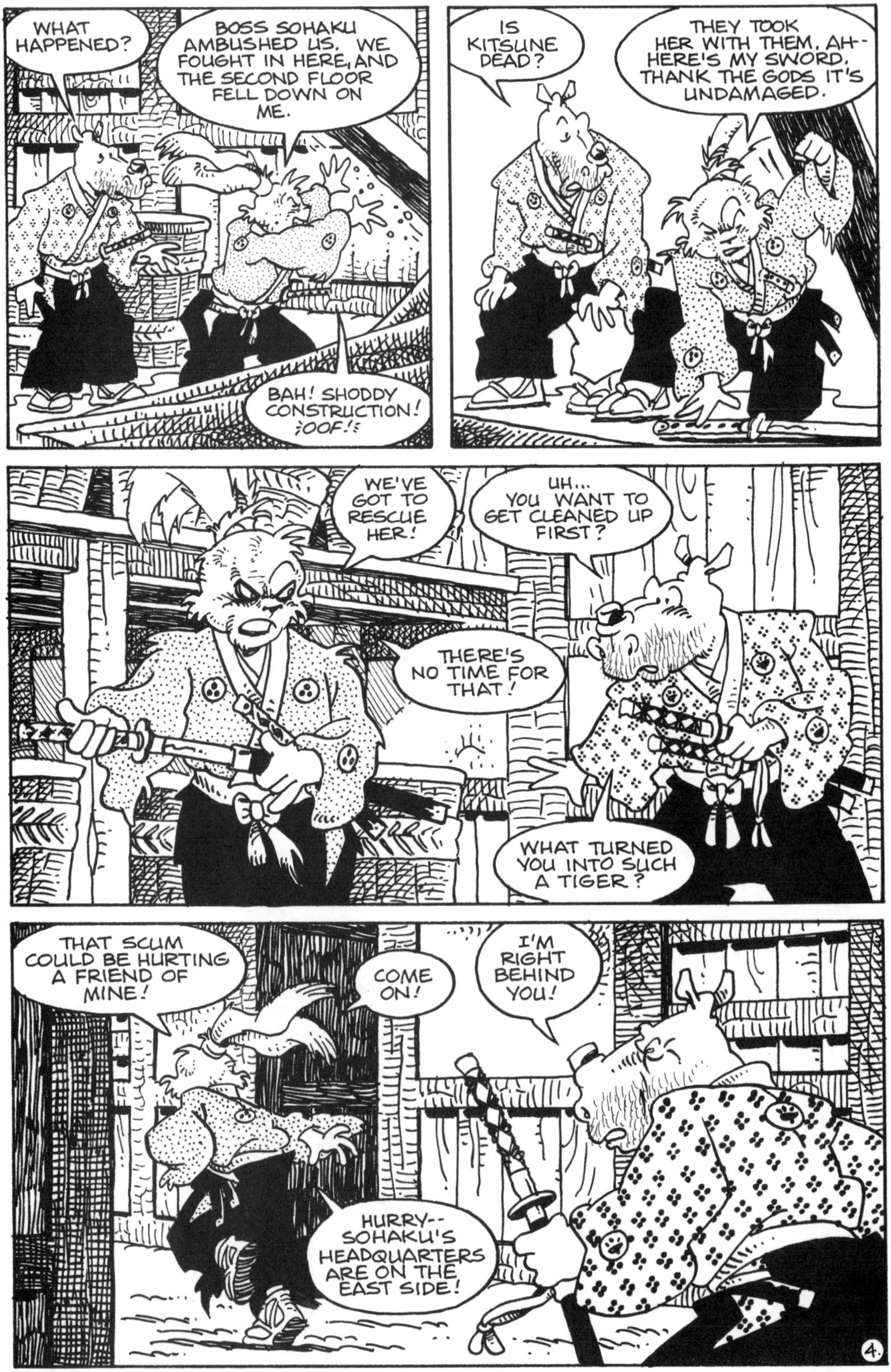
WHAT HAPPENED?
BOSS SOHAKU AMBUSHED US. WE FOUGHT IN HERE, AND THE SECOND FLOOR FELL DOWN ON ME.
BAH! SHODDY CONSTRUCTION! OOF!
IS KITSUNE DEAD?
THEY TOOK HER WITH THEM. AH-- HERE'S MY SWORD. THANK THE GODS IT'S UNDAMAGED.
WE'VE GOT TO RESCUE HER!
UH... YOU WANT TO GET CLEANED UP FIRST?
THERE'S NO TIME FOR THAT!
WHAT TURNED YOU INTO SUCH A TIGER?
THAT SCUM COULD BE HURTING A FRIEND OF MINE!
COME ON!
I'M RIGHT BEHIND YOU!
HURRY-- SOHAKU'S HEADQUARTERS ARE ON THE EAST SIDE!
4.

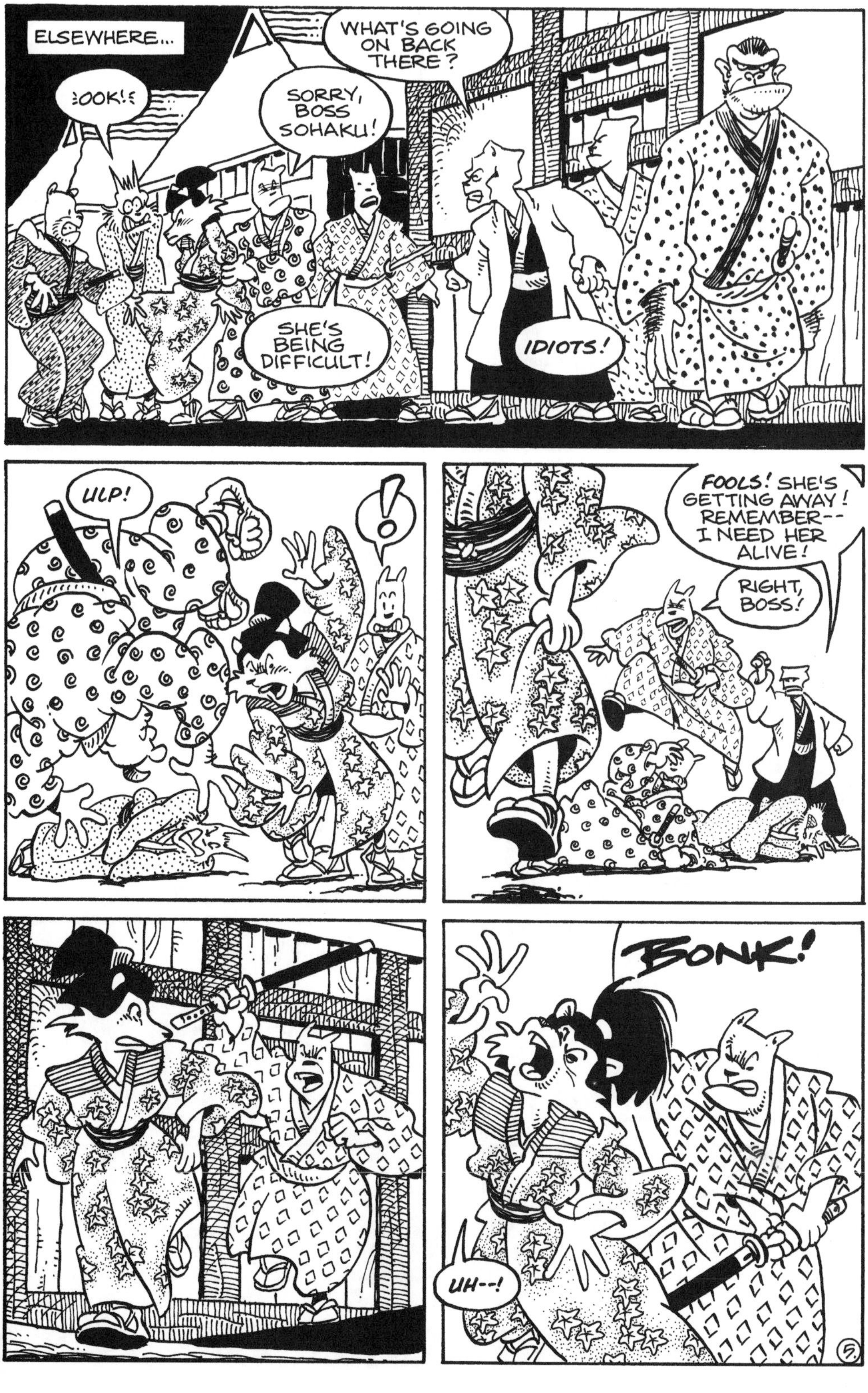
ELSEWHERE...
OOK!
SORRY, BOSS SOHAKU!
WHAT'S GOING ON BACK THERE?
SHE'S BEING DIFFICULT!
IDIOTS!
ULP!
!
FOOLS! SHE'S GETTING AWAY! REMEMBER-- I NEED HER ALIVE!
RIGHT, BOSS!
BONK!
UH--!
5

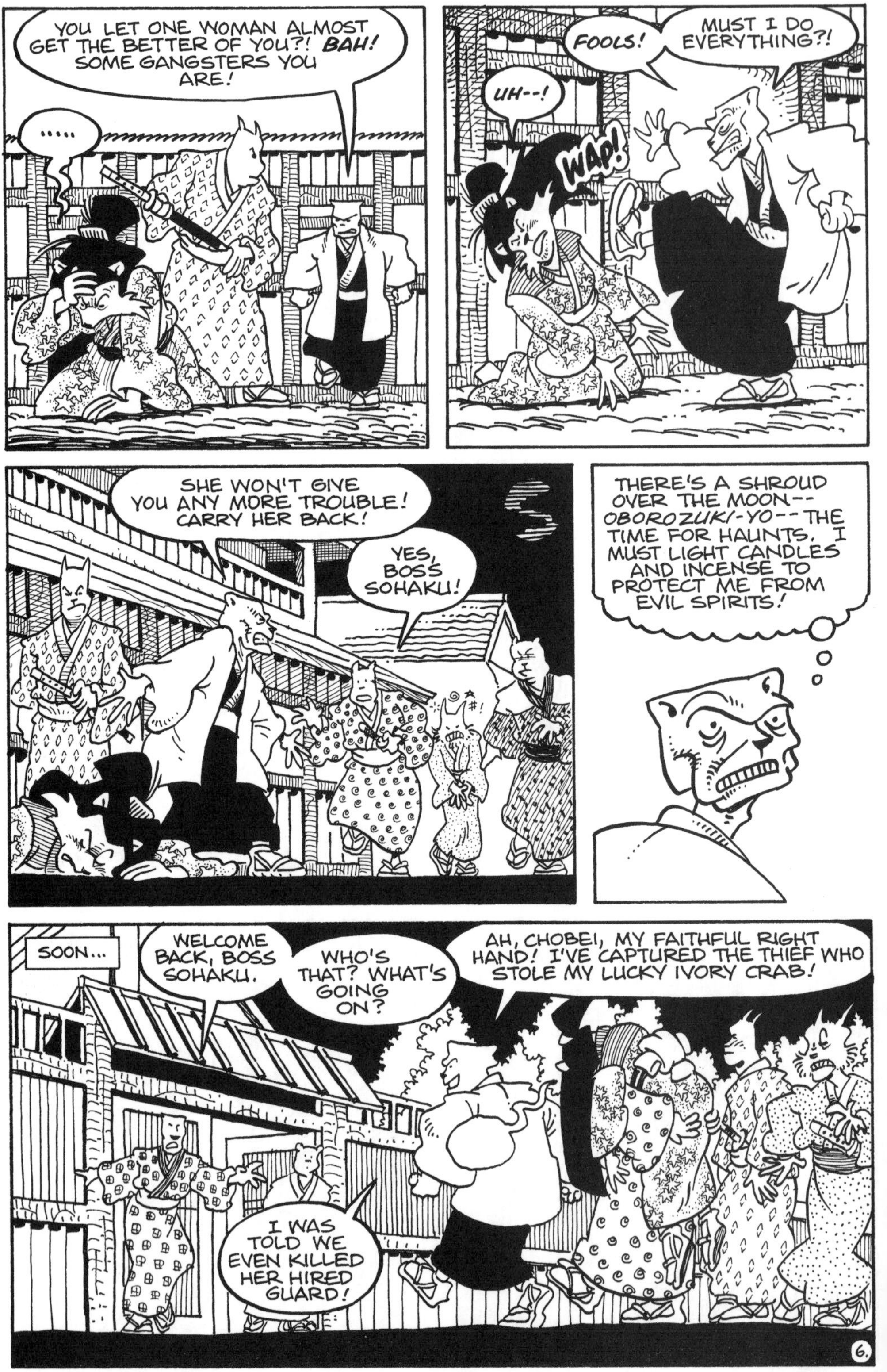

YOU LET ONE WOMAN ALMOST GET THE BETTER OF YOU?! BAH! SOME GANGSTERS YOU ARE!
.....
FOOLS!
MUST I DO EVERYTHING?!
UH--!
WAP!
SHE WON'T GIVE YOU ANY MORE TROUBLE! CARRY HER BACK!
YES, BOSS SOHAKU!
THERE'S A SHROUD OVER THE MOON-- OBOROZUKI-YO-- THE TIME FOR HAUNTS. I MUST LIGHT CANDLES AND INCENSE TO PROTECT ME FROM EVIL SPIRITS!
SOON...
WELCOME BACK, BOSS SOHAKU.
WHO'S THAT? WHAT'S GOING ON?
AH, CHOBEI, MY FAITHFUL RIGHT HAND! I'VE CAPTURED THE THIEF WHO STOLE MY LUCKY IVORY CRAB!
I WAS TOLD WE EVEN KILLED HER HIRED GUARD!
6.

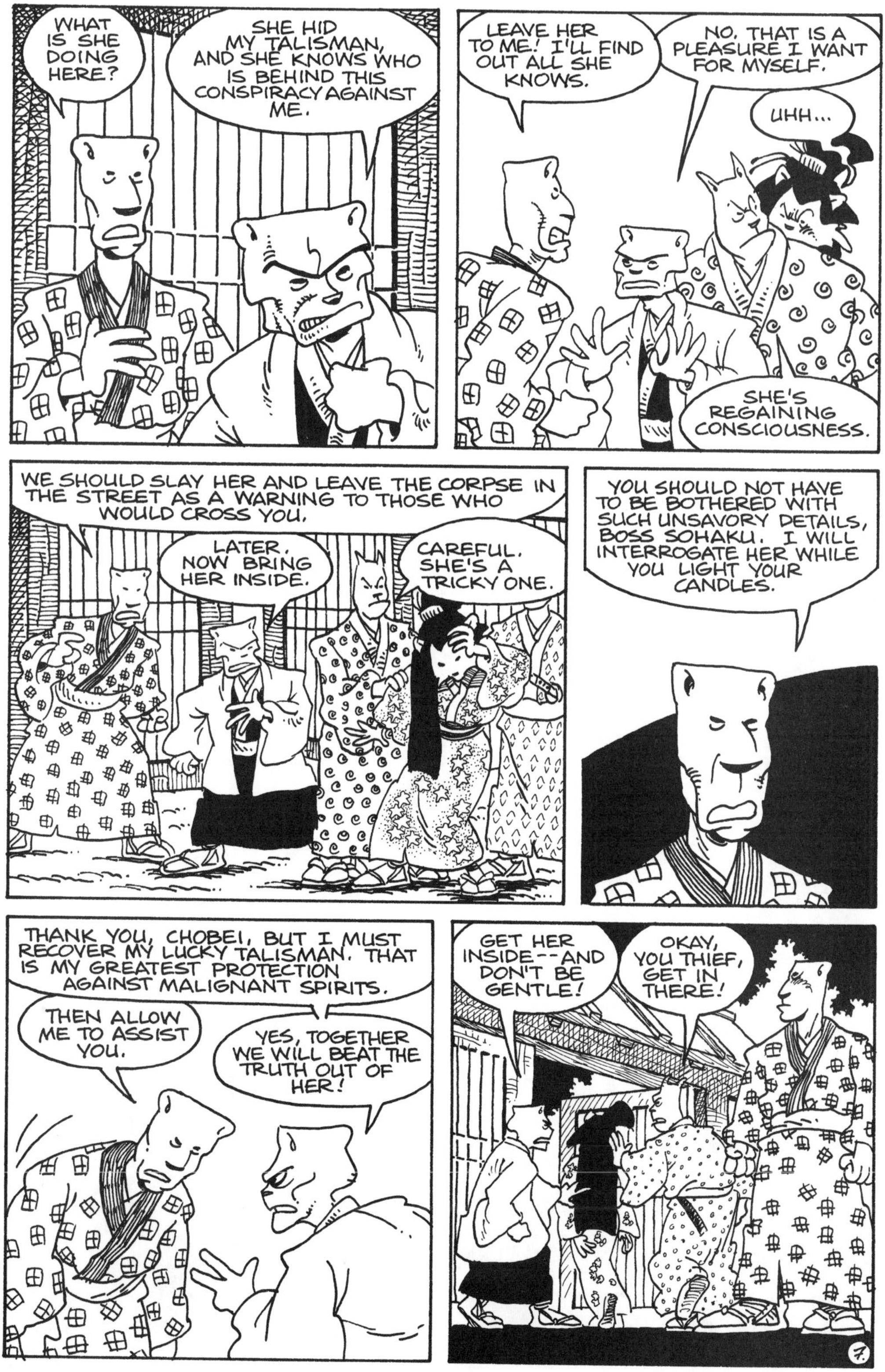
WHAT IS SHE DOING HERE?
SHE HID MY TALISMAN, AND SHE KNOWS WHO IS BEHIND THIS CONSPIRACY AGAINST ME.
LEAVE HER TO ME! I'LL FIND OUT ALL SHE KNOWS.
NO, THAT IS A PLEASURE I WANT FOR MYSELF.
UHH...
SHE'S REGAINING CONSCIOUSNESS.
WE SHOULD SLAY HER AND LEAVE THE CORPSE IN THE STREET AS A WARNING TO THOSE WHO WOULD CROSS YOU.
LATER. NOW BRING HER INSIDE.
CAREFUL. SHE'S A TRICKY ONE.
YOU SHOULD NOT HAVE TO BE BOTHERED WITH SUCH UNSAVORY DETAILS, BOSS SOHAKU. I WILL INTERROGATE HER WHILE YOU LIGHT YOUR CANDLES.
THANK YOU, CHOBEI, BUT I MUST RECOVER MY LUCKY TALISMAN. THAT IS MY GREATEST PROTECTION AGAINST MALIGNANT SPIRITS.
THEN ALLOW ME TO ASSIST YOU.
YES, TOGETHER WE WILL BEAT THE TRUTH OUT OF HER!
GET HER INSIDE--AND DON'T BE GENTLE!
OKAY, YOU THIEF, GET IN THERE!
7.

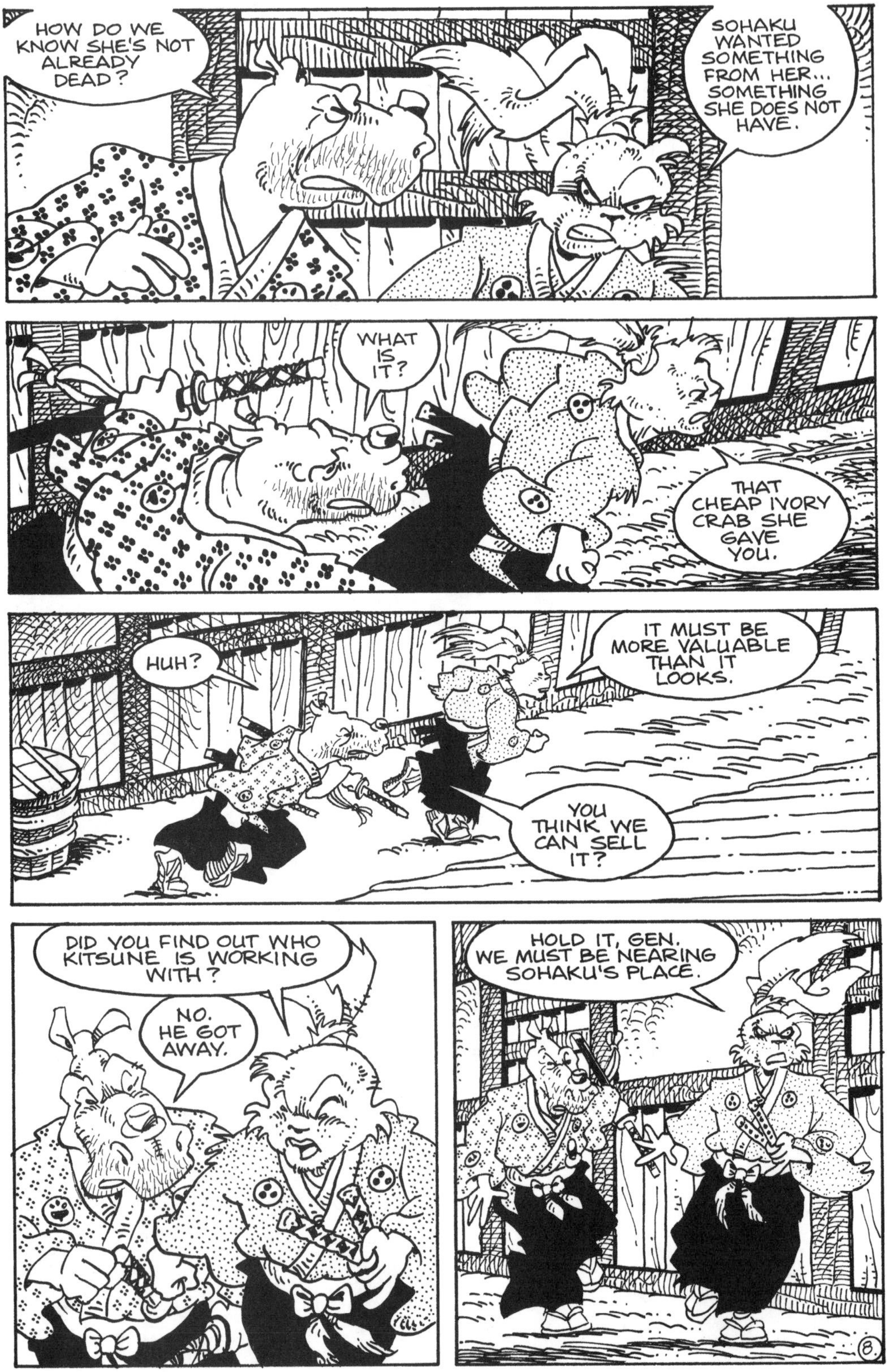
HOW DO WE KNOW SHE'S NOT ALREADY DEAD?
SOHAKU WANTED SOMETHING FROM HER... SOMETHING SHE DOES NOT HAVE.
WHAT IS IT?
THAT CHEAP IVORY CRAB SHE GAVE YOU.
HUH?
IT MUST BE MORE VALUABLE THAN IT LOOKS.
YOU THINK WE CAN SELL IT?
DID YOU FIND OUT WHO KITSUNE IS WORKING WITH?
NO. HE GOT AWAY.
HOLD IT, GEN. WE MUST BE NEARING SOHAKU'S PLACE.
8.

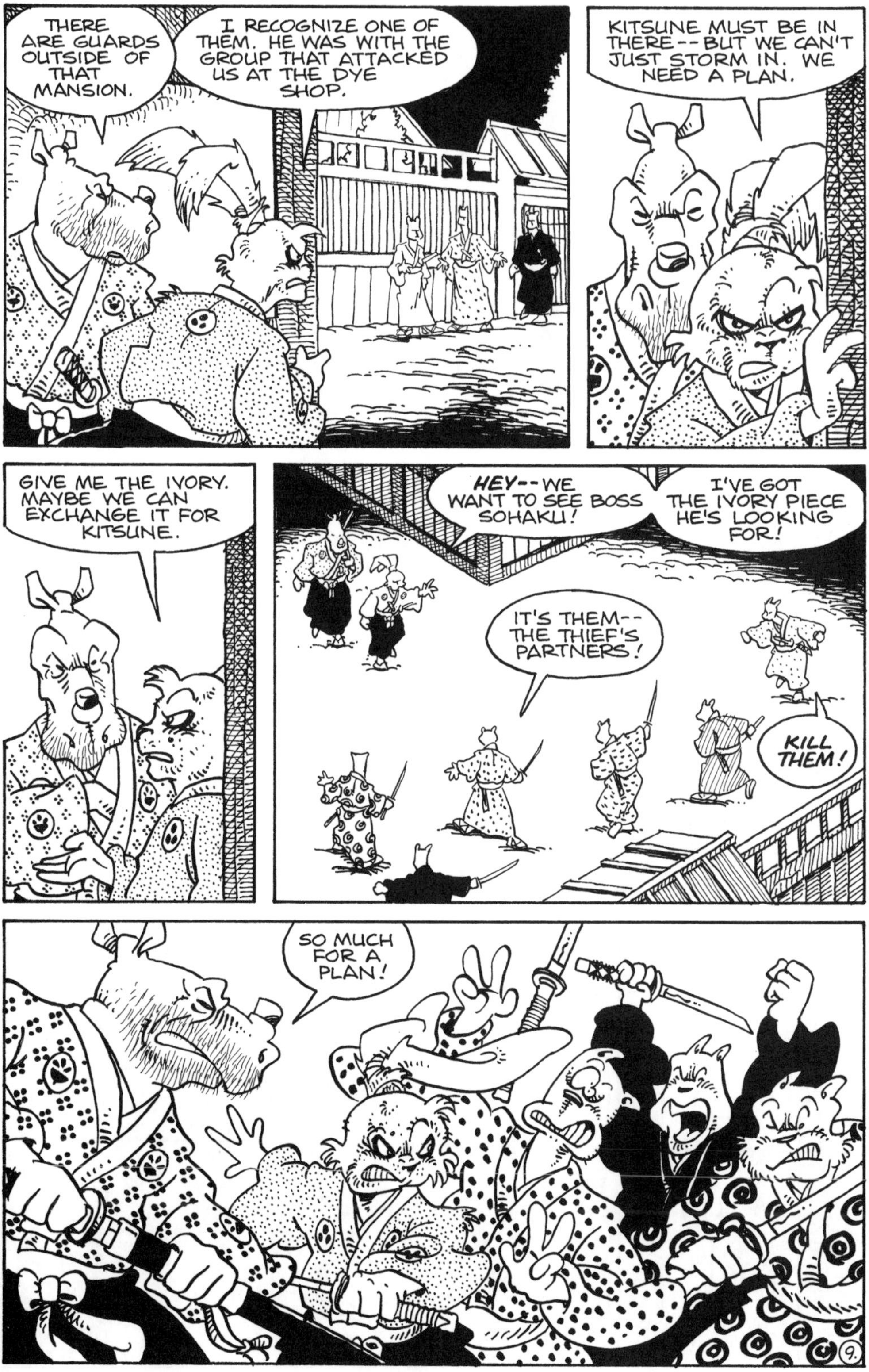
THERE ARE GUARDS OUTSIDE OF THAT MANSION.
I RECOGNIZE ONE OF THEM. HE WAS WITH THE GROUP THAT ATTACKED US AT THE DYE SHOP.
KITSUNE MUST BE IN THERE-- BUT WE CAN'T JUST STORM IN. WE NEED A PLAN.
GIVE ME THE IVORY. MAYBE WE CAN EXCHANGE IT FOR KITSUNE.
HEY-- WE WANT TO SEE BOSS SOHAKU!
I'VE GOT THE IVORY PIECE HE'S LOOKING FOR!
IT'S THEM-- THE THIEF'S PARTNERS!
KILL THEM!
SO MUCH FOR A PLAN!
9.

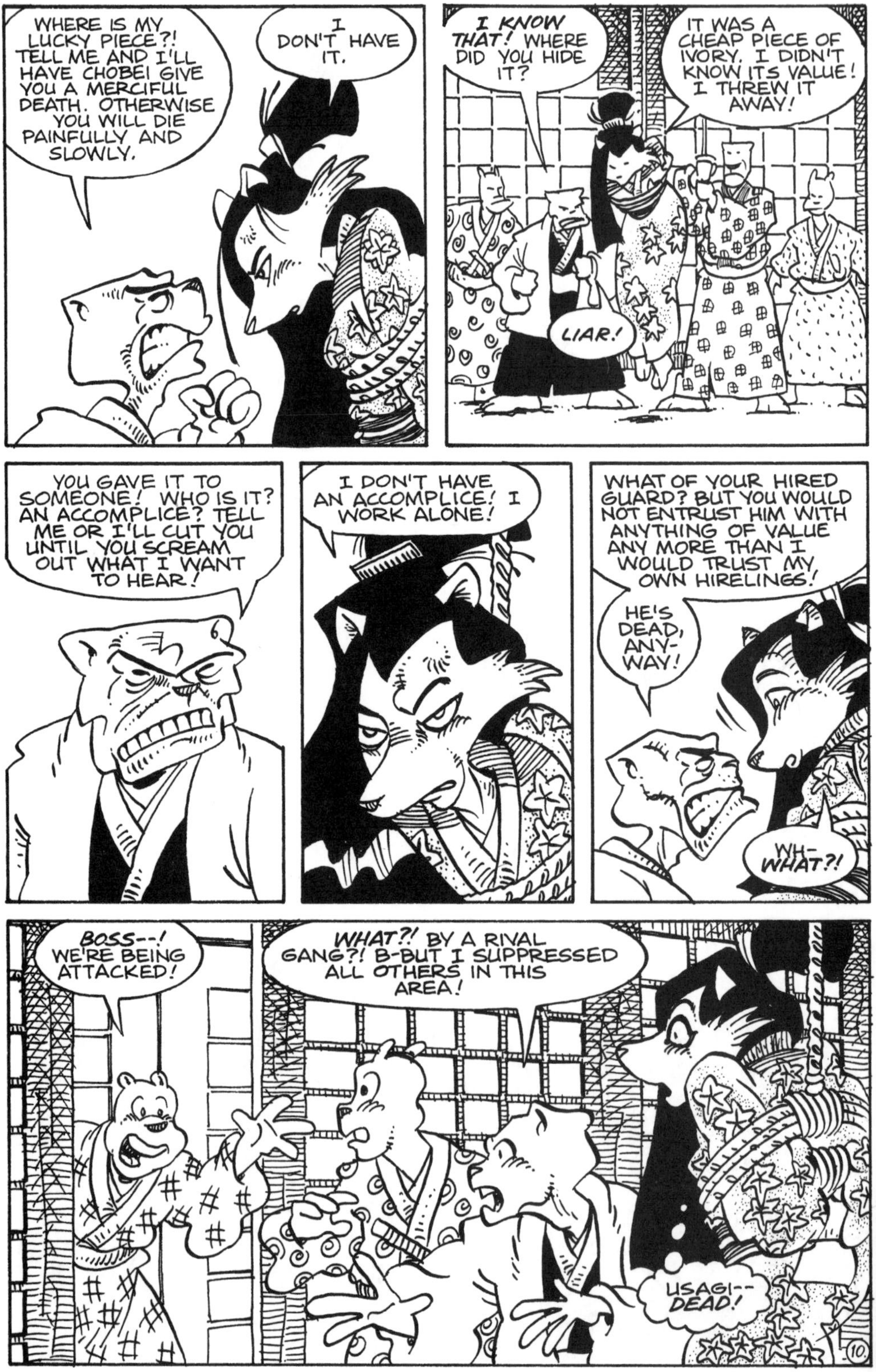
WHERE IS MY LUCKY PIECE?! TELL ME AND I'LL HAVE CHOBEI GIVE YOU A MERCIFUL DEATH. OTHERWISE YOU WILL DIE PAINFULLY AND SLOWLY.
I DON'T HAVE IT.
I KNOW THAT! WHERE DID YOU HIDE IT?
IT WAS A CHEAP PIECE OF IVORY. I DIDN'T KNOW ITS VALUE! I THREW IT AWAY!
LIAR!
YOU GAVE IT TO SOMEONE! WHO IS IT? AN ACCOMPLICE? TELL ME OR I'LL CUT YOU UNTIL YOU SCREAM OUT WHAT I WANT TO HEAR!
I DON'T HAVE AN ACCOMPLICE! I WORK ALONE!
WHAT OF YOUR HIRED GUARD? BUT YOU WOULD NOT ENTRUST HIM WITH ANYTHING OF VALUE ANY MORE THAN I WOULD TRUST MY OWN HIRELINGS!
HE'S DEAD, ANY-WAY!
WH-WHAT?!
BOSS--! WE'RE BEING ATTACKED!
WHAT?! BY A RIVAL GANG?! B-BUT I SUPPRESSED ALL OTHERS IN THIS AREA!
USAGI--DEAD!
10

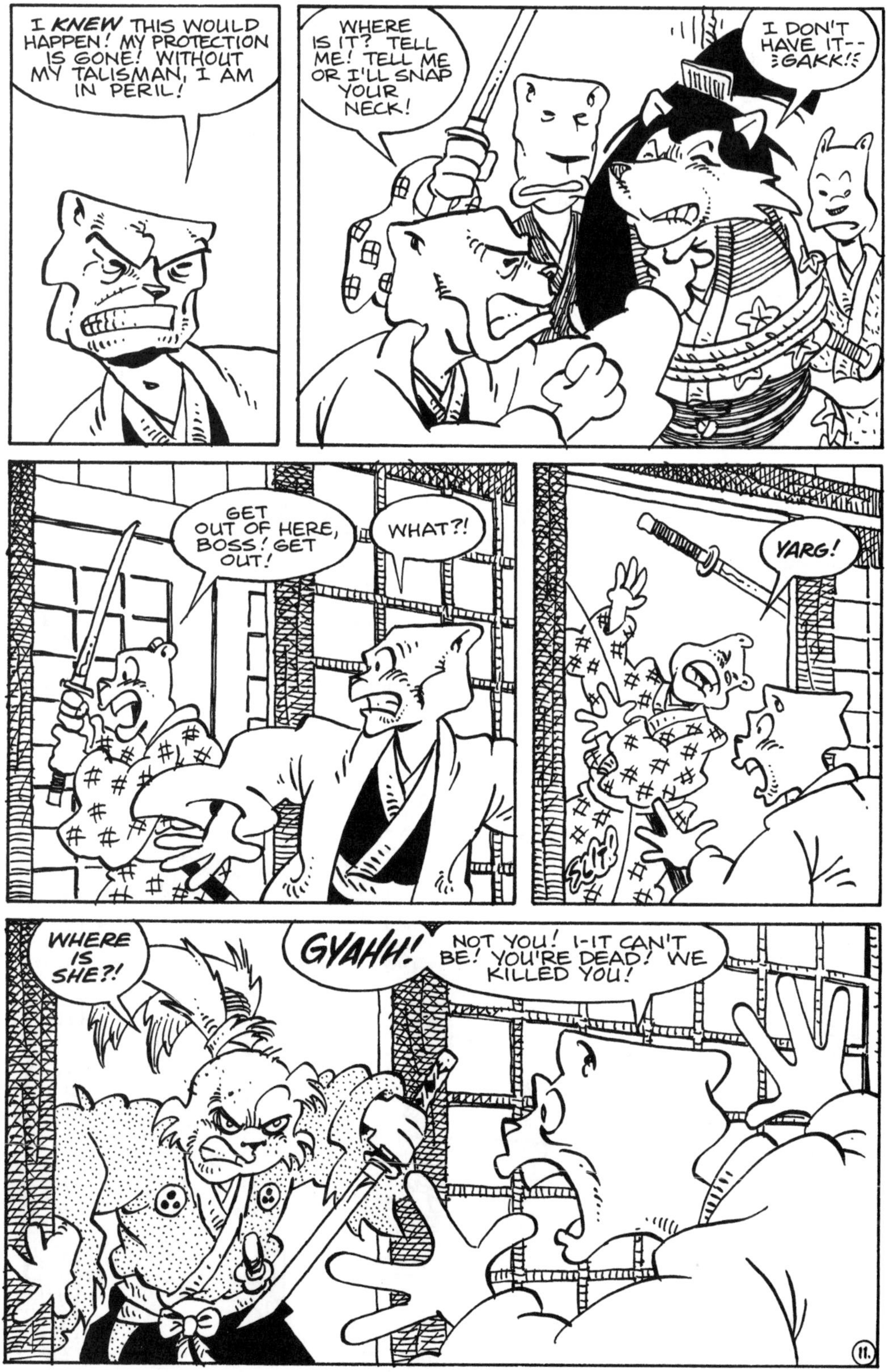

I KNEW THIS WOULD HAPPEN! MY PROTECTION IS GONE! WITHOUT MY TALISMAN, I AM IN PERIL!
WHERE IS IT? TELL ME! TELL ME OR I'LL SNAP YOUR NECK!
I DON'T HAVE IT-- GAKK!
GET OUT OF HERE, BOSS! GET OUT!
WHAT?!
YARG!
SLIT!
WHERE IS SHE?!
GYAHH!
NOT YOU! I-IT CAN'T BE! YOU'RE DEAD! WE KILLED YOU!
11.

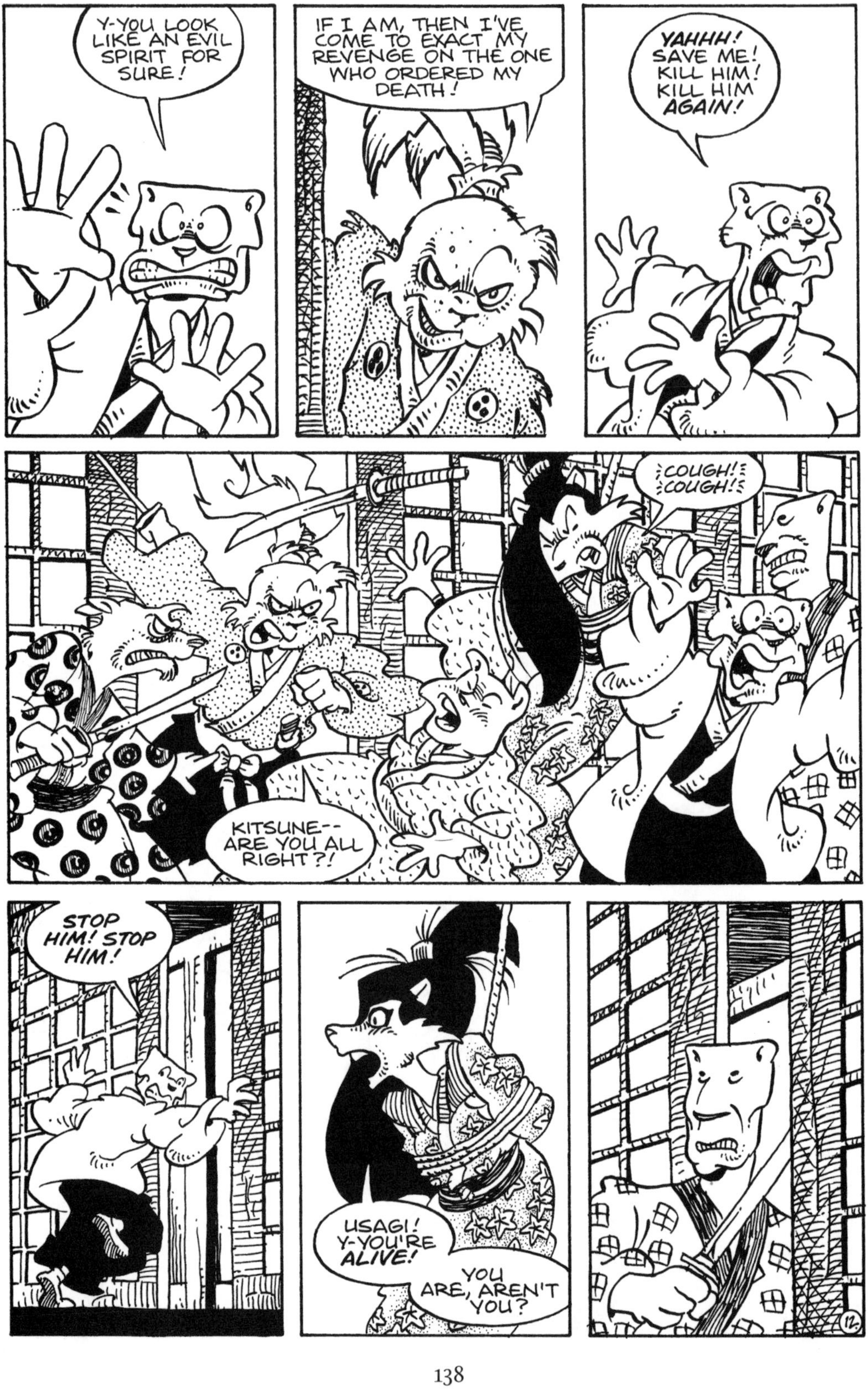

Y-YOU LOOK LIKE AN EVIL SPIRIT FOR SURE!
IF I AM, THEN I'VE COME TO EXACT MY REVENGE ON THE ONE WHO ORDERED MY DEATH!
YAHHH! SAVE ME! KILL HIM! KILL HIM AGAIN!
COUGH! COUGH!
KITSUNE-- ARE YOU ALL RIGHT?!
STOP HIM! STOP HIM!
USAGI! Y-YOU'RE ALIVE!
YOU ARE, AREN'T YOU?
12

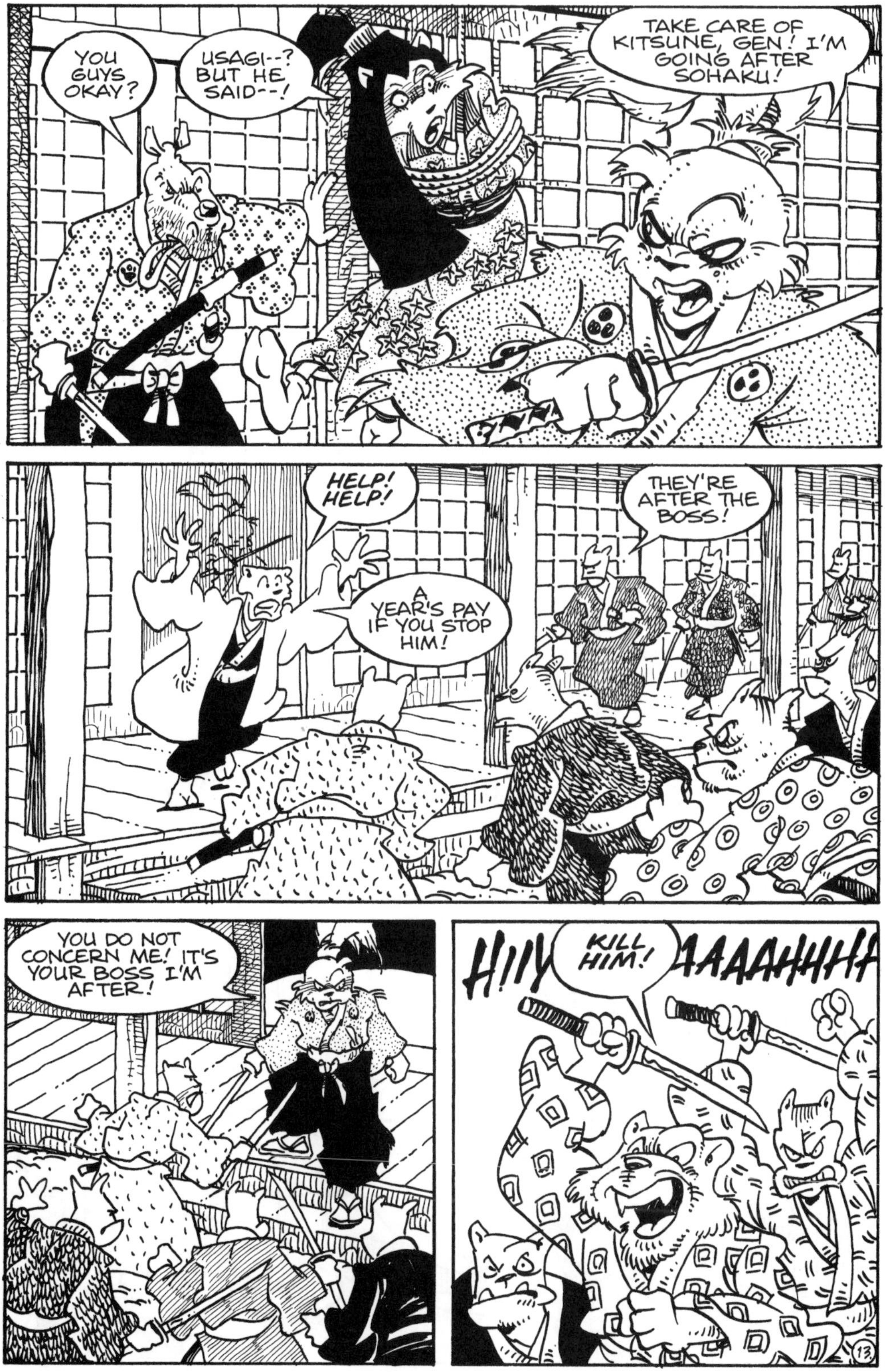
YOU GUYS OKAY?
USAGI--? BUT HE SAID--!
TAKE CARE OF KITSUNE, GEN! I'M GOING AFTER SOHAKU!
HELP! HELP!
A YEAR'S PAY IF YOU STOP HIM!
THEY'RE AFTER THE BOSS!
YOU DO NOT CONCERN ME! IT'S YOUR BOSS I'M AFTER!
HIIY
KILL HIM!
AAAAHHHA
13

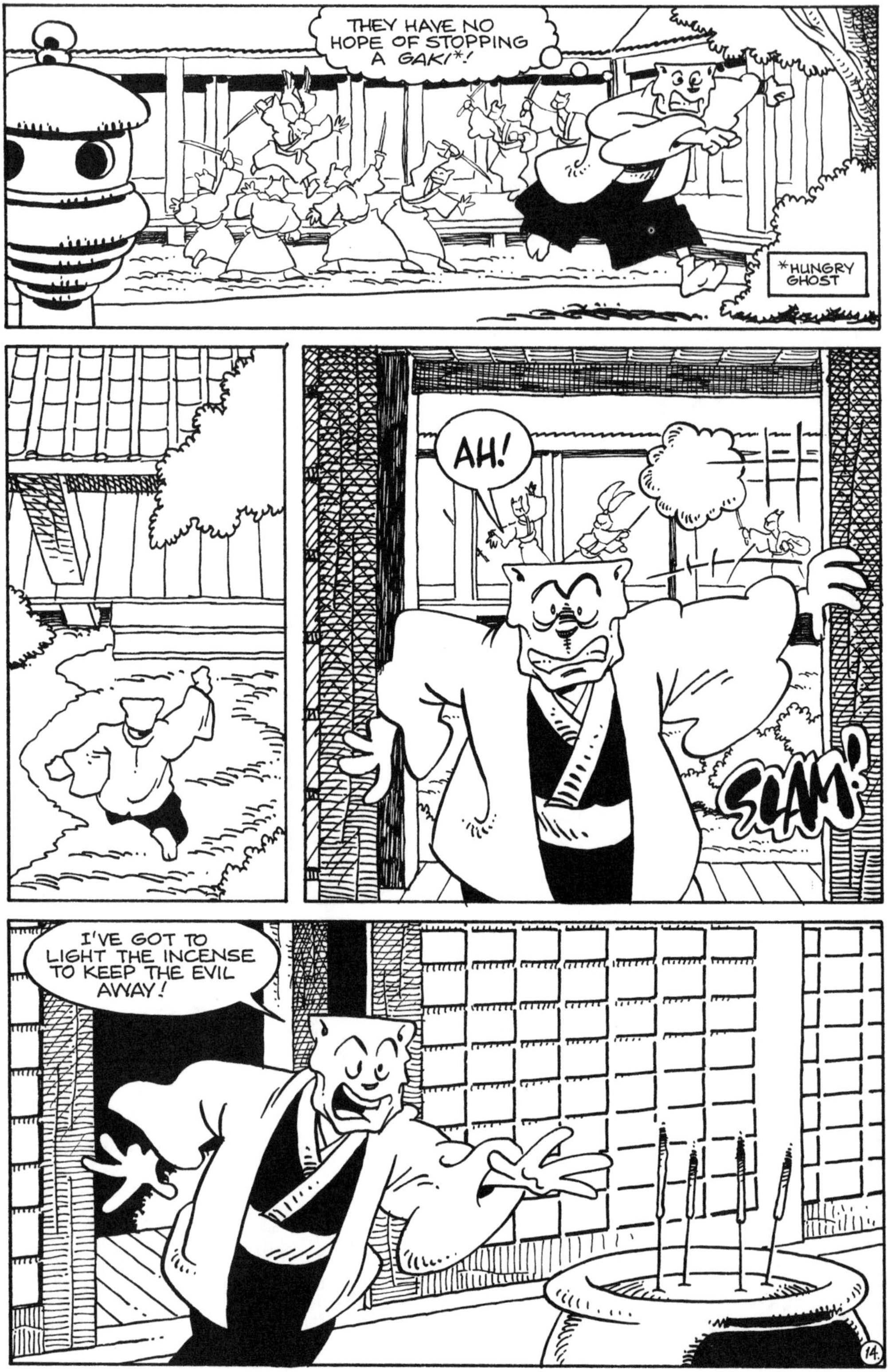
THEY HAVE NO HOPE OF STOPPING A GAKI*!
*HUNGRY GHOST
AH!
SLAM!
I'VE GOT TO LIGHT THE INCENSE TO KEEP THE EVIL AWAY!
14.

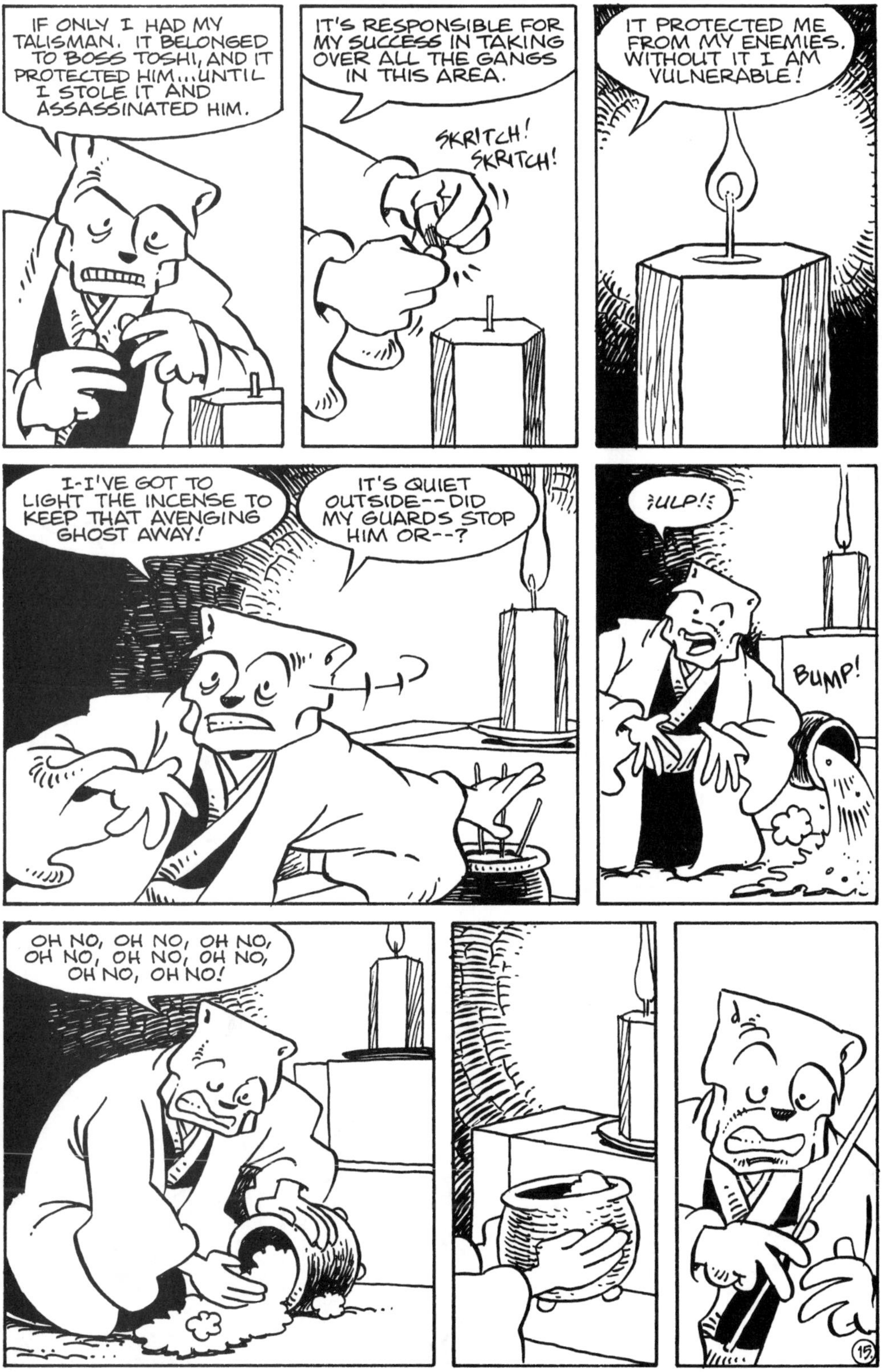
IF ONLY I HAD MY TALISMAN. IT BELONGED TO BOSS TOSHI, AND IT PROTECTED HIM...UNTIL I STOLE IT AND ASSASSINATED HIM.
IT'S RESPONSIBLE FOR MY SUCCESS IN TAKING OVER ALL THE GANGS IN THIS AREA.
SKRITCH! SKRITCH!
IT PROTECTED ME FROM MY ENEMIES. WITHOUT IT I AM VULNERABLE!
I-I'VE GOT TO LIGHT THE INCENSE TO KEEP THAT AVENGING GHOST AWAY!
IT'S QUIET OUTSIDE--DID MY GUARDS STOP HIM OR--?
ULP!
BUMP!
OH NO, OH NO, OH NO, OH NO, OH NO, OH NO, OH NO, OH NO!
15

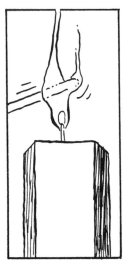
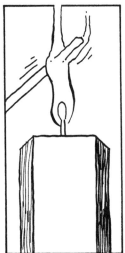
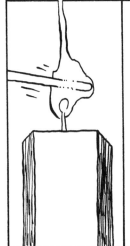
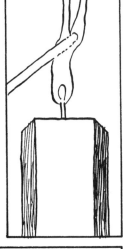

MY TALISMAN!

YOU'RE BACK!

;SNATCH!;

AH--YOU'VE RETURNED IN MY HOUR OF GREATEST NEED! NOT EVEN THE HUNGRY DEAD CAN HARM ME!

I CAN FEEL YOUR POWER FLOW THROUGH ME AGAIN! I CAN... I CAN--

...I...

16.

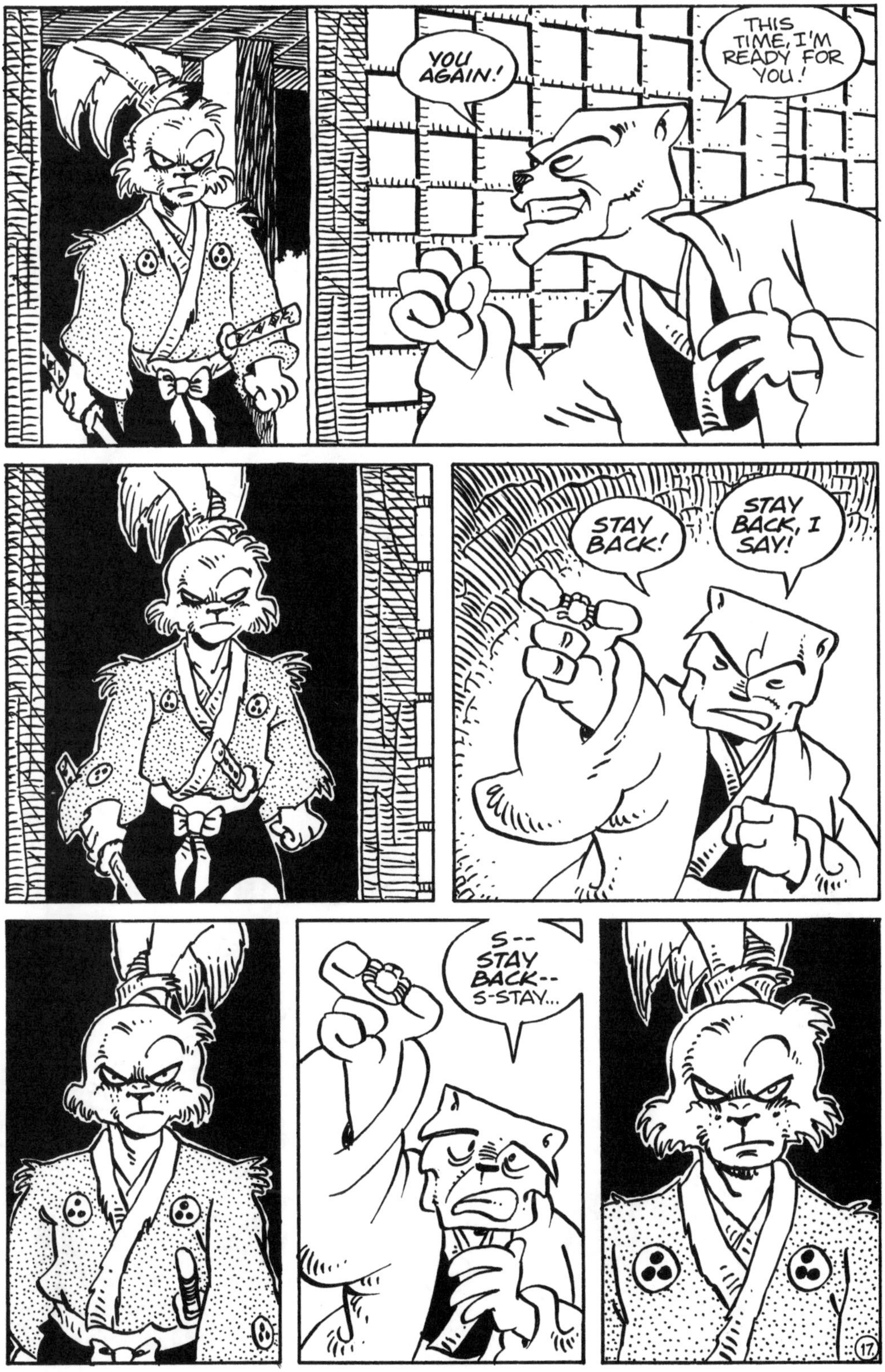
YOU AGAIN!
THIS TIME, I'M READY FOR YOU!
STAY BACK!
STAY BACK, I SAY!
S-- STAY BACK-- S-STAY...
17

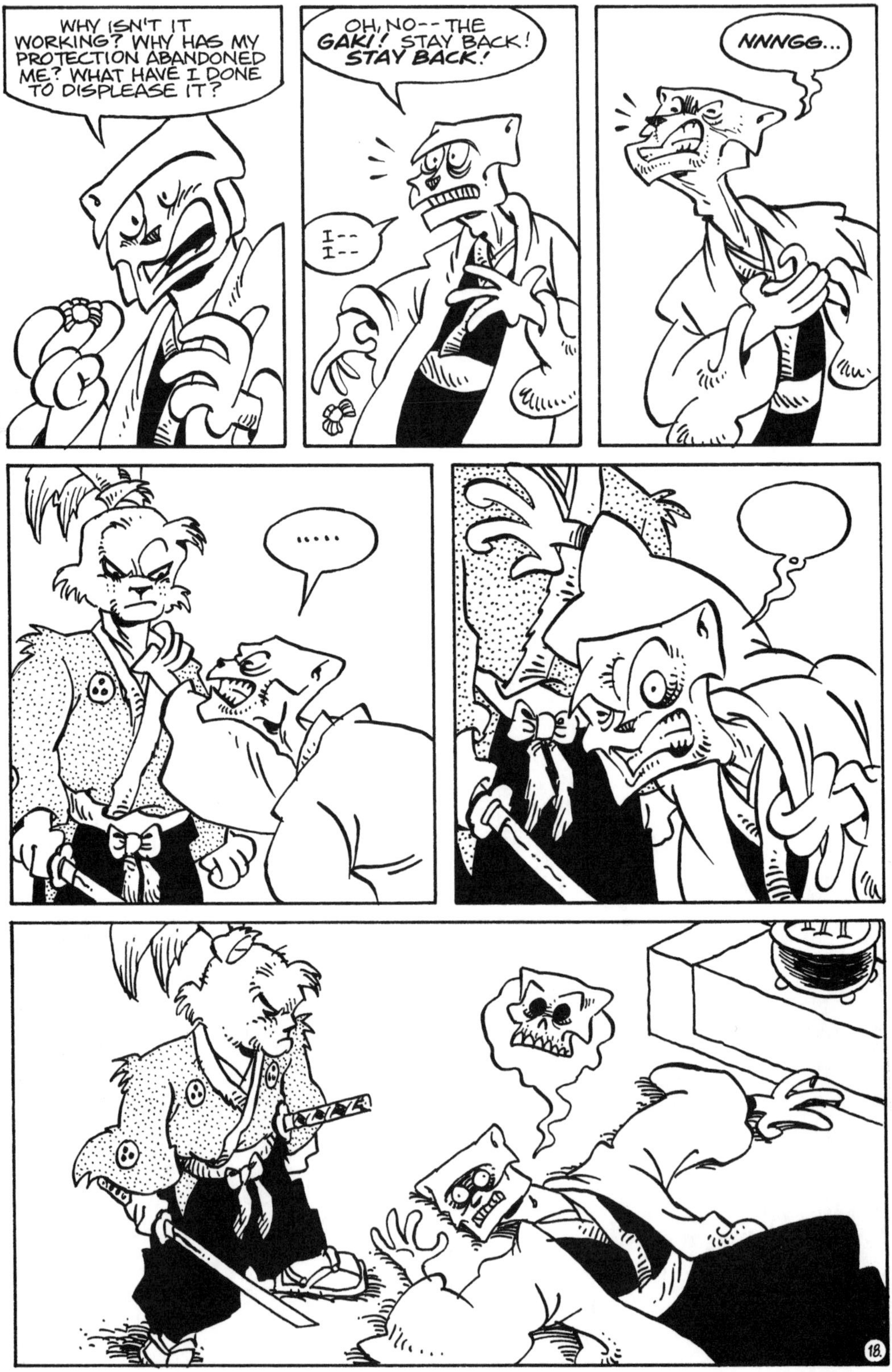
WHY ISN'T IT WORKING? WHY HAS MY PROTECTION ABANDONED ME? WHAT HAVE I DONE TO DISPLEASE IT?
OH, NO-- THE GAKI! STAY BACK! STAY BACK!
I-- I--
NNNGG...
.....
18.

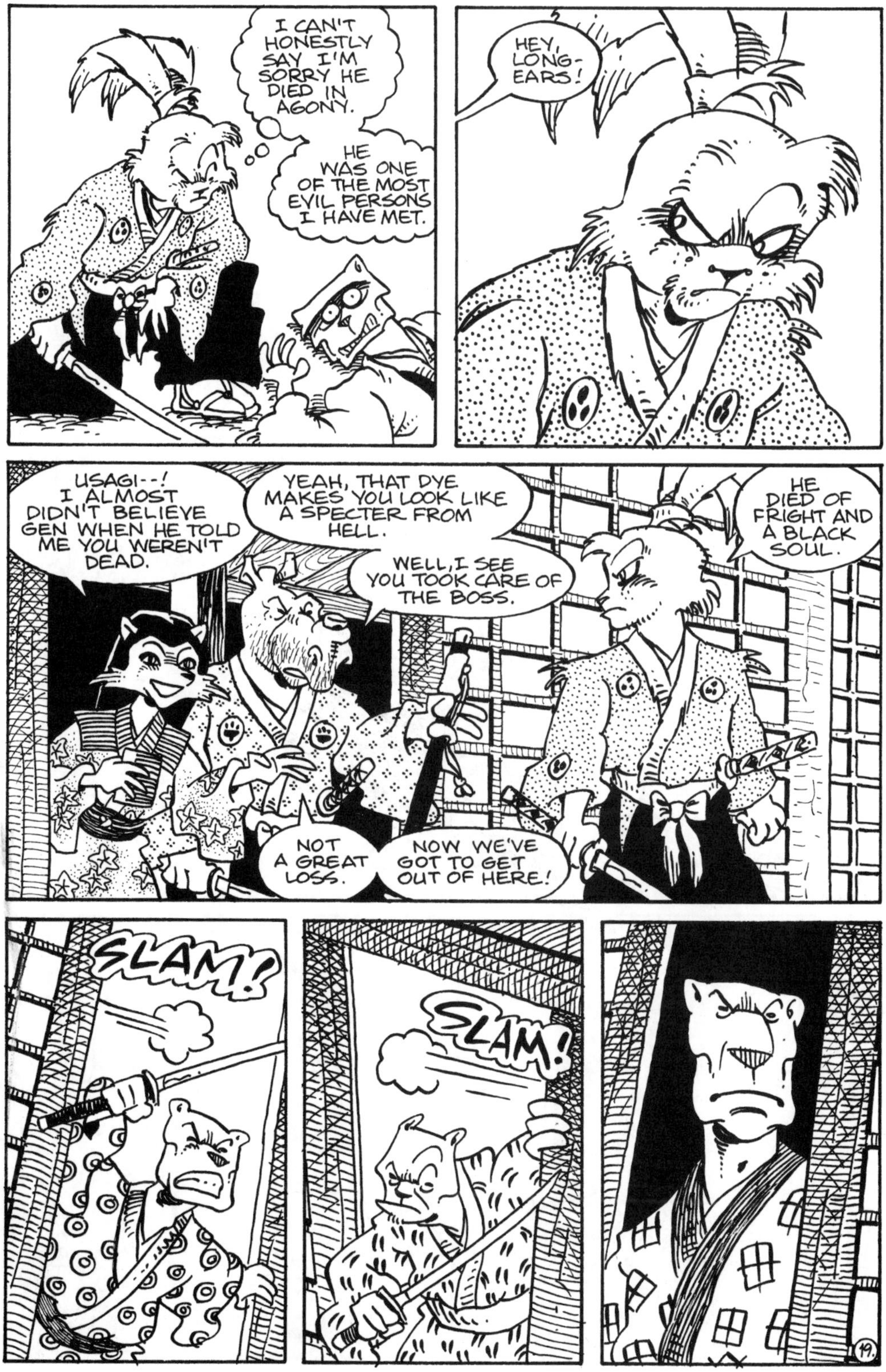
I CAN'T HONESTLY SAY I'M SORRY HE DIED IN AGONY.
HE WAS ONE OF THE MOST EVIL PERSONS I HAVE MET.
HEY, LONG-EARS!
USAGI--! I ALMOST DIDN'T BELIEVE GEN WHEN HE TOLD ME YOU WEREN'T DEAD.
YEAH, THAT DYE MAKES YOU LOOK LIKE A SPECTER FROM HELL.
WELL, I SEE YOU TOOK CARE OF THE BOSS.
HE DIED OF FRIGHT AND A BLACK SOUL.
NOT A GREAT LOSS.
NOW WE'VE GOT TO GET OUT OF HERE!
SLAM!
SLAM!
19.

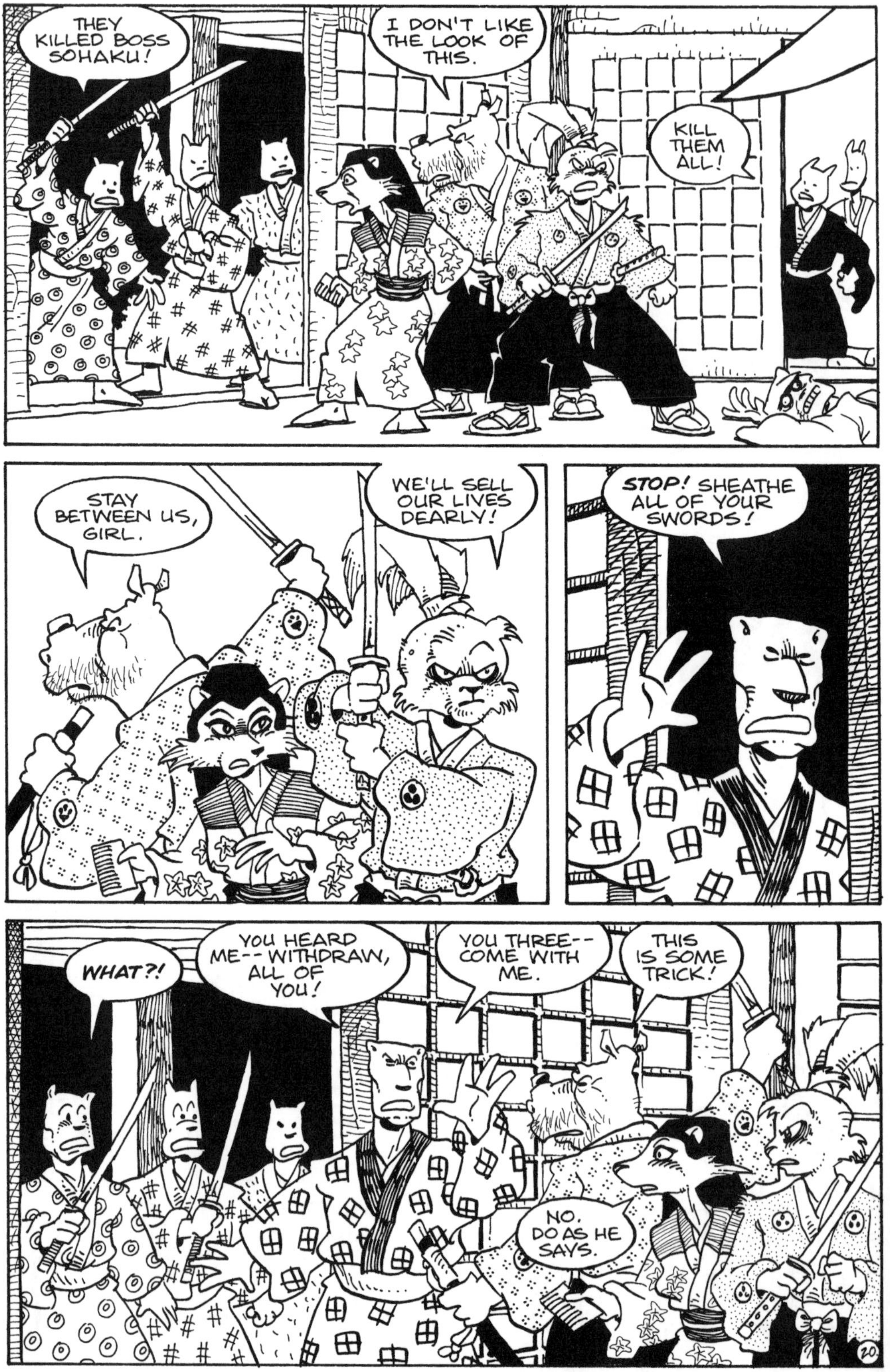
THEY KILLED BOSS SOHAKU!
I DON'T LIKE THE LOOK OF THIS.
KILL THEM ALL!
STAY BETWEEN US, GIRL.
WE'LL SELL OUR LIVES DEARLY!
STOP! SHEATHE ALL OF YOUR SWORDS!
WHAT?!
YOU HEARD ME-- WITHDRAW, ALL OF YOU!
YOU THREE-- COME WITH ME.
THIS IS SOME TRICK!
NO. DO AS HE SAYS.
20.

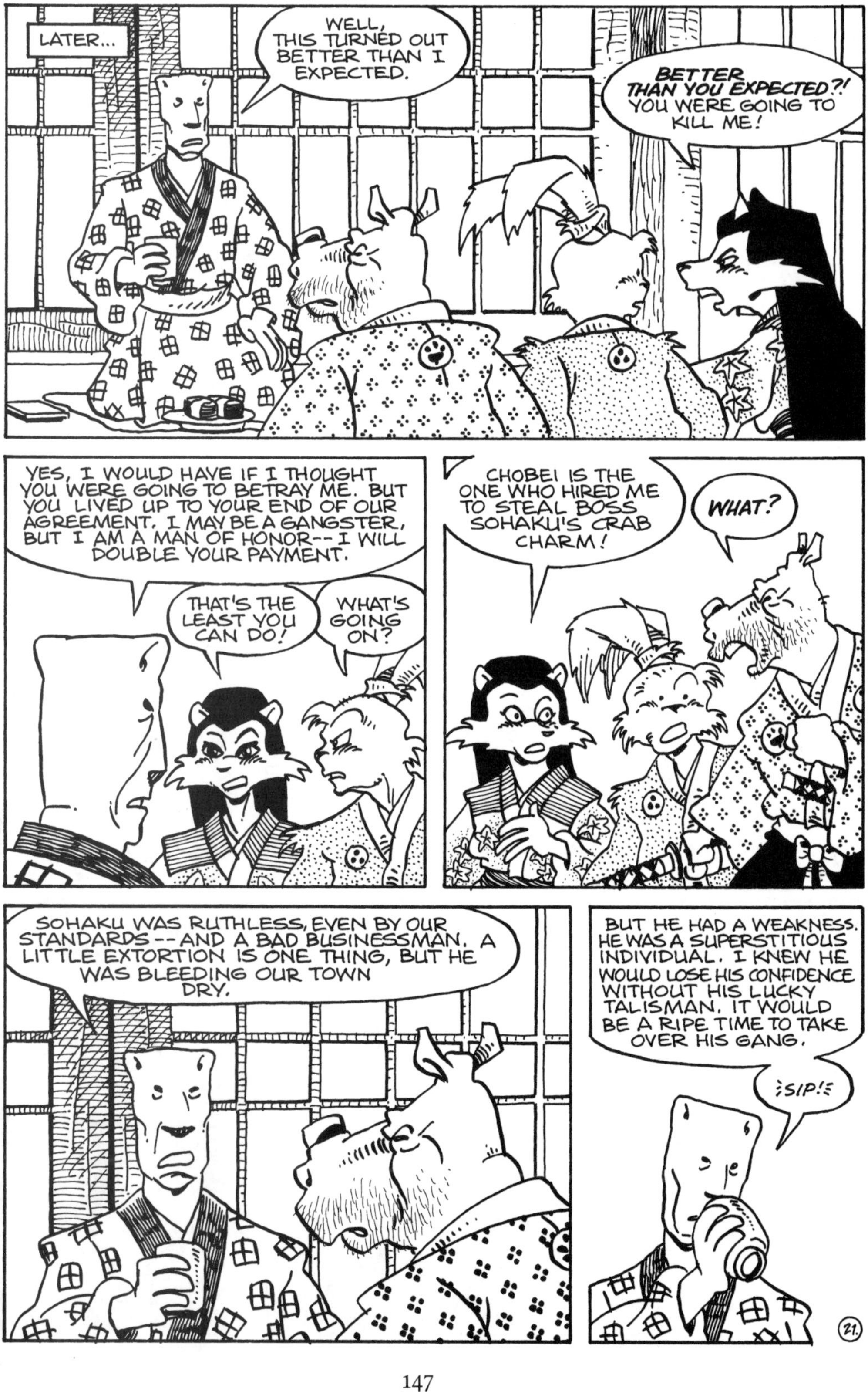
LATER...
WELL, THIS TURNED OUT BETTER THAN I EXPECTED.
BETTER THAN YOU EXPECTED?! YOU WERE GOING TO KILL ME!
YES, I WOULD HAVE IF I THOUGHT YOU WERE GOING TO BETRAY ME. BUT YOU LIVED UP TO YOUR END OF OUR AGREEMENT. I MAY BE A GANGSTER, BUT I AM A MAN OF HONOR-- I WILL DOUBLE YOUR PAYMENT.
THAT'S THE LEAST YOU CAN DO!
WHAT'S GOING ON?
CHOBEI IS THE ONE WHO HIRED ME TO STEAL BOSS SOHAKU'S CRAB CHARM!
WHAT?
SOHAKU WAS RUTHLESS, EVEN BY OUR STANDARDS--AND A BAD BUSINESSMAN. A LITTLE EXTORTION IS ONE THING, BUT HE WAS BLEEDING OUR TOWN DRY.
BUT HE HAD A WEAKNESS. HE WAS A SUPERSTITIOUS INDIVIDUAL. I KNEW HE WOULD LOSE HIS CONFIDENCE WITHOUT HIS LUCKY TALISMAN. IT WOULD BE A RIPE TIME TO TAKE OVER HIS GANG.
SIP!
21.

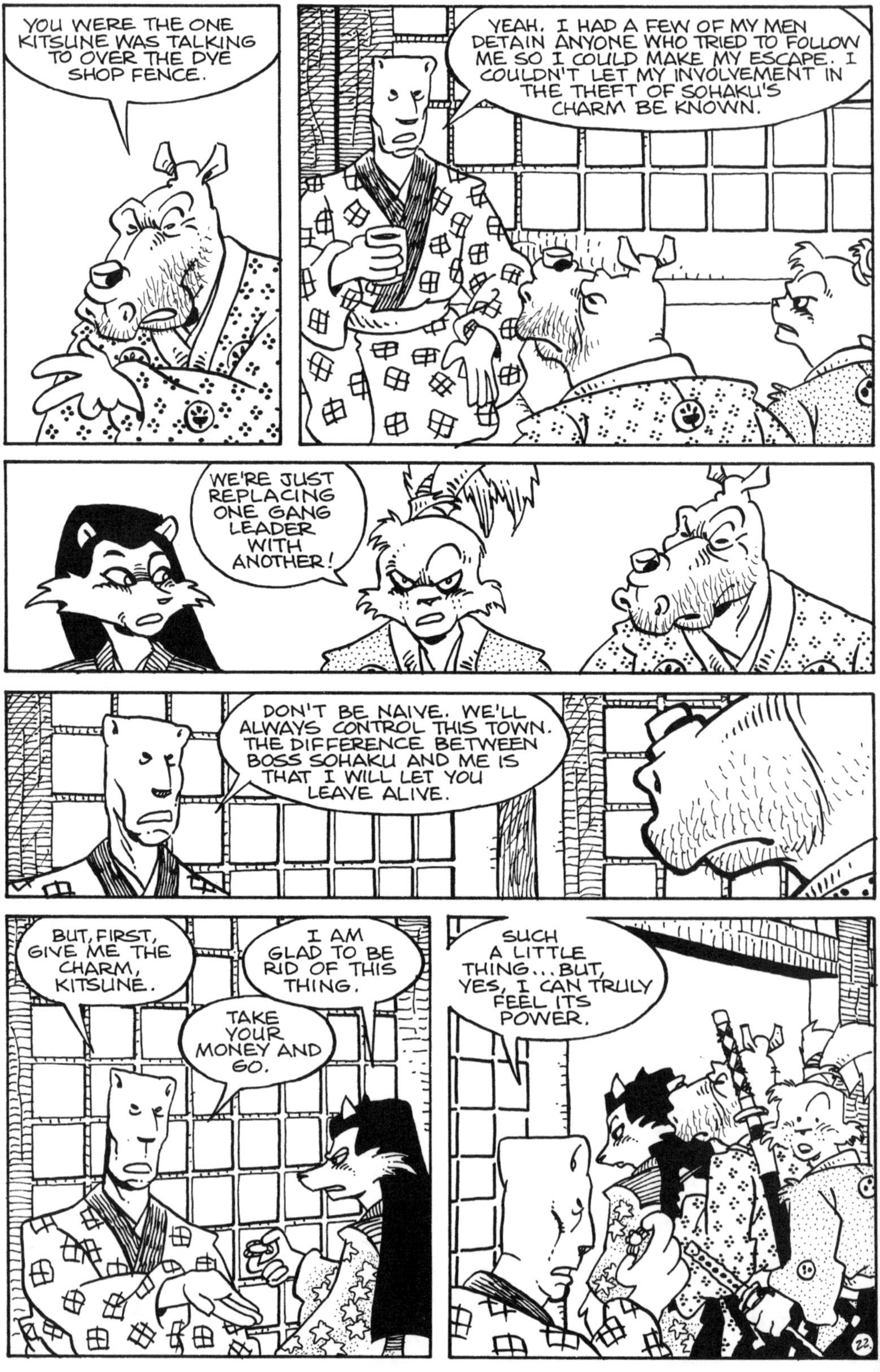
YOU WERE THE ONE KITSUNE WAS TALKING TO OVER THE DYE SHOP FENCE.
YEAH. I HAD A FEW OF MY MEN DETAIN ANYONE WHO TRIED TO FOLLOW ME SO I COULD MAKE MY ESCAPE. I COULDN'T LET MY INVOLVEMENT IN THE THEFT OF SOHAKU'S CHARM BE KNOWN.
WE'RE JUST REPLACING ONE GANG LEADER WITH ANOTHER!
DON'T BE NAIVE. WE'LL ALWAYS CONTROL THIS TOWN. THE DIFFERENCE BETWEEN BOSS SOHAKU AND ME IS THAT I WILL LET YOU LEAVE ALIVE.
BUT, FIRST, GIVE ME THE CHARM, KITSUNE.
I AM GLAD TO BE RID OF THIS THING.
TAKE YOUR MONEY AND GO.
SUCH A LITTLE THING... BUT, YES, I CAN TRULY FEEL ITS POWER.
22.

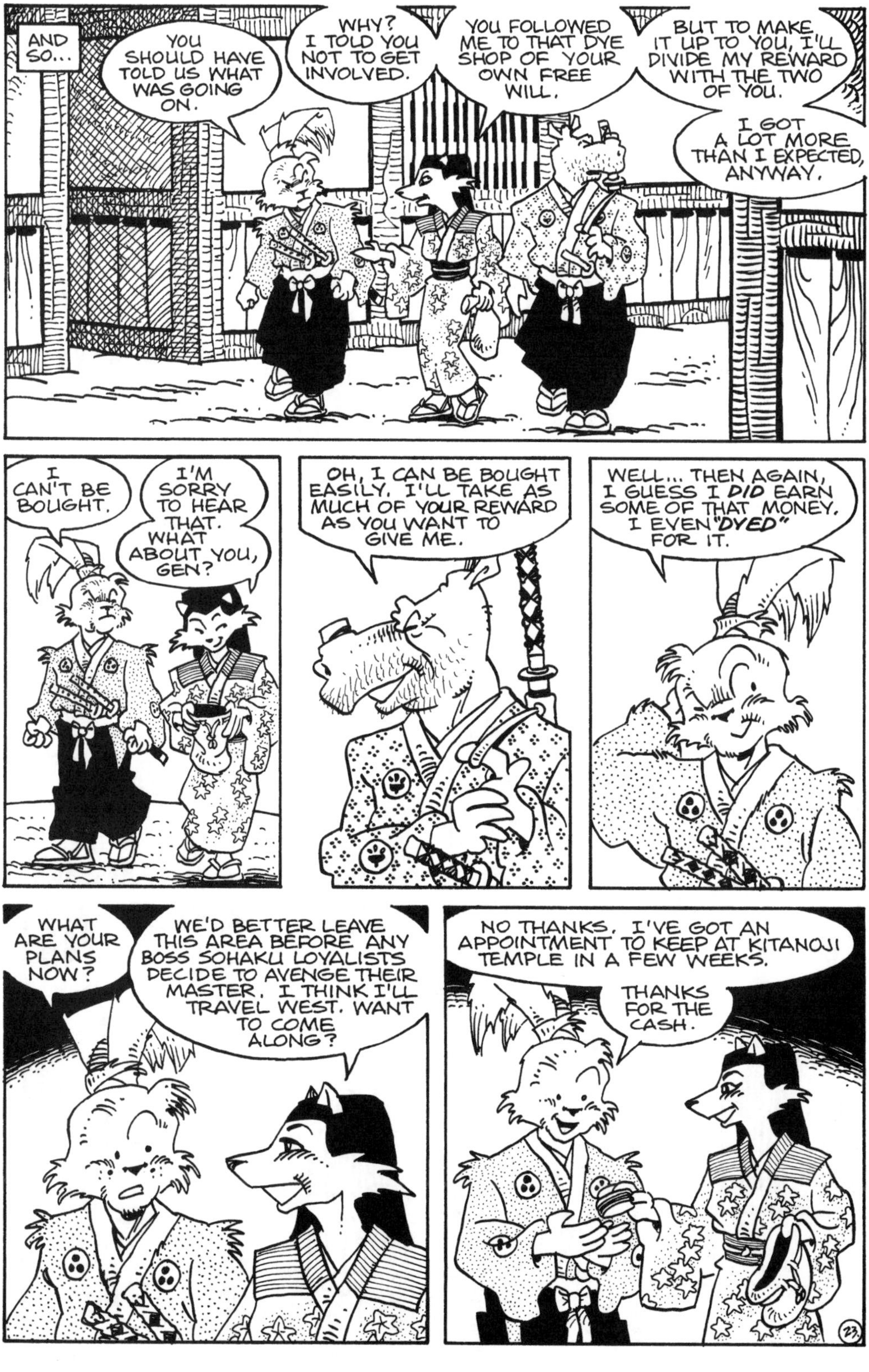

AND SO...
YOU SHOULD HAVE TOLD US WHAT WAS GOING ON.
WHY? I TOLD YOU NOT TO GET INVOLVED.
YOU FOLLOWED ME TO THAT DYE SHOP OF YOUR OWN FREE WILL.
BUT TO MAKE IT UP TO YOU, I'LL DIVIDE MY REWARD WITH THE TWO OF YOU.
I GOT A LOT MORE THAN I EXPECTED, ANYWAY.
I CAN'T BE BOUGHT.
I'M SORRY TO HEAR THAT. WHAT ABOUT YOU, GEN?
OH, I CAN BE BOUGHT EASILY. I'LL TAKE AS MUCH OF YOUR REWARD AS YOU WANT TO GIVE ME.
WELL... THEN AGAIN, I GUESS I DID EARN SOME OF THAT MONEY. I EVEN "DYED" FOR IT.
WHAT ARE YOUR PLANS NOW?
WE'D BETTER LEAVE THIS AREA BEFORE ANY BOSS SOHAKU LOYALISTS DECIDE TO AVENGE THEIR MASTER. I THINK I'LL TRAVEL WEST. WANT TO COME ALONG?
NO THANKS. I'VE GOT AN APPOINTMENT TO KEEP AT KITANOJI TEMPLE IN A FEW WEEKS.
THANKS FOR THE CASH.
23.

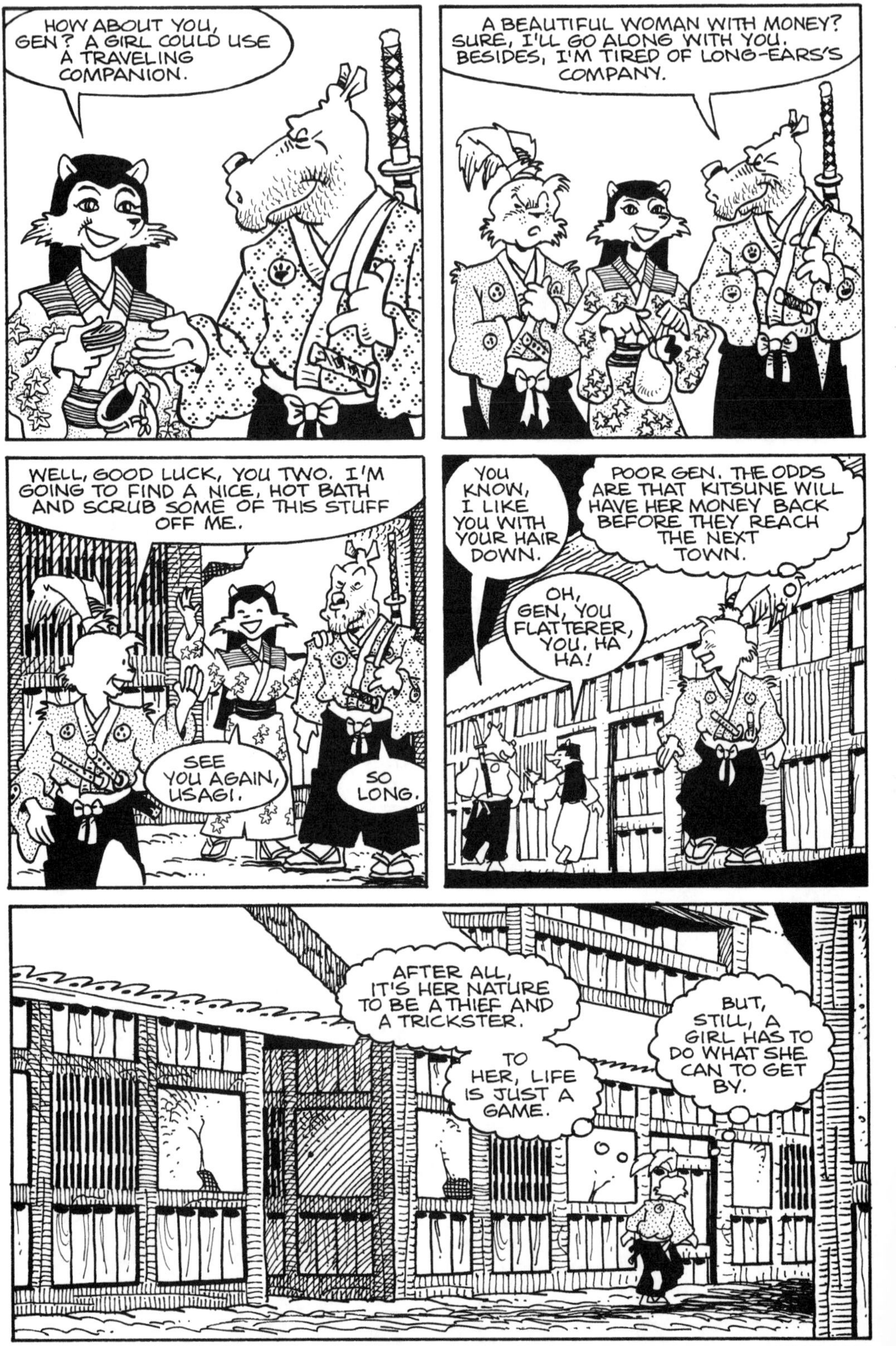
HOW ABOUT YOU, GEN? A GIRL COULD USE A TRAVELING COMPANION.
A BEAUTIFUL WOMAN WITH MONEY? SURE, I'LL GO ALONG WITH YOU. BESIDES, I'M TIRED OF LONG-EARS'S COMPANY.
WELL, GOOD LUCK, YOU TWO. I'M GOING TO FIND A NICE, HOT BATH AND SCRUB SOME OF THIS STUFF OFF ME.
SEE YOU AGAIN, USAGI.
SO LONG.
YOU KNOW, I LIKE YOU WITH YOUR HAIR DOWN.
POOR GEN. THE ODDS ARE THAT KITSUNE WILL HAVE HER MONEY BACK BEFORE THEY REACH THE NEXT TOWN.
OH, GEN, YOU FLATTERER, YOU, HA HA!
AFTER ALL, IT'S HER NATURE TO BE A THIEF AND A TRICKSTER.
TO HER, LIFE IS JUST A GAME.
BUT, STILL, A GIRL HAS TO DO WHAT SHE CAN TO GET BY.

THE END.

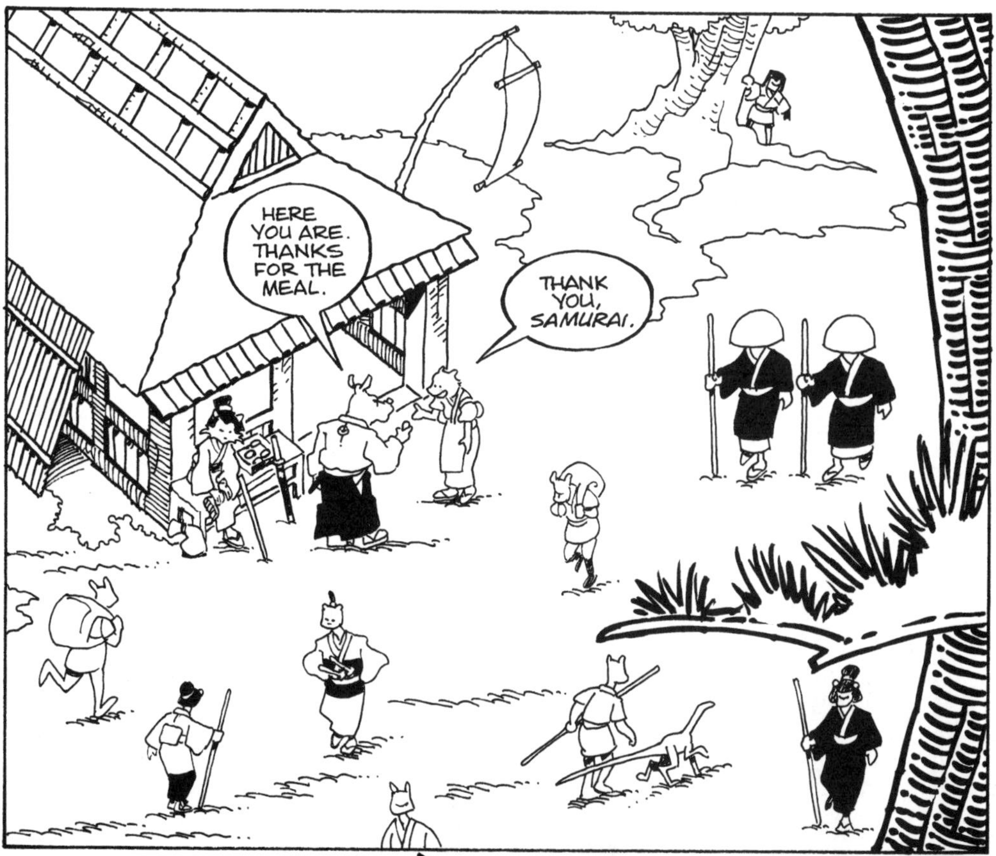
HERE YOU ARE. THANKS FOR THE MEAL.
THANK YOU, SAMURAI.

KITSUNE'S TALE

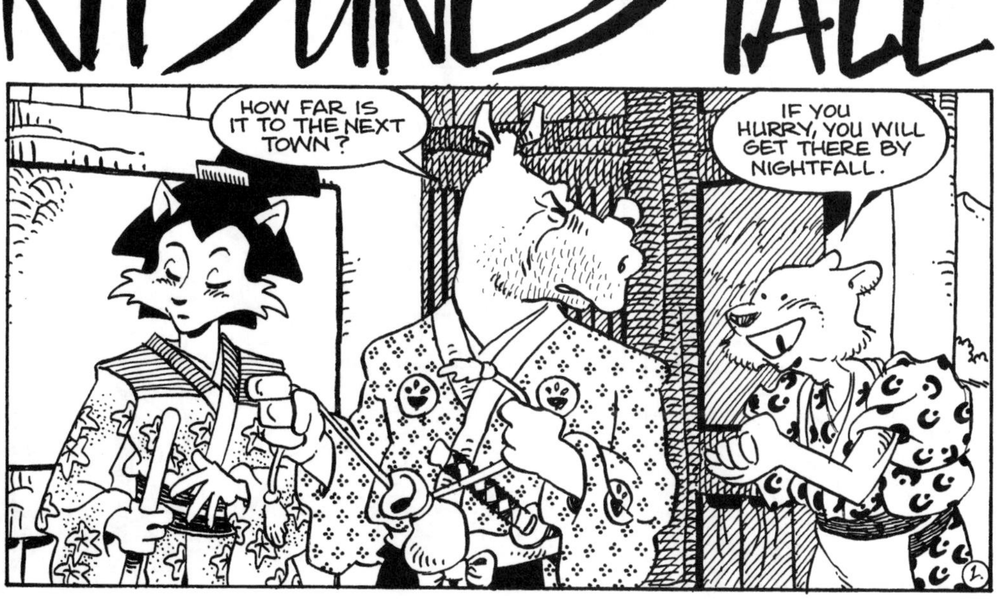
HOW FAR IS IT TO THE NEXT TOWN?
IF YOU HURRY, YOU WILL GET THERE BY NIGHTFALL.
2.

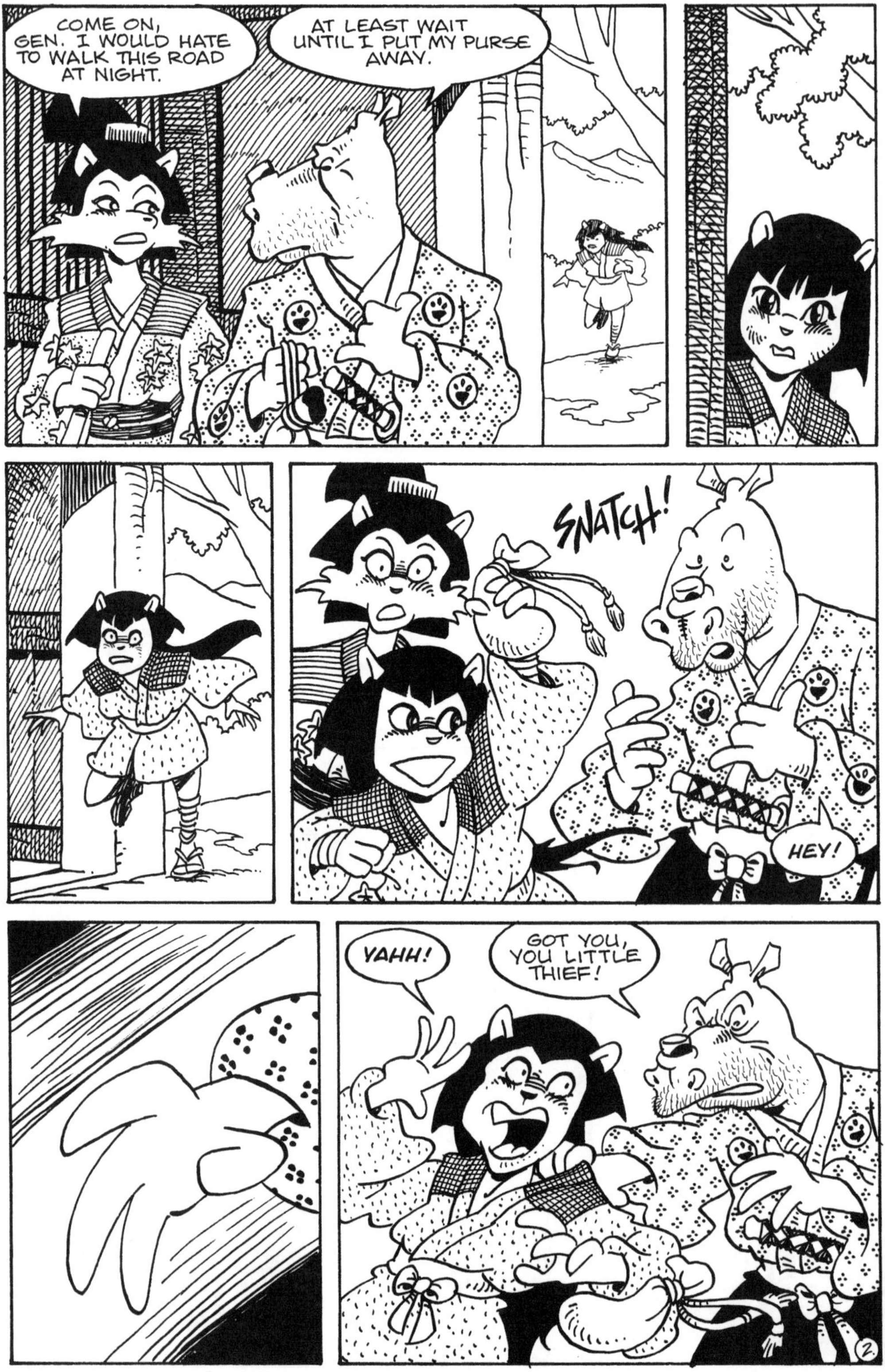
COME ON, GEN. I WOULD HATE TO WALK THIS ROAD AT NIGHT.
AT LEAST WAIT UNTIL I PUT MY PURSE AWAY.
SNATCH!
HEY!
YAHH!
GOT YOU, YOU LITTLE THIEF!
2.

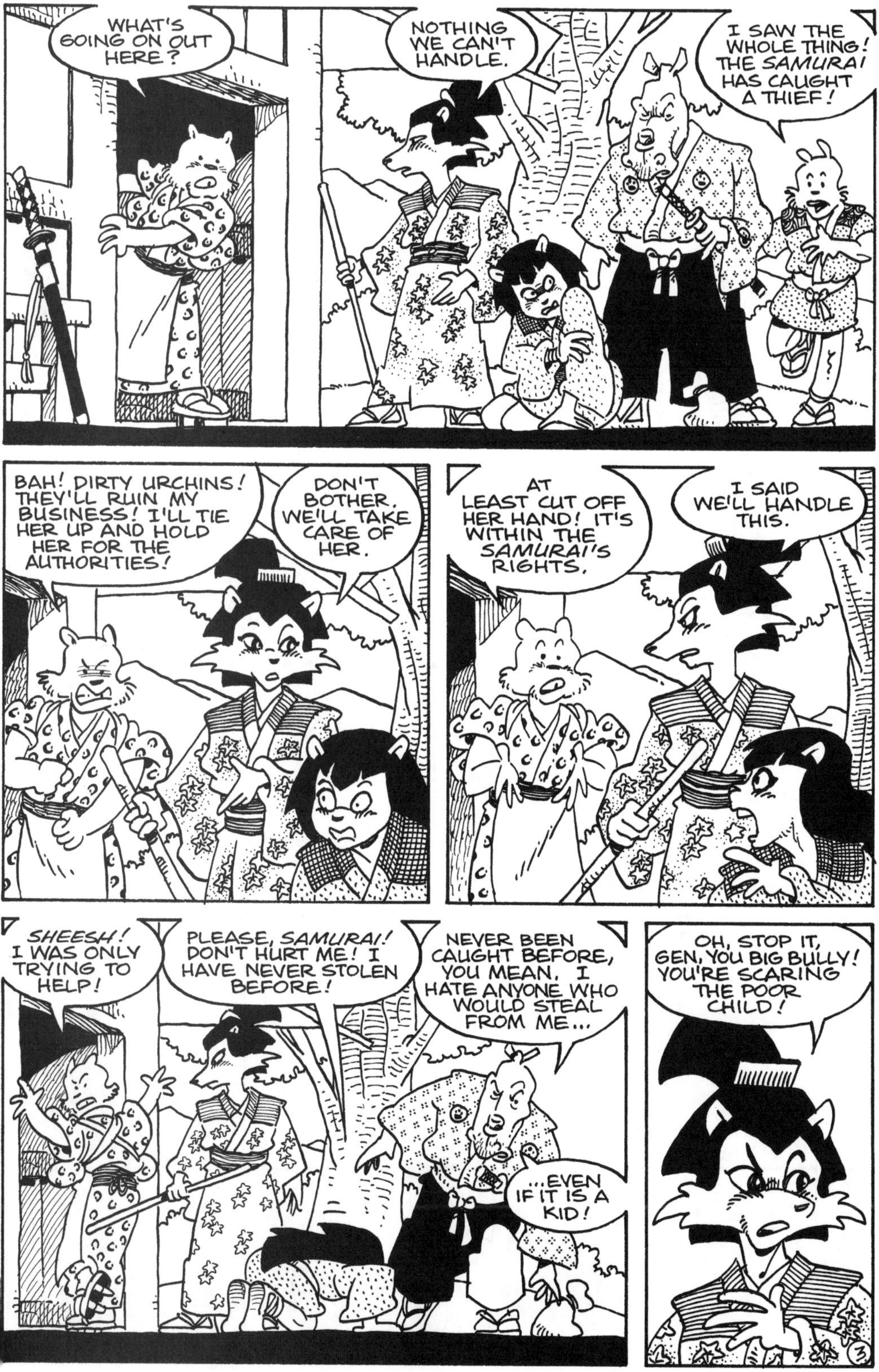

WHAT'S GOING ON OUT HERE?
NOTHING WE CAN'T HANDLE.
I SAW THE WHOLE THING! THE SAMURAI HAS CAUGHT A THIEF!
BAH! DIRTY URCHINS! THEY'LL RUIN MY BUSINESS! I'LL TIE HER UP AND HOLD HER FOR THE AUTHORITIES!
DON'T BOTHER. WE'LL TAKE CARE OF HER.
AT LEAST CUT OFF HER HAND! IT'S WITHIN THE SAMURAI'S RIGHTS.
I SAID WE'LL HANDLE THIS.
SHEESH! I WAS ONLY TRYING TO HELP!
PLEASE, SAMURAI! DON'T HURT ME! I HAVE NEVER STOLEN BEFORE!
NEVER BEEN CAUGHT BEFORE, YOU MEAN. I HATE ANYONE WHO WOULD STEAL FROM ME...
...EVEN IF IT IS A KID!
OH, STOP IT, GEN, YOU BIG BULLY! YOU'RE SCARING THE POOR CHILD!
3

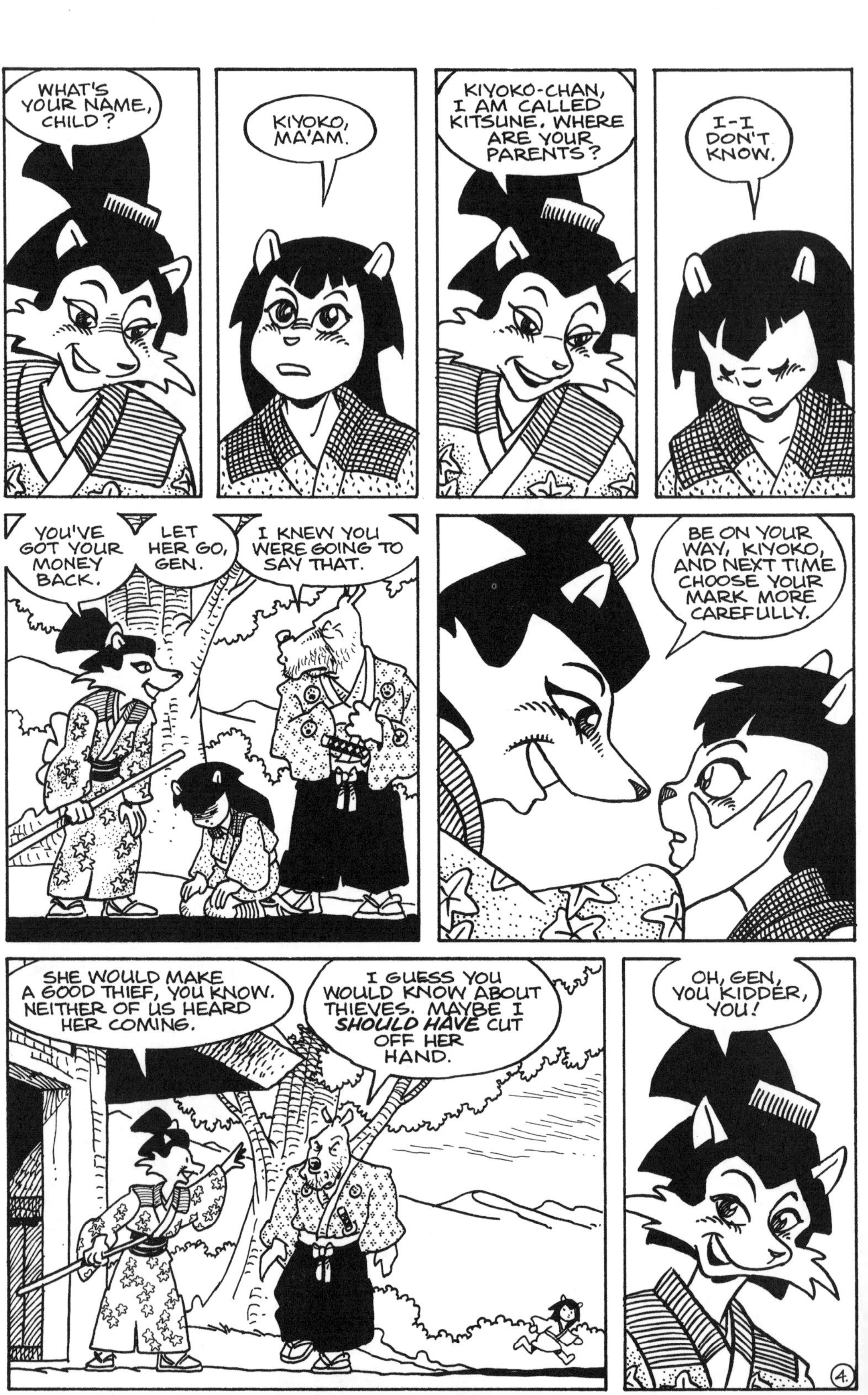
WHAT'S YOUR NAME, CHILD?
KIYOKO, MA'AM.
KIYOKO-CHAN, I AM CALLED KITSUNE. WHERE ARE YOUR PARENTS?
I-I DON'T KNOW.
YOU'VE GOT YOUR MONEY BACK.
LET HER GO, GEN.
I KNEW YOU WERE GOING TO SAY THAT.
BE ON YOUR WAY, KIYOKO, AND NEXT TIME CHOOSE YOUR MARK MORE CAREFULLY.
SHE WOULD MAKE A GOOD THIEF, YOU KNOW. NEITHER OF US HEARD HER COMING.
I GUESS YOU WOULD KNOW ABOUT THIEVES. MAYBE I *SHOULD HAVE* CUT OFF HER HAND.
OH, GEN, YOU KIDDER, YOU!
4.

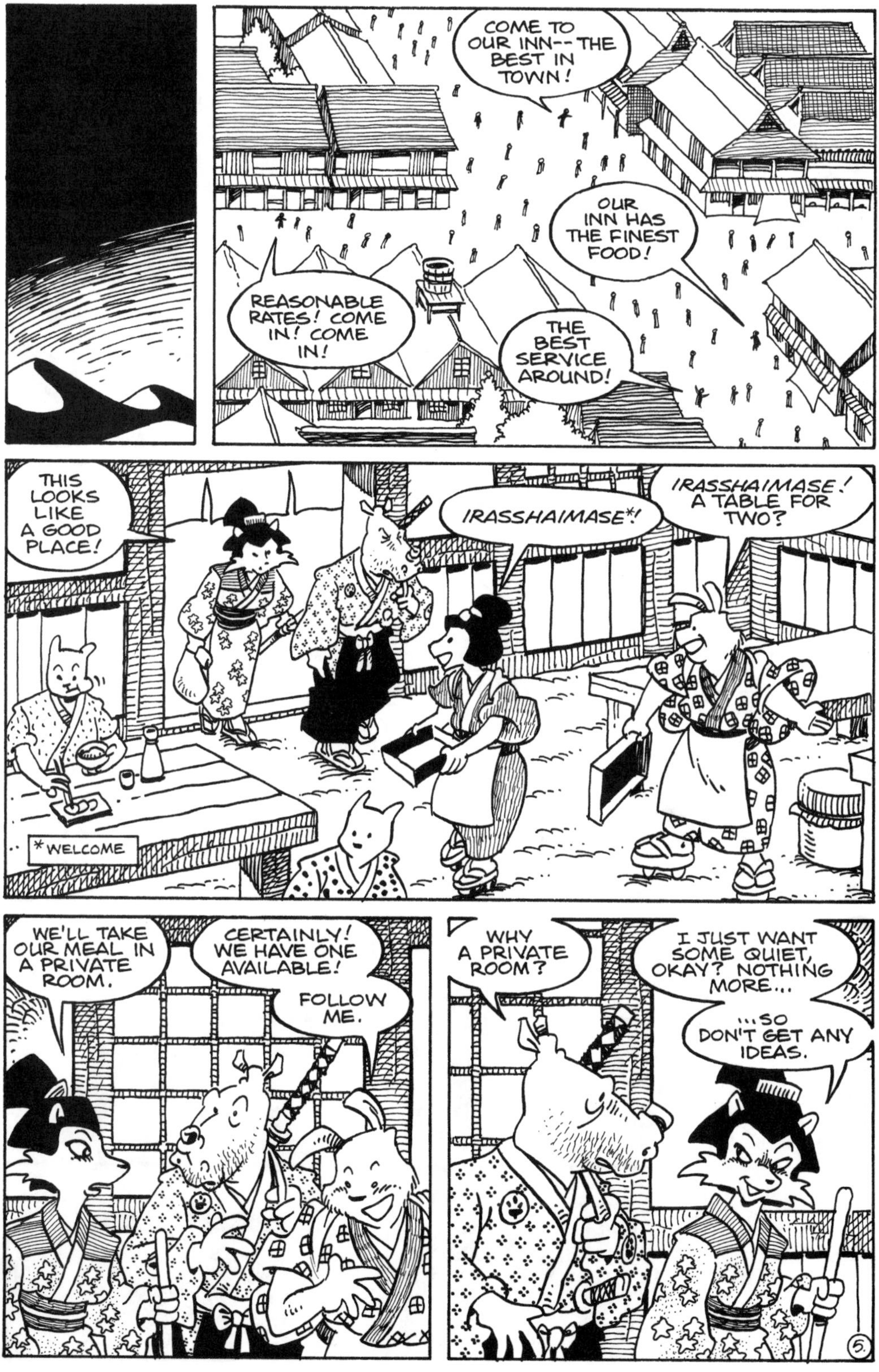
COME TO OUR INN-- THE BEST IN TOWN!
OUR INN HAS THE FINEST FOOD!
REASONABLE RATES! COME IN! COME IN!
THE BEST SERVICE AROUND!
THIS LOOKS LIKE A GOOD PLACE!
IRASSHAIMASE*!
IRASSHAIMASE! A TABLE FOR TWO?
*WELCOME
WE'LL TAKE OUR MEAL IN A PRIVATE ROOM.
CERTAINLY! WE HAVE ONE AVAILABLE!
FOLLOW ME.
WHY A PRIVATE ROOM?
I JUST WANT SOME QUIET, OKAY? NOTHING MORE...
...SO DON'T GET ANY IDEAS.
5.

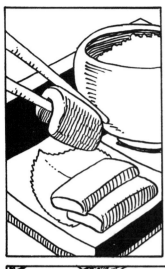

YOU'RE NOT EATING.

WHAT'S THE MATTER?

MUNCH! MUNCH!

I'M NOT HUNGRY, THAT'S ALL.

GOOD. MORE FOR ME THEN.

YOU'VE BEEN ACTING MOODIER SINCE WE LEFT THAT ROADSIDE INN. THAT LITTLE THIEF REALLY GOT TO YOU, DIDN'T SHE?

SHE JUST GOT ME THINKING OF SOMEONE, THAT'S ALL...A PERSON I HAD ALL BUT FORGOTTEN.

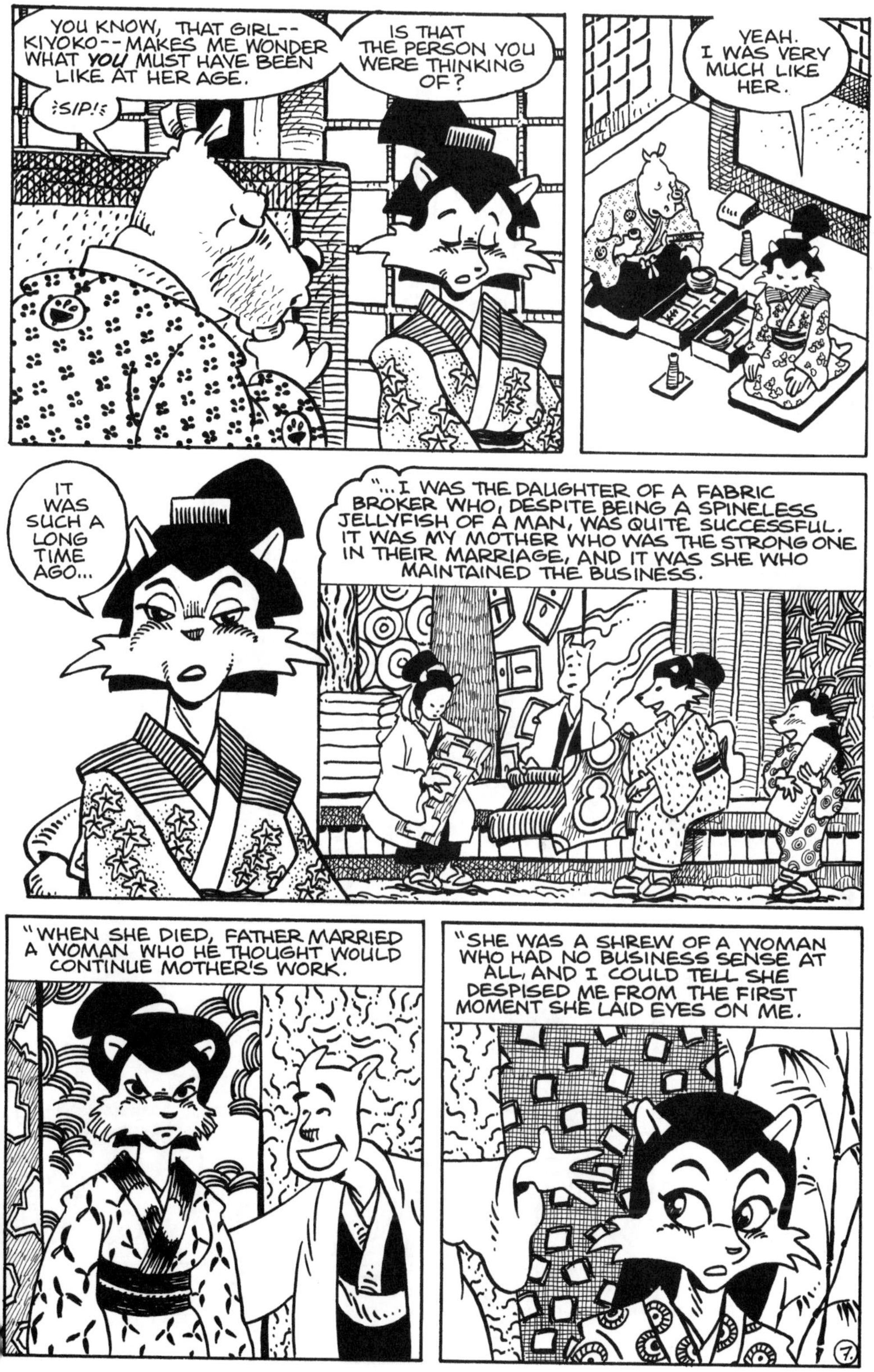
YOU KNOW, THAT GIRL-- KIYOKO--MAKES ME WONDER WHAT *YOU* MUST HAVE BEEN LIKE AT HER AGE.
SIP!
IS THAT THE PERSON YOU WERE THINKING OF?
YEAH. I WAS VERY MUCH LIKE HER.
IT WAS SUCH A LONG TIME AGO...
"...I WAS THE DAUGHTER OF A FABRIC BROKER WHO, DESPITE BEING A SPINELESS JELLYFISH OF A MAN, WAS QUITE SUCCESSFUL. IT WAS MY MOTHER WHO WAS THE STRONG ONE IN THEIR MARRIAGE, AND IT WAS SHE WHO MAINTAINED THE BUSINESS.
"WHEN SHE DIED, FATHER MARRIED A WOMAN WHO HE THOUGHT WOULD CONTINUE MOTHER'S WORK.
"SHE WAS A SHREW OF A WOMAN WHO HAD NO BUSINESS SENSE AT ALL, AND I COULD TELL SHE DESPISED ME FROM THE FIRST MOMENT SHE LAID EYES ON ME.
7.

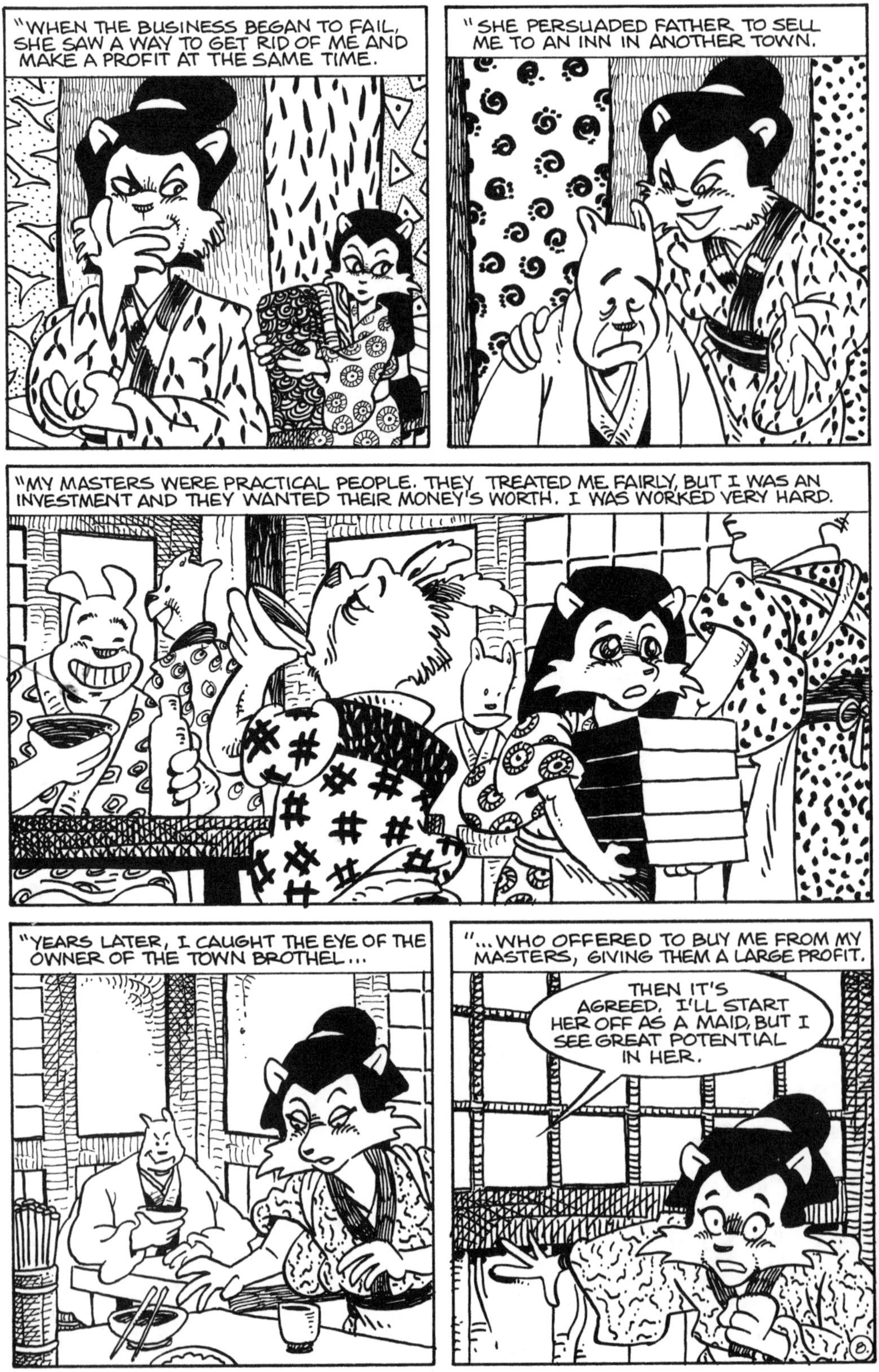
"WHEN THE BUSINESS BEGAN TO FAIL, SHE SAW A WAY TO GET RID OF ME AND MAKE A PROFIT AT THE SAME TIME.
"SHE PERSUADED FATHER TO SELL ME TO AN INN IN ANOTHER TOWN.
"MY MASTERS WERE PRACTICAL PEOPLE. THEY TREATED ME FAIRLY, BUT I WAS AN INVESTMENT AND THEY WANTED THEIR MONEY'S WORTH. I WAS WORKED VERY HARD.
"YEARS LATER, I CAUGHT THE EYE OF THE OWNER OF THE TOWN BROTHEL...
"...WHO OFFERED TO BUY ME FROM MY MASTERS, GIVING THEM A LARGE PROFIT.
THEN IT'S AGREED. I'LL START HER OFF AS A MAID, BUT I SEE GREAT POTENTIAL IN HER.
8.

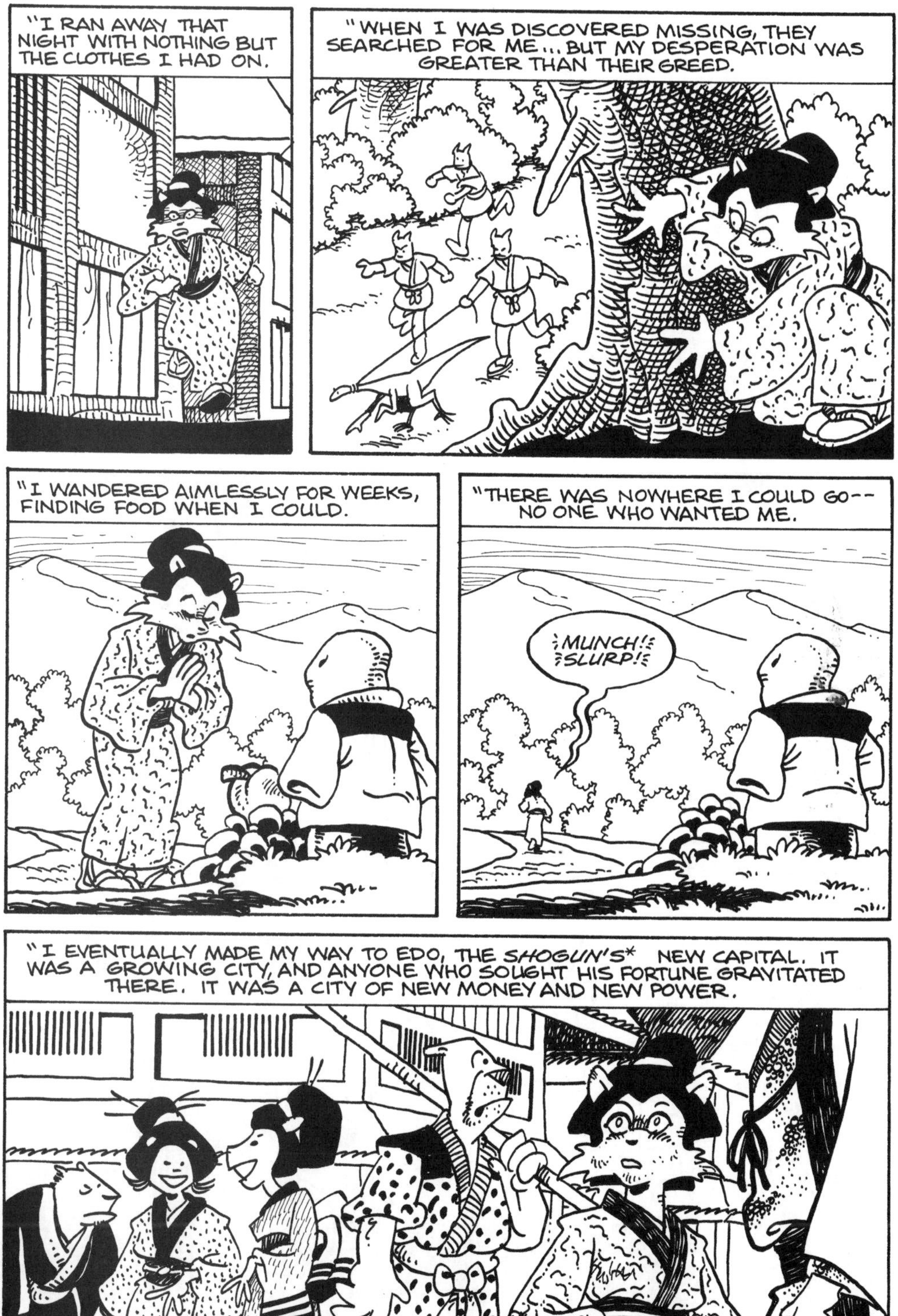
"I RAN AWAY THAT NIGHT WITH NOTHING BUT THE CLOTHES I HAD ON.
"WHEN I WAS DISCOVERED MISSING, THEY SEARCHED FOR ME... BUT MY DESPERATION WAS GREATER THAN THEIR GREED.
"I WANDERED AIMLESSLY FOR WEEKS, FINDING FOOD WHEN I COULD.
"THERE WAS NOWHERE I COULD GO-- NO ONE WHO WANTED ME.
MUNCH! SLURP!
"I EVENTUALLY MADE MY WAY TO EDO, THE SHOGUN'S* NEW CAPITAL. IT WAS A GROWING CITY, AND ANYONE WHO SOUGHT HIS FORTUNE GRAVITATED THERE. IT WAS A CITY OF NEW MONEY AND NEW POWER.
*MILITARY DICTATOR
9.

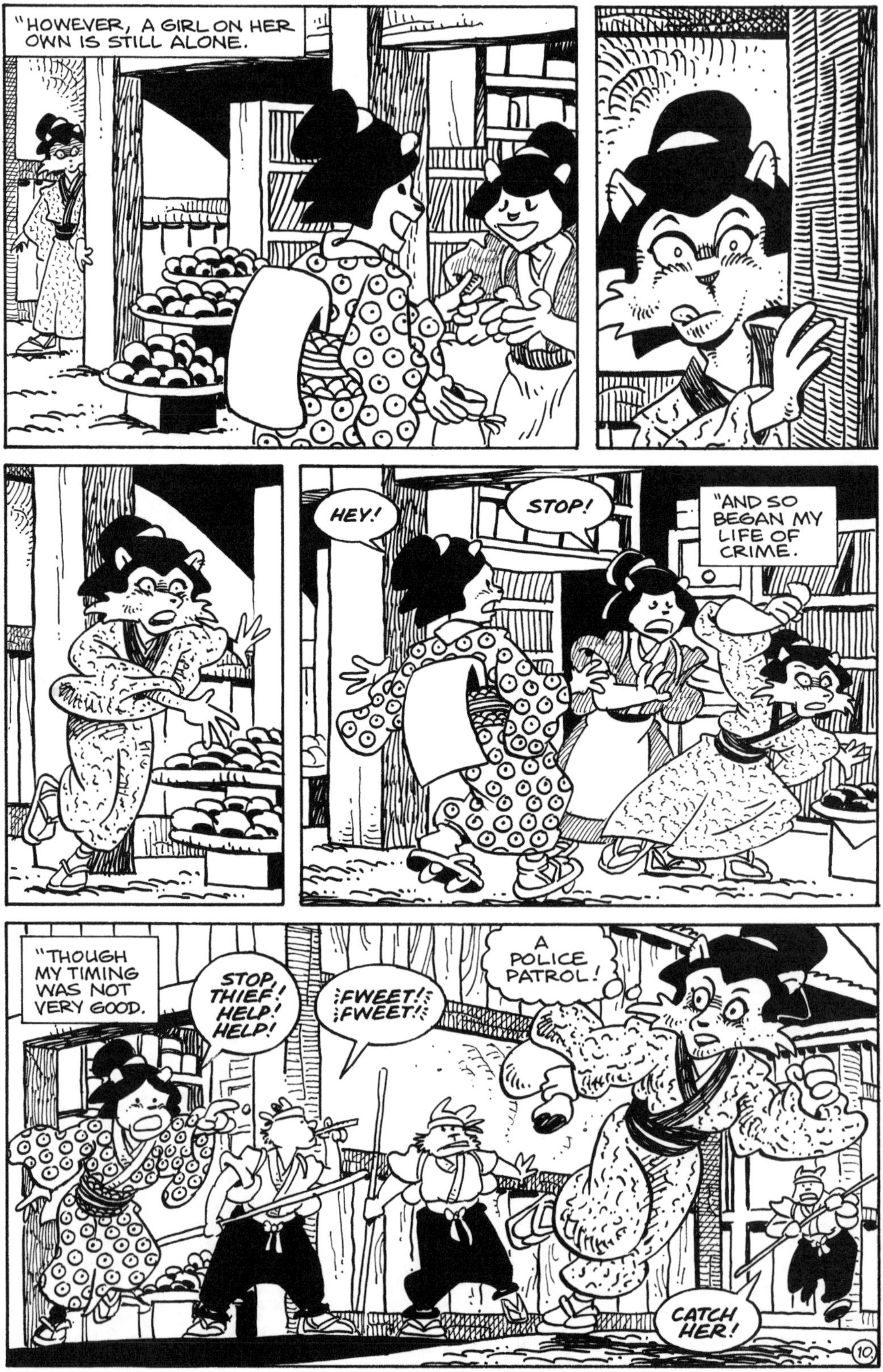
"HOWEVER, A GIRL ON HER OWN IS STILL ALONE.
HEY!
STOP!
"AND SO BEGAN MY LIFE OF CRIME.
"THOUGH MY TIMING WAS NOT VERY GOOD.
STOP, THIEF! HELP! HELP!
FWEET! FWEET!
A POLICE PATROL!
CATCH HER!
10

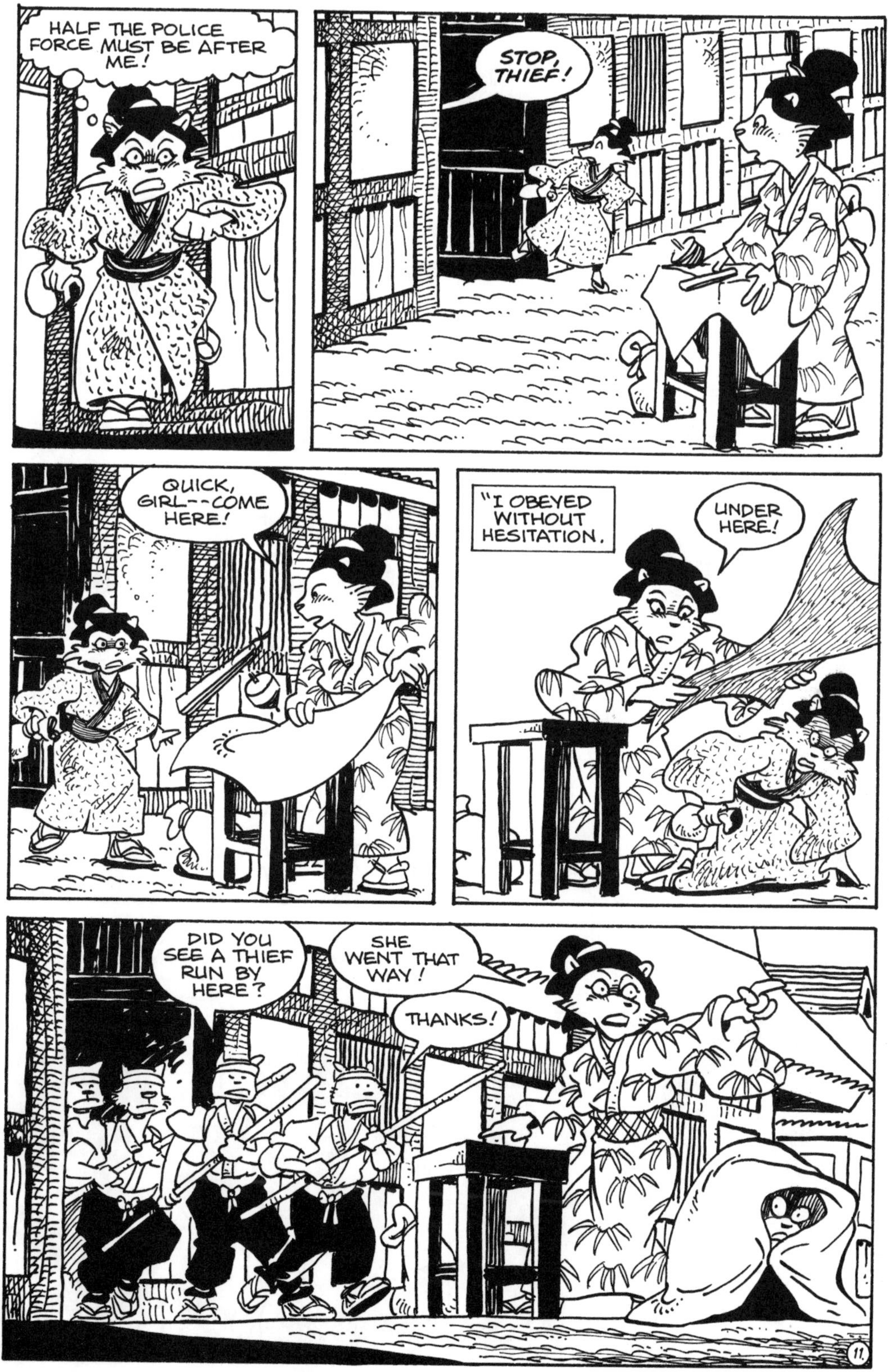
HALF THE POLICE FORCE MUST BE AFTER ME!
STOP, THIEF!
QUICK, GIRL--COME HERE!
"I OBEYED WITHOUT HESITATION.
UNDER HERE!
DID YOU SEE A THIEF RUN BY HERE?
SHE WENT THAT WAY!
THANKS!
11.

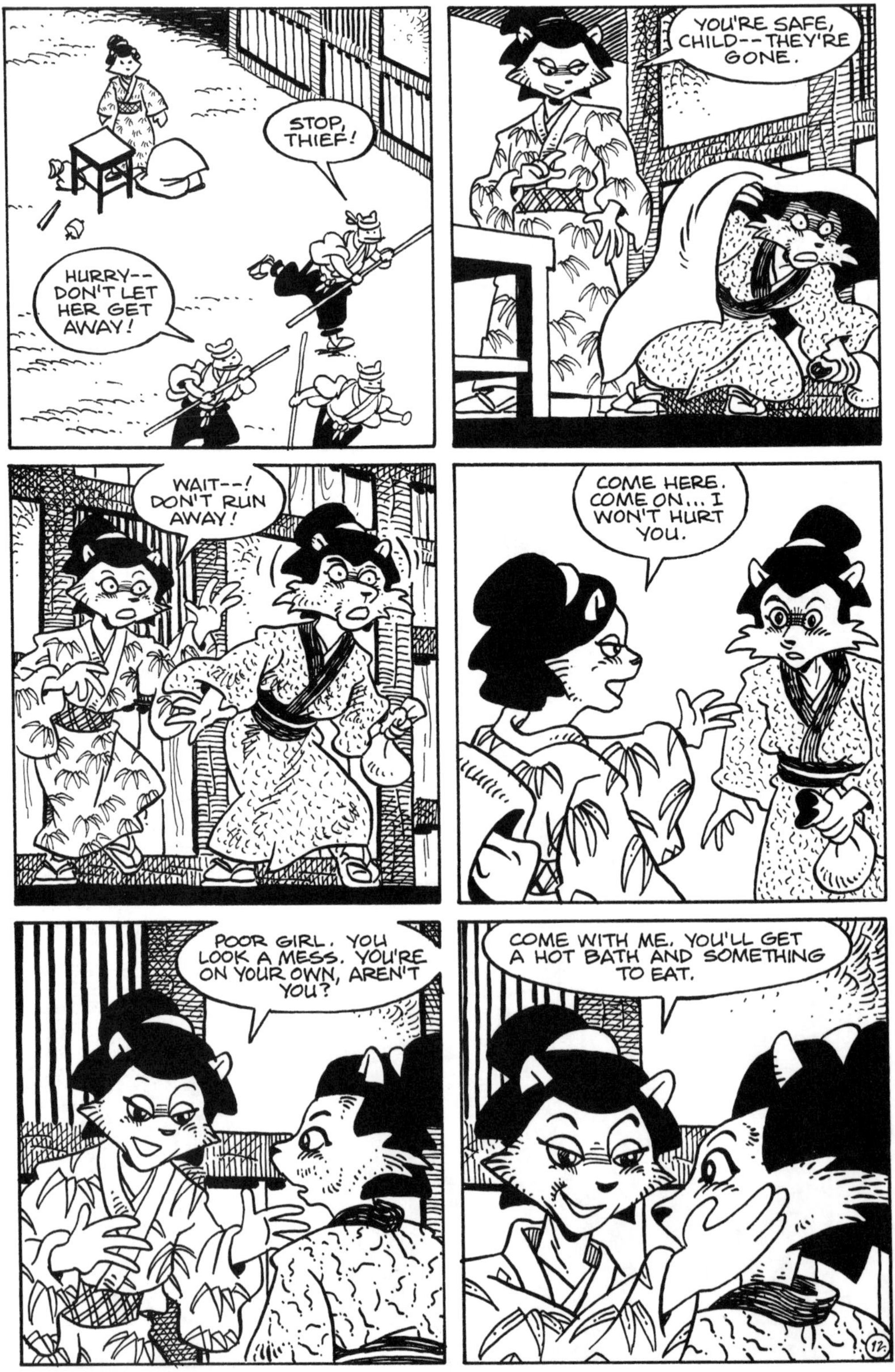
STOP, THIEF!
HURRY-- DON'T LET HER GET AWAY!
YOU'RE SAFE, CHILD--THEY'RE GONE.
WAIT--! DON'T RUN AWAY!
COME HERE. COME ON... I WON'T HURT YOU.
POOR GIRL. YOU LOOK A MESS. YOU'RE ON YOUR OWN, AREN'T YOU?
COME WITH ME. YOU'LL GET A HOT BATH AND SOMETHING TO EAT.
12.

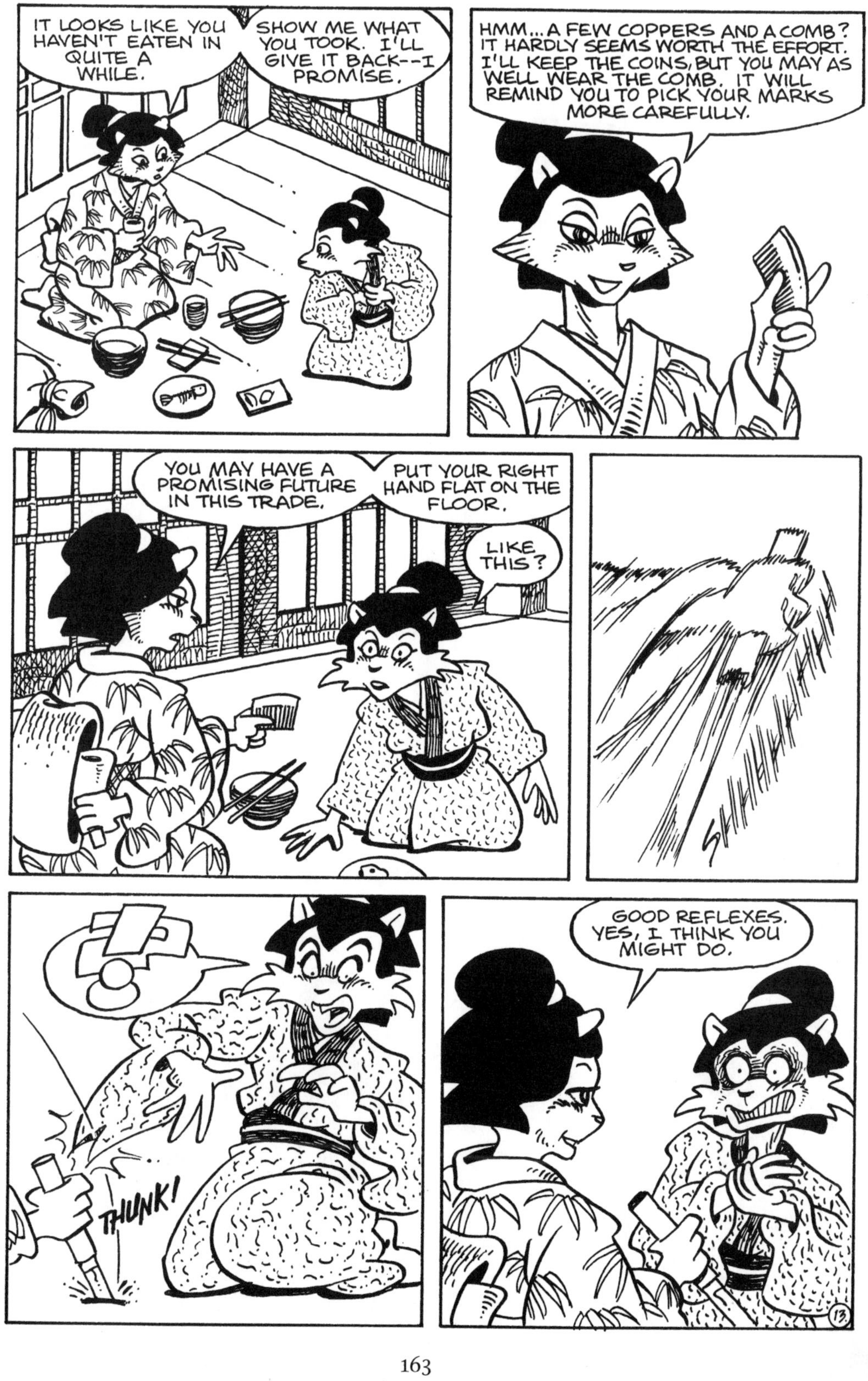
IT LOOKS LIKE YOU HAVEN'T EATEN IN QUITE A WHILE.
SHOW ME WHAT YOU TOOK. I'LL GIVE IT BACK--I PROMISE.
HMM... A FEW COPPERS AND A COMB? IT HARDLY SEEMS WORTH THE EFFORT. I'LL KEEP THE COINS, BUT YOU MAY AS WELL WEAR THE COMB. IT WILL REMIND YOU TO PICK YOUR MARKS MORE CAREFULLY.
YOU MAY HAVE A PROMISING FUTURE IN THIS TRADE.
PUT YOUR RIGHT HAND FLAT ON THE FLOOR.
LIKE THIS?
SHHHHHHHH
THUNK!
GOOD REFLEXES. YES, I THINK YOU MIGHT DO.
13

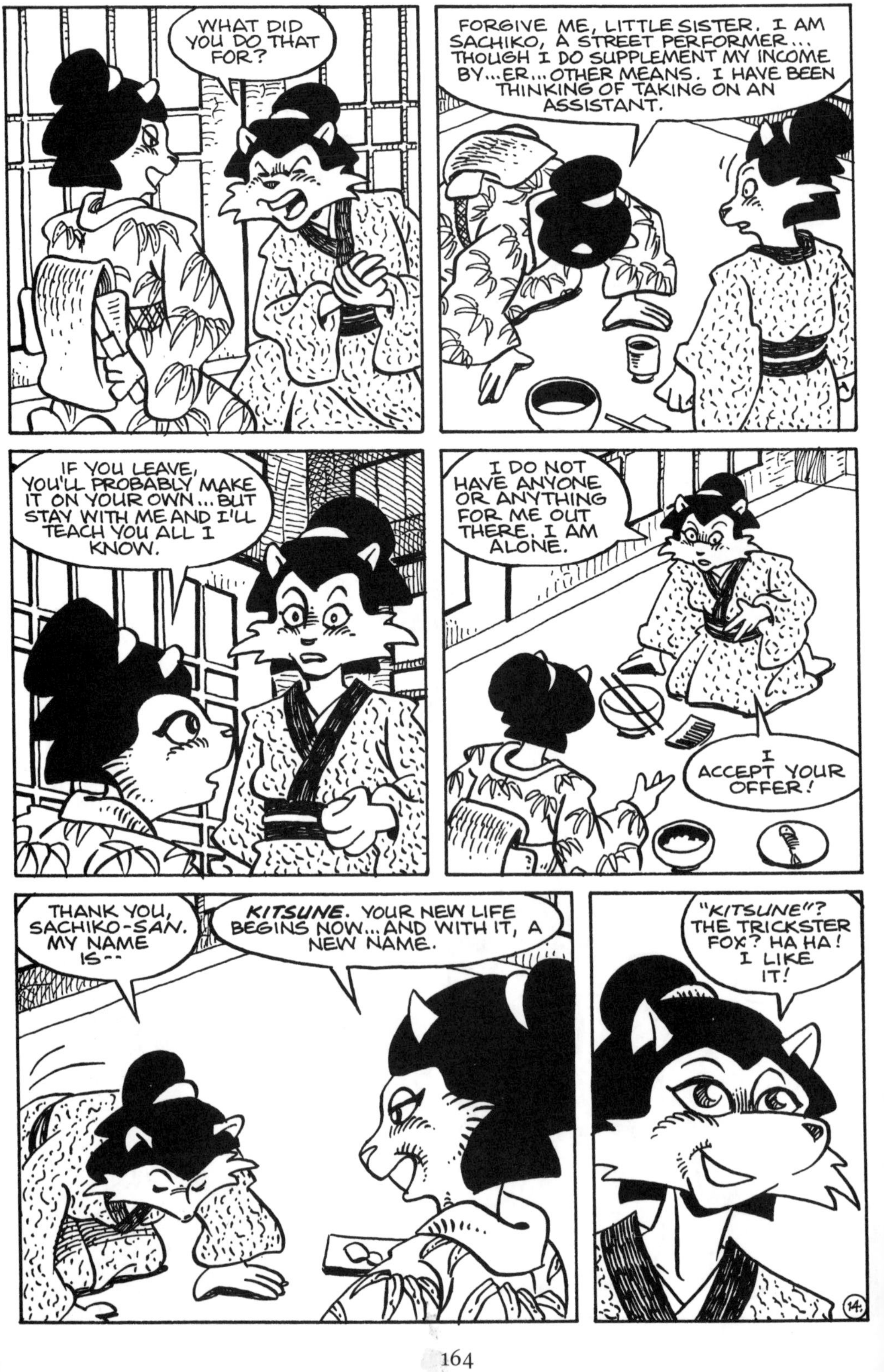
WHAT DID YOU DO THAT FOR?
FORGIVE ME, LITTLE SISTER. I AM SACHIKO, A STREET PERFORMER... THOUGH I DO SUPPLEMENT MY INCOME BY...ER...OTHER MEANS. I HAVE BEEN THINKING OF TAKING ON AN ASSISTANT.
IF YOU LEAVE, YOU'LL PROBABLY MAKE IT ON YOUR OWN... BUT STAY WITH ME AND I'LL TEACH YOU ALL I KNOW.
I DO NOT HAVE ANYONE OR ANYTHING FOR ME OUT THERE. I AM ALONE.
I ACCEPT YOUR OFFER!
THANK YOU, SACHIKO-SAN. MY NAME IS--
KITSUNE. YOUR NEW LIFE BEGINS NOW...AND WITH IT, A NEW NAME.
"KITSUNE"? THE TRICKSTER FOX? HA HA! I LIKE IT!
14.

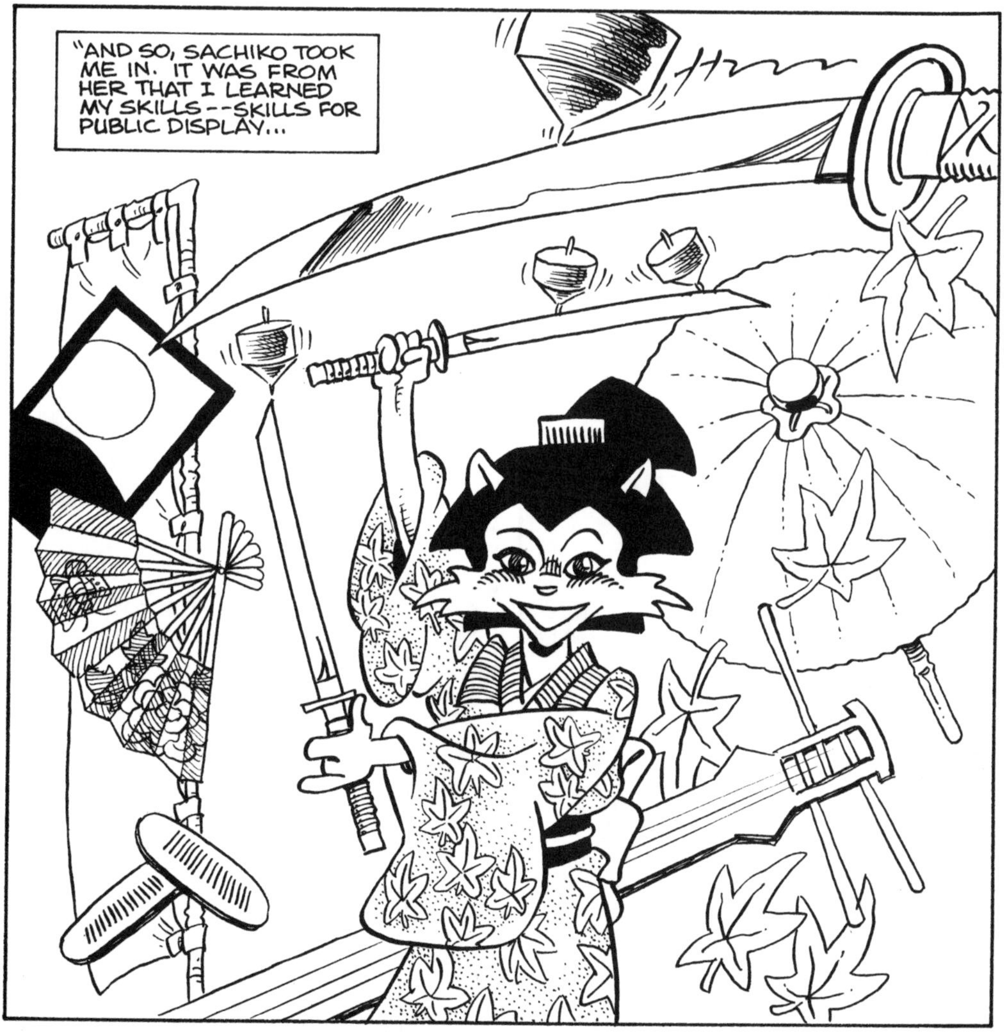
"AND SO, SACHIKO TOOK ME IN. IT WAS FROM HER THAT I LEARNED MY SKILLS--SKILLS FOR PUBLIC DISPLAY...

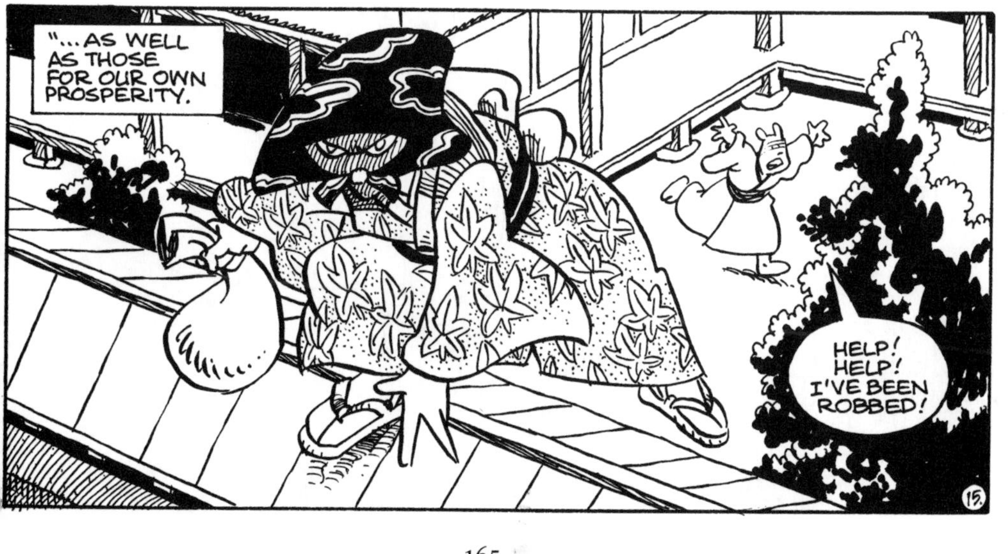
"...AS WELL AS THOSE FOR OUR OWN PROSPERITY.
HELP! HELP! I'VE BEEN ROBBED!
15.

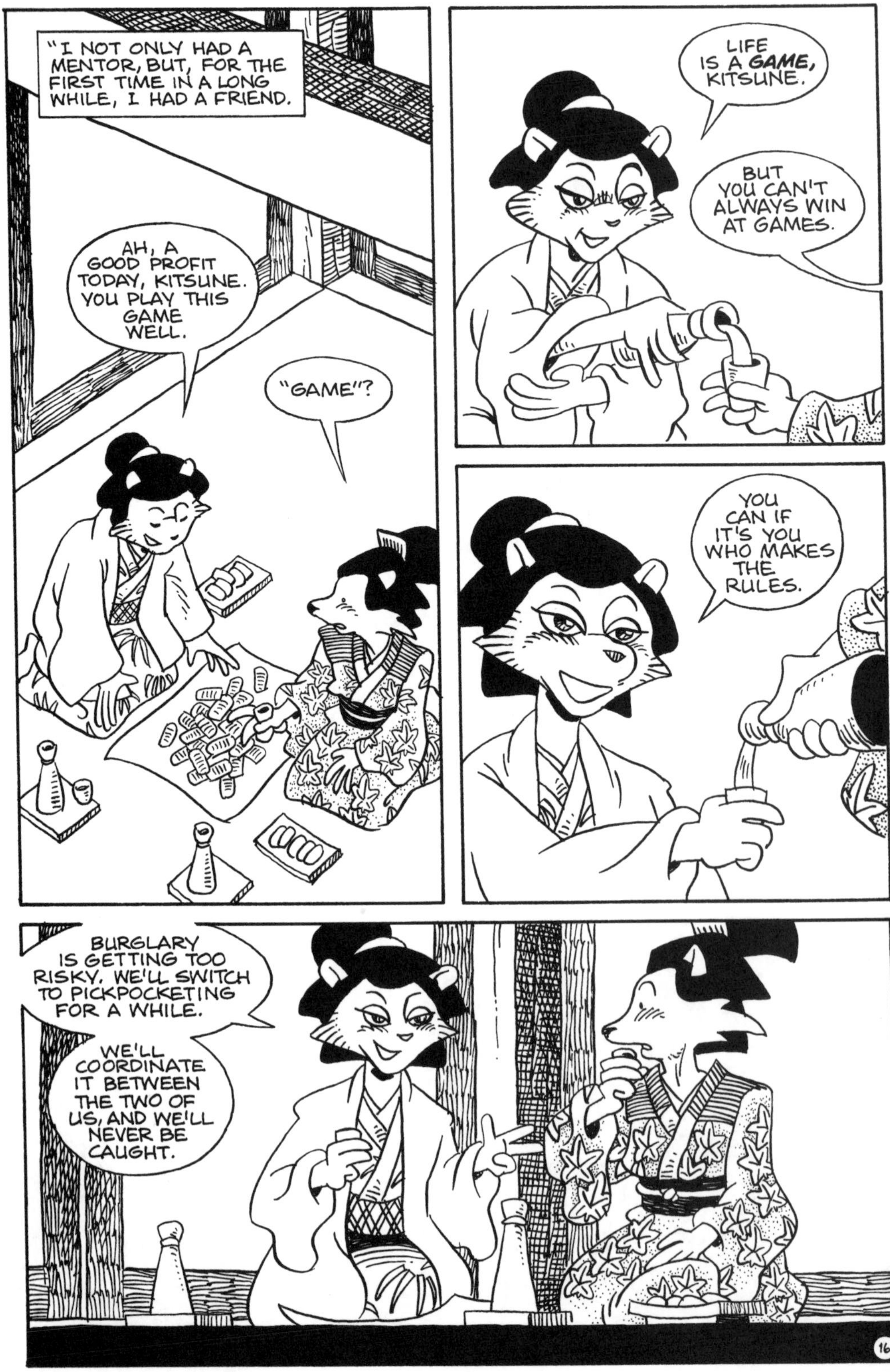
"I NOT ONLY HAD A MENTOR, BUT, FOR THE FIRST TIME IN A LONG WHILE, I HAD A FRIEND.
AH, A GOOD PROFIT TODAY, KITSUNE. YOU PLAY THIS GAME WELL.
"GAME"?
LIFE IS A GAME, KITSUNE.
BUT YOU CAN'T ALWAYS WIN AT GAMES.
YOU CAN IF IT'S YOU WHO MAKES THE RULES.
BURGLARY IS GETTING TOO RISKY. WE'LL SWITCH TO PICKPOCKETING FOR A WHILE.
WE'LL COORDINATE IT BETWEEN THE TWO OF US, AND WE'LL NEVER BE CAUGHT.
16.

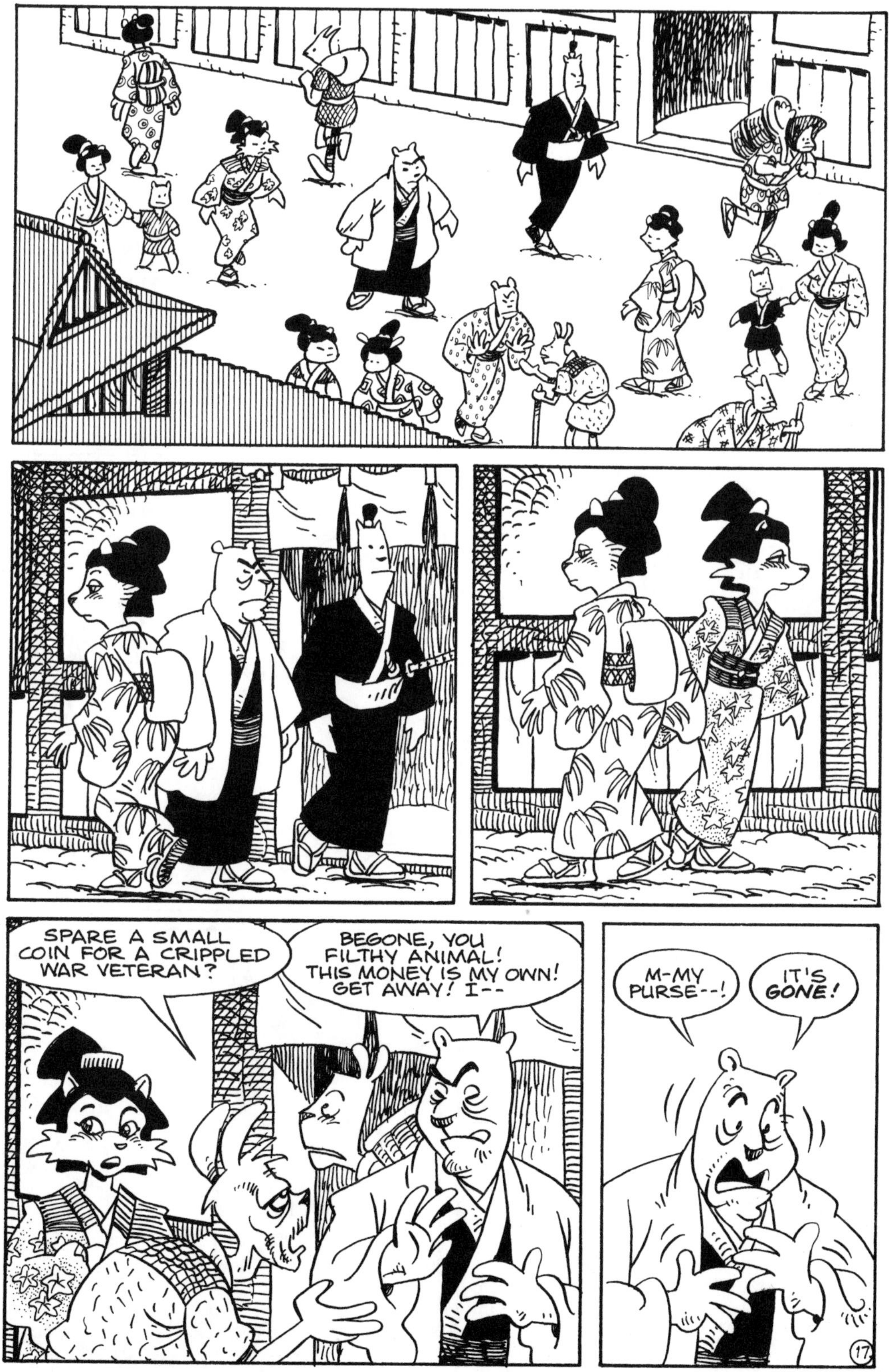
SPARE A SMALL COIN FOR A CRIPPLED WAR VETERAN?
BEGONE, YOU FILTHY ANIMAL! THIS MONEY IS MY OWN! GET AWAY! I--
M-MY PURSE--!
IT'S **GONE**!
17

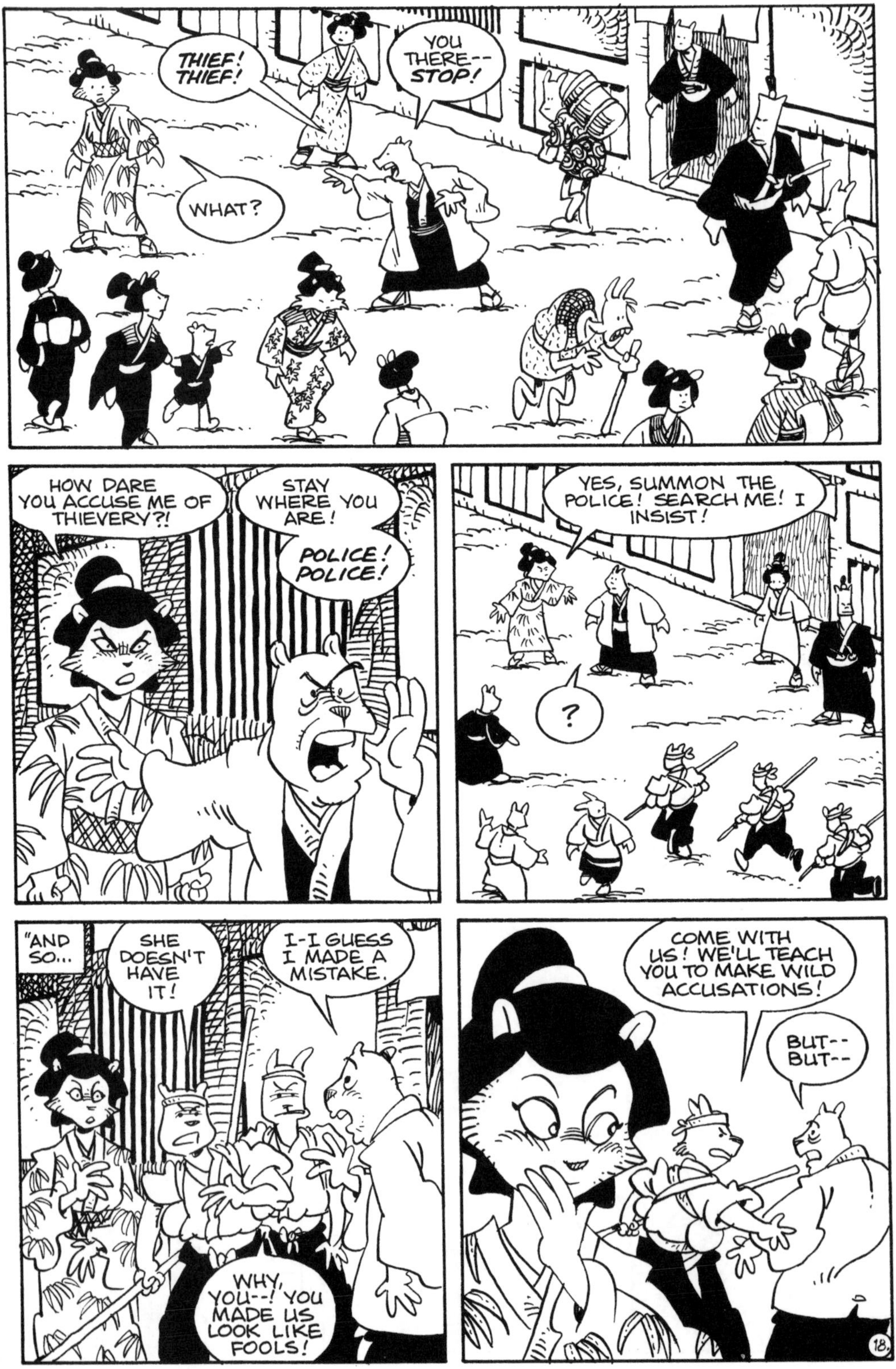

THIEF! THIEF!
YOU THERE-- STOP!
WHAT?
HOW DARE YOU ACCUSE ME OF THIEVERY?!
STAY WHERE YOU ARE!
POLICE! POLICE!
YES, SUMMON THE POLICE! SEARCH ME! I INSIST!
?
"AND SO...
SHE DOESN'T HAVE IT!
I-I GUESS I MADE A MISTAKE.
WHY, YOU--! YOU MADE US LOOK LIKE FOOLS!
COME WITH US! WE'LL TEACH YOU TO MAKE WILD ACCUSATIONS!
BUT-- BUT--
18

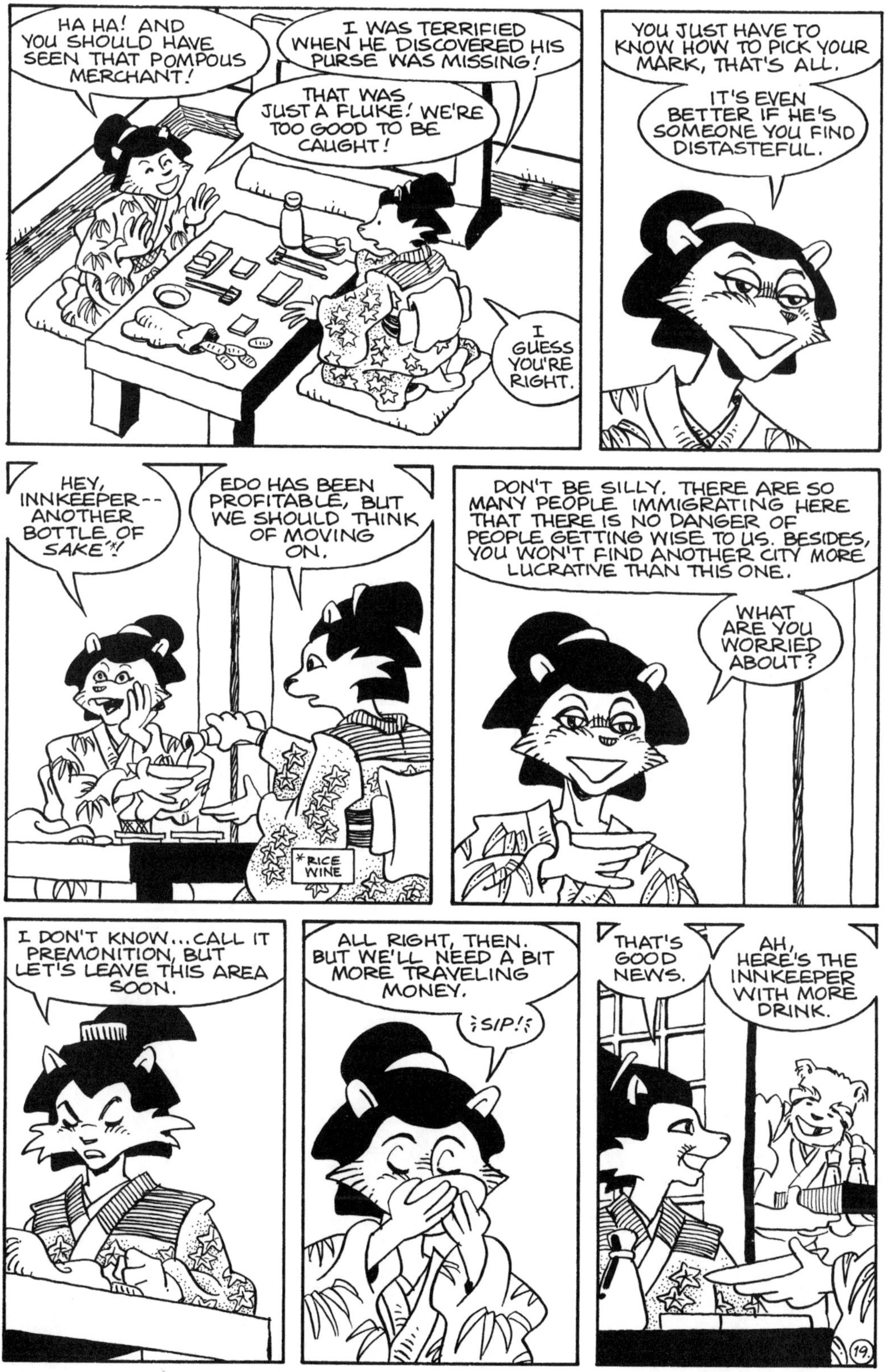
HA HA! AND YOU SHOULD HAVE SEEN THAT POMPOUS MERCHANT!
I WAS TERRIFIED WHEN HE DISCOVERED HIS PURSE WAS MISSING!
THAT WAS JUST A FLUKE! WE'RE TOO GOOD TO BE CAUGHT!
I GUESS YOU'RE RIGHT.
YOU JUST HAVE TO KNOW HOW TO PICK YOUR MARK, THAT'S ALL.
IT'S EVEN BETTER IF HE'S SOMEONE YOU FIND DISTASTEFUL.
HEY, INNKEEPER-- ANOTHER BOTTLE OF SAKE*!
EDO HAS BEEN PROFITABLE, BUT WE SHOULD THINK OF MOVING ON.
*RICE WINE
DON'T BE SILLY. THERE ARE SO MANY PEOPLE IMMIGRATING HERE THAT THERE IS NO DANGER OF PEOPLE GETTING WISE TO US. BESIDES, YOU WON'T FIND ANOTHER CITY MORE LUCRATIVE THAN THIS ONE.
WHAT ARE YOU WORRIED ABOUT?
I DON'T KNOW...CALL IT PREMONITION, BUT LET'S LEAVE THIS AREA SOON.
ALL RIGHT, THEN. BUT WE'LL NEED A BIT MORE TRAVELING MONEY.
SIP!
THAT'S GOOD NEWS.
AH, HERE'S THE INNKEEPER WITH MORE DRINK.
19.

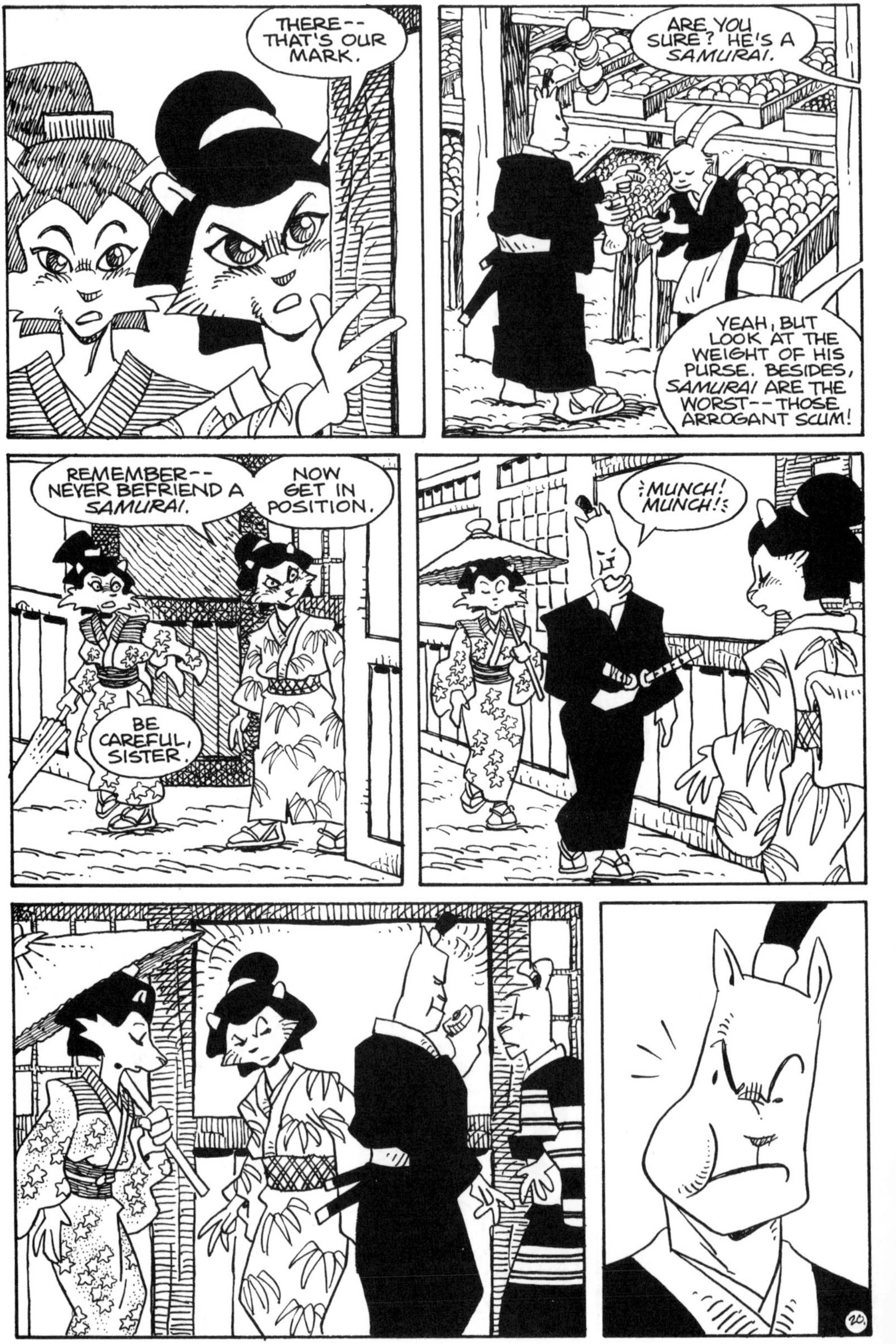
THERE-- THAT'S OUR MARK.
ARE YOU SURE? HE'S A *SAMURAI*.
YEAH, BUT LOOK AT THE WEIGHT OF HIS PURSE. BESIDES, *SAMURAI* ARE THE WORST--THOSE ARROGANT SCUM!
REMEMBER-- NEVER BEFRIEND A *SAMURAI*.
NOW GET IN POSITION.
BE CAREFUL, SISTER.
MUNCH! MUNCH!
20.

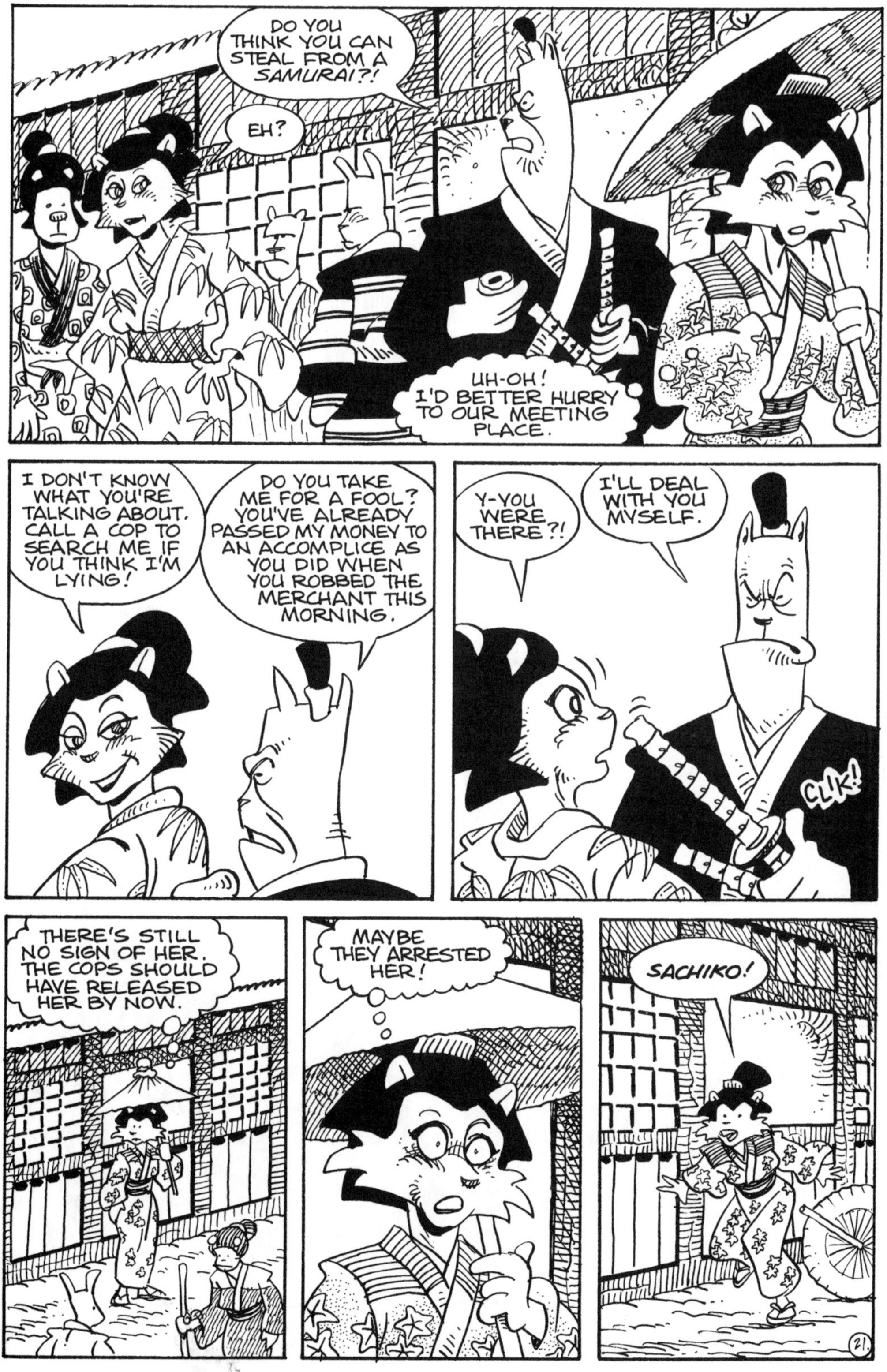
DO YOU THINK YOU CAN STEAL FROM A *SAMURAI*?!
EH?
UH-OH! I'D BETTER HURRY TO OUR MEETING PLACE.
I DON'T KNOW WHAT YOU'RE TALKING ABOUT. CALL A COP TO SEARCH ME IF YOU THINK I'M LYING!
DO YOU TAKE ME FOR A FOOL? YOU'VE ALREADY PASSED MY MONEY TO AN ACCOMPLICE AS YOU DID WHEN YOU ROBBED THE MERCHANT THIS MORNING.
Y-YOU WERE THERE?!
I'LL DEAL WITH YOU MYSELF.
CLIK!
THERE'S STILL NO SIGN OF HER. THE COPS SHOULD HAVE RELEASED HER BY NOW.
MAYBE THEY ARRESTED HER!
SACHIKO!
21.

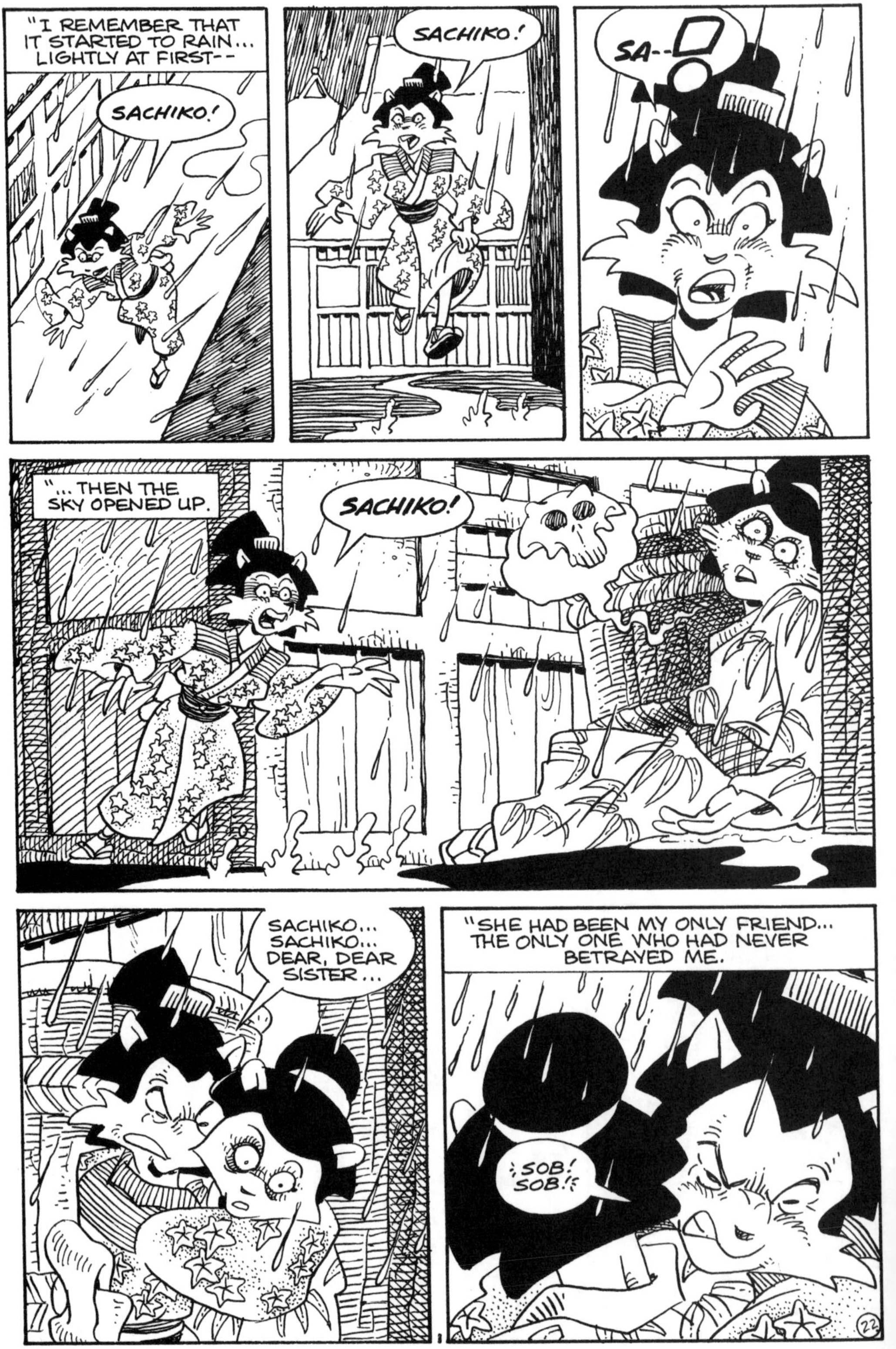
"I REMEMBER THAT IT STARTED TO RAIN... LIGHTLY AT FIRST--
SACHIKO!
SACHIKO!
SA--
"...THEN THE SKY OPENED UP.
SACHIKO!
SACHIKO... SACHIKO... DEAR, DEAR SISTER...
"SHE HAD BEEN MY ONLY FRIEND... THE ONLY ONE WHO HAD NEVER BETRAYED ME.
SOB! SOB!
22

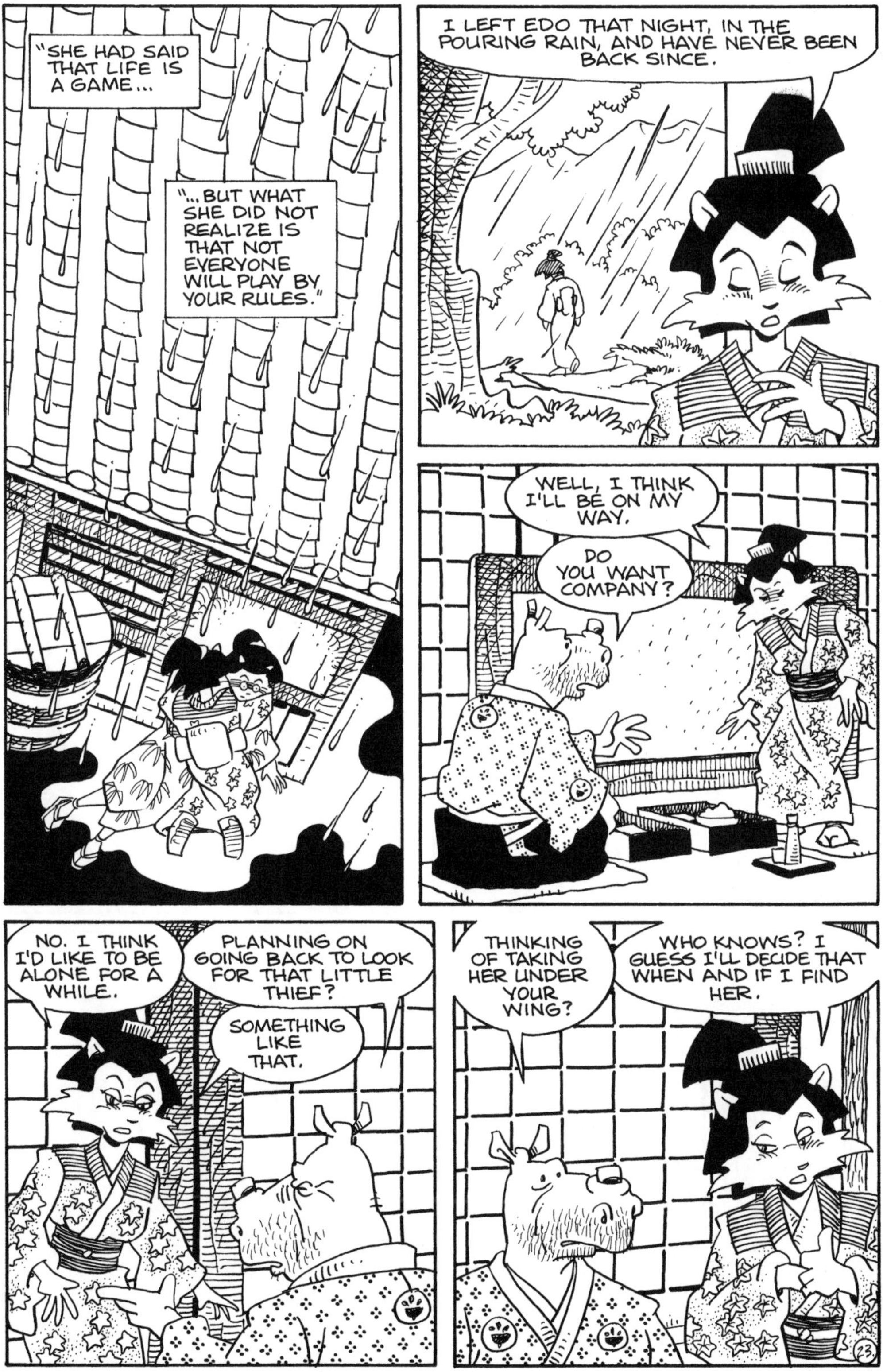
"SHE HAD SAID THAT LIFE IS A GAME...
"...BUT WHAT SHE DID NOT REALIZE IS THAT NOT EVERYONE WILL PLAY BY YOUR RULES."
I LEFT EDO THAT NIGHT, IN THE POURING RAIN, AND HAVE NEVER BEEN BACK SINCE.
WELL, I THINK I'LL BE ON MY WAY.
DO YOU WANT COMPANY?
NO. I THINK I'D LIKE TO BE ALONE FOR A WHILE.
PLANNING ON GOING BACK TO LOOK FOR THAT LITTLE THIEF?
SOMETHING LIKE THAT.
THINKING OF TAKING HER UNDER YOUR WING?
WHO KNOWS? I GUESS I'LL DECIDE THAT WHEN AND IF I FIND HER.
23

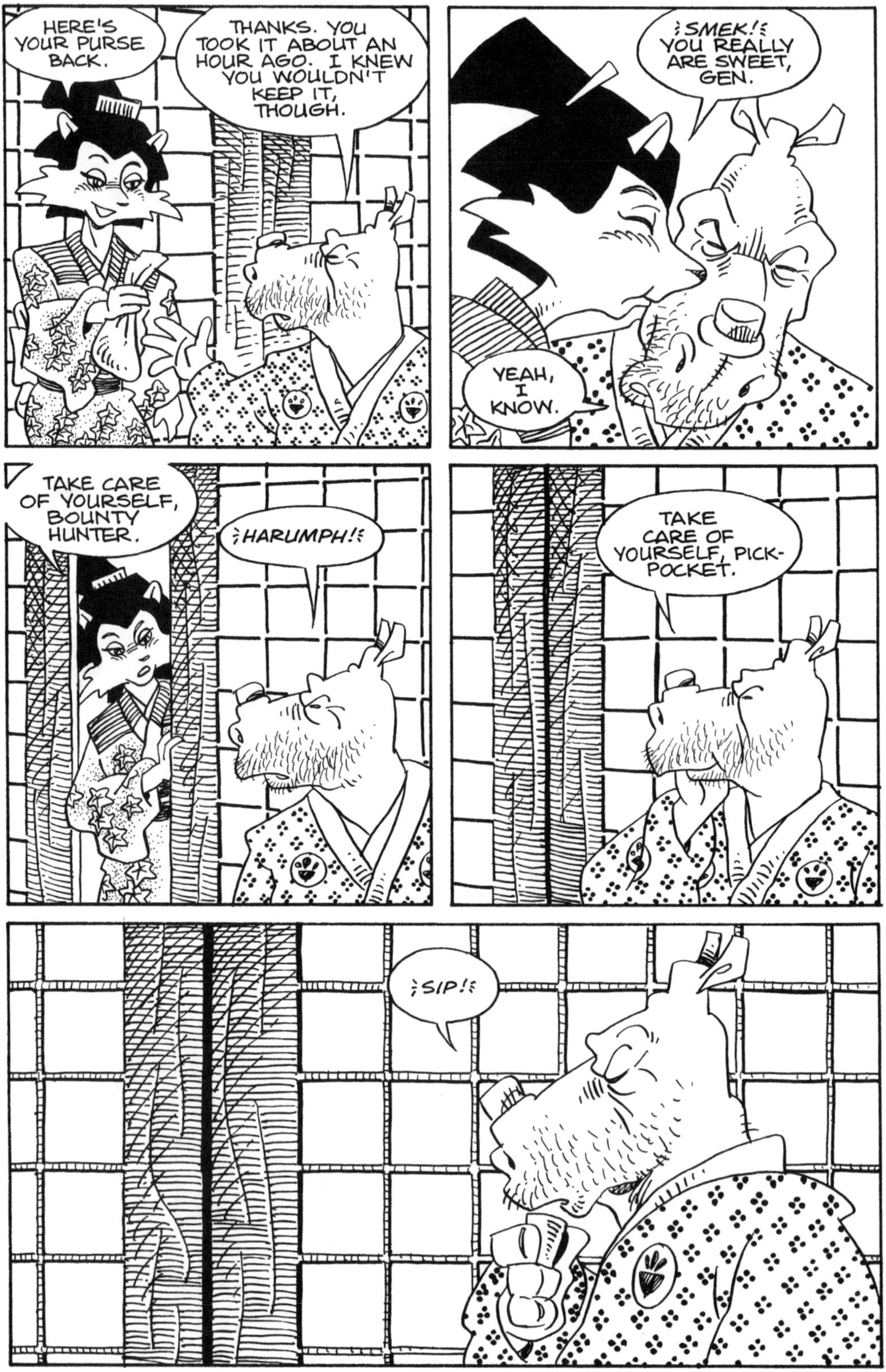
HERE'S YOUR PURSE BACK.
THANKS. YOU TOOK IT ABOUT AN HOUR AGO. I KNEW YOU WOULDN'T KEEP IT, THOUGH.
SMEK!
YOU REALLY ARE SWEET, GEN.
YEAH, I KNOW.
TAKE CARE OF YOURSELF, BOUNTY HUNTER.
HARUMPH!
TAKE CARE OF YOURSELF, PICK-POCKET.
SIP!
THE END.

Gallery

The following pages feature Stan Sakai's cover art from issues forty-six through fifty-two of Dark Horse's Usagi Yojimbo Volume Three *series.*

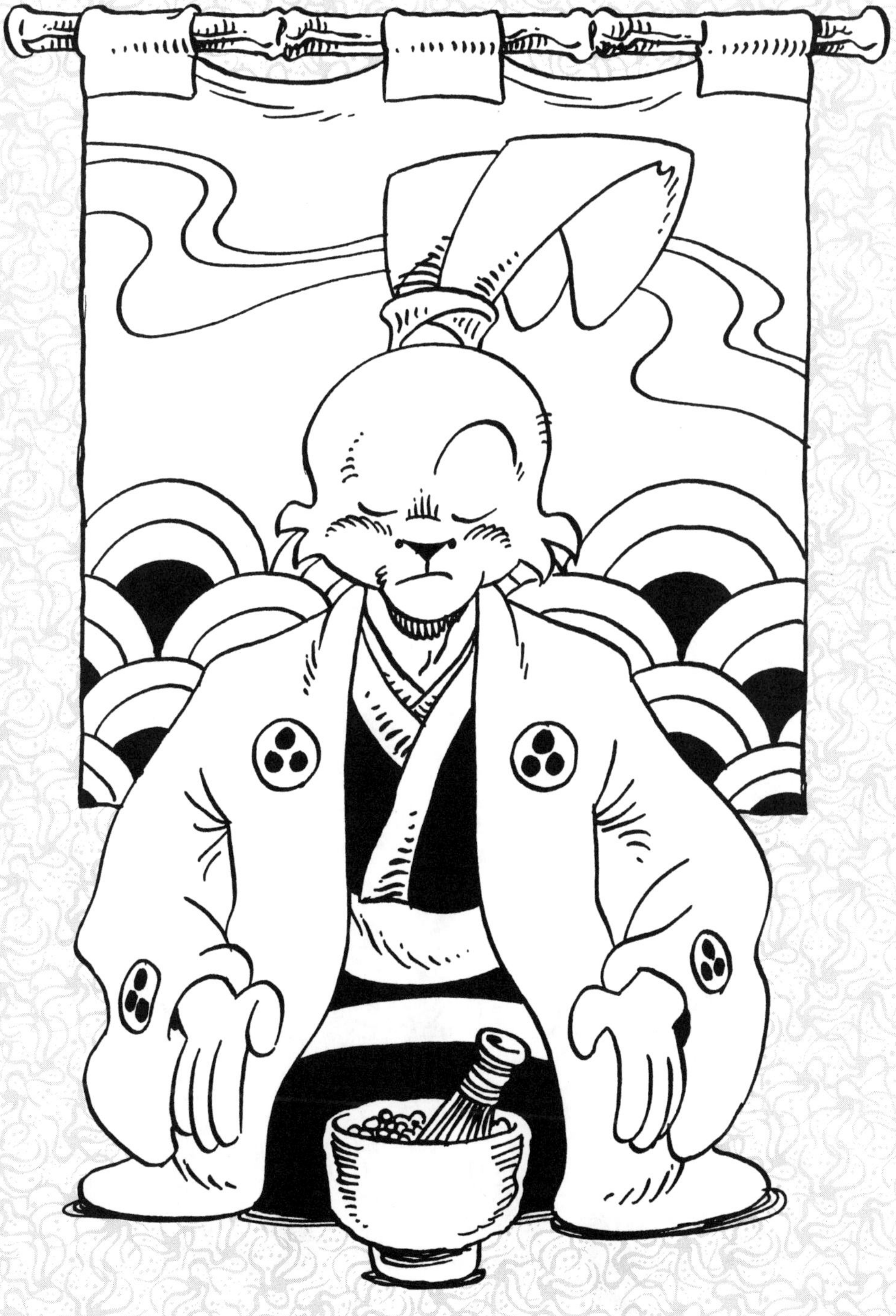

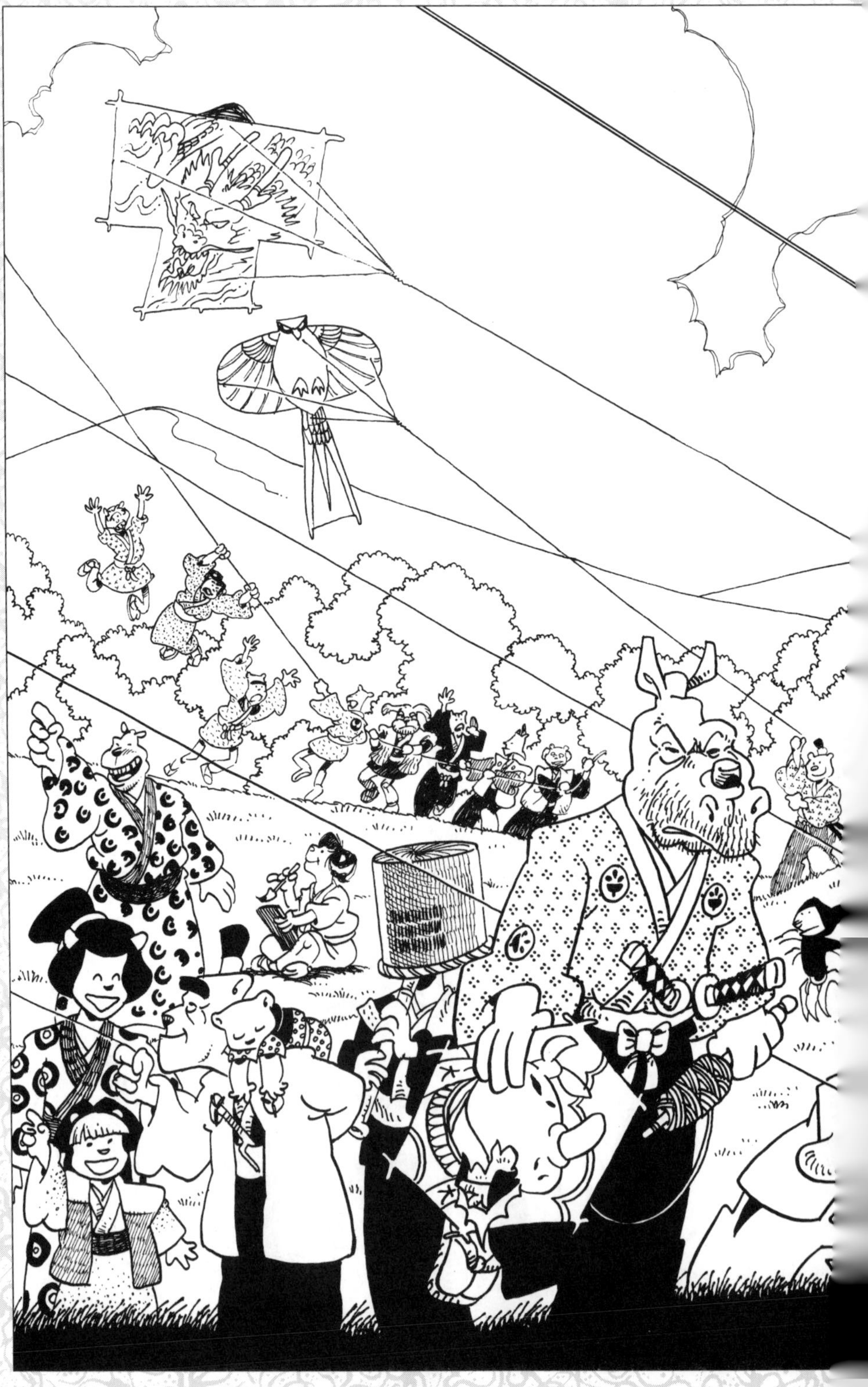

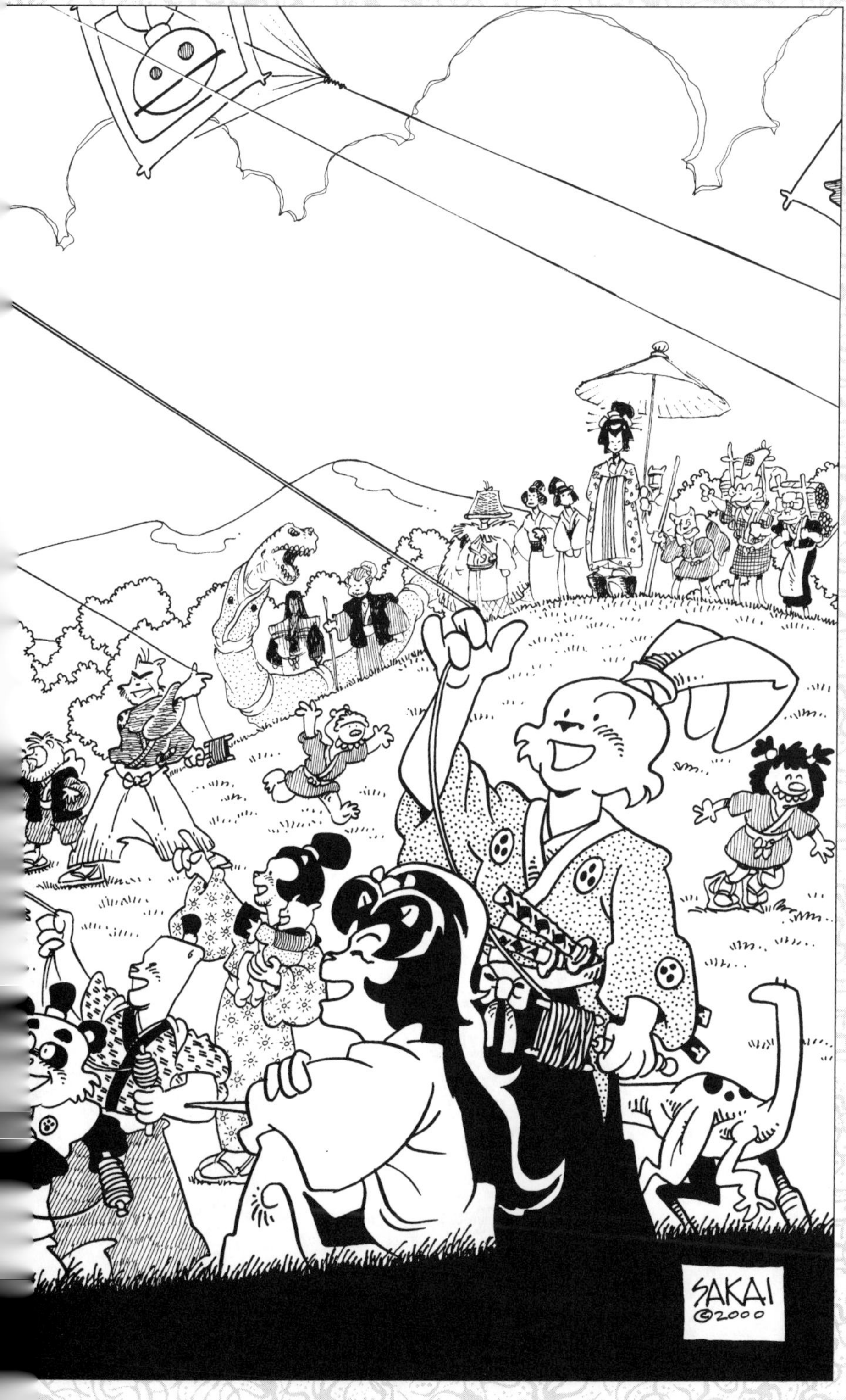
SAKAI
©2000

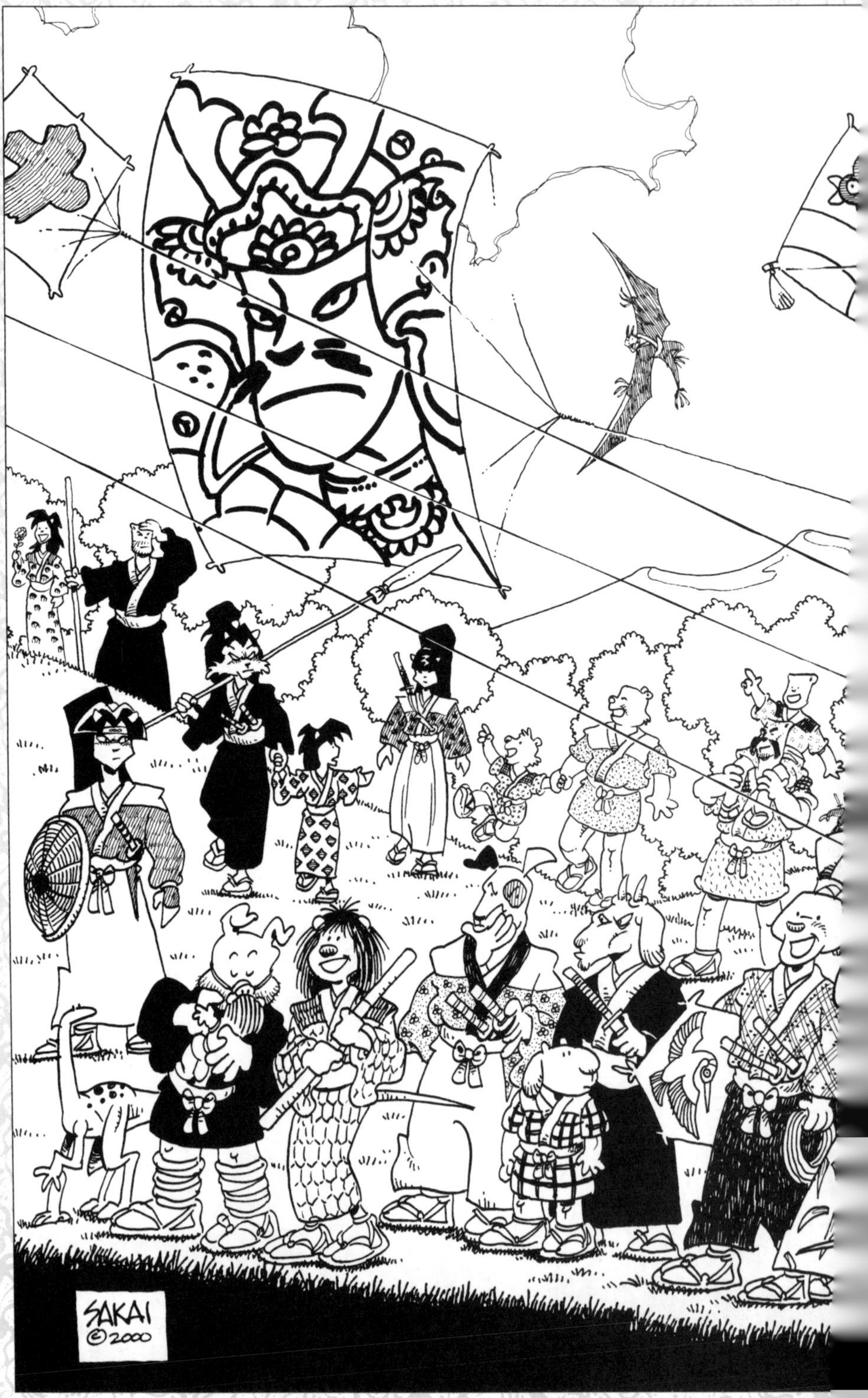
SAKAI
©2000

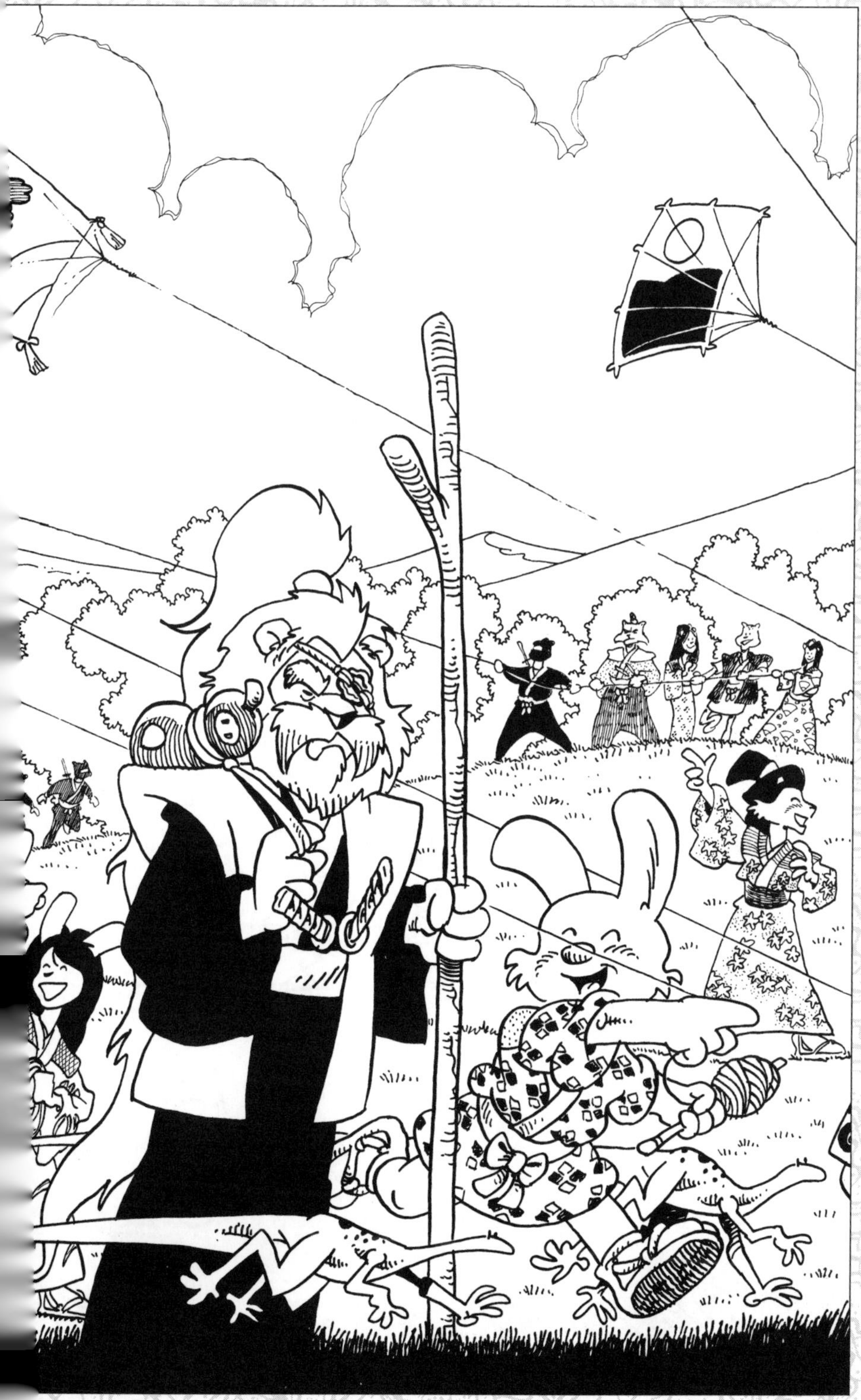

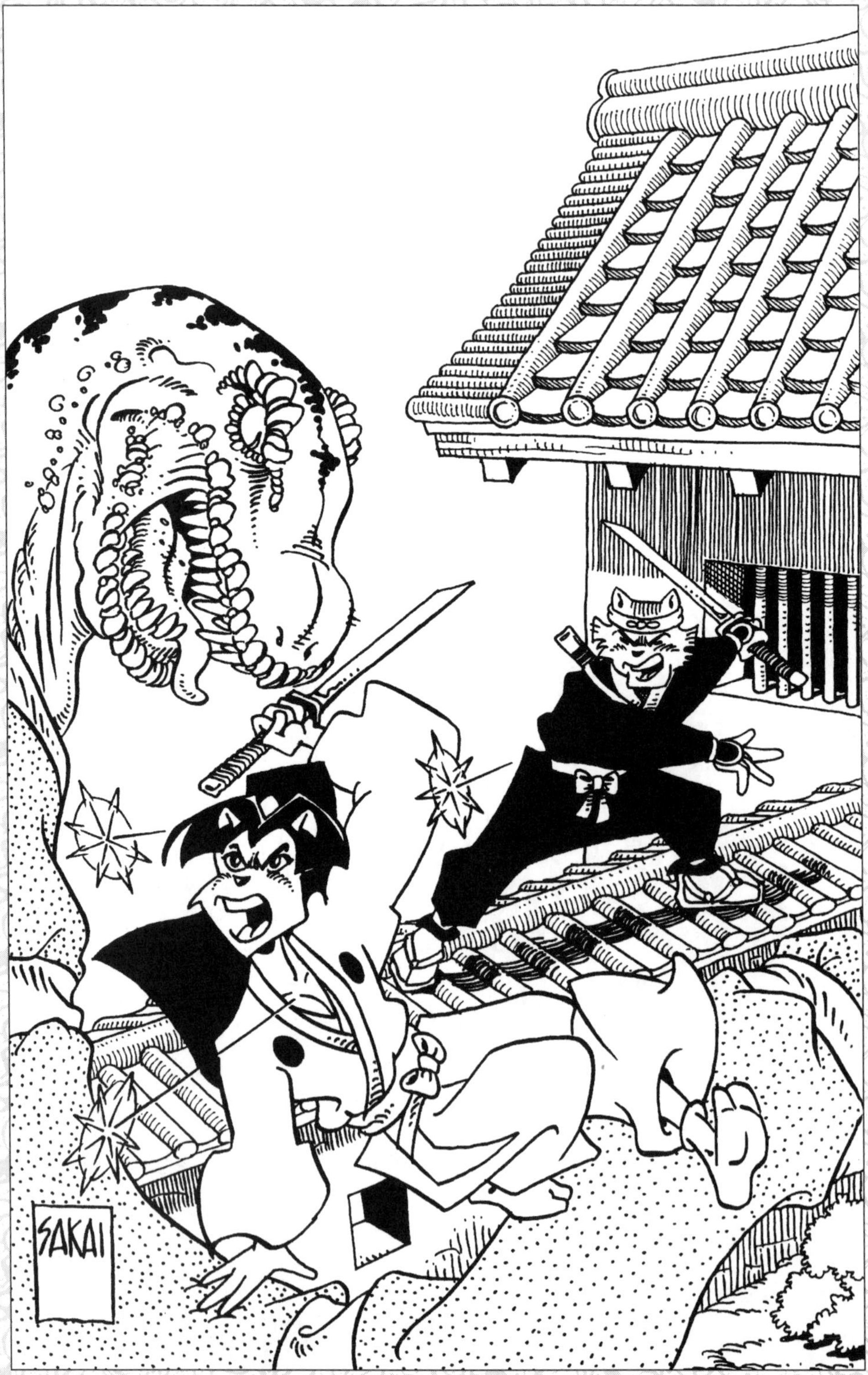
SAKAI

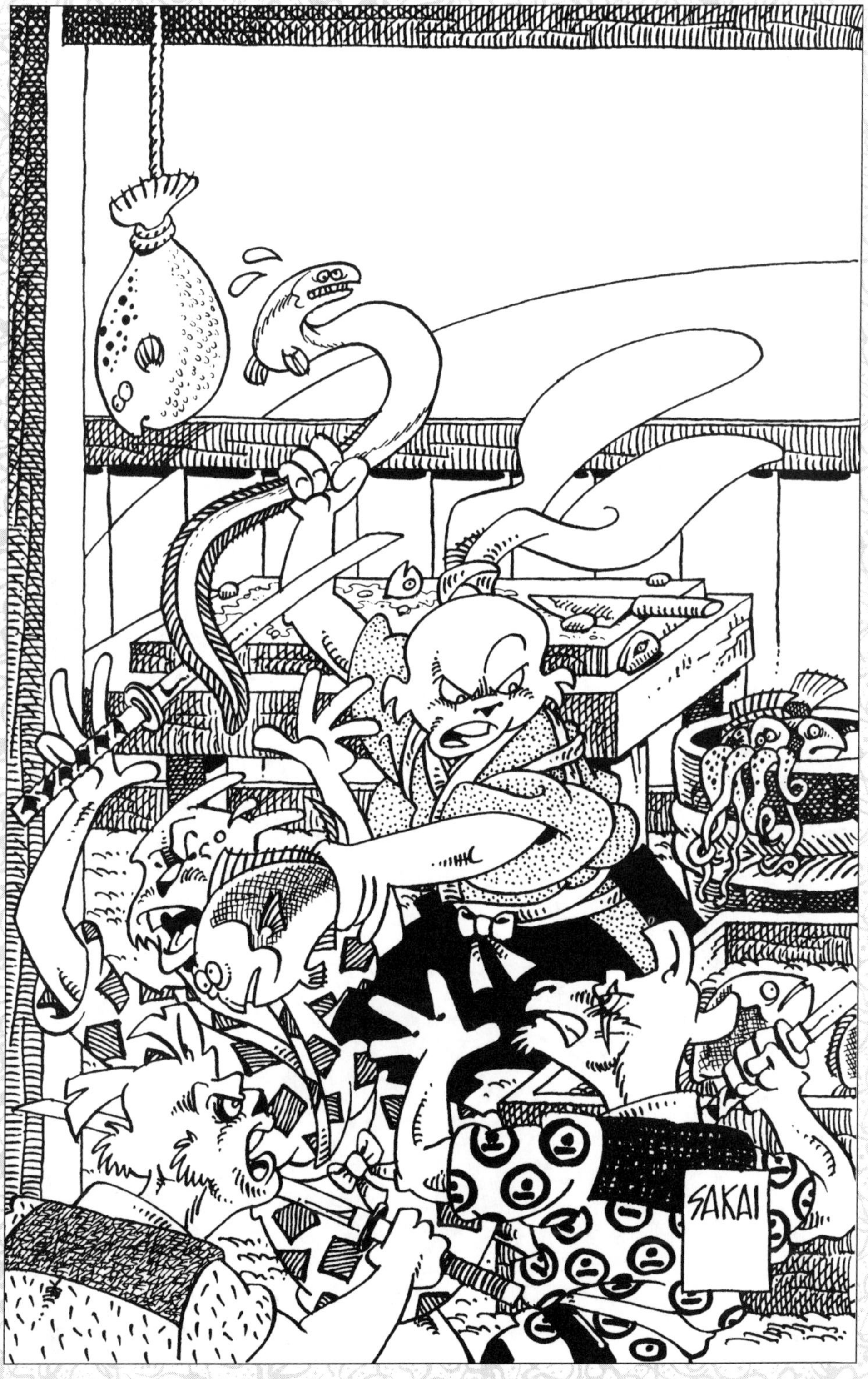
SAKAI

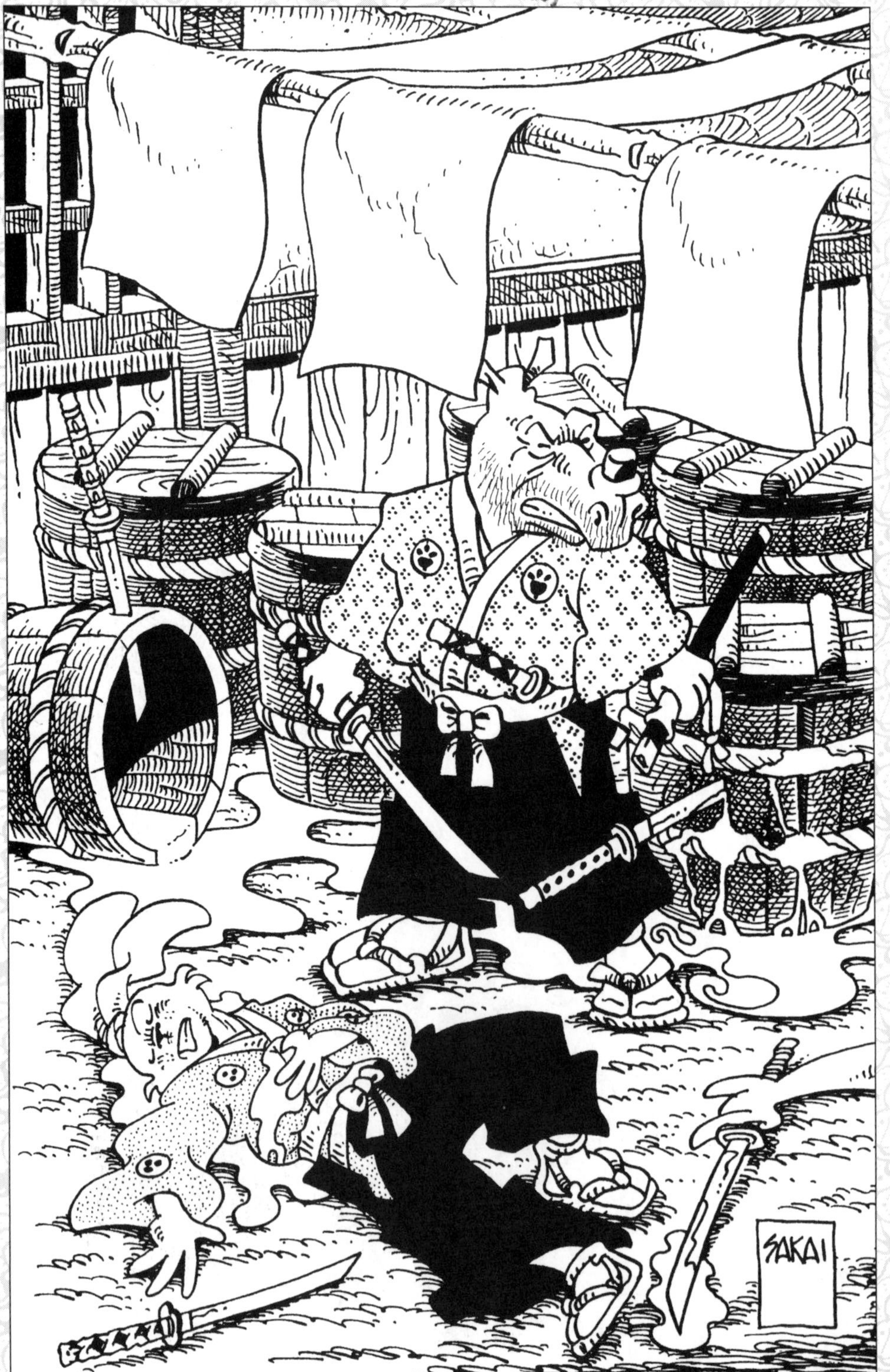
SAKAI

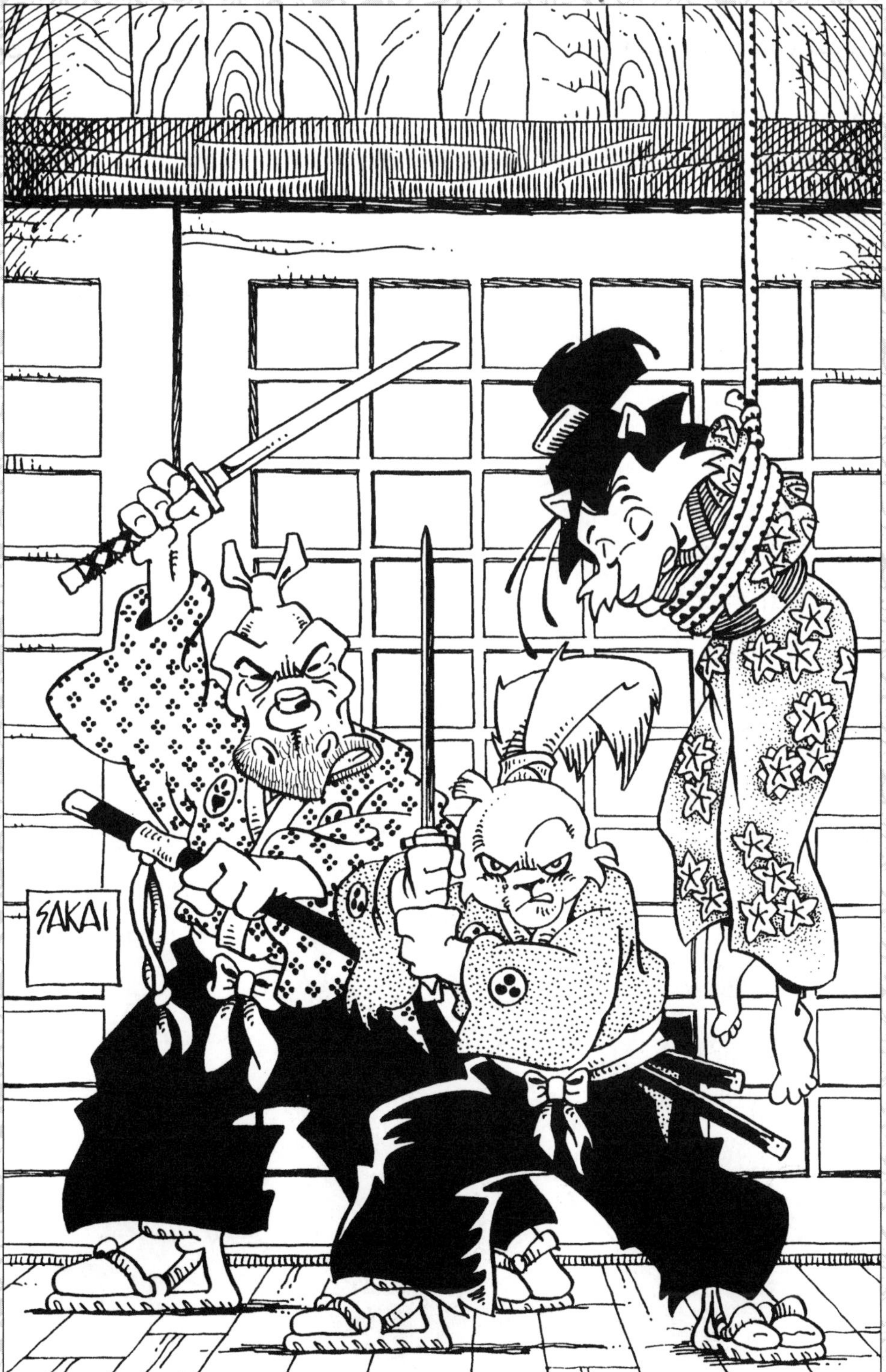
SAKAI

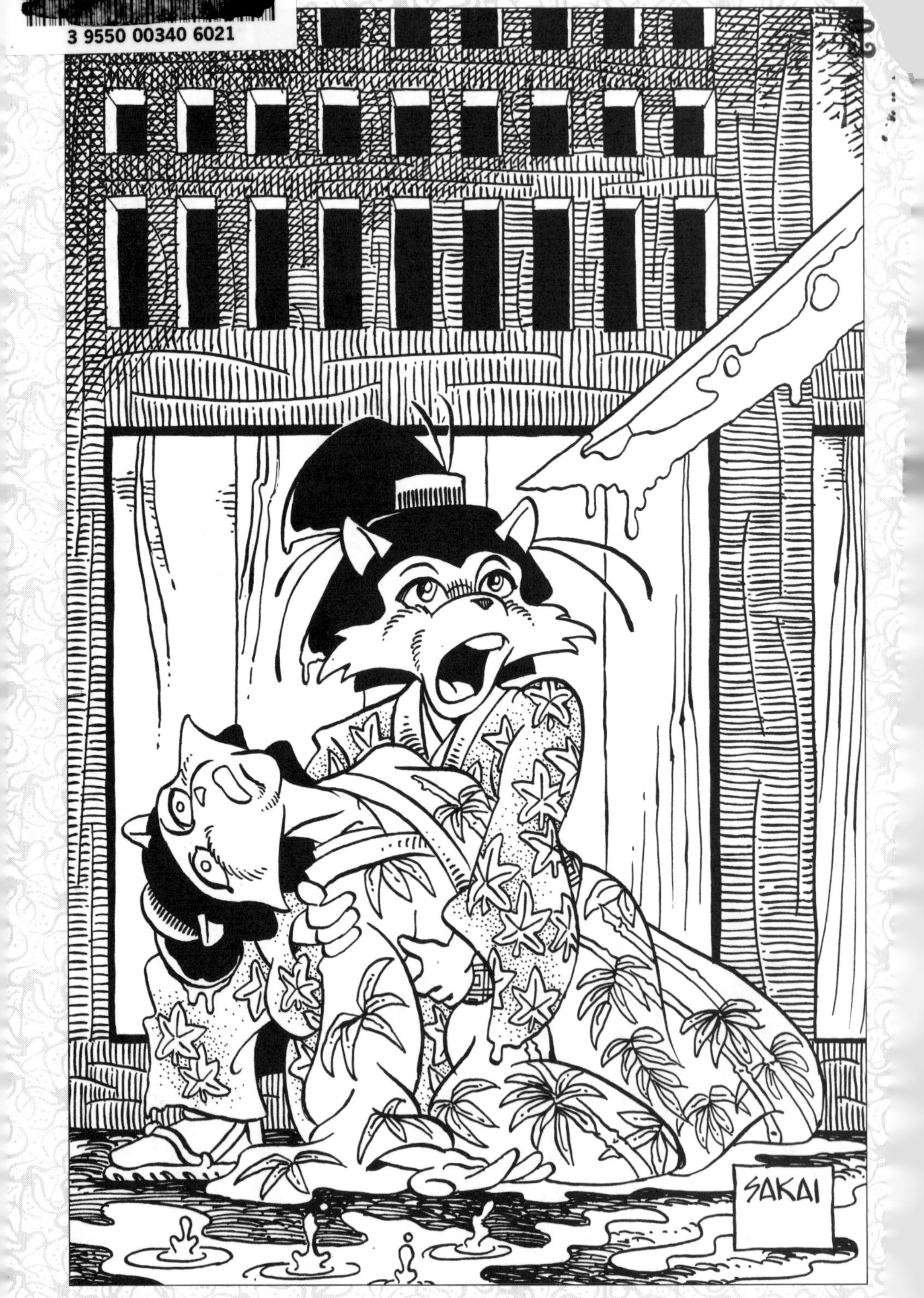
SAKAI